THE
LIBRARIAN

MIKHAIL ELIZAROV

THE
LIBRARIAN

Translated from the Russian by
Andrew Bromfield

PUSHKIN PRESS

LONDON

Pushkin Press
71–75 Shelton Street, London WC2H 9JQ

The publication of this book was negotiated through Banke,
Goumen & Smirnova Literary Agency (www.bgs-agency.com)

The Librarian first published in Russian as
Библиотекарь in 2007

This translation first published by Pushkin Press in 2015

ИНСТИТУТ ПЕРЕВОДА

AD VERBUM

Published with the support of the Institute for Literary Translation, Russia.

0 0 1

ISBN 978 1 782270 27 0

Set in Monotype Baskerville by Tetragon, London
Printed and bound by CPI Group (UK) Ltd, Croydon CRO 4YY

www.pushkinpress.com

The working man should have the firm understanding that you can make as many buckets and locomotives as you like, but a song and a thrill cannot be made. A song is more precious than things...

ANDREI PLATONOV

PART I

The Books

GROMOV

THE WRITER Dmitry Alexandrovich Gromov (1910–81) lived out his days in total obscurity. His books sank without trace in a bottomless abyss of recycled paper, and when political catastrophes finally demolished his Soviet Homeland, it seemed that there was no one at all left to remember the writer Gromov.

Not many people had read him. Of course, there were the Soviet editors who assessed the political loyalty of texts, followed by the critics. But it was hardly likely that anyone had ever pricked up their ears in startled interest at the titles *The Proletarian Way* (1951), *Fly On, Happiness!* (1954), *Narva* (1965), *By Labour's Roads* (1968), *The Silver Channel* (1972) and *The Quiet Grass* (1977).

Gromov's life story progressed step by step in parallel with the development of his Socialist Motherland. He was educated at a Soviet seven-year school and a teacher-training college, and subsequently worked as the executive editor of a factory's in-house newspaper. The purges and repressions passed Gromov by and he calmly carried on as he was until June 1941, when he was drafted into the army and found himself on the front line as a war correspondent. In the winter of 1943 Gromov suffered frostbite in his hands—they managed to save the left one, but his right hand was amputated. After the victory was won, Gromov took his family from Tashkent, the city to which they had been evacuated, to the Donbas and stayed there, working in the editorial office of a municipal newspaper until he retired.

Gromov took up the literary pen late, as a mature forty-year-old. He often drew his subjects from the development of the country as a whole, celebrating the everyday, plain, cotton-print life of small provincial towns, settlements and villages, writing about mines, factories, boundless expanses of virgin soil and battles fought for the harvest. The heroes of Gromov's books were usually "Red Directors" or collective-farm chairmen, soldiers newly returned from the front, widows who had preserved inviolate their love and their civic courage, and Young Pioneers or Young Communist League activists—resolute and jovial, ready and willing to perform some heroic "feat of labour". Good triumphed with excruciating regularity: metallurgical combines sprang up in record times; a young man who only yesterday had been a student was transformed into a seasoned specialist after a mere six months of practical work in an industrial plant; a factory workshop over-fulfilled the plan and took on additional obligations; in autumn golden rivers of grain flowed into a collective farm's storage bins. Evil was always re-educated or clapped in jail. And amorous passions also developed—but they were very chaste: following Chekhov's axiom on firearms in plays, the gunshot of a kiss that was promised at the start of a book was fired as a damp, slobbery blank to a cheek in the final pages. But so much for the subject matter—all of this was also written in a dreary style, in soundly wrought but incredibly insipid sentences. Even the covers, with their tractors, combine harvesters and miners, were made out of some trashy kind of cardboard.

The country that gave birth to Gromov could afford to publish thousands of authors that no one read. The books lay in the shops, their prices were reduced to a few copecks, they were carted off to a warehouse and handed over for pulping, and more books that no one wanted were published.

The last time Gromov was published was in 1977, but after that all those people in the editorial offices, who realized that Gromov's writings were the harmless verbal trash of a war veteran and that, while there was no particular social demand for them, society had nothing against the actual fact of their existence, were replaced by different people. Everywhere he went, Gromov received polite refusals. The state, already celebrating its own imminent suicidal demise, was hatching out the demonic literature of its own destroyers.

Gromov, a solitary widower now, realized that his allotted time had expired, and he too quietly expired, to be followed ten years later by the USSR, for which he had once written his books.

Although altogether more than half a million volumes of Gromov's works were printed, only scattered, individual copies had found miraculous refuge in the libraries of clubs in remote villages, hospitals, corrective labour camps and orphanages, or been left to rot in basements, bound round crosswise with string and squeezed in between the documents of some Party Congress and multiple volumes of the *Collected Works of Lenin*.

And yet Gromov did have his own genuine devotees. And they scoured the country, collecting the surviving books, willing to go to any lengths to get them.

In everyday life Gromov's books bore titles with references to river channels and steppe grass. But the titles used among Gromov's collectors were quite different—the Book of Strength, the Book of Power, the Book of Fury, the Book of Endurance, the Book of Joy, the Book of Memory, the Book of Meaning...

LAGUDOV

V ALERIAN MIKHAYLOVICH LAGUDOV could undoubtedly be
considered one of the most influential figures in the universe
of Gromovian discourse.

Lagudov was an only child, born to a family of teachers in
Saratov. He demonstrated significant talent from early childhood.
In 1945, as a youth of seventeen years, he set out for the war as
a volunteer, but never reached the front—in April he contracted
pneumonia and spent a month in hospital, and in May the war was
over—the theme of a soldier who missed the war was an extremely
painful one for Lagudov.

In 1947 Lagudov was admitted to the philological faculty of
a university. After successfully defending his graduation thesis, he
worked as a journalist on a provincial newspaper for twelve years,
and in 1965 he was invited to join a literary journal, where he
became the head of the review section.

Lagudov's predecessor had departed from his post after letting
a novel of dubious loyalty slip through. Khrushchev's thaw had
already taken place, but the boundaries of censorship remained
blurred, and it wasn't always easy to tell apart a text in the spirit
of the new times and anti-Soviet propaganda. As a result both the
journal and the publishing house had received a severe reprimand.
And therefore Lagudov paid attention to everything that arrived
on his desk. After glancing briefly through a story by Gromov one
evening, he decided to polish the book off quickly and never come
back to it. He had a positively warm review in mind—Lagudov's

conscience wouldn't allow him to criticize a front-line veteran, even if the veteran's politically correct text about anti-aircraft gunners was mediocre from an artistic point of view. Before nightfall he had finished the book. Without even suspecting it, the assiduous Lagudov had thus fulfilled the Condition of Continuity. Maintaining his vigilance, he had read the story from the first line to the last, without skipping the dreary paragraphs of nature description or any patriotic dialogue. And thus Lagudov had also fulfilled the Condition of Zeal.

He had read the Book of Joy, otherwise known as *Narva*. According to his former wife's reminiscences, Lagudov experienced a state of turbulent euphoria and couldn't sleep all night long; he said that he had subjected existence to a comprehensive analysis and had magnificent ideas about how to do good for mankind. He said that previously he had been enmeshed in life, but now everything had become clear, and he laughed loudly as he said it. By morning the emotions had subsided, and he drily informed his alarmed wife that it was too early to proclaim his ideas openly. That day he couldn't go to work because he was in a depressed state, and he didn't express any more ideas on the subject of universal harmony.

The substantive aspect of the euphoria that Lagudov experienced did not possess any conceptual points of intersection with Gromov's storyline, and Lagudov himself did not link the events of the night with the book in any way. But nonetheless a certain emotional scar was left on his soul, which ensured that Lagudov did not forget the writer by the name of Gromov.

Eighteen years later Lagudov saw a short novel by Gromov in a seedy little shop at a railway station. Inspired by nostalgia for the happiness of that distant night, Lagudov bought the book; after all the reductions it cost only five copecks and it was not very large, about two hundred small pages—just right for the journey ahead.

In the suburban train circumstances once again assisted Lagudov in fulfilling the two Conditions. Some tipsy young louts travelling in his carriage were pestering the passengers. Lagudov, no longer young and not very strong, chose not to get involved with the burly yobs. As a man he felt ashamed of not being able to pull the villains up short, and so he stuck his nose into the book's pages, pretending to be someone extremely interested in what he was reading.

The volume Lagudov had picked up this time was the Book of Memory (*The Quiet Grass*), which cast him briefly into a drowsy state. The book implanted in him a phantom of brilliant radiance, a mythical, non-existent memory. Lagudov was engulfed by such overwhelming tenderness for the life he dreamed of that he trembled in tearful ecstasy at this all-consuming, pure, lambent feeling.

Reading a second Book by Gromov wrought an abrupt change in Lagudov's destiny. He left his job, divorced his wife and disappeared, leaving no tracks behind him. Three years later Lagudov surfaced again, and a mighty clan had already assembled around him, although its members called themselves a "library". This was the term that came in time to be applied to all organizations of a similar nature.

In the first instance Lagudov's library was joined by people on whom he had tested the Book of Memory. Initially he rather arrogantly took the miraculous effect to be the result of his own personal qualities. However, experiments showed that if the Conditions were observed, the Book affected everyone without exception. The psychiatrist Artur Friesman became Lagudov's closest associate, although for the first few months Lagudov had doubted his mental health.

Lagudov was cautiously selective, recruiting members of peaceable professions that had been reduced to poverty—teachers, engineers, modest workers in the cultural sphere—those who had been intimidated and morally crushed by the sweeping changes of recent times. He assumed that the intelligentsia, humiliated by these new times, would provide amenable and reliable material, incapable of rebellion or betrayal, especially if the Books—and, by inference, Lagudov—could help realize the intelligentsia's eternal yearning, as a class, for spirituality.

In many respects this supposition was mistaken. Gromov's Books induced global personality change, and the circumspect Lagudov was merely fortunate with most of his new comrades, in addition to which he received professional assistance from Friesman, who by no means recruited anyone and everyone.

Those who joined the library usually felt profound respect and loyalty to Lagudov, and that was understandable—Valerian Mikhaylovich gave back hope to most of these despairing people tormented by poverty, offering them a meaning for their existence and a close community united around a single idea.

For the first two years the people whom Lagudov gathered under his banner were mostly humiliated and insulted members of the intelligentsia, but then he decided that the library was clearly lacking in a more robust kind of strength. And at this point Friesman came to Lagudov's rescue. Men who had been shattered by the war in Afghanistan often came to his clinic for help. Friesman worked on these men first, and then handed them over to Lagudov. In 1991 the library was augmented by retired soldiers who had no wish to betray their Soviet oath. The former officers transformed the intelligentsia members into a serious combat unit with strict discipline and a security service. The library could turn out up to a hundred fighting men at any time.

Naturally, the system of selection did fail sometimes. Thoughtless prattlers appeared, who blabbed about the Books at every opportunity. On several occasions the shoots of conspiracy broke through the surface of the ground. But the mischief-makers all suffered an identical tragic fate—they disappeared without trace.

There were also cases of Books being stolen. Lagudov was betrayed by a rank-and-file reader, a certain Yakimov. After being issued the Book of Memory from the reserves when his turn came round, Yakimov duped the curator and fled to parts unknown.

Lagudov had enough books, and the library was not impoverished, but the precedent was abhorrent in itself and, in addition, the traitor had managed to make his escape.

Other readers took their lead from this successful crime. These ones were caught. To restore Lagudov's shaken authority and to deter any future miscreants, the book thieves were quartered in front of the entire library.

Yakimov was discovered by chance a year after the daring robbery. He had taken refuge in Ufa. A punitive assault force was immediately dispatched there, its mission to eliminate the thief and return the Book. Lagudov's soldiers were greatly surprised when they discovered that Yakimov had not wasted his time in Ufa and had organized a library of his own.

Lagudov's small detachment took the courageous decision not to wait for reinforcements to arrive. They openly informed Yakimov about the showdown in the laconic "we're coming to get you" style. Cold weapons were agreed on and a spot outside the city, as remote as possible, was chosen.

It's worth noting that the readers of Yakimov's library lived according to the principle "the dead know no shame". No one won the victory that night. Both adversaries withdrew, exhausted by the sanguinary conflict.

Lagudov didn't hazard another punitive expedition. He needed to protect the book depository against the enemy closer to home and not send detachments off to the back of beyond, getting faithful readers killed in order to satisfy his own ambitions. His library was in any case surrounded by numerous aggressive rivals.

For a long time Lagudov assumed that knowledge of Gromov was being spread by traitors from his own library. He believed too strongly in his own chosen status and couldn't possibly imagine that anyone apart from him had proved capable of penetrating the secret of the Books independently. Lagudov regarded all those who founded their power on *his* discovery as second-rate individuals, corrupt thieves. Even subsequently, when he was forced to abandon his ideas of exclusivity, he only accepted contact on an equal basis—and even then grudgingly—with initial, natural librarians: those who had solved the mystery of the Books with their own brains, without any prompting.

However, the proportion of those who became familiar with Gromov through information leaks was actually rather large and many new clans were organized around fugitive readers, without any theft necessarily being involved—at the end of the Eighties it wasn't all that difficult to get hold of the Book of Memory if you really wanted to. The most important role was not played by renegades or by rumours, but by the missionary activities of the first "apostles", whose names have long since occupied their post-humous places in the pantheon of this cruel and secretive society. Some of them are worth mentioning.

Pyotr Vladimirovich Shepchikhin. He worked in a print shop and typeset the Book of Memory. After confusing the dust jackets, instead of the detective novel he had set his mind on, he took home Gromov. By pure chance he got stuck in the lift with the book for the entire night, and when he was freed by lift engineers early in the morning, he came out a different man. A sensitive individual, Shepchikhin immediately realized that the reason lay not in his own physiology, but in the mysterious Book. Shaken by the mystery, he left his job and set off to wander the country, becoming one of Gromov's most fervent propagandists.

Shepchikhin was killed—in fact he was probably bumped off by neophytes whom he himself had once told about the Book. They did away with him after deciding that Shepchikhin's propagandist activities were too dangerous to the hermetic isolation of the Gromov world.

Yulian Olegovich Doroshevich. He was undergoing compulsory treatment at an occupational detoxification centre, and in order to avoid being driven insane by the sober boredom, he read. All sorts of garbage had settled in the libraries of those semi-punitive institutions—books that were even slightly worthwhile didn't linger there for long. But thanks to that detoxification centre Doroshevich discovered Gromov and the Book of Endurance (*The Silver Channel*). This Book brought any afflicted soul a feeling of great consolation and reconciliation with life. It was said to be of help in cases of physical pain, acting as a general anaesthetic. The Book apparently had no substantial effect on feelings other than grief, fear and pain, but simply froze them into a general indifference. Doroshevich's own psychological make-up determined the selective nature of his missionary work. He revealed the Book only to those people who, in his view, were the unhappiest. Doroshevich's life was broken off in circumstances that have never been clarified; it is not known who killed him—probably someone who regarded the sin of murder as far less important than his own suffering.

It is possible that history exaggerates the spiritual qualities of the wandering "apostles" and that in actual fact they, like all librarians, coveted personal ascendancy and also tried to establish book communities, but failed to complete their mission.

Their strange selflessness rather contradicted the specific nature of the mystery. Every new reader who was introduced to Gromov realized that there would not be enough Joy, Endurance or Memory for everybody and it was better to keep mum about the author. In an organized community it was easier to keep the Books safe and increase their number, and therefore those lone wandering pathfinders died out. A library chose its own new readers, more readily recruiting solitary individuals without families and with some kind of mental problem, and examining each candidate at length to make sure they were worthy of communing with the miracle, and would be able to guard and protect it, and even, if necessary, give their lives for it.

In short, Lagudov had plenty of competitors. Soon not only the Books, but also the bibliographies of Gromov disappeared from every public library that was even slightly significant. Even in Moscow's "Leninka" someone removed all the information from the card index. Consequently, during computerization the data on the missing author were not entered anywhere and Gromov formally disappeared. Someone also made free with the books on the shelves. Without the card index it was only possible to guess at the true number of publications.

By the beginning of the Nineties collectors of Gromov had a list of six already tried-and-tested Books. They also had information about a seventh, which they called the Book of Meaning. It was believed that when it was discovered the true purpose of Gromov's creations would be revealed. As yet, however, no one could boast of having found a copy of Meaning, and some sceptics asserted that no such book actually existed.

All the libraries regarded a full collection of the works as an immensely powerful spell that ought to produce some kind of global result.

Lagudov's theoreticians spoke of a "godlike condition" that lasted for the same length of time as the action of any particular Book. No one knew what benefits could be derived from this condition, correctly assuming that the ideas which occurred to someone inside God's skin would transcend the human level. The rank-and-file readers were informed that, on becoming God, Lagudov would immediately make provision for his comrades-in-arms.

There were discussions about the end of the world, "book poisoning" that threatened the reader with death, or how all the Books, read straight through, would raise the dead. But these were only hypotheses.

It was assumed that Gromov himself might have had a complete set of works, but when Lagudov started searching, Gromov had been dead for a long time. When he died his apartment had gone to strangers and they had cleared out all the junk in the first week.

Gromov's only daughter, Olga Dmitriyevna, lived with her family in Ukraine. One of Lagudov's men paid her a visit, posing as a journalist, and was dismayed to discover that she had given the two Books she possessed to a casual visitor who had introduced himself as a literary scholar who was studying her father's work. Olga Dmitriyevna did not remember the titles of the books either. They seemed to have been the Book of Memory and the Book of Joy.

Of course, Lagudov found out who had got there before him, but that was not much help. He didn't engage in armed conflict with the competitors involved. After all, no one had deceived him, they had simply been quicker off the mark, and he only had himself to blame. Lagudov drew the appropriate conclusions for the future and tripled his efforts.

Gromov had a brother, Veniamin, to whom he also sent his books, and Lagudov had a stroke of luck with this brother—in addition to the Book of Memory and the Book of Joy, which Lagudov already had, a rather rare and valuable copy of the Book of Endurance (*The Silver Channel*) was discovered. Acting like morphine, this book held all who were afflicted with pain and suffering firmly cemented into the library...

The years of systematic work were not entirely wasted. Rumour had it that Lagudov's depository contained eight Books of Joy, three Books of Endurance and no fewer than a dozen copies of the Book of Memory (*The Quiet Grass*), which had been published last and was better preserved than the others: there were as many as several hundred copies of it in the world. The Book of Memory was strategically useful; its use made it easy to recruit and retain readers who were susceptible to tender feelings.

Two Books of Memory and an apartment in the very centre of Saratov were exchanged for a dangerous Book of Fury (*By Labour's Roads*), which was capable of arousing a state of battle trance in even the most timid of hearts.

The other Books still had to be searched for. Lagudov had high hopes for the country's outlying regions and its Central Asian neighbours, where Gromov's Books could theoretically have been preserved, because by the beginning of the Nineties all the Books lying "on the surface" in Central Russia, eastern

Ukraine and Belorussia had been picked up by collectors from various libraries.

But when the search became harder, methods that were far from noble came into play. Violent raids on depositories became more and more common.

At about the same time the so-called copyists became active— readers who made copies of the Books to sell for their personal enrichment. The copyists claimed that the effect of a copy was no different from that of the printed original.

But a manuscript almost always contained errors of some kind, or some words that had been omitted, and therefore proved ineffective. Photocopies that should have excluded the possibility of error also had no effect. It was thought that the decisive factor was the printing, and certain Books were reprinted. Rumours concerning the quality of a reprint "fake" were contradictory. In any case it was universally asserted that a copy would never compare with an original.

Forgeries provoked numerous skirmishes, which led to the demise of more than one library that had gone astray. The copyists were outlaws; they were liquidated by their own people and others alike. But they were highly successful in one regard—quite a lot of copies appeared.

That was when the cases of vandalism began. Original Books were sold and exchanged with a page skilfully removed and replaced by any other that was made of similar paper. Naturally, the mutilated Book had no effect. Whereas formerly people had restricted themselves to a cursory glance through a Book, after these incidents they went through the pages, comparing the typeface and the quality of the paper.

There had never been any great trust between the libraries—no one wished to reinforce the power of a rival. Exchanges or sales were extremely rare, and any fraud sparked a bloody conflict.

The resulting battle took place at a remote spot, with all due pomp and solemnity—members of the libraries brought Books attached to poles like holy banners. At first they were originals, later they were often replaced by replicas. Firearms were categorically forbidden. This was more than just some special noble warrior's code. It was always easier to disguise stab wounds or crush injuries as accidents or ordinary "domestic incidents" for the outside world, with its morgues, hospitals and law-enforcement agencies. Bullet wounds could only be interpreted in one way. And apart from that, weapons of that sort were noisy.

Usually household items were employed in the fighting—knives as big as butchers' cleavers, axes, hammers, crowbars, garden forks and rakes, flails. In general terms, the detachments of fighters armed themselves in the manner of Yemelyan Pugachev's peasant army or the Czech Hussites, and the sight of these people inevitably brought to mind the idiom "battle to the death", because with a scythe and a meat cleaver the sensation of death was especially keen...

No one saw Lagudov during his final years, apart from his very closest associates. It was said that Valerian Mikhaylovich went into hiding, fearful of hired killers from competing libraries.

SHULGA

NIKOLAI YURYEVICH SHULGA was born in 1950. He grew up a shy, timid boy, was a good pupil in school, but suffered from indecisiveness. A catarrhal infection left Shulga with a facial tic and he underwent several unsuccessful operations that left deep scars. Shulga was very embarrassed by his problem, which was emphasized by unwieldy glasses. He had almost no friends. In 1968 Shulga went to a teacher-training college, but in the third year he abandoned his studies and enlisted for a Young Communist League construction project in the north, where, as he put it, "people are not valued for their appearance, but for their labour valour".

Defying his own nature as a member of the intelligentsia, Shulga spent a couple of years as a labourer in oil prospecting. The work was heavy and boring, and people laughed at Shulga anyway because he, with his far from heroic appearance, explained his tic and scars as the legacy of an unsuccessful bear hunt.

In 1972 Shulga signed on with a group of fur trappers. The team also included two hunters and a guide from the local population. A blizzard drove them into a hut and interred them under snow for a month. Centuries of human experience in the taiga warned of the dangers of collective incarceration and the guide worked a spell so that the men wouldn't start shooting each other in their claustrophobic desperation.

The folk magic failed, overwhelmed by a mightier enchantment, and it all ended in disaster. In addition to salt meat and buckshot, the previous occupant had left behind about a dozen books, jumbled together with newspapers—as kindling. Out of sheer boredom Shulga started reading Gromov. He found himself with the Book of Fury (*By Labour's Roads*). He didn't understand much about literature, and the dreariness of the text suited his temperament. And so Shulga fulfilled the two essential Conditions of Zeal and Continuity.

And after the Book had been read, death came to the hut. In an attempt to conceal the crime, Shulga dismembered the dead men and carried them out into the taiga. The remains were discovered by a search party and the bodies were identified. Shulga appeared in court. He didn't deny his guilt and sincerely repented of what he had done, attributing his appalling actions to intoxication by the sable poison that the hunting party carried—to avoid damaging the precious skins, the little animals were poisoned. He claimed that somehow the poison had found its way into his food.

Shulga told the court that he was reading by candlelight when he felt a "change of state", as if boiling water had run through his entire body.

Very probably an offensive comment had been cast in Shulga's direction. For instance, someone said: "Stop wasting the candles on useless crap, you twitchy wanker." Men rendered bitter and exasperated by enforced incarceration are not particularly choosy about how they express themselves, and cramped conditions offer plenty of occasions for crudity.

Shulga experienced a surge of superhuman aggression, grabbed hold of an axe and did away with the guide and the hunters. After a few hours his fury evaporated and the realization of what he had done hit home.

Shulga underwent the relevant tests and no traces of poison were discovered in his body. Taking into account his confession, his cooperation with the investigation and the claustrophobic psychogenic aspect of the crime, the death penalty was commuted to fifteen years in a strict-security camp.

Shulga's fearsome offence was no help to him in the camp. Ignorant as he was of the finer casuistic points of criminal culture, when questioned he mentioned in his ingenuous answers that he had spent two years studying in a teacher-training college. Lanky and scrawny, with spectacles and a twitching cheek, Shulga had already been dubbed "Head Teacher" at the pre-trial detention centre. He was a perfect target for mockery. Already depressed by his own unattractive appearance, he determined his own status in the camp: somewhere between a downtrodden "skivvy" and a lowly "gofer"—a perpetual "cleaner".

Shulga was tormented by despair and fear. He was unable to put anything right in his life. On the front lines it was genuinely possible to make the move from coward to hero by performing some feat of heroism. But he didn't know of any feat or action of any kind that would improve his position in the criminal world, and probably no such action even existed.

Shulga mostly befriended the same kind of misfortunates as himself, the "skivvies" and the "abused". His neighbours in the barracks, who were "regular guys", were loath to associate with him, realizing that he was sinking down the hierarchy, and they tried to avoid any unnecessary contact with a man whose excessive helplessness could lead at any moment to his being awarded "a plate with a hole in it", that is, a demotion to the most despised and abused level of the prison hierarchy.

Shulga was unfamiliar with the prison-camp caste structure. Hoping to get his sentence reduced and receive privileges of some kind, he took the bait offered by the camp administration and joined the crime prevention section. And then he discovered that he had joined the ranks of the "scum"—that was what convicts who agreed to collaborate with the camp authorities were called.

Shulga became a member of the "team". Wearing his arm-band on his sleeve, he stood watch at the checkpoint between the "living zone" and the "production zone" of the camp. Bearing in mind his liberal education, incomplete as it was, and his state of health—the tic had grown worse—Shulga was moved to a job in the library. Things were a bit easier there.

Shulga had been in prison for more than five years. In his free time he read compulsively, devouring anything and everything in order to occupy his mind. His fear had diminished somewhat and at moments of inner calm or in the peace of the night he often thought about what it was that had turned him, a good-natured and timid man, into a murderer. His reminiscences led him to that little book with the dirty grey binding that had perished in the fire.

Shulga found Gromov's short novel *Fly On, Happiness!* in the prison-camp library. It was a completely different book, not the one that he had read, but he still remembered the author's name. On Sunday evening, with his typical thoroughness, Shulga read the whole of the Book of Power. At a specific moment he sensed the inner transformation that had come over him, and his mind was suddenly filled with a pulsating awareness of his own impor-tance. Shulga liked this new sensation very much and, even more importantly, he realized why it had happened and where it had come from.

Shulga observed that, thanks to the Book, he was capable of influencing people around him and imposing his will on them. Naturally, it wasn't the world outside that had changed, but the man who had read the Book. A mysterious force temporarily transformed Shulga's facial expressions, the look in his eyes and his bearing, operating on his opponent through his gestures, tone of voice and the words that he spoke. You could say that the Book helped Shulga to recruit the souls of those who were part of his social circle—the "scum", "skivvies", "gofers", "stooges" and "lowlifes" (the downtrodden and sexually abused)—all the untouchables of the criminal world.

Meanwhile in the camp the old thieves' elite was gradually sup-planted by a generation of young bandits who no longer honoured the unwritten code of previous times that forbade the humiliation of anybody at all for no particular reason. The school of excess that had been born in the low-security camps invaded the relatively smooth-running strict-regime environment. Life became much more bitter for the lower castes. Downtrodden convicts were humiliated and even sexually abused for mere amusement, out of boredom. The reason for it could be anything at all—a cute appearance, weakness, excessive intellectual refinement.

One day an absolutely outrageous incident occurred in the camp when the lowlife Timur Kovrov "hit on" a young, promising criminal boss—Kovrov flung himself on the other man and started licking him. The high-status thief beat the lowlife almost to death, but he forfeited his previous authority for ever; even worse, now tainted himself, he joined the ranks of the outcasts and soon afterwards was found hanged by his own hand. Kovrov recovered in hospital and rumour has it that his sentence was reduced because of his serious injuries.

Probably no one even noticed that two days before this strange attack Shulga had a talk with Kovrov and urged him to commit the act. This Kovrov had been reduced to the status of a lowlife through trickery—as a novice he had been sat on the "sod's seat" in the camp cinema. And certainly no one remembered that previously the young criminal boss had openly mocked and bullied Shulga, threatening to "shaft the four-eyed brainy scumbag up the back entrance".

In this way Shulga invented his own means of defence against the criminal world—employing the inarticulate, filthy, tormented creatures with holed plates as badges of their humiliation and alienation, whose lot in life was merely to open their mouths and assume the pose.

In the space of a month several respected criminal bosses were hit on—all the ones who had ever molested Shulga. It should be noted that high-ranking thieves reduced to low status by a "kamikaze lowlife" didn't live long afterwards; they slashed their veins and hanged themselves, otherwise their former victims would have raped and abused them with highly inventive cruelty...

Shulga read the Book regularly and every day it lent him an artificial, but nonetheless effective, charisma. Even seasoned convicts, quite unable to understand what was happening to them, couldn't stand up to Shulga.

Word that he was inciting the lowlifes against the brothers reached the big boss himself—there were informers among the outcasts. The big boss was puzzled by how a worthless scumbag like that could suddenly have started radiating such psychic power. He had a gut feeling that Shulga was cheating in some incomprehensible fashion—and after pondering for a long time, he drew the right conclusion. That night the Book was stolen from Shulga. The big boss never figured out its secret, but essentially he guessed correctly about the source of the mysterious spell.

In the morning Shulga discovered his loss. And the barracks-hut skivvy passed on the message that the elders had summoned the Head Teacher for a parley. Shulga guessed how the meeting would end, but repeated experience of the sensation of power had turned him into a quite exceptional individual.

The showdown took place in the forestry plot. It was February and darkness came early. The big boss was not expecting any resistance. He only had one fighter from his immediate entourage with him, plus a "bull", a man who had gambled away his life and become a "torpedo"—he was the one who was supposed to take out the upstart Head Teacher. But the big boss wasn't expecting things to get that far. He intended to suggest that Shulga hang himself, so that the "bull" wouldn't have to take the sin on his own soul. The noose had already been set up on a convenient branch.

Shulga looked so limp and jaded that no one even thought of checking to see if he had a weapon. But they should have. Hidden up his sleeve he had a heavy section of steel pipe, stuffed with sand to give it extra weight.

Gratified to note that the Head Teacher was no longer pulsating with self-confidence, the big boss was convinced yet again that he was dealing here with a faker who pulled off his trickery by using some kind of unusual hypnosis.

After hearing his sentence pronounced, Shulga merely asked where the Book was now, promising to reveal its fantastic secret. Intrigued, the big boss took the Book out.

Without hurrying, Shulga scooped up a handful of snow and waited for it to thaw into water, then shook his sleeve so that the pipe slid down into his hand and froze solid to his wet palm. He crashed the first blow down onto the head of the "torpedo". The two thieves drew their knives, but the crushing weapon demonstrated its superiority. Shulga sustained serious damage too. He had just enough strength left to pick up the Book before he passed out.

There was a secret witness to the duel—the prisoner Savely Vorontsov, who had been under Shulga's magical influence for a long time. Sensing that something was wrong, he had decided to follow Shulga, and had been proved right. Vorontsov's help could not have been timelier for the librarian, who was bleeding to death. Prising the length of pipe out of Shulga's hand, Vorontsov flung it over to the dead "torpedo" and raised the alarm.

After some stage-setting the scene looked different: the "bull", who had lost at cards, had taken violent revenge on the criminal elite and Shulga had been injured when he tried to intervene.

The camp authorities didn't really believe in this fairy tale, but they accepted it as their primary scenario, especially since there were only two witnesses—Vorontsov and the injured Shulga—and they both said the same thing. Shulga spent a month in a hospital bed and then returned to the camp.

Shulga was able to thwart a second attempt on his life by preventative measures. The thief who was preparing to attack that night was "tainted" that same day by the lowlife Volkov, who died from knife wounds on the spot, but saved his master.

The thieves wisely decided not to tangle with Shulga any more. They couldn't show him respect, but it would have been stupid to mess with a man who could have an authoritative criminal boss shamed with a single word.

After that Shulga's life was subjugated to an unvarying routine. In the morning he read through the Book and for the rest of the day he lorded it over the skivvies and abused lowlifes. The authorities thought it best not to interfere in this situation. Shulga's role as a social counterweight had brought the camp the calm and order that the authorities needed, and for that he was given secret support. As long as Shulga remained in the camp, the thieves tried not to commit any more outrages, and all the castes coexisted more or less peacefully.

Shulga's closest associates in his future library were the former lowlife Timur Kovrov, and the skivvies Savely Vorontsov, Gennady Frolov and Yury Lyashenko. They were released several years earlier than Shulga, who got out in 1986 after serving fourteen years of the fifteen to which he had been sentenced.

Shulga sought out his old camp comrades, and together with them he immediately began strenuous efforts to collect the Books, since life itself had appointed him a "librarian". He didn't share the secret with anyone at first, speaking only in allusions and innuendo. In fact Shulga didn't disclose the entire truth for a long time, even to the devoted Kovrov. When the first Book of Memory and Book of Joy were found, Shulga was always present at the readings, insisting that the Books' effect was the result of his own presence.

Shulga surrounded himself with ordinary human material that he dredged from the depths of society, from the low dives and rubbish dumps. Former "shit-shovellers", "scumbags" and "cocksuckers" became a dangerous force under Shulga's leadership. Their prison-camp humiliation merely gave them a sense of solidarity, an implacable hatred of society and a single great desire for vengeance—on anyone, on everybody at once. This contingent was the main difference between Shulga's library and other structures of a similar nature.

As opposed to Lagudov, who had put his money on the intelligentsia, Shulga based himself on the outcasts. In addition to the humiliated strata of criminals, recruits were also gathered from among disenchanted members of religious sects, street bums, bottle collectors, low-grade lumpens who had taken to drink and handicapped individuals who were capable of working. We know that the library was joined by an entire workmen's cooperative of deaf and dumb carpenters—fifteen hulking great men who were very handy with axes. At the beginning of the 1990s the number of readers had passed the 150 mark.

To finance the clan, its "civilians" skilfully practised their customary professions of begging, petty theft and extortion. The "infantry"—dedicated trackers—got hold of the Books.

Shulga was not mistaken in his choice of social milieu. It was a delusion on the part of the greater society to assume that its outcasts were weak, unreliable and cowardly. On the contrary, the status of outcasts bordered on that of the chosen. Shulga's men, who communed with the mystery every day, were in their own way no less spiritual and intellectual than Lagudov's engineers. For them Gromov's books opened the door into a new universe—a secret, awesome universe, full of riddles and thrilling mystery; there was a struggle taking place there too, there were many dangerous adversaries, there were codes of law for life and for battle, and there was a place for nobility and valour. Everything was decided in honest combat, face to face, like in the olden times. There was an emotional reward, far more powerful than the lift from vodka—hope and faith in the as-yet-unknown gifts that would be bestowed by Books to be found in the future, the Books that had not yet been read.

But of course, not everything went smoothly. In 1989 the library suffered a schism, initiated by Frolov and Lyashenko. They hid the Books of Power that had been found on one of the numerous search expeditions. Frolov and Lyashenko were the leaders of that expedition and, once they got their hands on the books, they wanted leadership for themselves.

Shulga realized that any harsh intervention would only make things worse. A schism was inevitable, and in order to avoid its ending in bloodshed, Shulga decided to lead it himself. A general meeting was held, at which the establishment of two more libraries was announced.

The division went through peacefully. According to the rumours, Frolov took forty men away to Sverdlovsk, and about thirty followed Lyashenko to Sochi. Shulga wasn't mean with the new librarians; he gave each of them some start-up capital—three Books of Memory and three Books of Joy each—so that the new libraries would have no difficulty in recruiting readers.

Of the "old guard" from the prison camp, Kovrov and Vorontsov remained with Shulga. The clan had been reduced by half, but there was no immediate prospect of any threat to Shulga's absolute authority. Kovrov and Vorontsov were both reliable and would never think of trying to take his place. Shulga's library possessed six Books of Memory, nine Books of Joy, four Books of Endurance, a Book of Fury and a Book of Power.

MOKHOVA

I N THE LATE EIGHTIES and early Nineties skirmishes between clans for Books were especially frequent and especially bloody. The viciousness of Yelizaveta Makarovna Mokhova's library became legendary. The story of this woman, which in many respects determined the fate of all collectors of Gromov, deserves close attention, especially since a great deal is known about it.

Mokhova grew up in a family without a father. She was a withdrawn little girl who was an average pupil at school and had no close friends, since from the earliest classes she was distinguished by a morbid vanity. After graduating from medical college she lived for two years at her mother's expense, officially working somewhere as a cleaner, then passed the exams to join the evening department of an institute of pharmacology. During the day she worked in a chemist's shop.

After receiving her second professional diploma in 1983, Mokhova found herself a job in an old folk's home.

She enjoyed preparing the medicines there and the laboratory was cool and quiet. Among her powders and test tubes Mokhova secretly revelled in the covert power she held over her decrepit wards, aware that her mere wish was enough for any medicine to be transformed into a deadly poison, and it would be quite impossible to expose the poisoner—Mokhova had been an assiduous student and had a good grasp of the finer points of her trade.

Sometimes, just for a joke, Mokhova would sprinkle some caustic muck into an ointment for bedsores, imagining some old woman scrabbling away in bed as she struggled to reach the source of that fiery itch with her arthritic hand, or goggling blankly at the black ceiling for hours, trying to fall asleep after taking a sedative half composed of stimulant caffeine.

Another few years were passed with these amusements. Mokhova didn't marry, and for that she blamed her mother, with whom she shared an apartment. As a result of these reproaches, or perhaps of some inner melancholy, the mother died. Without her pension Mokhova didn't have enough money to live on, and she got herself another job, working half time as a nurse in the women's section of the Home.

She found it hard there at first. There was a terrible stench in the wards—the bedridden old women relieved themselves where they lay. It wasn't possible to wash a good hundred patients several times every day, and some nursing assistants preferred to keep the windows open to maintain the flow of fresh air. At first the old women caught cold and died, but the ones who survived actually grew hardier, and the staff suffered more seriously from the freezing cold than they did.

Attempting to fight the stench at its origin, the nursing assistants frequently didn't feed the especially messy patients adequately. The only thing that the old women were not denied was food for thought; they were always given newspapers, the magazines *Health* and *Working Woman*, or the books that were in the library.

Mokhova rapidly found her feet in her new job and, what's more, she resolved the problem of the overpowering smells far more humanely than her colleagues. Her professional knowledge prompted the answer. Mokhova made up a binding medicine that the nursing assistants added to the old women's food, and after that even the worst "poopers" relieved themselves in goat's pellets, and no more frequently than once a week.

The decisive milestone in Mokhova's life was the day when the extremely rare Book of Strength, known to the outside world as *The Proletarian Way*, came into the hands of eighty-year-old Polina Vasilyevna Gorn.

It was more than a year since Gorn had lapsed into senile dementia. She didn't talk much, having lost the skill of speech, but her memory retained the ability to read. She didn't understand the words very well, but was still able to construct graphic symbols out of them—she no longer needed the meaning. Because of her insomnia Gorn read the entire Book of Strength in a single session, satisfying the two Conditions, and arose like Lazarus. For a while the Book gave her back her pep and part of her mind.

Mokhova glanced into the ward at the noise and saw a bizarre scene.

Gorn, who always lay there in a filthy, soiled nightshirt, was dashing about between the beds with a rapid, mincing gait, grabbing at everything that came within reach. Suddenly halting in the middle of the ward, Gorn gave an agonized cry, as if she had forced a cork out of her dumb throat—"Ilya Ehrenburg!"—and burst into violent laughter. After that the words came tumbling out one after another, like grains of hail falling on a tin roof: "So long ago! It worked! Soldier, soldier! Lady's! Raw! Lady's! I forgot, you know!" Gorn tried to name the objects she came across, but her memory couldn't manage that, and she described their qualities out loud. Grabbing the cushion out from under the head of the woman next to her, she growled: "Lopill? Wollyp? Soft, comfy! Sleepy time!" Or, when she knocked over a box of sewing accessories, she cried out: "Fumble, thumble. Mustn't prickly! Jab-jab!"

The other old women started falling asleep and Mokhova got ready to tie Gorn down and give her a sedative injection.

Gorn saw the syringe of cloudy liquid in Mokhova's hand and her eyes flashed spitefully. But she didn't dare to attack Mokhova and chose a tactical retreat instead. Gorn skipped lightly over lockers and beds, like a goat. Mokhova, who was fifty years younger than her, simply couldn't keep up. She felt ashamed of her slowness and vented her spite on the women who had now woken up, all popping up on their beds like little roly-poly dolls and following the chase. Mokhova dealt out stinging slaps left and right, knowing that the unfortunate old women's sclerosis would never let the truth be known.

Mokhova pursued the nimble Gorn with the syringe for a long time, dreaming of jabbing her with the medicine that would freeze her high spirits just as soon as possible. Eventually Mokhova drove Gorn into a corner and tumbled her over onto a bedside locker. Gorn tried furiously to fight Mokhova off, kicking off her slippers and scratching furiously like an animal with all four limbs at once. She wheezed out words that almost made sense: "You'll dirty! Prostitute! Infect me! Whore! How old are you?" And her hooked nails, which looked like excrescences of amber, ripped Mokhova's white coat.

After her night-time injection Gorn lay without moving for two days, then she revived slightly and, early on the third evening, reached out her hand for the book. Mokhova didn't bother Gorn, but as she walked through the ward occasionally, she heard intermittent muttering—Gorn was monotonously reading the book aloud.

At about midnight a racket broke out in the ward again. The same story was repeated, with the difference that Gorn had grown even stronger now and didn't run away, but joined full-blooded battle.

Soon Gorn was lying strapped down on a bed, tossing her head about wildly, with a crimson bump swelling up on it.

Mokhova had been mauled as badly as Lermontov's novice in his battle with the badger: her neck, face, breasts and arms were covered with deep, bloody scratches. She was very finicky about her appearance, and the wounds made her absolutely furious.

Mokhova darted across to the bed, swung her hand and punched Gorn hard on the jaw. Her fist felt the crack of the dental plate as it broke.

The old woman pushed the two fragments out with her swollen tongue and suddenly said quite lucidly: "Don't hit me, Lizka!"

Mokhova had just raised her hand for a second punch… The old woman started squirming about and added resolutely, building sentences out of the growling words: "I'll. Do. What. I'm. Told. Read. The. Book. There's. Strength. In. It."

Gorn told Mokhova everything that she'd understood about the Book. At first Mokhova didn't believe what Gorn said, but she wiped away Gorn's blood and applied a cold compress to the bump. Mokhova spent all the next day pondering something, then she volunteered to take a night shift out of turn. The nursing assistant who was supposed to help Mokhova was allowed to go home.

Mokhova hadn't been intending to read the book herself; she was expecting Gorn to do that, and she was planning to observe her. But the bump on the head affected Gorn's health badly: after the effect of the Book of Strength wore off, she didn't even return to her former feeble, semi-demented state; she just slept, groaning intermittently.

Mokhova sat down not far from Gorn, in order to follow her reactions, and started reading aloud. It wasn't easy; her voice gradually became hoarse and her attention faded. But Mokhova had completed courses in a training college and a higher institute, and she knew how to cram.

Early in the night Mokhova completed the Book. Silence reigned in the ward. Mokhova looked at Polina Gorn and shuddered in surprise. The old woman was already sitting up on the bed with her legs dangling over the side like black branches.

"Lizka!" Gorn barked, but in a perfectly amicable manner, and started darting about the ward, working off her excess strength.

Suddenly the other old women started getting up. A cold shudder ran down Mokhova's spine. The Book hadn't started to affect her yet. Reading aloud, directing the words outward, not into herself, had retarded the effect. Slipping out into the corridor, Mokhova locked the door of the ward and set a chair against it, in order to observe what was going on through the window above it.

What she saw was both terrifying and amusing. The old women were making extremely strong, sweeping movements with their arms, making it look as if they were hugging themselves, and jerking their legs out forward like the soldiers who guarded Lenin's mausoleum. At the same time the expressions on their faces were a succession of every possible contortion and grimace. Sometimes the old women blurted out words—"intestine", "health", "labour merit"—or else they simply laughed.

Like Gorn on that first night, they tried to name the objects around them. "Spenil, Pilsen!" an old woman with tangled hair shouted out, looking at a ballpoint pen. "Make letters!"

"Plamp!" howled another, staring at the ceiling.

A third one chanted: "Kittle! With warm water!"

A fourth one grabbed hold of an alarm clock and wheezed intensely: "Lome! Lome! Tefelome! Don't remember!" And she growled furiously: "Tame!"

When they crashed into each other, the old women tried to introduce themselves; "What name? Anna Kondratyevna! Forgot what I wanted! How old? And my name's Tarasenko! What name? Krupnikova. Anyway, it was a good dress. And we ate well! What did you eat? Is your name Alimova? Galina! Alimola? I told you, old you, sholed you. You're called Galina? Galila. Dalila. How old are you? Six point two roubles. No, point three roubles!"

When she saw Mokhova's face pressed up against the glass in the door, the old woman with the alarm clock shouted out ferociously: "Mirror!"

Mokhova's fear left her when she felt the Strength. And from that moment on she thought about how to make use of this property of the Book that had been revealed to her. Naturally, she didn't intend to write a sensational article for a medical journal.

Her thoughts were interrupted by a heavy blow against the door. The old women had lined up into a live battering ram, determined to break out.

Mokhova wasn't afraid of the encounter. She already knew that the berserk old women could be subdued and pacified. Gorn's example proved that. Mokhova had prepared a club in advance—a length of high-voltage cable with a heavy tin-bound core of metal wires.

A blow shook the door. Bed castors squeaked across the lino-leum. Mokhova understood the tactical concept when the glass in the window above the door flew out and an old woman appeared in the aperture. The metal mesh of a bed had served as an excel-lent trampoline, tossing the old woman two metres up into the air. There were still fragments of glass in the frame and the old woman had impaled her stomach on them. Bleating in fury, she carried on trying to crawl through. Inverted Himalayas of blood slowly oozed down the door, making it look as if the old woman had put out bloody roots.

The second assault was launched more successfully. First a mop flitted about in the broken window, knocking out the shards of glass. A metal mesh bed base creaked again and a different old woman flew into the opening and started climbing down the door into the corridor.

Before the old woman could crawl out, Mokhova stunned her with a blow of the club. Then she opened the door and skipped back a few metres.

The old women came piling out of the ward and surrounded Mokhova. Gorn stood beside the door, indicating that she wasn't getting involved in the fight.

The old women raged and howled, but they didn't dare attack. Anyone who bared her teeth, as if she was about to pounce, earned a heavy blow from the club. Eventually an old woman by the name of Reznikova assumed the role of leader.

Stepping forward, she fended off a blow from the club with the mop. She raised her hand, calling for silence. Mokhova was in no hurry and she let the old woman have her say. An utterance vaguely resembling coherent speech followed; "Now, in the first place, first of all! We have to do! The same way as yours, that time! Today I did forgot, as they say! I did very bad today!"

The old women started murmuring approvingly in response to this gibberish and only Polina Gorn asked: "Reznikova, are you married?"

"Four years already!" Reznikova snarled, then swung round ferociously towards Mokhova, flinging up the mop.

The heavy cable whistled through the air and reddish-brown glop splashed out of Reznikova's mouth onto the wall. Mokhova swung her arm back again and the old women trudged into the ward, whimpering discontentedly.

The pacification was achieved with minimal casualties: Reznikova had a broken jaw and the old woman who got stuck in the window over the door had deep cuts on her stomach. The injured were carried onto beds and Mokhova gave them first aid.

The effect of the Book was soon exhausted and the old women started dropping where they stood, like wind-up dolls in which the spring has run down.

Mokhova dragged the bodies onto beds, washed the blood off the door and swept up the glass.

The second group reading was not accompanied by any outbursts of aggression against Mokhova. The old women submitted to her completely, for which most of the credit belonged to Gorn, who influenced her comrades by using both argument and the club, which Mokhova had personally handed over to her, conferring upon her local authority.

Polina Gorn's former garrulity did not return; her mind became rational and her thoughts succinct.

On Gorn's advice Mokhova held new readings in different wards during the week. Gorn herself and about ten pacified old women attended the reading in order to suppress any possible focal points of rebellion.

The militia expanded every time that Mokhova was on duty. The Book had a salutary effect on senile organisms. In their normal condition, of course, the old women still did not possess even a hundredth part of the strength that the Book gave them, but their minds remained relatively clear.

In part they attributed the miraculous effect of the Book to

Mokhova. They were old, lonely and abandoned by their own children, and the lingering spark of motherhood still glimmered in their hearts. Not the raucously domineering kind, but the self-sacrificing kind.

Gorn picked up this mood among the old women. The next night Mokhova was dubbed the "little daughter" and the old women were dubbed the "mums". Gorn had thought through the ritual of adoption very thoroughly. In Mokhova's view it was not particularly pleasant or hygienic, but Gorn persuaded Mokhova to go through with it.

Every old woman smeared Mokhova's face with her vaginal secretions, as if symbolizing in this way that Mokhova had appeared in the world via her womb, and swore to protect the "little daughter" to her last breath.

Sixty old women went through the ritual. Twenty or so recent converts watched them, raging and roaring—and in the meantime they were pacified by overseers who dealt them slaps round the back of the head to drive home the idea that the greatest happiness they could ever be granted was to become a "mum" as soon as possible.

That same night Gorn said to Mokhova: "The staff! Get rid!"— and ran her hand across her throat, imitating the movement of a butcher's knife.

The time had come for decisive action. Someone had snitched to the director about the noise at night, the broken window panes and the bruises. It was obvious that these emergencies occurred during Mokhova's shift, and she could have faced serious unpleasantness. To carry out the operation Mokhova had the faithful Gorn and a militia of about eighty old women in total.

Mokhova informed the director, Avanesov, that at the weekend she intended to hold a recreational reading session in the women's section, because she believed that the old female patients needed it. Avanesov did not object.

At eleven in the morning the female half of the old folk's home started stirring. The corridors were filled with the creaking of beds being trundled about as the ambulatory old women moved their bedridden friends to the site of the assembly.

Mokhova was already experienced in reading rapidly and intelligibly, and she ran through the text in record time. Curious nurses came down several times from the men's floor above. They were told that everything had been agreed with the director. One way or another, Mokhova won herself three hours' grace. And when the duty sister called the director at home and complained about the pandemonium that Mokhova had caused, it was too late.

Avanesov arrived in time for the final pages. He curtly ordered the patients to be taken back to their wards. Mokhova openly raised her voice. Avanesov repeated his order, again in vain. He threatened to sack Mokhova for these outrageous excesses. The nurses and nursing assistants came running at the sound of his shouting. Taking hold of the heads of the beds, they started trundling the old women away to their wards. Seeing Mokhova still not responding to what he said, the director started walking towards her. And in that second Mokhova shouted out, "The End!"—and clapped the Book shut.

At that very moment the old woman Stepanida Fetisova grabbed the drip tube out of the vein of her ward neighbour Irina Shostak and deftly flung this improvised garrotte round Avanesov's neck. Deprived of her flow of medication, Shostak fell into a coma, from which she emerged a minute later when the Book took effect.

The rebels were unstoppable. The slaughter began and Avanesov, strangled with a drip tube, became the first victim.

Mokhova's army went through its baptism of fire at its official place of residence. As victims for its lynching it had four nurses, five nursing assistants, three female cooks, two dishwashers-cum-servers, the building manager, the caretaker, who also doubled as the electrician and plumber, and all the patients in the men's section, about fifty in total.

The old women had been divided in advance into squads of ten. Each squad was led by a sergeant-mum, who took her orders from Mokhova or Gorn.

Two squads were dispatched urgently into the yard to guard the gates and the fence—no one could be allowed to slip away.

The approaches to the director's office and the reception area were blocked off to exclude the possibility of a phone call. From the cubbyhole of the caretaker Chizhov, who was drinking his vodka for the last time in his life, they took a wood cleaver, a carpenter's axe, a small sledgehammer, a screwdriver with a long blade, a crowbar, a shovel and a spade for clearing snow.

The old women infiltrated the kitchen, where they found half a dozen knives and a meat cleaver, with which they promptly and pitilessly dispatched two of the female cooks and the dishwashers. The third cook, Ankudinova, was a massive woman: scattering the old women with her mighty arms, she managed to get to the door and hid somewhere on that floor of the building. They didn't pursue her for the time being.

The cutting weapons were given to the strongest old women, those who in their previous lives had been used to slitting the throats of cattle and poultry. The sledgehammer went to a large individual of proletarian origin, a former structural fitter.

The death squads scattered across the various floors. The nurses mistakenly thought they could escape by locking themselves in the wards. The sledgehammer broke down the door and the old women poured in through the breach, jostling and growling. They threw the nurses on the floor and, not having any cold weapons, tore at them with their hands and gnawed on them with their false teeth or removed the rubber pad from a crutch so that it wouldn't soften the blow and beat the nurses on the face, the breasts and the stomach with the wooden frame.

Three nursing assistants managed to get up onto the roof and batten the hatch behind them. They tried to get down the fire-escape ladder. Old women, prepared to die themselves in order to prevent an escape, jumped out of nearby windows and clutched on tight to the fugitives' dressing gowns. Dragged down by the extra weight, the nursing assistants tumbled off the ladder with a squeal and fell, breaking their bones.

In the men's section a squad of ten old women with pillows ran from bed to bed, suffocating the paralysed old men. On Gorn's orders the men who could walk were herded together and driven onto the knives. The old men went as meekly as sheep, making no attempt to escape.

Only one man managed to flee—a war veteran, the retired colonel Nikolai Kaledin. Despite his age, he had retained the ability to think and fight.

Kaledin, the cook Ankudinova, the nursing assistants Basova and Shubina, and the building manager Protasov offered worthy resistance. They managed to break through to the firefighting-equipment point and get hold of two crowbars and a gaff.

With courage worthy of the Ryazan folk hero Yevpaty Kolovrat, the small group broke through the lines of old women several times, but there was nowhere they could go to escape from them. The first to fall was Shubina, and then the building manager was killed. The cook Ankudinova, the nursing assistant Basova and the colonel were pinned against the wall and held there with crutch blows from a distance until the old women with the axes and knives arrived.

The old women piled corpses on beds to increase the force of the blow. Loaded up with bodies, the beds smashed into the small group like trucks with battering rams. The colonel, Ankudinova and Basova were crushed against the wall. Kaledin fell and was finished off immediately, and Mokhova ordered the old women not to finish off the courageous cook and nursing assistant

These women were no longer young and they possessed exceptional strength and fighting spirit—Gorn had informed Mokhova of this and suggested luring Ankudinova and Basova over to their side.

The outcome was that the nursing home was taken in less than an hour. Mokhova's army lost only six old "mums". Another ten of them were slightly injured.

On Monday a new shift came to work—a female doctor, a senior nurse and nursing assistants. These were easily captured, frightened and enslaved. No further killings were necessary; the old women had already realized their own strength.

Paradoxically, no one found out about the bloody battle. The building stood out on the very edge of town. Not many people visited the old folk. The last check had been a month before the skirmish and no review committee was expected now until the New Year. In any case, times were getting difficult and the authorities had no time for the elderly.

Mokhova made a careful study of the personal files on each employee of the Home who had been killed. In all cases personnel without families had been selected.

The old director Avanesov lived alone. They put an old woman in his flat, and she told everyone she was Avanesov's sister. Any visitors and review commissions could be dealt with by the tamed doctor and senior nurse. Mokhova herself attended meetings at the social-security department, presenting a fake letter with Avanesov's seal.

The nursing assistants proved to be gratifying material. These women, who had come here twenty years earlier from remote villages, had been completely written off by their relatives. Their lives were failures, they had worked hard, never married and vegetated in hostels. Mokhova sent appropriate letters to the hostels, saying that so-and-so had finally been allocated her own living space.

The caretaker Chizhov, two unmarried nurses and the dish-washers had been living temporarily in an outhouse on the grounds of the Home, so no problems at all arose with them. The dead continued to receive wages for many years and were then sacked retrospectively.

A document was cooked up, supposedly from Protasov, to say that he had been recruited to a job somewhere in the Urals. False documents were also used to dispatch the dead cooks to some remote back-of-beyond. The cohabitee of one nurse was sent a fake letter from her, saying that she was leaving for the Soviet Far

East with her lover. Another nurse was divorced and had only a mother and a son. They were finished off by a suicide granny who was sent to them and poisoned both her victims and herself with carbon monoxide.

That left the numerous dead old men and the problem of burying them. Even with the strength that the Book granted them, the old women could not have buried so many corpses rapidly. Mokhova simply hired an excavator, explaining that a foundation pit needed to be dug for a new laundry.

The excavator dug the pit in one day and they piled the corpses into it. The old men didn't have any near and dear ones, and if any were to show up suddenly, there was an appropriate record of death ready and waiting.

The captured Home became Mokhova's citadel. In civilian terms, it was effectively impregnable, with a three-metre-high wall and sturdy gates. A vigilant female guard was always on duty at the checkpoint and the wall was patrolled by an armed detachment.

The army was distinguished by iron discipline and obedience. Mokhova had found something with which to oppose both Lagudov's select representatives of the intelligentsia and Shulga's lumpens—the principle of collective motherhood proved to be a reliable ideological platform.

As a former dean of a faculty of Marxism-Leninism, Polina Vasilyevna Gorn knew many things, and in particular that no organization would survive for long without a General Line. "Promise them eternal life. And then we'll see how it goes," Gorn wisely suggested to Mokhova.

Mokhova lined up her militia in the yard and told them the story of the Books and the Great Goal. The conclusion to be drawn from her story was that anyone who stayed with Mokhova to the end would be rewarded with eternity. When they heard these dubious good tidings, the old women set the parade ground ringing with roars of triumph. They had acquired a Great Dream.

THE MOKHOVA THREAT

G ROMOV'S BOOKS still had to be sought out, and in this area
Mokhova was exceptionally successful. She began a lot later
than her competitors, but she quite rapidly made up for lost time
and overtook the leading libraries where collecting was concerned.

Like the "steel bird" in the well-known Soviet song, the old
women found their way into places that no armoured train could
streak into, no surly tank could creep into and no search parties
from hostile clans could penetrate.

The old women's world was a separate, expansive universe, rich
in opportunities and connections. The old women knew people
right across the country, and the "mums" wrote letters, got on
the phone and sent telegrams to their friends. Quite often trivial
"natter sessions" at the entrance to some building were more pro-
ductive than the months-long expeditions undertaken by Shulga's
or Lagudov's scouts. There were old women everywhere who had
access to bulk stores of information as they supplemented their
pensions by working part time for pitiful rates as cleaning ladies
or attendants in libraries and archives. Mokhova's rivals referred
to these women who wormed their way in everywhere as "mops".

The old women entangled the Gromov world in the web of
their espionage networks. They easily intercepted hostile agents
returning home, all unsuspecting, with their booty. They filled those
agents with fatal amounts of drink in trains, ambushed them in
the night at railway halts and in pitch-dark entrances on deserted
streets. The books flowed to Mokhova.

If the libraries had not taken countermeasures, Mokhova would certainly have acquired a complete set of works. They say that the list of Gromov's works was stolen from the Lenin Library for Mokhova, but it never reached her—for which the credit must go to the now-defunct clan of Stepan Guryev, a former gold prospector.

His library was located in the Altai Mountains, close to the Bagryany and Severny gold mines. The gold works had been abandoned for a long time and the "readers" began working them again, thereby earning the means to live and to search for the Books. These men were old hands who had been around: we know that migrant Chechen marauders took a passing interest in the mines, but the overconfident sons of the Caucasus were burned alive, after being lured into a trap in a barracks hut…

Guryev's men caught a female courier carrying material. Demonstrating exceptional self-sacrifice, the old woman ate the tablets of cheap cardboard. Hoping to reconstitute the books somehow, they dissected the old woman's gastrointestinal tract. They extracted only thoroughly chewed, unreadable shreds, but from the number of cardboard scraps they could conclude that there had originally been seven Books.

Searches required not only patience, but also money. Mokhova conveniently got one of her women hired as senior accountant in the social-security department. This adroit bookkeeper managed things so that the nursing home somehow dropped out of the authorities' field of view, and yet continued to be financed with government money for many more years.

The Home could hold as many as four hundred "mums". The flow of pensioners was continuous: following established practice, the men were exterminated immediately and the women were put under armed guard.

After two years Mokhova possessed the largest and most powerful army of all the clans. And in addition, the relative age profile of the "mums" gradually grew younger. From the example of the cook Ankudinova and the nursing assistant Basova, Mokhova realized that the army needed younger recruits. The decrepit old women had shown that they were outstanding warriors, but only when the Book transformed them. For the rest of the time most of the army had only a third of that strength. Literally a week after the Home was captured the recruitment of fresh forces began.

The idea of eternal life in one's own body had a lot in common with the ideology of the Jehovah's Witnesses. Perhaps that was why Mokhova often reinforced the ranks of her middle-aged warriors with members of the sect, who gladly made the switch to her, preferring the knife and the axe to handing out stupid leaflets.

The old women involved their own elderly, but still sound, daughters. Semi-alcoholics, divorced or simply solitary, bitter and angry at the whole world, they stayed in the Home, opting to commit to the struggle for immortality.

No one was taught to fight. Gorn wisely assumed that there was no point in disturbing old reflexes. The women were given items with which they had been familiar throughout their lives. The village women were equally skilful with an axe, a knife, a scythe or a flail. Those who had worked at transport depots, factories and construction sites or mended roads were issued with the familiar orange waistcoats, crowbars, sledgehammers, spades and picks.

It should be said that to believe these women were weak was a serious error. In years and years of heavy labour their bodies had all accumulated immense muscular strength. They had simply become psychologically decrepit and forgotten that they once used to swing crowbars and axes untiringly at construction sites, lug sleepers and sections of rail on the railways or carry buckets and stretchers filled with immensely heavy cement.

No one was surprised by the ability of some Chinese martial-arts master, a frail little man, to handle dozens of young opponents. The women, having worked all their lives, also possessed immense reserves of physical strength. The Book was necessary only to help them recall the blunted sensation of Strength.

This infantry of female road labourers and collective-farm

women, whose bodies seemed to consist of flesh that was moulded like lead, crushed the clans of Shulga's former comrades in arms, Frolov and Lyashenko. In particular the fifty-year-old crane driver Olga Petrovna Dankevich distinguished herself in these bloody campaigns. She had grown so strong that her preferred weapon was the hook of a crane, which she carried on a three-metre-long pole. A blow from that mace would have flattened a rhinoceros. Dozens of readers, and even librarians, met their death from that monstrous hook.

When Guryev's clan was liquidated and Mokhova took cruel revenge for the courier's dissected gastrointestinal tract, the imminent danger became clear. For a long time after that an old woman was a symbol of danger and a synonym for cruel cunning.

In 1995 the libraries united against Mokhova's tyranny. The coalition also had another highly important goal—to wrest from Mokhova the Book of Strength that she possessed. It was said that any copies of the extremely rare Book of Strength that showed up had been assiduously destroyed and perhaps there was now only one copy left in existence. Just how the libraries intended to divide it up among themselves afterwards was not clear.

The opinion was expressed that the Book of Strength would have to be burned or become common property, but no one explained exactly how. The question was swept under the rug to avoid introducing confusion and disunity. In any case everyone was unanimous that Mokhova had to be disposed of.

The coalition army included detachments from sixteen librar-ies—about two thousand men from various different cities: Saratov, Tomsk, Perm, Kostroma, Ufa, Krasnoyarsk, Khabarovsk, Lipetsk, Sverdlovsk, Penza, Belgorod, Vladimir, Ryazan, Vorkuta and Chelyabinsk. They were joined by a militia of six hundred people fielded by reading rooms.

Mokhova flung almost three thousand mums into the battle. She herself wisely did not take part in the fighting. The army was commanded by Polina Gorn.

LIBRARIES AND READING ROOMS

A READING ROOM was the name given to a small group organized round some particular Book—of Joy, Memory or, more rarely, Endurance.

The entire Gromov world had begun with small communities like this. When a solitary individual who had penetrated the mystery of a Book turned up, a reading room would form around him, including those comrades whom he had decided to take into his confidence. If someone with a family became a member of a reading room, then soon his nearest and dearest became members too, and that was tolerated indulgently. But every piece of string comes to an end, and at a certain stage the community stopped expanding.

A reading room was the foundation or basis on which, in time, a library could spring up. The opposite also occurred. Following an armed clash a small clan might be reduced to a reading room.

All kinds of people were taken in, from all age groups and all professions. Every reader was free, both morally and—more importantly—financially. This was an advantage that reading rooms had over libraries, where people donated part of their income, the so-called "membership fee", to fund the search for Books and support the administrative structures.

Just like a library, a reading room had a leader, who was known as the librarian. He or she was the owner of the Book or the person to whom the reading room had entrusted it. Reading rooms did not become involved in the search for Books; people were satisfied with what they had and honestly waited their turn to use it.

At first there were no points of intersection between the libraries and the reading rooms, although they knew about each other. Later the libraries built up their strength and accumulated more Books. The existence of competitors was incompatible with their totalitarian plans.

Reading rooms were blackmailed and intimidated. Suggestions were made that they should voluntarily give up their Book, and they were promised a place in a library if they did so. Sometimes Books were expropriated. There was an official explanation for this blatant banditry: the reading rooms were declared a hotbed of copyists and the leaders of large libraries called for copying to be halted at any price.

From out of a black void the "torch-bearers" appeared—hellhounds spawned by the will of the large clans. The torch-bearers attacked reading rooms, stole their books and burned them. These losses had practically no impact on the libraries, which had numerous spare copies in their depositories, but the wretched readers who had been deprived of their only Book were left with nowhere to go except into a library.

Against the background of this contradictory situation Mokhova's star rose high in the Gromov firmament. Following several successful raids on the depositories of influential libraries it became clear that a major battle was inevitable. An appropriate field for it was found in the north of Russia, beside the abandoned village of Neverbino.

And then the members of several clans, including Lagudov's and Shulga's, appealed to the reading rooms for help in the struggle against Mokhova, promising them absolute immunity from all financial levies in the future. That was why so many volunteers assembled near Neverbino. They came from every corner of the country to bear arms and stand up for their own reading rooms and Books.

THE BATTLE OF NEVERBINO

THE COALITION'S DETACHMENTS were organized in a primitive fashion, after the example of the Russian forces at the Battle of Kulikovo Field. The individuals in its staff headquarters were remote from modern military tactics, but nonetheless—as became clear later—quite practical in their approach.

The avant-garde of the formation consisted of the patrol and advance regiments, made up of reading rooms. Located behind them was a large regiment made up of brigades from six libraries, with its flanks protected by right-flank and left-flank regiments, each consisting of four combined brigades. Sheltering behind the large regiment was Shulga's clan, which called itself the reserve regiment, and the ambush regiment stationed in a small stretch of forest nearby was the detachment from Lagudov's clan, which also had only moderate claims to excellence as a fighting force.

Books of Endurance were extracted from secret depositories. Special readers, gathering groups of fifty people around them, read through the Books, straining their voices as they rendered the listeners' bodies insensible to wounds.

The allusion to Kulikovo Field was reflected in the challenge to a duel issued to all comers by the crane driver Dankevich as she whirled her terrible hook round her head. No duel took place, however—no Peresvet could be found among the ranks of the libraries.

Battle commenced at about two o'clock in the morning. Pumped full of strength, the "mums" moved in to attack the patrol and advance regiments. After suffering heavy losses, the reading-room militias pulled back.

Polina Gorn issued orders from a low hill where she was surrounded by her guard. Seeing that the frontal attack had run out of momentum and was threatening to turn into a pointless, drawn-out battle, Gorn created an advantage of numbers on the flank by throwing six units of a hundred women against the left-flank regiment, which fifteen minutes later no longer existed, having been crushed by the hammers of former railway workers.

Shulga's reserve regiment, which was responsible for preventing outflanking movements, abandoned the left-hand regiment to its fate, swung round the right-hand regiment and made straight for the high ground where Gorn's headquarters was located.

The detachments led by the mighty Dankevich emerged at the rear of the combined forces, creating a genuine threat of encirclement. Lagudov's ambush regiment struck at the rear of the mums who had broken through. The sudden introduction of fresh forces did not change the situation significantly. What saved the coalition was the passage of time. The effect of the Book of Strength had partially worn off—it had been read to the old women in advance, to provide the strength required for the forced march from the railway line to Neverbino.

Gorn's bodyguards perished in the cruel skirmish. An old woman who looked very much like Gorn was cornered by Shulga's soldiers. She fought desperately until she suddenly weakened and Shulga, goaded on by the Book of Fury, split his opponent's head open.

The death of their general was the signal for mass flight by Mokhova's army. Weakening as they ran, the old women were pursued like Mamai as far as the railway station. No more than a few dozen survived.

Rumours circulated that Gorn herself did survive, that it was her double who had been killed, that Gorn and two dozen of her closest comrades in arms who had retained their agility managed to hide and several days later reached their citadel, the nursing home. But it was preferred not to broadcast this information widely.

Many clamoured that Mokhova should be polished off in her lair and the Home should be taken by storm, otherwise the hydra would sprout more grey-haired heads, but this suggestion was stifled with the argument that Mokhova was finished anyway and "her fangs had been drawn": a scorched fragment of the Book of Strength was found at the site of Gorn's headquarters—it was believed that Gorn, sensing defeat, had destroyed this unique copy, probably the only one still in existence.

The price of victory was great. The combined forces had lost about a thousand men in the battle and hundreds had been wounded or maimed. Needless to say, the reading rooms had lost most of all.

The bodies of the dead were carried to a deep ravine, covered with caustic fertilizer to accelerate decomposition, and earth was scattered over everything, so that no pit remained. Seeds of common burdock and other fast-growing weeds were also thrown into the earth. In spring, burdock of gigantic size sprouted across the ravine, concealing for ever the bodies of those who had fallen at Neverbino.

On their way home, the reading-room militiamen and even the leaders of libraries that had taken a mauling spoke bitterly, in half whispers, saying the Neverbino bloodbath had been deliberately planned by Mokhova's, Lagudov's and Shulga's analysts in order to cut back the exorbitantly swollen numbers of people who knew about Gromov. The battle had reduced that world by a quarter.

At about the same time a new agency of power and administration was established—the Council of Libraries. Lagudov, having emerged from the battle with minimal losses for his clan, had more influence than ever, and he promoted the idea that only "natural librarians"—that is, those who had independently penetrated the essence of Gromov's Books—should have the right to be the chairman of the council. And after the Battle of Neverbino, there were officially only two of those left—Lagudov and Shulga. The Krasnoyarsk librarian Smolich, Nilin from Ryazan and Avilov from Lipetsk had been killed.

The council confirmed the official decision to grant the reading rooms financial immunity. A thorough census was carried out; reading rooms were normally named after the places where their members lived, or sometimes the name was derived from the surname of the librarian or founder.

All the reading rooms, with the exception only of those who fought at Neverbino, undertook to pay the council a tax of ten per cent of members' income. Naturally the proceeds were deliberately reduced by readers who concocted false documents. The council therefore toughened up the rules and replaced the moderate tithe with a unitary annual tax—a specific sum was set for every individual Book.

At the risk of getting ahead of ourselves, it should be said that the council did not rest on its laurels at this stage and went on to repress the independent groups completely. The reading rooms were coerced into becoming branch lending libraries. Henceforth a Book only nominally belonged to a reading room—the true owner of the Book was the council, which rented it out.

A table of fines was also drawn up. Any reading room that was heavily fined twice was disbanded in the name of the council and its Book was subject to confiscation. Non-compliance was punished with great severity.

Offences included, for instance, the presence of a copyist among a reading room's members, excessive garrulity on the part of any reader, theft and concealment of a newly found Book—any action capable of posing a threat to the conspiratorial secrecy of the Gromov universe.

Unfortunately the edict of immunity was systematically violated, if only because by no means every library accepted its legality—those who had not taken part in the Battle of Neverbino, for instance. These clans, who were not members of the council, acted crudely and cruelly, like all aggressors. Even if a reading room successfully defended its Book in battle, it lost so much blood in the process that it became easy prey for looters or other predatory clans.

Artfully engineered provocations also took place. It was enough to discredit an undesirable reading room twice for the council to take an immediate decision to disband it. For situations like this several programmes of social rehabilitation were developed. It was considered a great stroke of luck if the readers were all registered with the nearest library, without being broken up—and the concept of "near" was distinctly relative: quite often people had to travel more than a hundred kilometres to a Book. Membership dues and the cost of travel together took a heavy toll on readers' pockets

More often a different, tragic scenario was played out. Local or regional libraries refused to take all the strangers at once, arguing that they were already overfull. Preference was given to applicants who earned at least a minimally acceptable wage, out of which membership dues were then deducted. The readers with low incomes were scattered to any libraries where there were vacancies. We can imagine what an assignment to Irkutsk or Krasnoyarsk meant for someone who lived in Omsk. Many refused to make the move and joined the queues of "victims". As a rule these broken people went to seed, becoming vicious and violent. It was from their numbers that the council formed its brigades of torch-bearers. These mercenaries willingly carried out even the very vilest of missions since, after all, the reward for the job was a Book.

Readers who rejected this situation could only accept the challenge and face up to an enemy who outnumbered them many times over. It is obvious how these battles ended, when twenty brave defenders of a reading room fought against hundreds of choice warriors sent by the council…

During these troubled times I became a librarian. My reading room owned a Book of Memory and was frequented by seventeen readers.

PART II

The Shironin Reading Room

THE BOOK OF MEMORY

I MYSELF DID NOT read the Book of Memory until a month after I took up the job, and I must confess that I have not reread it often. The "memory" induced has always been the same, and it sometimes seemed to me that it might be worn out by repetition, like a pair of trousers.

Actually the sensation experienced cannot really be called memory or recall. Dream, vision, hallucination—these words also fail to capture the essence of the complex condition in which the Book immersed me. Its gift of deception to me personally was an entirely invented childhood, full of warm emotion and joy, and I immediately believed in it, because the sense of living this vision was so total: in comparison, real memories were mere bloodless silhouettes. In fact this three-dimensional phantom was experienced more brilliantly and intensely than any life and consisted only of little crystals of happiness and tender sadness, shimmering with the bright light of one event after another.

The "memory" had a musical lining, woven out of many melodies and voices. I caught echoes of 'The Beautiful Distance' and 'The Winged Swing', a polar-bear mother sang her lullaby to little Umka, a troubadour lauded a "ray of golden sunlight" in a velvety baritone, a touching little girl's voice asked a deer to whisk her away to magical deerland, "where pine trees sweep up to the sky, where what never was is real". And following those pine trees, my heart tore itself out of my breast and flew away, like a bird released out of warm hands.

To the accompaniment of this pot-pourri filled with rapturous tears, I saw New Year round dances, fun and frolics, presents, sleigh rides, a puppy with dangling ears yelping clamorously, thawed patches in spring, little streams, May Day holidays with banners and streamers, the unbelievable height of a flight on my father's shoulders, a vast expanse of smoky dandelions sprawling in front of me, cotton-wool clouds drifting across the sky, a picturesque little lake, pierced through with reeds, trembling in the wind, silvery small fry darting through the warm, shallow water, grasshoppers chirring in grass tinted yellow by the sunlight, purple dragonflies suspended motionless in the air, swivelling their precious, spangled, glittering heads.

I "recalled" my school years. There was a new little satchel, coloured crayons lying on a desk and an open copybook with my favourite words for ever—"Motherland" and "Moscow"—scrawled in awkward handwriting. My first teacher, Maria Viktorovna Latynina, opened her register and gave me a red "A" for penmanship. There was a new maths textbook with a wonderful smell, in which rabbits were added together and apples were taken away, and a nature-studies textbook as fragrant as the forest.

Imperceptibly the lessons matured, moving on to algebra and geography, but all this knowledge was grasped with mirthful ease. The winter holidays spilled out into the smooth, frosty surface of the skating rink and a snowball fight started up; then came spring with its chatter of starlings and a hand traced out some funny love note that was passed two desks along to the girl with the cute, light-brown plaits.

Holidays soared through the air like balloons, bright with the rainbow colours of flower beds, and the sun glinted in every window. Summer came and the euphorically blue sky of July swept across over the earth and fell, becoming the Black Sea with cloud foam on its waves. The cornflower-blue mass of Kara Dag loomed through the southern heat haze, the air was a-rustle with cypress trees and fragrant with juniper. With every caressing gust of the wind the bright two-storey building of the Young Pioneer Camp surfaced out of the greenery. Lenin, as white as sugar, towered up on his granite pedestal and bright-coloured alleys of flowers ran out in all directions from the statue like the rays of a star. Scarlet, resounding happiness fluttered on the slender mast of the flagstaff...

Described in words, of course, this doesn't sound particularly impressive. But that evening, when the effect of the Book came to an end, I gazed for a long time at a cloud as dark as a liver, creeping across a stormy sky. And I realized then that I would fight for Gromov's Book and my invented childhood.

It's incredible how easily my memory accepted this distinction. The phantom from the Book had no claim to kinship with me, and in the final analysis it was no more than a glossy heap of old photographs, the crackle of a home movie projector and a lyrical Soviet song.

Even so, my real childhood—that long, hateful caravan of commonplace events, for which I cared nothing—was immediately relegated to the sidelines.

But all that happened much later; for the first few weeks in the Shironin reading room I cursed my inheritance—without even wishing it, my late Uncle Maxim had played a really dirty trick on me. Together with my uncle's apartment I had inherited the position of librarian and the Book of Memory.

UNCLE MAXIM

M Y UNCLE WAS a doctor by profession. At first his life worked out remarkably well. He graduated from school with a silver medal, second in his class, and went to study at the Medical Institute. After two years of practical work for an institute in Siberia, my uncle was recruited to work in the Arctic.

I remember Uncle Maxim when he was still young. He used to come to visit us and always brought foodstuffs that were in short supply or things that were impossible to buy in the shops—imported anoraks, jumpers and shoes. One time he gave me a Panasonic twin-cassette deck that was the envy of many of my friends for years.

We would sit at the family table—Dad, Mum, me and my sister Vovka… Actually her real name was Natasha, and Vovka was just her nickname at home. When Natasha was born, my father took me, two years old at the time, to the maternity home, promising to show me a real, live Thumbelina there. I stood outside under the window and called, "Mummy, where's Thumbelina?"—and a half-deaf nurse, as kind-hearted as a St Bernard, who was gathering up the rubbish on the steps, smiled every time I said it and told me, "Don't shout, little one, they'll bring out your Vovochka in a moment…"

Well, we would sit there, and Uncle Maxim would tell us all sorts of amazing stories, almost like fairy tales, about the Far North. "In one village a reindeer herder shot himself. They buried him and the next night a murrain broke out among the deer. An old shaman said that they hadn't buried the suicide properly and he had turned into a demon that was killing the cattle. They dug up the body, buried it again face-down and nailed it down with a walrus tusk. And believe it or not, the murrain stopped immediately…"

Unlike timid Vovka, I enjoyed these frightening stories. My father, it's true, claimed that my uncle was rather partial to my mum and inclined to boast a bit in order to impress her. I suppose my father was simply envious of Uncle Maxim, who led such a colourful life.

But then my uncle stopped visiting us. I heard from my parents that he wasn't working with the expeditions any longer and had moved from the romantic tundra deep into the boring heart of Russia. But for me my Uncle Maxim remained the hero of an adventure film, a Siberian "Pathfinder", for a long time.

As the years passed, my uncle's halo faded noticeably. "He's a degenerate" and "He's a disgrace to the family" my father used to say about him. Apparently while he was in the cold climate my uncle had developed a taste for alcohol, and perhaps the constant availability of surgical spirits—because of his profession—had also played its part, or perhaps he had just fallen in with drinkers.

When his contract ended, my uncle worked as the head of a department in a hospital and tried to write his Ph.D. thesis. He never started a family of his own. Vodka ruined all his plans. First he was demoted to a neighbourhood doctor, and then sacked altogether for his drunkenness. Uncle Maxim rode around in an ambulance for several years, but then they got rid of him too.

In the last fifteen years he had only appeared at our place twice. The first time he arrived on a plane for my grandfather's funeral, drank heavily at the wake and even had a fight with my father, and the second time was when my grandmother died. My uncle arrived late for the funeral because he was on a bender and there weren't as many flights as in the old Soviet days, so he had to come by train. My uncle made a trip to the cemetery, stayed with us for a couple of days, quarrelled with my father and went away again.

After my grandfather and grandmother died my father used to say bitterly: "It was Maxim who drove them into their graves!"

And he was partly right—the old folks suffered terribly over how badly their son's life had turned out.

Uncle Maxim only phoned us rarely, and always with the same request—to send him a money order. My father, who had learned from bitter experience, always refused him and one day my uncle called his older brother a "Yid" and disappeared for a very long time.

Then he started calling again, but he didn't ask for money any longer; he simply asked how we were getting on. There were rumours that he hadn't drunk for five years. We found out about it from an old army colleague of my uncle's, a doctor, who stayed with us when he was passing through and handed on some money from my uncle—two hundred dollars that Maxim had once borrowed from my father. My uncle's army colleague told us that Maxim Danilovich had given up alcohol, but he suspected that my uncle had been sucked into a different kind of quicksand—apparently some religious organization or other, perhaps the Baptists or Jehovah's Witnesses.

Uncle Maxim himself didn't tell us anything specific; his voice on the phone was always cheerful, and when my father asked, "Maxim, have you drunk yourself completely out of your mind? Can't you even be open with your own brother?"—he just laughed and sent greetings to Mum, Vovka and me.

CHILDHOOD, BOYHOOD, YOUTH

I ONCE USED TO DREAM of studying at the Medical Institute, so that, like my Uncle Maxim, I too could roam the country in search of romantic adventure. At the time I never even thought about the fact that a doctor's profession is a stationary one and medical personnel don't usually travel much.

In the final year of school my plans changed. Everything was turned upside down by a theatre club that was organized at school. Unfortunately it was led by an adventurer who had absolutely no talent. After a year we had been irrecoverably inoculated with every imaginable failing of the actor's art, but the most terrible thing of all was that each one of us firmly believed in his own genius. Instead of preparing for our future lives and choosing a profession to match our abilities, with a decent and stable income, we started dreaming about art.

In its short existence the club didn't stage even a single production; all we did was rehearse. Yevgeny Schwartz's play *An Ordinary Miracle*, which we had arrogantly chosen to stage, never got any farther than the first act, but we already thought of ourselves as stage artistes.

I remember what a terrible state of alarm I threw my father and mother into when I announced that I intended to go to Moscow, no less, and join the Theatrical Institute to become an actor.

I must give my parents due credit, for they did try to rescue their son from the impending catastrophe. The only one who supported me in my vainglorious dreams was Vovka, but only until it was made clear to her that her brother Alyoshka was not going to end up on the practice stage at the Moscow Art Theatre, but go straight into the army. After this sudden enlightenment, Vovka fell silent and I lost my only ally. My parents had already launched a new educational campaign. Now, to spare my vanity, they started denouncing the nepotism inherent in theatrical institutions: "No one ever gets in there without graft."

My courage failed me and they cunningly tempted me with a different prospect. My father said that he didn't want to destroy my dreams, but wouldn't it be better first to acquire a solid profession in a technical college? And then, five years later, if I still couldn't live without art, I would be more mature, I would know myself better, and I could go to college to study directing, which already sounded more respectable in itself. I thought about it and agreed to the technical college and a "solid profession".

To this day that expression reminds me of something rectangular and heavy, resembling simultaneously a silicate brick and a reinforced concrete pillar. I chose the most solid area of all—"Machinery and Technologies for Foundry Engineering". In the entrance exams in Maths and Physics I made a whole heap of mistakes and got a pretty bad fright, but they pulled me up to a "B". After an entirely fictitious exam—a composition—I was accepted for the first year of the course.

I wasn't interested in my studies; every subject was alien to me. But I didn't skip lectures and for the exams I dutifully copied out heaps of cribs, which they didn't take away from us.

After the mid-year exams many students were kicked out of the institute, but not out of the Faculty of Mechanics and Metallurgy. They hoisted up our grades as high as they could, and I tried hard not to fall behind too. Doing all those drawings was hard, but even that problem could be solved—for a small reward, students who specialized in perspective geometry would do them for me. My grant was just enough to cover the especially hideous course requirements in the Theory of Machines and Mechanisms—TMM—which had been known since time immemorial as "This Murders Me". I lived with my parents and didn't have the kind of financial problems that students from out of town might face.

It was 1991 and my assessments still contained, as a final flourish from the Soviet age, an examination on the history of the Communist Party of the Soviet Union, which I passed with a "B", and a test on Scientific Atheism.

Of course, I didn't forget what my true calling was and why I was there—to acquire that "solid specialization", that indulgence from my parents and myself, so that, with a mechanical engineer's diploma tucked under my jacket, I could stride fearlessly into the artistic world with a clear conscience.

When they started developing a team at their institute for the Club of the Jolly and Ingenious competition, I dashed to join it. My first trial appearances on stage made it clear that I was "not funny". Everyone realized it. I attributed this acting failure to my noble, entirely unclown-like stature and dramatic talent. Disappointed, I consoled myself with the thought that my natural gifts were not those of a buffoon in amateur dramatics, but of a serious artiste.

I managed to make up two feeble jokes. One played on the name of Ukrainian vodka with pepper, *horilka*—"In Ukraine they've started making vodka for monkeys—Gorillka…"—and the other developed that Russian saying, "There's no virtue in standing"— "There's no virtue in standing. Take the weight off. Virtue's in the backside." They laughed at the second joke and ditched it. I also reworked the song 'The Beautiful Distance' to include the words, "I promise I'll be cleaner and I'll shave."

My hour of stardom arrived when our institute's team got involved in the municipal festival. Three days before the quarter-finals, it turned out that the competition sections "Greetings" and "Homework" were still not ready. The Jolly and Ingenious were headed for the bottom, taking their captain with them. They laid out witticisms written on scraps of paper like a game of patience and couldn't gather them together into a single whole. The mournful prospect of an exit from the festival loomed over us.

The manager of the student club, Dima Galoganov, dropped in to see us. He was a recent graduate of the institute and now a petty bureaucrat. Galoganov sombrely swore to disband the team in the event of failure.

During the castigation I looked through the archive, which contained the rejected dross, jumbled it up together with some lightweight jokes, and suddenly a complete plan of the performance took shape in my mind.

Raking up the pieces of paper and the notebook, I announced that by the next day I would write a complete programme for all the sections. In one night of work I managed to sew those dismal scraps together into a colourful and entirely original performance. One leitmotif was particularly successful, using songs in which the words "go crazy" figured at least in passing: "He's wearing a camouflage tunic, it'll make her go crazy", "I'm going crazy or ascending to a higher plane of lunacy", "And the postman will go crazy trying to find us", "I'm going crazy over you". The moment the singer reached that phrase with "crazy" in it, he suddenly started pulling dumb faces, smiling, gurgling and dribbling. In the final song we really cracked the audience up when our entire line-up started gurgling like idiots. Our team triumphantly won through to the semi-final, and a star of Moscow's Club of the Jolly and Ingenious who was on the jury said that our performing skills were worthy of a higher league.

The president of the institute congratulated the manager of the student club, Galoganov, on our victory, and Galoganov didn't forget about me. In three days I had become number one in the team. From being a rank-and-file writer of jokes, I was elevated to a position with obscure contours, within which the functions of a director could be vaguely discerned. Moreover, no one objected to my elevation. On the contrary, I was loudly congratulated and thanked.

I made haste to inform my family about my success and they nodded smugly—"Well, what did we say?", "Well, well, only a second-year student and already a director…"—and they winked at me cunningly, as if to say, "The best is yet to come."

My new purpose in life eventually robbed me of my "solid profession". From the second year I hardly studied at all, but worked on the CJI. I was granted most of my course tests and exams as a gift, thanks to the vice-president for cultural affairs.

My own gift for compilation, which had previously manifested itself in the writing of reports, came in handy in my new position. It was easy for me to design programmes for all the amateur concerts and celebrations devoted to the institute's anniversaries, and I became an indispensable assistant to our club manager.

A half-hour film about the institute was shot under my supervision. We timed the presentation just right, combining two round dates: the president's sixtieth birthday and the institute's sixtieth anniversary, and we said it was a modest gift from the student club.

The film was called *Our Beloved Polytech: Yesterday, Today, Tomorrow*, and it was pompously eulogistic. For several years the flattering video was always shown to high-placed guests from the ministry.

The president was very touched by his present and money started being allocated to the club. Following these subsidies Galoganov, who bought himself a new television, a video player and a music centre, really doted on me.

The institute's petty bureaucracy invited me to its parties as one of its own. Sensing imminent promotion, Galoganov, in his drunken generosity, started predicting more and more frequently that I would be his successor in the post of club manager and was genuinely offended because I wasn't ecstatic at the prospect.

At the time I couldn't understand that life had handed me a perfectly tolerable little pattern for a career—a calm, swampy haven. I indignantly rejected these gifts of fate. Instead of consolidating my friendship with Galoganov and the vice-president for cultural affairs, time after time I informed my benefactors with a condescending smile that I intended to take up art seriously and couldn't give a damn for a future as a petty functionary in a college.

My parents, of course, tried to change my mind, but I replied harshly that I had promised them a "solid profession" and not a life obliterated by boredom.

Vovka kept quiet, because she had been morally compromised. She was a second-year student then, and I can't remember which came first—the melon-shaped bulge of her stomach or the words about getting married soon. And so Vovka didn't butt in with any clever advice, but devoted assiduous efforts to cajoling passing marks for her exams out of her lecturers, in order not to lose a year of study. For our part, we tried to like Vovka's fiancé Slavik, a member of her study group. This didn't prove too hard; at the very first viewing the defiler of virtue won us all over with his meek and obliging manner. He seemed really to love Vovka. They soon married and moved into our old folks' empty apartment. In June Vovka gave birth to a boy, whom they called Ivan.

In two years pride had blinded me. I associated freely with the vice-president of the institute and had my own desk in the office of the club manager. I wasn't writing any diploma thesis at all. At Galoganov's request an old diploma work entitled 'Casting from Lost-Wax Models' was extracted from the archives and the title page was changed.

What else was there? In summer, at the end of the fourth year, I got married. At that time student marriages had assumed the proportions of an epidemic. My wife was called Marina. She had a rather pleasant appearance, with features so generically regular that she looked like a statistically average model of an attractive girl. That was the way the propaganda posters used to depict the striding ranks of Young Communist League girls, all with that same collective prettiness. After the first day we met, I wouldn't have recognized her in the street. The only distinctive thing about

Marina was her laugh. It was very melodic and resonant, and she mostly laughed when I flaunted my wit. Eventually I noticed her.

Throughout my polytechnic years I was never short of girlfriends. I was a rather well-known celebrity. Even so, this Marina saw off her rivals pretty quickly, but I didn't take that seriously at all: I was genuinely amused by the girl's hunt for a husband.

Marina wasted no time and cranked up the relationship so smartly that six months later I was surprised to learn that people were already talking about us as a soon-to-be family, and the strangest thing of all was that I didn't feel the slightest desire to correct this evident misunderstanding. Even the vice-president, running along the corridor, congratulated me on my imminent wedding.

My parents were also wholeheartedly in favour. They thought that marriage would make me settle down, forget my stupid dreams and opt for a happy family life instead.

The part of my soul that was infected by the universal wedding fever falsely reassured me that a wife would not be any obstacle to the career of a future stage director. Everything was decided by a phrase uttered by my boss Galoganov: "What are you afraid of? If you don't like it, you can get divorced."

Somehow it was that possibility of a future divorce that reassured me, and I proposed to Marina. The wedding was attended by a narrow family circle—Vovka was in her eighth month and charmed everyone at the feast with her impressive stomach. As a wedding gift my father-in-law and mother-in-law gave us an apartment, which, however, they registered in Marina's name.

Our marriage lasted just over a year. In that relatively short period of time I had learned that my spouse's weeping, unlike her laughter, was incredibly unpleasant

After receiving my diploma as an engineer, I started assiduously preparing to join a faculty of stage direction. I set out to reconnoitre Moscow. The Russian capital struck me a sly blow with the rouble. It had never even occurred to me that now I was a citizen of a different country and my education would have to be paid for.

This woeful fact immediately put an end to any idea of attending a college in Russia. When I got back, I was able to look my acquaintances in the eye with no shame and say that the only reason Moscow was off the agenda was money. I reproached my parents: you see, I ought to have gone then, five years ago, when the Soviet Union still existed.

What my home city had to offer for the realization of my dream was an institute of culture, a cauldron in which the flayed flesh of all the Muses seethed and bubbled. In among the faculties of music and those offering drilling in leftist decorative and applied arts, the custodians of academic and folk choirs, guardians of orchestras consisting of dombras and balalaikas and mentors of choreographic ensembles, there was a theatre faculty with departments for the art of acting, directing drama and directing theatricalized performances and festivals.

More mature now, I took a more sober view of my abilities. My self-confidence had evaporated together with my youth. A week before the exams I found out that the competition for drama was rather high, eight applicants for each place, which was rather strange for our back of beyond.

The competition for the acting department was a bit lower, but I suddenly felt ashamed of my age; at the age of twenty-two I felt like that late developer Lomonosov, smelling of coastal fish, among the crowd of young seventeen-year-old school-leavers.

That left the direction of theatricalized performances and festivals, which had a tolerable level of competition at three applicants per place. They also required a document demonstrating experience of working with a collective. Galoganov's secretary banged out one of those for me in five minutes flat, and the vice-president appended a positive reference to the note.

I consulted my family. My parents and Vovka said unanimously: "Don't take any risks—the important thing is to get in. You can change departments afterwards if you like."

Yet again I let myself be guided by cowardice. The documents were submitted for "performances and festivals".

But even so I was indescribably happy that summer. The girls applying for the acting faculty were so alluring, perched on long high heels and just barely covered by transparent chiffon that fluttered in draughts, baring their youthful charms to the July heat and the male glances of the entrance committee.

When they heard that I had joined the direction department (I wisely didn't specify which one), these beauties asked me not to forget about them. They laughed as they said: "You just whistle, young director, and we'll come flying instantly. You'll see how affectionately we'll thank you for a role, dear director…" they promised, laughing and glowing tenderly.

And then, inspired by my summer ecstasy and my eagerness to whistle to those young actresses just as soon as possible, I showed up at home and informed my odious Marina that I was divorcing her.

My wife responded with a howl like a police siren, which, fortunately, zoomed by as quickly as a yellow car with a flashing light. Literally one week later I was once again a bachelor and full of hope. My parents grieved for a while and calmed down, and kind Vovka said that she had never liked Marina anyway.

My memories of the next five years are bitter ones. "Producing folk spectacles" turned out to be much the same as metal studies, only in the field of art. The people studying there were all grown-up and ugly—dumpy young women, pushy thirty-year-old guys from the depths of the provinces, directors of small-town clubs who simply needed a diploma to hang on the wall.

Acting skills were limited to the development of diction for the first six months: "Betty bought a bit of butter, but she found the butter bitter, so Betty bought a bit of better butter to make the bitter butter better." The teacher of stage art taught us to bow and to deliver swingeing slaps to cheeks. The acrobatic classes would have done any rest home proud—forward roll, backward roll, half split, arms out wide.

In directing class we ran through scenes with "justified silence". These clashes between underwater divers, spies waiting in ambush and married couples who had quarrelled—that is, characters who were logically silent—inevitably turned into series of deaf and dumb convulsions.

For the second time I took up sociology, philosophy and the forever-foreign English language. New things that were added included the incomprehensible subject of pedagogics, cultural studies and literary studies.

After my first session in the dean's office I learned that I wouldn't be able to transfer to drama except "on a paid basis". This news hit me so hard that for the next three years I meekly allowed them to mould me into an entertainer of the masses with a tin bucket on my head and a carrot for a nose.

I should have offered my honest, thunderous repentance to my dream and fled from that den of putrescence, but I suddenly started lying monstrously to myself and everyone else, saying that I was very happy with my studies.

I practised self-deception. Vovka and Slavik had survived the torment of their institute and little Vanya was going to kindergarten. Soon Slavik got a good job in a company that sold office furniture and Vovka fell pregnant again and delighted us all with a second child, Ilya, so she, Slavik and my parents had even more joyful cares to occupy them…

By the fourth year of study the veil had fallen from my eyes. A belated rescue plan was hatched—to switch from the day faculty to the extramural one and immediately get a job in the old student club. I dashed headlong to the alma mater I had derided, but I was too late. No one remembered the creator of the film *Our Beloved Polytech* any longer. The president had retired, Galoganov had been thrown out for embezzlement and the post of club manager had long ago been occupied by a man worthy of it.

Overwhelmed by the panic of an antiquated twenty-six-year-old, I transferred to the extramural faculty and laid siege to every House of Culture in the city in my search for work. Both the "Builders" and the "Railwaymen" rejected me scornfully. I was given refuge by the local television channel, where I tacked together scripts out of inarticulate raw text. Then I squeezed my way into a smalltime radio channel, where I edited an ignominious comedy programme.

At the age of twenty-seven I was awarded my second degree diploma. In September I took part in a shoddy mass spectacle entitled *Day of the City*. The artistic director turned out to be shrewd and sticky-fingered. We presented the municipal executive committee with an impressive budget for all sorts of folk costumes, round bread loaves and linen towels representing Slavic hospitality and fees for the groups taking part, then made do with less and divided up the remainder among our artistic group.

The petty copecks paid by the television channel and the radio were humiliating. I was short of money. In late December I was invited to play Grandfather Frost and, casting shame aside, I pulled on the cotton-wool beard and eyebrows, flung the sack over my shoulder and set off round the kindergartens. Our pitiful trio—Grandfather Frost, the Snow Maiden and an accordion player—gathered the toddlers together and swiftly taught them to sing 'A fir tree was born in the forest' and 'Merrily we stride together through the wide expanses'. The ones who "sang along together" loudest were handed presents. After the children's matinees, having parted from the accordionist and now drunk, I fornicated with my Snow Maiden, who was perhaps not especially beautiful, but most amenable.

Thanks to my connections at the institute I was given a part in a New Year's play for a children's party, held in a former House of Young Pioneers. Dolled up in flared pants, a pink shirt and a tie, I shouted, "Oh!" in a hoarse voice through a hole in a papier-mâché mask that was supposed to represent a wolf's jaws every time I saw the rabbit—this one was female—and pursued her clumsily round the stage. "Just you wai-ai-ait!" I growled, planting my feet wide, stumbling and falling flat, like a wardrobe, bruising my knees.

The plot-line had me and Old Lady Shapoklyak playing all sorts of tricks on the positive characters—we stole the trunk with the fairy tales in it, we were exposed, we repented and were forgiven, and then we danced round the beautiful New Year tree with the sticky-handed children.

The humiliation concluded with a modest buffet meal and the lovable rabbit led me away to spend the night in her burrow.

THE INHERITANCE

A ND THEN, at the Russian Orthodox Christmas, the notification of Uncle Maxim's death arrived. The police report informed us that M.D. Vyazintsev had been found dead with multiple contusions and knife wounds. A slip of paper attached indicated the row and sector of my uncle's burial place in the Second Municipal Cemetery. The letter had reached our foreign parts only after a long delay—a month after the funeral.

We were very upset by this tragic news. My dad pressed his fist against his lips and whispered, "Oh, Maxim, Maxim." My mum burst into tears—she had always felt sorry for my dissolute uncle. I remembered that seven years earlier she had wanted to invite him to Vovka's wedding, but Dad tried to dissuade her: "Maxim will get drunk and make a scene." In the end we didn't invite him. And now my uncle was gone.

As far as we could tell, no one had found the killer and probably no one had even looked for him. My uncle's former reputation would have suggested that he had fallen victim to his asocial acquaintants. But that was strange, after all, according to what we had heard; he hadn't drunk alcohol for many years already. In any event the police had simply written him off and had him cremated. Dad kept planning to go to visit his grave, but the idea never got beyond words.

It's shameful to admit it, but my uncle Maxim's death moved on quite quickly from the stage of grief to the routine of receiving the inheritance, in which the main item was a two-room apartment. My uncle didn't have any family and we were his only blood relatives. This was worth doing. There was absolutely no hope that I could earn enough for my own living space independently.

When I got married, everyone had assumed that the question of a domicile for me had been resolved. We had immediately given my deceased grandparents' apartment to Vovka and her husband. My parents had once acquired a dacha plot outside the city, with a little house like the one that Nif-Nif the little pig built. My father kept trying to turn this hovel into a genuine house, but all in vain. A year later I presented my parents with my divorce and returned to my native hearth and home. From May to October my mother and father went away to the dacha, but we spent the winter together, and we were cramped...

But now I could hope to acquire a little pad of my own at last. The only catch was that my uncle had not left a will. And that entailed a whole heap of exhausting bureaucratic formalities.

According to law, if no claim to the inheritance was received within six months of the death, the apartment reverted to the city, and it had to be won back through the courts.

We contacted the state notary's office for the area where my uncle lived and exchanged letters with the Russian consulate. There were no grounds for refusing us. In March we received a document stating that from 1 June my father, as a blood relative, would come into the inheritance. We only had to pay some outstanding fees or taxes.

The family council decided that I would go to arrange the business.

I was taking on the difficult task of selling my uncle's apartment. It was anticipated that if a potential buyer were found, my father would come to help me and collect the proceeds, so that he could check everything and make sure we weren't swindled.

We had serious discussions about the problem of moving the money across the border and even considered the possibility of transporting it in the urn with my uncle's ashes. Mum immediately spoke up against such a sacrilegious conspiracy and said she had better come with my father, and then, with three of us in the same train compartment, we would get the money through safely. But in any case my father wanted to bury my uncle's urn beside my grandfather's and grandmother's graves.

We had a letter of attorney drawn up, giving me the right to decide all the legal questions, and I packed for the journey, hoping to have the sale completed in a few short weeks and start patching up my leaky life.

The journey took almost three dreary days. I travelled in a third-class sleeper, so the ticket wasn't all that expensive. A grey-haired woman who looked like a kindly schoolteacher timidly asked me to swap places with her. I gave up the lower bunk, and the grateful "teacher" plied me with home-made potato pies.

Perched opposite us was a red-cheeked maiden in the collective-farm style. She was travelling with a large bundle wrapped in check cloth, which wouldn't fit under the seat. During the day the farm girl guarded it vigilantly and at night, just to be sure, she lowered her solid foot, still in its shoe, from the bunk and set it on the bundle.

A sharp-nosed little man, as frisky as a mouse, settled in above the maiden with a small plywood suitcase. The little man drank tea and told the maiden about his difficult lot in life, repeatedly intoning, "When you're poor, you're poor." He had already managed to soften the female conductor's heart and get a mattress for free, and every now and then he ran to fill up his glass with hot water, because he was carrying his own strong brew with him.

I tried to remain reticent and when the "kindly schoolteacher" asked: "Where are you going to?" I replied curtly: "To visit my uncle"—and then deftly stuck my nose in a book and didn't allow myself to be drawn into conversation.

On the first night we crossed the border. About a dozen snorers had congregated in the carriage and so I slept badly; even covering my head with the pillow wasn't much help.

In the morning the train got stuck at the small station of Zhelybino. My window was opposite a memorial plaque screwed to the peeling station wall: "Here died a valiant death Sergeant Stepan Yakovlevich Gusev, Private First Class Ivan Matveyevich Usikov, Privates Khamir Khafunovich Khazifov, Pavel Kuzmich Fyodorov and Husein Izmailovich Alikperov." After an hour I had learned this list of the dead off by heart and then the train finally set off again. At midday we passed through Moscow.

It was hot in the carriage. I gazed interminably at the fleeting whirligig of the landscape. The sky blazed bright blue, little lakes glinted brilliantly. When a bird launched itself off a tree and flew into the grass, the wind carried it away, spinning it round like a scrap of paper. Hills of crushed stone sprang up, only to be replaced by sparse green forest with a clearing full of dandelions spreading through it like a hole. A pine forest began, with reddish-brown bogs stretching away behind it: the rotten trunks of birch trees stuck up out of the water. Then a spruce forest started and was broken off by a bridge. On the other side of the river a modern-looking village with three-storey prefabricated apartment blocks was fenced off by poplar trees. After that came an open field, overgrown with weeds, with a rusty goal frame for football and a spotted goat tethered to it.

Looking at the abandoned goal, for some reason I imagined a disaster: children were playing football, the ball flew off onto the rails and a child didn't notice the train. In keeping with my sad thoughts a cemetery and a gingerbread church appeared.

Station platforms looking like airport landing strips hurtled by so fast that I didn't have time to read the names. The district towns with their endearing, simple names followed one after another: Pozyrev, Lychevets. The stations there often had only two tracks. While we were standing, local pedlars slouched through the train, offering newspapers and magazines, beer and simple provisions— sunflower seeds, meat pasties, dried fish.

On the third day I was already sick and tired of travelling and was glad when we passed Kolontaysk in the morning. A few hours later the massive grey, watery expanse of the Urmut Reservoir appeared outside the window, followed by the smoking funnels of a nuclear power station, like chess pieces, and endless stretches of industrial plants, barracks-style buildings with walls of smoke-stained glass.

The old station building was like a high-domed church, and deep inside it faded Soviet frescoes depicted the Socialist happiness of the past.

After tumbling out onto the station platform the passengers were surrounded by taxi drivers clamouring insistently like gypsies to offer their motorized services. I asked the one who looked the least mercenary to me how I could get to Chkalov Street. The driver worked his lips a bit, figuring out the profit in his head, and named a price, but I still couldn't tell if it was acceptable or not—I was confused by the difference between Russian roubles and Ukrainian hryvnias. In roubles it sounded more expensive.

I apologized, said I didn't have much money and asked if he could tell me how to get there on public transport. The taxi driver hesitated for a moment before taking pity on me and showing the way. He waved his hand in the direction of a McDonald's mast with a neon "M" on the top, which was visible beyond the roofs of the buildings.

Skirting round the buildings I saw a trolleybus-turning circle and a route-taxi stop. To be on the safe side I asked a cultured-looking old woman about the central market and she confirmed what the taxi driver had said, that it was five stops away. Then she asked me if I could remember which tree had come into leaf first this year: the alder or the birch? She explained, "If it was the birch, it will be a good, warm summer. But if the alder was first, we've had it, it's going to be rainy and cold."

I already liked the town because it was filled with festive sunshine, and I could smell the blossoming lilac's intoxicating scent even through the windows of the trolleybus. Most of the buildings were pre-revolutionary, with large windows, ornate moulding work that had come away in places on the walls and wide front doorways. The atmosphere of modest merchant-class serenity was spoiled by numerous kiosks with clumsily daubed signs: "Pies", "Ice Cream", or "Irina Ltd". I was delighted to see the Russian letter "y" at the end of so many Russian shop-name signs "Produkty" ("Groceries"), "Soki, Vody" ("Juices, Waters"), "Sigarety" ("Cigarettes"). In my native parts, where Ukrainian *nezalezhnyst* ("independence") had been raging for almost nine years, this letter had disappeared completely.

The town centre was green and spacious. The intersection of Gagarin Prospect and Komsomol 50th Anniversary Prospect formed a small square, which had a bronze Lenin three metres high. Standing to the right of the statue was an armoured car of Civil War vintage, and to its left was a T-70 World War II tank, as if Lenin were being urged to choose more contemporary military technology but wasn't taking the hint, stubbornly thrusting out his hand in an attempt to flag down a foreign automobile on the main avenue.

Right beside him was a cosy little park. A granite pedestal with a howitzer gun towered over the flower beds. Below the golden figures "1941–1945" lay wreaths and flowers, evidently left over from the Victory Day celebrations on 9 May. Rising up behind the little park was a cathedral with reddish, samovar-shaped domes and a bell tower with a steeple covered with a dull, mossy-emerald patina.

The trolleybus stopped beside an old brick wall surrounding the cathedral that had grass sprouting through it. I walked along a short little street smothered in lime trees and came out directly opposite the metal fence of the market, at the point where the fish stalls began and there was a smell of riverine scum.

I asked some women with stuffed shopping bags where the number eighteen bus stop was. They explained that it was at the other side of the market, but advised me against taking the bus— "it's not reliable"—it was better to wait there for the route taxi, which also ran along Chkalov Street.

I found the Trust agency that I needed in the semi-basement of a sleek nine-storey building faced with tiles, between a delicatessen and a hairdresser's.

The interior was a standard example of a modest "Euro-standard" renovation. The black imitation-leather furniture, white blinds and rambling pot plants inspired a distinct feeling of trust.

There was only one woman ahead of me in the queue, but I was mistaken to feel glad about this—she stayed in the notary's office right up to the lunch break, so I was forced to spend the best part of another hour browsing through the local newspapers.

By the time the seals had been applied and I had spent more time in the queue to the little window in order to pay the required fee and handed in the receipt to the notary, the day was already declining into evening.

In the delicatessen I bought a bottle of Absolut vodka and a large gift box of chocolates. Who could tell which sex of bureaucratic individual I would encounter at my uncle's local housing department? I needed gifts to accommodate both possibilities.

The Comintern-era housing complex was a collection of five-storey, prefabricated slums on the very edge of town. Housing Department Office No. 27 seemed to have disappeared into thin air. Tired and angry, I repeatedly asked local people to help me, but no one knew where it was. Eventually a woman with a garbage pail volunteered to show me the way.

As if in deliberate mockery, the metal doors of the Housing Department Office, with a crookedly attached schedule of water outages for June, were locked with a large metal bar. And there were no encouraging notes such as "Back soon".

The woman studied the schedule and the hollows under her eyes were instantly flooded with black melancholy. She looked at me reproachfully, as if I were to blame for the imminent outage. As she left, shaking her head, the garbage pail in her hand squeaked pitifully.

At that moment I realized that I now faced either a search for a cheap hotel or a night out on the street. In helpless despair I started pounding on the door, which rumbled like theatrical thunder.

A little old man in a taut singlet, with a tattoo on his skinny shoulder and grey curls on his chest, stuck his head out of the closest window on the first floor. He swore at me amiably—so that I wouldn't abuse him in return, and struck up a conversation.

I explained that I had just arrived from out of town, I needed to get into an apartment, otherwise I had a night on the street ahead of me, and the keys were in the housing department office.

The old man pondered for a moment and disappeared into the room. Just when I had already decided that he had satisfied his curiosity, he emerged from the entrance, tucking his singlet into a pair of tracksuit trousers with side stripes as he walked along.

"Wait here," he said and set off, flapping his slippers briskly, towards the next high-rise. Ten minutes later the old man came back, and he was not alone. Plodding along behind him was a plump woman of about forty in a polka-dot dress with a black belt round her stomach. Her chubby calves were completely covered in terrible bites, so she occasionally stopped and scratched her legs fervently. She smiled at me coquettishly, displaying gold teeth that looked like grains of maize. "A sweet woman, look, even the mosquitoes love me…" Then she introduced herself as Antonina Petrovna.

Behind the steel door there was a set of prison-style bars through which I could see a small corridor covered with scuffed linoleum and a rusty barrel with the word "Sand" on it. Hanging on the wall at the entrance were a fire extinguisher and an old poster showing a shaggy-haired Valery Leontyev, the pop idol of the Eighties, looking like a spaniel.

The old man squirted a small gob of spit onto the poster and declared profoundly: "Has all the virtues of a man, apart from his faults."

I put my passport, a stack of documents and the letter of attorney down on the desk, secretly hoping that my unshaven features did not provoke suspicion. To be on the safe side I explained: "I've come straight from the train. It took me three days to get here."

Antonina Petrovna took a perfunctory look at the documents and the passport—my name was the same as my uncle's, after all—then opened the safe, rummaged inside it and pulled out a bunch of keys.

I said, "This is for the inconvenience"—and handed Antonina Petrovna the box of chocolates. I presented the bottle of vodka to the old man, who said, "There was no need for that"—and stuck it in the pocket of his trousers, which immediately slipped down under the weight of a litre of liquid.

I learned from Antonina Petrovna that no one had reported the death of the former owner of the apartment to the telephone exchange. She advised me that to keep the telephone line I should contact them and pay the outstanding charges as soon as possible.

The building in which my uncle used to live was a five-storey structure from the Khrushchev era, standing on Shironin's Guards Street, right on the edge of town, beside a flooded construction pit overgrown with sedge. If not for the poplars that had been planted there, the building would probably have slipped down the slope in a few years' time. I was distressed when I figured out how much could be realized from selling an apartment in such a seedy spot.

Led by Antonina Petrovna, I walked along the path past a couple engaged in conversation—a man and a woman, both middle-aged. I caught a scrap of their talk: "I'd tear that bastard Yeltsin apart with hooks myself."

"And not just him either," the woman replied.

The man was large and well-fleshed, with a bald patch that was on the offensive, and he was gesticulating militantly with a long paper bundle. The woman was clutching some sort of kitchen-garden implement—the metal head of it was wrapped in a rag. With her faded anorak and plaited hair, she looked as if she had just come back from her dacha. There was a bag standing by her feet, with a plastic bottle protruding from it.

The pitiful grin of the doorway was flanked by two old women sitting opposite each other like a pair of rotten teeth. Anticipating their curiosity, Antonina Pavlovna said, "This is the late Vyazintsev's nephew."

It seemed to me that the chatting couple also noticed us—the woman glanced round, and the man was already looking in our direction anyway. He stopped talking for a moment, then carried on waving his bundle about even more vigorously, apparently devising further forms of execution for the retired president.

We walked up to the top floor, the fifth. Antonina Pavlovna removed the plasticine seal with its thread. I signed a piece of paper, and Antonina Pavlovna wished me good luck and plodded off heavily down the stairs.

First of all I locked myself in the toilet and relieved the pressure that had built up during the day. As I flushed, I thought that now I had marked the apartment as mine, like some wild animal. Then I took a stroll round my two-room estate.

The telephone wasn't working. The windows were still sealed with paper from the last winter. I immediately tore the paper off and flung the balcony door in the sitting room wide open to get rid of the musty smell.

The horizon was already pink and the low sun had turned into a slow-moving egg yolk. A strong wind created an impression of flight, amplified by the high-rise buildings in the distance, somewhere beyond the quarry and the highway. My fifth floor seemed to be on the same level as them. Two wires for hanging washing out to dry stretched along the length of the balcony like musical strings, and the wooden clothes pegs hanging on them looked like small gudgeons. The dried-out railings were thickly entwined with Virginia creeper.

All in all, I liked my uncle's residence. The entrance hall was hung with the "brick-effect" wallpaper that had once been so fashionable. The sitting room contained a cumbersome sofa-bed, two armchairs, a standard lamp with a brass pole, a coffee table and a maroon wall unit that held tableware, crystal, books and a radiogram set in a deep glassy niche.

I examined the drawers for any "treasures". What I discovered was a heap of receipts, a box of gilded teaspoons, a stethoscope, an eye-pressure tonometer and a pile of crumpled cardboard boxes of medicine.

In the bedroom, in addition to the bed, there was a writing desk, a set of shelves with books and a walnut wardrobe. To my surprise, among the clothes I discovered a motorcycle helmet, a whopping great hammer and several broad pieces of tyre tread, cut from the tyres of some massive truck—to be quite honest, I couldn't figure out the function of these neat slabs of rubber.

But in the narrow side cupboard, between the sheets and the towels, my uncle had hidden two pornographic magazines, both in some incomprehensible European language, perhaps Dutch or Swedish. My heart ached as I thought how lonely my Uncle Maxim had been…

The bathroom made an even more painful impression on me. Lying there on the washbasin in front of the mirror, beside the toothbrush and the tube of toothpaste, was a safety razor with dried-out stubble on the blade—all that was left of Uncle Maxim…

The kitchen was small, with barely enough space for the cooker, the Northern refrigerator, the table, the stools and the cupboard hanging on the wall above the sink. There was a small portable television set standing on the wide window sill.

Although the apartment didn't look a total wreck, it was definitely in need of renovation. Assessing my own strength and experience, I realized that I wouldn't be able to manage the wallpaper and the tiles that had come away all on my own—I would have to hire workmen in order to get the apartment into marketable condition.

I scoured the bathtub thoroughly with baking soda and took a bath with a sliver of pink soap that I scraped off the washbasin. My uncle's kitchen reserves yielded up macaroni, canned mackerel and a tin of peas. I relieved the tedium of my supper by watching some episode or other of the TV serial *The Eternal Call*.

I spent the night on the sofa-bed in the sitting room. Although I was worn out, I couldn't get to sleep for a long time. I was obsessed by the thought that the phone line had been disconnected and without it the price of the apartment was sure to fall, and I was also haunted by dreams of a generous buyer showing up immediately and offering me six thousand dollars without even bargaining. Then I imagined a bad buyer, greedy and cunning, who wouldn't give me more than three thousand and tried to swindle me. I tossed and turned, grinding my teeth.

First thing in the morning I drank some tea and ran off to the local post office, which I had spotted during my wanderings around the area the day before. I called home from the international phone there and reported to my father on the work that had been done so far.

I also enquired at the post office where the local telephone exchange was. I had primed myself unnecessarily for difficulties here. They gave me a bill that had to be paid at the savings bank (the accumulated debt amounted to an insignificant sum, even including the penalties) and promised to reconnect the phone within a week. Absolutely delighted by how easily the matter had been resolved, I immediately set off to visit my uncle at the cemetery.

There weren't any graves in the crematorium section—only concrete walls in which the urns were immured. My uncle had been placed close to the ground, I had to squat down to read the words engraved on the brass plaque:

MAXIM DANILOVICH VYAZINTSEV. 1952–1999.

And in slightly smaller letters:

REST IN PEACE.

I put off the conversation with the administration of the cemetery until the sale of the apartment was settled.

THE BUYER

BUT AT HOME a surprise was waiting. A note, folded in four and wedged in the door, with a message for me from a certain Vadim Leonidovich Kolesov. He wrote that in Housing Department Office No. 27 he had heard from the manager, Mukhina, that I intended to sell the apartment and, as an extremely interested party, he wished to meet with me. His aged parents lived nearby, so the purchase of accommodation in this precise location would be ideal, and he asked permission to call round that evening at about ten.

The polite tone of the letter suggested a man of delicate manners. True, the thought did briefly flash through my mind that I hadn't really told Antonina Petrovna anything much, but it was easier to convince myself that in my tired state I had simply not attached any significance in that situation to the question: "What are you thinking of doing with the apartment?"—and had replied automatically, without even realizing it.

Everything, of course, was suddenly going rather too well, but after a long sequence of setbacks in this worldly life, a minor indulgence from destiny seemed entirely justified.

A quick sale was the outcome that suited my plans to return home soon better than any other. I reread the message excitedly and put the sheet of paper in my pocket, promising myself that in the event of a successful deal I would give Antonina Petrovna a more substantial present than a box of sweets.

I still had half a day in reserve, so I put my feet up for a while and took a nap, and then tidied the apartment, washed the floors and slipped out for half an hour to the grocery shop. Outside I saw the couple from the previous day chatting to each other again—the bald man with the bundle and the dacha lady in the headscarf. On my way back, they had been joined by another two: a man with a moustache, who was clearly another vegetable gardener, clutching the handle of the spade on which he was leaning with strong, sinewy hands, and a floppy-haired young guy in a threadbare mechanic's boiler suit, with a toolbox. The young guy was cracking simple-minded little jokes to the dacha lady, and the sinewy man with the spade was laughing loudly.

An elderly woman in horn-rimmed spectacles who was sitting at the entrance to the building set aside her knitting and asked me sternly: "Who are you visiting, young man?"

I replied politely, "Only myself. I'm the late Vyazintsev's nephew."

Satisfied with my answer, the stern woman took up her needles again.

I spent the time until Kolesov's arrival sorting through my uncle's bunker. In addition to preserved goods and all sorts of builder's lumber, the cupboards under the ceiling in the hallway contained a photographic enlarger, a Kharkov electric shaver in a box, a slide projector and a whole bundle of copies of the old *Outlook* magazine, with the flexible blue plastic records that came with them. I even tried to play one, but the speakers of the radiogram had a loose connection somewhere, and the sound kept cutting out. While I was edging my way in behind the wardrobe to drag out the wires, someone rang the doorbell.

At this point I must admit that Kolesov did not at all resemble the ideal buyer nurtured by my dreams—the bashful father of a small family consisting of a wife and a five-year-old daughter.

Vadim Leonidovich was bony and lanky, with intensely black slicked-back hair that was receding deeply above the temples, like Mickey Mouse. He smiled and gesticulated continually, and he had a very shrewd look about him, but in theory a shrewd man ought not to be interested in my apartment.

Instead of a wife and a little fair-haired daughter, Kolesov had brought with him a friend by the name of Alik. Vadim Leonidovich introduced him and immediately broke into profuse, staccato apologies for descending unannounced on me and for bringing his workmate along as well. Apparently this Alik—a character with a face as red as sunburn—had kindly given Vadim Leonidovich a lift in his car. Alik stood in one spot with his fists thrust into the pockets of his leather jacket, swaying to and fro from his heels to his toes with a springy movement, like a rocking chair, and only once asked for some water.

Vadim Leonidovich scampered round the sitting room as nimbly as a spider, glanced briefly into the kitchen, and soon I heard him cry out in joy from my uncle's bedroom:

"Alik, Alik, come here quickly!"

"What's up in there?" the sullen Alik muttered, but he answered the summons anyway.

Kolesov was standing in front of the shelves, exultantly leafing through a book.

"Would you believe it, eh?"

His eyes met Alik's and Alik coughed.

"*The Quiet Grass*! Have you read it?" Kolesov asked, skewering me with a piercing glance.

"No," I replied drily. I was thoroughly fed up of Kolesov's scurrying about and fatuous exclamations. "Is it worth reading?"

"I don't think so," he said with a smile. "It's a rubbishy little book. It's just that for me it's associated with a certain romantic memory that can't be expressed in words. Koktebel, the sea… Alik here knows about it. I can tell you if you like…"

I took the book out of his hands and examined it cursorily. Published in the late 1970s. The narrow spine was half worn away and it was hard to understand how Kolesov could possibly have discovered this "romantic memory" on my uncle's shelves.

"Listen!" he suddenly exclaimed. "You don't need the book. Sell it to me, eh?"

I said guardedly that if we made a deal, I would make him a present of this piece of trash.

Vadim Leonidovich started fussing.

"Didn't I say that everything suits me just fine?… I'm willing to lay out er, er, er… eight thousand greenbacks. What do you say?" he asked, and froze with an anxious air.

It was two thousand more than my very boldest forecasts. Inwardly exultant, I paused sagaciously to maintain gravitas, as if I were weighing up all the pros and cons, and then nodded.

Vadim Leonidovich declined tea and delighted me by taking a tape measure out of his pocket and measuring the walls, drawing the conclusion: "The suite will be a perfect fit." Then, in confirmation of the seriousness of his intentions, Kolesov informed me that he would like to start registering the deal the next day. I reminded him that on a Saturday everything would be closed. He clicked his tongue in annoyance, postponed our meeting until Monday and dictated his home and work telephone numbers for me.

Vadim Leonidovich wheedled *The Quiet Grass* out of me anyway. "Oh, please, now we've struck a deal," he whined jokingly, and I decided not to be petty and mean-spirited.

Vadim Leonidovich pressed the book to his chest and said it was this "lucky find" that had decided everything; for him it was a "good sign" about the apartment. He suddenly recollected that an acquaintance was waiting for him in the car and it was terribly impolite to keep him waiting. Vadim Leonidovich hadn't mentioned any third party before that…

Now I realize it was my obliging nature that saved me. Who knows what would have happened if I had refused to let Kolesov have his present…

Somehow it happened, no doubt because the conversation ran on, that I followed my visitors out. As we walked down the stairs, Kolesov joked happily, saying that he had been searching for *The Quiet Grass* for a long time, and now a stroke of luck had brought the book to him.

In the hours that had passed since I came back from the shop and then received Kolesov, it had turned completely dark. The yard was empty. The woman knitting by the entrance, the garrulous dacha folk, the bald man with the bundle and the mechanic had all gone home.

The car, a Zhiguli 2106, had two people in it: the driver and a passenger sitting beside him. When we appeared, they got out and Vadim Leonidovich waved the little book to them, after which the driver relaxed and leaned back against the car, while his companion came towards us. I had just enough time to realize that my visitors were not even a threesome, but a foursome…

THE AMBUSH

ND THEN CAME the whirlwind, breakneck sequence of bloody events with which my new life began. It all happened literally in seconds.

The man who was walking towards us suddenly shuddered and collapsed to his knees, holding one hand to his temple, and beside him the short crowbar that someone had flung out of the darkness landed on the ground with a dull thud. The previous day's Yeltsin-hater, the bald, husky man with the paper bundle, was already beside the driver. He made a stabbing movement and the bundle suddenly buried itself in his adversary's stomach, so that the paper folded up concertina-wise around the bald man's fist. He jerked his hand back out, and I saw a long, straight blade. The bald man drove his weapon into the driver's side for good measure and the driver slumped down, lifeless, onto the ground. The killer deftly wiped down the blade with the crumpled paper.

Kolesov manage to run off a couple of metres, but he was over-taken by the false dacha folk. I heard the dull sounds of a struggle.

Alik tried to say something, but instead of words he belched out blood. The point of a knitting needle was protruding from his throat. Standing behind him was an elderly woman, the same one who had been knitting on the bench. Alik shuddered and another needle ran through the hand that he was holding over his Adam's apple.

The mechanic appeared, picked up the fallen crowbar and finished off the dying man with a sharp blow to the back of the head, then informed the elderly woman who had done in red-faced Alik with her needles:

"This one's finished, Margarita Tikhonovna."

Tucking the crowbar into his belt, he gave me a conspiratorial wink and said, "No noise now!"

A dark-coloured RAF minibus drove up with its lights off. Two men jumped out of it and started deftly throwing the corpses into the back. The men acted swiftly, in unison.

Repeatedly casting anxious glances at me through her glasses, Margarita Tikhonovna whispered:

"Quietly now, quietly, everything's fine, just keep it quiet…"

The dacha lady came running up to her. Her vegetable-garden implement turned out to be a short pike. She held out the confiscated book and called in a whisper:

"Pal Palych, hurry up."

The man with the moustache dragged over Kolesov, bound and gagged, and flung him crudely into the RAF.

The bald man said to Margarita Tikhonovna:

"I'll go with Palych in their car and we'll follow you."

"No, Igor Valeryevich, you come with us and Pal Palych will manage on his own," she said, carefully tucking the book into the cuff of her cardigan before adding the command: "Let's clear out!"

Nudging me gently in the back, the bald man moved me onto a side seat in the minibus and perched on the seat beside me. The mechanic and the women also climbed in, the door slammed, and the RAF set off into the darkness.

I should say that while the massacre was taking place I stood there without stirring a muscle, as if I had turned to stone, and probably couldn't have given a shout, even if I had wanted to—I was struck completely dumb by the shock.

Scenes flashed in front of my eyes from television reports about bandits who found out about apartment sales from inside informers. If Kolesov himself were not in a rather sorry state, I would have assumed that he had set everything up, but since we hadn't signed any documents yet, such behaviour made no sense.

Nightmarish questions buzzed around inside my head like an enraged swarm of bees: "Could the bandits really have made a mistake in their haste? What's going to happen to me? I have been left alive and they haven't even laid a finger on me. But why, or more to the point, for how long? Until it becomes clear that I don't have any money and the sale hasn't taken place?"

Kolesov squirmed in his bonds on top of the corpses on the jolting floor of the RAF. It occurred to me that he had every reason to assume that I had set him up, although that also seemed absurd—no one takes the money with him to look at an apartment.

Of all the people around me, the mechanic could certainly be taken for a genuine bandit—he had a really brazen face. The bald, husky man, who looked like a butcher from the market, also made a sinister impression. But looking at Margarita Tikhonovna and the dacha lady, it was impossible to believe that these genteel-seeming women had proved to be cold-blooded killers.

The elderly woman immediately rebuked the mechanic:

"Sanya, have you got any brains at all? If that crowbar had fallen on the asphalt, what a clang it would have made!"

The young guy apologized.

"Margarita Tikhonovna, honest to God, I was going to throw a mallet at first, but then I suddenly felt afraid—he was such a big, strong brute." The mechanic prodded the dead man with his foot. "What if it didn't stun him…"

"Don't scold Sasha," the dacha lady interceded for her partner in crime. "I think it all went off quite excellently."

"Exactly," the driver agreed. "Clean as a whistle."

"Tanechka, I know what I'm saying," Margarita Tikhonovna objected. "And another thing, all of you; I asked you not to mention any names on an assignment! And there you go, like little children, 'Margarita Tikhonovna', 'Pal Palych'…" she said, mocking them. "What did you think you were doing?"

The dacha lady and the mechanic smiled guiltily.

"Oh, come on now, Margarita Tikhonovna," the bald man put in, "they were whispering… And you yourself, as it happens, addressed me in full form, name and patronymic, you just didn't mention my surname," he laughed.

"I'm sorry, Igor Valeryevich, I should be thrown on the scrap heap too," Margarita Tikhonovna said dejectedly. "But nonetheless, you young people, be more vigilant next time."

The mechanic, who had been sitting there, hanging his head, stopped acting out his contrition and suddenly held his hand out to me.

"Alexander Sukharev."

"Alexei Vyazintsev," I forced out.

"Pleased to meet you," the mechanic said, smiling. He looked about the same age as me, perhaps a little younger. "Well, how are you doing? Your pants are probably filled to overflowing, right?"

While I was still pondering my reply to this familiar suggestion, Margarita Tikhonovna rapped the mechanic over the knuckles first.

"Stop that, Sasha!" She gave a deep sigh and said in an exceptionally solemn tone of voice, "Alexei… Dear Alexei Vladimirovich, I can only imagine the conclusions you must have drawn from what you have seen. But let me tell you that you are in no danger whatsoever in our company. If only because all of us…"—at these words the mechanic, the dacha lady, bald Igor Valeryevich, the driver and his navigator nodded in unison—"… loved and respected your uncle Maxim Danilovich Vyazintsev… I swear on his cherished memory, we did not wish to frighten you, but unfortunately we could not warn you either. Too much would have had to be explained, you might not have believed us, and the criminals would have escaped unpunished. I hope that in the near future you will be able to make sense of everything for yourself and will not condemn us for this violence. Six months ago these… monsters…"—her voice trembled—"… villainously waylaid and murdered Maxim Danilovich…"

The bald man turned over the lifeless Alik (a knitting needle protruded from his throat, running through his hand and holding it in place), threw back the leather flap of the dead man's jacket and took out a very long awl, as slim as a needle, covered up to the handle with a narrow plastic tube.

"There, feast your eyes on that," he said, turning to me, "just so you won't have any doubts about these characters. Their own make. They temper them specially in sealing wax—the blade's as strong as diamond, it'll pierce anything you like."

"Ooh, the bastards!" said the mechanic Sasha Sukharev. He grabbed Kolesov by the scruff of the neck, shook him a few times and tossed him back onto the dead bodies, throwing in a heavy punch to the kidneys. Kolesov groaned.

Margarita Tikhonovna observed this scene without the slightest sign of sympathy, and then mockingly waved the confiscated book under Kolesov's nose.

"Well, then? What's that your name is? Vadim Leonidovich? How did you make such a mess of things, eh?"

Kolesov squirmed in his bonds and his eyes flashed, full of torment and fear.

"Now listen carefully. Your informer Shapiro has been detained. And therefore I hope you will be appropriately forthcoming at the interrogation… I can't guarantee you your life, by the way, but even in the worst-case scenario, you'll still see Saturday. Is there anything you want to say?"

The mechanic Sukharev lifted Kolesov up, ripped the plaster off his mouth and pulled out the brownish, blood-soaked gag. Kolesov gurgled: "I didn't kill anyone. That's nothing to do with me… It was Marchenko who gave the orders…" Then the gag stopped his mouth again.

"So you are prepared to cooperate?" Margarita Tikhonovna asked severely. "Or… were you killed during arrest? In principle Shapiro is enough for us. What do you think, Igor Valeryevich?"

The bald man pressed the confiscated awl to Kolesov's side and the miserable Vadim Leonidovich started nodding his head rapidly. What else could he do? In his place I would have accepted any conditions too.

The mechanic frisked the bodies while the false dacha lady Tanya gazed at me with tenderness in her eyes, then suddenly said:

"Alexander Vladimirovich, you behaved quite splendidly, and you are very, very much like Maxim Danilovich…"

"Very true," said the driver, turning round for a moment. "I noticed that too. The same face."

"I can hardly believe it," said the navigator. "A dead ringer for his uncle…"

"Alexei Vladimirovich," said Margarita Tikhonovna, touching my knee cautiously, "I realize that you are perturbed and shocked. If you wish to collect your thoughts, please, do not speak. Rest and recover your equilibrium."

In fact I had a lot of questions. What did they kill Uncle Maxim for? Who are these people who supposedly killed him? And finally, most important of all: what's going to happen to me? However, complying with Margarita Tikhonovna's categorical proposition, I spent the rest of the journey looking out through the black window at the agitated cardiogram of roadside lights.

Along the way they discussed where to take me. Margarita Tikhonovna urged me to come to her place, but bald Igor Valeryevich insisted that his place was better, since Margarita Tikhonovna's address might be known to the foe. This argument proved decisive and the RAF swerved off the lit street and wound its way between faceless buildings of precast concrete panels—it turned out that Igor Valeryevich lived somewhere around here.

At the entrance to the building the company divided. The driver and his navigator, having been instructed to guard Kolesov, immediately drove off with their dead cargo.

THE FIRST NIGHT. THE FIRST DAY

I CAN'T SAY NOW that it was the most terrifying night of my life. Rather, it was one of a series of terrifying nights.

We went upstairs, and in the doorway of the apartment Igor Valeryevich told me to make myself at home. The others didn't need any special invitation. Tanya went off to the kitchen to play housewife. Sukharev whistled as he locked himself in the toilet. Margarita Tikhonovna showed me into the sitting room and Igor Valeryevich pointed to the adjoining room: "Alexei, the bedroom's all yours for the night."

I politely declined tea—what if they slipped something into my cup? My fear had subsided slightly and my legs no longer felt rubbery, although my stomach was still on fire with adrenaline intoxication. I tried to behave with dignity, but my voice betrayed my condition and I preferred to keep silent and restrict myself to a nod for "yes" or a brief shake of my head for "no".

Margarita Tikhonovna did not forget to repeat: "Alexei Vladimirovich, the important thing is not to forget that you are among friends and perfectly safe." But I didn't really believe it.

Still smiling, Margarita Tikhonovna sat down to speak on the phone. The words she heard in the receiver jerked her clean out of her previous state of calm.

"What do you mean 'got away'? When?" Margarita Tikhonovna exclaimed plaintively. "Now calm yourself, Timofei Stepanovich, no one is accusing you of anything! What about the others? Oh, you kill the very heart in me... I'm speechless... All right, let them search… Yes, come immediately. We're at Igor Valeryevich's place!"

She put the phone down and, struggling to conceal her own agitation, announced:

"Comrades, stay calm now. We have an enormous problem. Shapiro has escaped. Vadik Provotorov is wounded…"

A tense silence enveloped the room. Then Igor Valeryevich's fist crashed down onto the table. Cups rattled and hopped up in the air. Tanya gasped. Sukharev started dashing around the room, swearing.

"Stop all this emotion!" Margarita Tikhonovna ordered. "What way is that to behave? At least show some dignity in Alexei Vladimirovich's presence!"

Sukharev immediately fell silent and slumped down into an armchair, breathing noisily through his nose.

Igor Valeryevich exclaimed bitterly:

"Well, there you have it, never count your chickens before they're hatched…"

"Perhaps they'll still manage to catch him?" Tanya suggested timidly.

"I doubt it," Margarita Tikhonovna sighed. "Shapiro's already gone to ground, and the most ghastly thing of all is that he has warned Marchenko."

Igor Valeryevich picked up a saucer that had flown off the table.

"Then get in touch straight away with Tereshnikov, or whoever it is that's in charge of things now, and…"

"Igor Valeryevich…"

"Otherwise Marchenko will do it first. If he hasn't already." Seeing Margarita Tikhonovna hesitate, he added: "Marchenko knew all about Shapiro's plans anyway, and the raiding party was acting with his knowledge too. He would have sounded the alarm himself in a day."

Margarita Tikhonovna gave me a compassionate look.

"How I wish, Alexei Vladimirovich, that I could tell you every-thing, so that you would calm down at last… But it's a long, complicated story. It's better if we put it off for later. You must have realized that we have run into unexpected difficulties…"

Margarita Tikhonovna spent the next fifteen minutes or so calling essential people, while I clutched at every word in the hope of investing it with meaning and clarifying my own fate.

"Good evening, Comrade Tereshnikov. I'm sorry to trouble you, this is Selivanova here, from the Shironin reading room. We have an emergency situation… A meeting is required, tomorrow… Twenty hundred hours, as usual. Please understand, this is a matter of extreme urgency! If they go to the station today, then by tomorrow evening they could… We really shouldn't drag this out… I can hint that we have something that could spoil… Yes, in triplicate. The fourth is alive and willing to talk about the Gorelov reading room… I am astounded by your perspicacity… Yes, by all means, inform Lagudov and Shulga… And don't try to intimidate me with the Council of Libraries… All to the way to the Supreme Soviet if you wish! And don't you dare address me in such a tone of voice! I'm not some young girl! Thanks be to God, I'm sixty-three years old! Yes!… Good night to you!"

"What a scoundrel!" she concluded, after the receiver clattered into its cradle.

Mind you, Margarita Tikhonovna spoke to the others far more cordially.

"Comrade Burkin, how do you do… I was just talking to Tereshnikov. We've arranged a meeting for Saturday. What do you think, will you support us? Well, thank you so much… Vasily Andreyevich, it really requires more than just a couple of words… In general terms, we're going to expose the Gorelovites' true colours… Caught in the act… Yes… Three-quarters were liquidated, one-quarter with a battered face is bound and under guard… Nothing good about it. Shapiro has got away from us… We're clarifying that… I'm far from delighted myself… Yes, thank you…"

"Zhannochka Grigoryevna… Good evening… How is your health?… We really need you very badly tomorrow… A meeting…

The Gorelovites have blundered… Today… We liquidated three of them. But it's still too early to congratulate us on our good fortune—the key witness, who is also the accused, has escaped… Yes, Shapiro, the very same… What do I think? I think that Sunday is going to be a very hot day… Yes… Zhannochka Grigoryevna, I have always counted on you… Thank you for those kind words, my dear…"

"Comrade Latokhin, good evening. This is Selivanova. There's a meeting on Saturday… Dear man, I realize this is a bolt out of the blue… I called Tereshnikov… We'll dot all the i's and cross all the t's tomorrow… Our own initiative… We had a little fox hunt here… With mixed results… We let the most important one get away. He escaped just as we had things….Pilipchuk was in charge, Timofei Stepanovich… Well, he blames himself, he's in a desperate state… A heart attack is just what we need at the moment… And how am I doing? Comrade Latokhin, I'm like that speckled hen in the fairy tale; I calm everyone down: 'Don't cry, Granddad. Don't cry, Grandma…' Yes… Tereshnikov? His usual self, trying to intimidate me with the Council of Libraries… Thank you, Comrade Latokhin, we never doubted you…"

I caught the gist of what had happened. The escape of a certain Shapiro had totally confounded my abductors' plans, so that the murderous attack on Kolesov and his comrades had spawned serious problems. Margarita Tikhonovna used the words "library", "reading room" and "council" rather often, but it seemed to me that in this context they had a somewhat different meaning.

"I've done everything I can do. Burkin, Simonyan and Latokhin are on our side, I never expected any different," Margarita Tikhonovna summed up.

The doorbell trilled abruptly and insistently. Then someone knocked.

"That's Timofei Stepanovich," Margarita Tikhonovna said with a start. "At least, I hope it is…"

Grabbing his blade, Igor Valeryevich went to answer the door. A few seconds later the new arrival's rasping voice could be heard in the hallway.

"We let him get away! He tricked us! He's scum, the bastard! Forgive me, comrades!"

There was a clatter of iron-shod boots as an old man with shaggy hair and broad shoulders came running into the room. He was dressed like a collective-farm chairman, but he looked as if he'd been fighting with the partisans for at least a year: his baggy-kneed, mud-smeared trousers were tucked into his boots, and here and there patches of pine needles and wood resin were clinging to his jacket.

"It's my fault!" the old man exclaimed, wrenching a grey strand out of his tousled thatch. "I let Shapiro get away! I'm prepared to accept the severe consequences of my failure!"

"Timofei Stepanovich, please calm down at once!" Margarita Tikhonovna declared quietly but imperiously. "How is Provotorov? Alive?"

"They took Vadka off to hospital…" said the old man, examining the strand of hair clutched in his fist. "The doctors said it's nothing serious… Shapiro stunned him and hopped out through the window…" He unclenched his fingers and the wrenched-out tuft dropped onto the carpet.

"Timofei Stepanovich, my dear, how could you have?" Tanya asked dejectedly. "Where were you?"

"In the privy…" said Timofei Stepanovich, almost crying. "Provotorov and Lutsis were left with Shapiro… You told me just a while back, 'Shapiro's a traitor.' But it was Maxim Danilovich himself who brought him into the reading room! I just couldn't believe that he… I thought we were wrong to suspect the man, one of our own comrades, that we'd be ashamed afterwards and have to apologize for it!" Timofei Stepanovich suddenly hesitated with a strange air. "And who's this?" he asked, gawping wild-eyed at me.

"Maxim Danilovich's nephew," said Margarita Tikhonovna. "Alexei Vladimirovich Vyazintsev. I told you…"

"Take my word…" Timofei Stepanovich wheezed, darting towards me.

I hid ingloriously behind Margarita Tikhonovna.

"Alexei Vladimirovich, take my word for it, I will make amends…" said Timofei Stepanovich, thumping himself on the chest with a resounding thud. "I'll gnaw that Shapiro's heart out…"

"Timofei Stepanovich, my dear," Margarita Tikhonovna implored him wearily, "curb your heroic temperament for now. Alexei Vladimirovich has suffered enough as it is. He has had more than enough new impressions to cope with today. Why don't you just tell me where Ogloblin and Larionov are?"

"They're guarding that one you captured," said Timofei Stepanovich, reluctantly backing away from me, "in the Vozglyakovs' shed."

"And the others?"

"Searching for Shapiro…" said the old man with a dismissive gesture. "They divided into two groups. Dezhnev and Ievlev are in charge."

"I'll tell you what I'm afraid of…" Igor Valeryevich put in. "If Kolesov finds out that we haven't got Shapiro, he'll refute all his testimony. We have to hand him over to the observers tomorrow in any case. He'll have time to talk to Marchenko…"

"Boys and girls," said Tanya, pointing at me, "we have Alexei Vladimirovich! He's a witness too!"

A sudden foreboding brought me out in a sweat.

"And why not," said Sukharev, perking up feebly. "He was there, wasn't he? He saw the whole thing. Right, Alexei?"

"I'm against it," Margarita Tikhonovna said after pondering briefly. "I wouldn't like to get Alexei Vladimirovich involved…"

"Maybe just as a back-up option?" Igor Valeryevich put in cautiously. He sat down beside me. "Of course you're not in the mood for all this right now… But what did happen at Maxim

Danilovich's place, I mean at your place, when Kolesov showed up? Only in detail, now."

As far as I was able, I recited the sequence of events: the note in the door, the strange visitors and the book that was found on the shelves, which Kolesov cadged from me.

"In principle, Tereshnikov is obliged to take this into account," said Margarita Tikhonovna. "Even if Kolesov tries to squirm out of his testimony, we have the letter, which is evidence of a kind… By the way, where is it, Alexei Vladimirovich?"

"I'll go for it," Sukharev piped up. "If Alexei just tells me where…"

"Here it is," I said, taking the creased sheet of paper out of my pocket in the feeble hope that it might somehow serve as my ransom.

"Alexei Vladimirovich! My ray of sunshine!" Margarita Tikhonovna exclaimed. "How excellent that you brought it with you!"

She tucked the letter into her handbag and spoke words that transformed the floor into a lurching deck.

"Alexei Vladimirovich, I really am most reluctant to impose on you, but I think that tomorrow we shall require your help after all. Could you repeat to the meeting everything that you have told us?"

I didn't dare to risk saying "no", recalling the manner in which problems of "cooperation" were dealt with in this company. Sukharev had the confiscated awl, tempered in sealing wax, tucked into his belt, and bald Igor Valeryevich hadn't put his fearsome blade away yet.

Margarita Tikhonovna thanked me, old Timofei Stepanovich rushed to shake me by the hand, Tanya smiled, Sukharev patted me on the shoulder, Igor Valeryevich said that my agreeing to help was a tribute to the memory of Uncle Maxim. And I realized in horror what an inescapable quagmire today's events had turned into.

In conclusion Margarita Tikhonovna said:

"Igor Valeryevich, we leave our guest in your keeping. Let him rest. We'll come for you early tomorrow evening."

*

They left. I meekly withdrew into the other room, but of course I had no intention of sleeping. And, to all appearances, neither did my guard. I heard the sound of ponderous steps, and then the springs of an armchair sighed under his weight. A strip of light came in under the door. I heard the rustle of a newspaper and the jingle of a circling teaspoon.

About halfway through the night the light went out and, after waiting for the sound of regular snoring, I tried to get out into the sitting room without making any noise. The treacherous door didn't merely creak, it whinnied like a horse. The snoring immediately broke off, Igor Valeryevich lifted his head up off the cushion, sleeked down round his bald patch the hair that had straggled across his temples and the back of his head, and turned on the standard lamp with his other hand.

"Alexei, the toilet's right beside the front door, only the tank's acting up," he said, screwing his eyes up drowsily against the bright light. "That's Sanya's fault, the pest, he broke the handle again last night. There's a green bucket in there, fill it with water and pour that in, and I'll fix the tank in the morning…" Igor Valeryevich was wearing tracksuit trousers and a singlet that emphasized his bovine fleshiness. The knife was lying beside him on a nightstand. "Finding it hard to sleep in a strange place?"

"I'm sorry, I didn't mean to wake you."

"It's no big deal, I was only half dozing anyway… If you need anything, don't stand on ceremony, just go ahead and get me up…"

As I came out of the toilet, I noticed an oval plaque on the door, with a bas-relief image of a little urchin peeing into a chamber pot. One exactly like it used to hang in our home about twenty years earlier, but then it had got lost somewhere. Strangely enough, the sight of this tranquil urination that had been going on for decades in apartments of the most various kinds suddenly relieved my anxiety. Or perhaps the fear had simply drained out of me spontaneously and I had flushed it away with water out of the green bucket.

I suddenly felt terribly tired. And the back of my neck hurt, as if someone had been stubbing out fag ends on it with his boot. I closed my eyes and dreamed of a headache.

In the morning Igor Valeryevich buzzed annoyingly with his electric shaver and worked away noisily in the kitchen—dishes clattered in the sink while the frying pan hissed.

"How did you sleep, Alexei?" he shouted, hearing that I was up, and glanced out, holding a fork with a slice of bread stuck on it. "Have a wash, we're going to have breakfast in a minute. Do you like toast? With ham and cheese?…"

Igor Valeryevich's surname was Kruchina, a word signifying "grief" in Russian, but nothing could possibly have been more inappropriate to his bright, sunny temperament. He acted as if we were old friends and spoke in the cheerful manner of the presenter of *Morning Exercise* on the radio. I tried to avoid meeting his glance, but every time he ambushed me with a broad smile.

"Don't be shy now, Alexei, pile it up and I'll toast some more. That's it, good lad! Maybe I should make a salad?"

I hastily declined, because the sight of Igor Valeryevich with a knife—even a kitchen knife—would have been too much for me.

"How about some tea with lemon? You don't mind? That's grand, then!" And he immediately started crooning some bouncy little tune to himself.

Half a day of this excessive bonhomie wore me out finally and completely. I didn't trust him and was expecting this performance to come to an abrupt end at any moment, after which Igor Valeryevich would reveal his true, ferocious face.

But in the meantime he enquired enthusiastically about what I'd done in my life. On learning that I had a degree in metallurgy he positively blossomed.

"Alexei! We're colleagues, you and me. I'm a foundry engineer!"

I listened to him, but kept casting anxious glances at the nightstand with the previous day's weapon lying on it. It wasn't really a knife, more like a bayonet with a very long blade.

Igor Valeryevich spotted my glance, but interpreted it in his own way.

"Like it? It's an antique. From the First World War. How it came to be in our parts is a mystery, probably it was during the Civil War..." He reached out to the nightstand, and my heart suddenly contracted painfully.

But in fact nothing terrible happened. Igor Valeryevich carefully placed the bayonet in my hands. I touched the letters inscribed in an arc on the long, sturdy blade—"Modelo Argentino 1909" and "Solingen"—and the smooth wooden facings of the handle, then followed the cliché and ran the ball of my thumb along the edge of the blade.

"Sharp," Igor Valeryevich confirmed proudly. "Why, of course it is! Handsome, isn't it?" It was clear that he loved his weapon and valued it highly.

Then Igor Valeryevich brought over a photograph album and I leafed right through it out of politeness.

"The old man and my mum... No longer with us," Igor Valeryevich commented as I turned the pages. "My brother Nikita— he's in Arkhangelsk now... That's me in the army. I served in the Transcarpathian region... My college... I studied in the evening faculty, and I worked as well, of course. I've been in a foundry shop almost twenty-five years... My ex-wife. We didn't get on... And this is me being awarded my medal. Believe me, I would have been nominated for a Hero of Socialist Labour if the Soviet Union hadn't collapsed, the documents were all ready, and then... Fucking disaster struck and they cut back production. We were lucky they didn't shut down the plant..."

The final pages were filled with group photographs; Igor Valeryevich in the company of various people, among whom I recognized my abductors of the previous day and my Uncle Maxim.

"Our reading room. That's me with Fedya Ogloblin, who was driving yesterday, and beside him is Sasha Larionov, they're kind of backwards namesakes—one's Fyodor Alexandrovich and the other's Alexander Fyodorovich… Pavel Pavlovich, only without his moustache—he grew it for conspiratorial purposes… Sasha Sukharev and Tanya Miroshnikova, Margarita Tikhonovna… Well, you'll meet the others today anyway… The Vozglyakovs: Maria Antonovna and her daughters Anna, Svetlana and Veronika. Denis Lutsis… and Marat Andreyevich Dezhnev, our family doctor. A remarkable man… Vadka Provotorov, Grisha Vyrin… And this," he said, jabbing his finger at a Gigantopithecus with a shaved head, standing behind everyone and embracing almost the entire freak show in his huge, immensely long arms, "is Nikolai Tarasovich Ievlev. No words can possibly express how strong he is. You're never afraid with a comrade like that around… And here, to the left of Margarita Antonovna, this is Pashka Yegorov… he's dead and gone now, Pashka. Like Maxim Danilovich… And this here, with Sveta Vozglyakova…"—he pointed to an individual in dark glasses, clinging to the very edge of the photo like some kind of polyp—"… is a very bad man, Boris Arkadyevich Shapiro in person. Yes, indeed… You could say he's the reason for all our troubles." Igor Valeryevich's face darkened.

"But what kind of meeting is this, and who's going to be there?" I asked, plucking up my courage.

"All sorts of people. Both friends and enemies… All considered, it's a long story." Igor Valeryevich smiled guiltily. "It's just that Margarita Tikhonovna asked me not to alarm you by filling your head up with too much information…"

After suddenly recalling that I was due to "testify" that evening, Igor Valeryevich left me in peace. I spent the time until Margarita Tikhonovna arrived sitting on the sofa, pretending to prepare my "speech", but really only scribbling fitful squiggles on the sheets of paper that Igor Valeryevich had issued me with.

THE MEETING

T HE RAF PULLED UP at a pair of tall iron gates. A curly spiral of barbed wire ran along the top of the concrete wall. Our driver sounded his horn briefly and the gates opened. It looked to me as if we had driven into the grounds of some kind of factory, because through the twilight that was brightened slightly by a single lamp I could make out barrack-style workshop buildings, as identical as cattle sheds.

"Up you get, Alexei Vladimirovich…" Margarita Tikhonovna had dressed herself up for the meeting in a severe, dark-blue suit with a large malachite brooch adorning the lapel. She had piled her hair up high and put on lipstick, mascara and rouge. Only her shoes were the same as the day before—black, with wrinkled bows. "We're getting out…"

I was overwhelmed by fear again, and even the considerate way she addressed me as "Alexei Vladimirovich" could no longer reassure me. No, I wasn't afraid of bloody violence. It was a premonition, a realization that what was happening now could never be undone, that this was a Rubicon, a boundary line, and once I crossed it I could never go back to my former life again.

Margarita Tikhonovna repeated her summons, but I didn't budge, as if I were stunned. Then Sasha Sukharev and Tanya took me under the arms and practically carried me out of the minibus.

Immediately we were surrounded.

"Greetings to the glorious Shironin reading room," said a smiling, grey-haired old man with the majestic features of a field marshal, although he was dressed in a most unsoldier-like manner—canvas trousers and a knitted sleeveless jumper over a shirt.

"And good evening to you too, Comrade Burkin."

"How are you feeling, Margarita Tikhonovna? Did you see them? Lagudov's oprichniks?" He pointed to a small group of men standing apart, beside a battered old Volga with its black-and-white checkerboard taxi signs painted over. "Blasted observers... Oh, here's Simonyan... Hello, Zhanna Grigoryevna!"

An elderly woman with a tear-stained-looking Armenian face walked up to us.

"Margarita Tikhonovna, has Comrade Burkin told you? The Kolontaysk comrades have arrived. The entire reading room. All on our side... Oi!" she exclaimed suddenly. "Is he?... Could he be Maxim Danilovich's son?"

"No, Zhannochka Grigoryevna. His nephew. Alexei Vladimirovich Vyazintsev."

"Please, just call me Alexei," I said, feeling awkward at the way Margaret Tikhonovna was leading me around like a blind man.

"This is only his second day here," she said. "He hasn't had a chance to come to grips with anything yet, I'm managing things for him in the meantime. We didn't have a chance to warn him; he arrived right in the thick of things."

Simonyan folded her hands as if in prayer.

"I understand. The poor boy."

"What boy?" Burkin put in with ostentatious vivacity. "He's an assault commando! Parachuted straight in!"

"That's very true," Margarita Tikhonovna agreed. "He behaved with exceptional heroism. But what else would you expect? He's a Vyazintsev!"

A horn sounded outside. The gates screeched open and an ungainly-looking truck drove into the yard. Men started popping out from under its tarpaulin cover, as if they were emerging from the Trojan Horse.

"The Gorelovites are here," Simonyan whispered.

I saw Larionov and Pal Palych hand over the captured Kolesov to the observers. Once surrounded by the observers, he immediately went limp, as if his legs had been cut from under him, and held himself up by clutching at people's sleeves, although before that he had moved about without any kind of assistance at all.

The crowd poured into a workshop. Someone asked for the lights to be switched on. Dim neon lamps started buzzing on a metal beam below the ceiling. Entirely emptied of its equipment, the workshop looked like a sports hall. The only thing left was the motionless black ribbon of a conveyor belt along one wall, and many of those who had come in immediately decided to make use of it as a bench.

All in all about a hundred people crowded into the workshop. The brigade of twenty-something men who had arrived on the truck—the Gorelovites—stood apart from all the others. They made a strange impression, like members of the technical intelligentsia who had suddenly lost their veneer of intellectual culture and reverted to the condition of factory hooligans.

People I already knew gathered round Margarita Tikhonovna: Tanya, Sasha Sukharev, Pal Palych with his moustache, Igor Valeryevich Kruchina, old Timofei Stepanovich. Soon the driver of the RAF, Ogloblin, came over with his navigator, Larionov—the mirror-image namesakes Fyodor Alexandrovich and Alexander Fyodorovich.

We were joined by the Vozglyakov family: the mother Maria Antonovna and her three daughters—Anna, Svetlana and Veronika. These four gigantic women looked tremendously impressive. They were all red-cheeked blondes, with identical button noses. I felt narrow-shouldered and puny beside their mighty, broad-boned physiques.

A young man squeezed his way through to me.

"Denis Lutsis," he said, introducing himself. In marked contrast with Sasha, who was also about my age, he was definitely some kind of exemplary postgraduate student. Thin and angular, in glasses, beside the robust Vozglyakov family he looked even less impressive than I did. "Pleased to meet you."

"Alexei," I said for the umpteenth time that evening and shook his fragile hand.

"Denis," Margarita Tikhonovna called. "Where are Grisha, Marat Andreyevich and Nikolai Tarasovich?"

"They couldn't come, Margarita Tikhonovna," Lutsis whispered. "Dezhnev is on duty in the clinic—he couldn't get out of it. And Grisha and Nikolai Tarasovich are at Vadik Provotorov's place."

A solitary male voice cut through the general hubbub that was gradually subsiding.

"Silence! Silence, please, I can't shout!" he waited for a few seconds. "Comrades, the agenda for this evening includes two complaints…"

"That's Tereshnikov," Lutsis whispered in my ear. "The district observer, something like a judge…"

Margarita Tikhonovna gave us a severe look, and Denis stopped speaking.

"The first complaint was submitted by the Shironin reading room. Acting librarian Comrade Selivanova, please come out to the centre… There is a parallel complaint from the Gorelov reading room. Librarian Comrade Marchenko… If you please," said Tereshnikov, gesturing for Marchenko to come out. A man who looked like some belligerent head of department walked out of the Gorelov brigade, his cheek displaying either a fresh haematoma or a bright-crimson birthmark.

"I wouldn't touch a comrade like that with a bargepole!" some joker shouted out. People in the crowd laughed and Tereshnikov grimaced in annoyance.

"This is not a court of law, of course, but it's not a fairground either. Take this more seriously. Three bodies, by the way…"

"Five," Margarita Tikhonovna corrected him in a resounding voice. "Add on another two."

"Comrade Selivanova," said Tereshnikov, "as far as I understood from the report, you accuse the Gorelov reading room of attempting to seize a Book of Memory by force…"

"And also of the murder of our librarian Vyazintsev and our reader Yegorov."

Tereshnikov assumed an expression of moderate anguish.

"Six months ago all of us here mourned Comrade Vyazintsev… You know that the council held a supplementary investigation. Vyazintsev was killed by street hooligans. And your reader Yegorov, if my memory does not deceive me, was run over and killed by some drunken villain who fled from the scene in a base and cowardly manner. These tragedies could be blamed on our society's total lack of spirituality and the extent to which life in this country encourages criminal behaviour…"—Tereshnikov's tone became sterner—"… but yesterday the Gorelov reading room lost three of its members! I very much hope that you will be able to provide adequate proofs in justification of this act."

The people in the workshop started murmuring, discussing what they had just heard. Marchenko nodded and frowned at Tereshnikov's words.

"Absolutely," Margarita Tikhonovna declared, staring menacingly at Marchenko. "The meeting will be presented with the proofs this evening."

"Very well," Tereshnikov declared. "Who wants to begin? You, Comrade Selivanova?"

"Let him begin!"

"I cede that right to my colleague," Marchenko rejoined smartly. Tereshnikov frowned.

"We're not in school here. Stop wrangling… All right, let us hear Selivanova!"

Margarita Tikhonovna quietly cleared her throat and began.

"The recent incident has its roots in the events of two years ago, when our reader Pavel Yegorov was knocked down in strange circumstances by a truck that was being driven erratically—that was the conclusion of a forensic medical examination on the basis of his injuries. I do not draw any hasty conclusions regarding trucks, and let me remark immediately that we do not regard the fact that this is the form of transport used by the Gorelov reading room as proof of their guilt…"

"Well, thank you kindly…" Marchenko snarled.

A buzz ran round the workshop, but whether in support or condemnation of his remark wasn't clear.

"Silence!" Tereshnikov snapped severely and nodded to Margarita Tikhonovna. "Continue."

"Indeed, there are a great many trucks in Russia, and no shortage of drunk drivers either, and one of them killed our comrade Pavel Yegorov. An accident. But a month later, here in this hall, Comrade Marchenko suggested to Maxim Danilovich that we accept into our reading room a certain worthy individual, Boris Arkadyevich Shapiro, a former member of the Severodvinsk reading room."

"I protest," Marchenko exclaimed. "It was not a recommendation. I merely stated the situation. In addition to me, there were representatives present from Smolensk and Belgorod, as well as librarians from our district—comrades Burkin, Latokhin and Simonyan. They can confirm that. Your Vyazintsev took Shapiro in of his own volition, mentioning that the Shironin reading room had recently lost a reader!"

"Of course, of course," Margarita Tikhonovna said with a baleful smile. "But why have you suddenly started making excuses, Comrade Marchenko? I have not as yet reproached you with this Shapiro, have I? Could it be that you have a presentiment of something to come?"

"All I know is that yesterday three of my people were brutally murdered and a fourth was seriously injured, and also that absolutely outrageous, false accusations have been levelled at me and my reading room!" Marchenko hissed furiously.

"Silence!" Tereshnikov shouted yet again, to still the hubbub that had erupted in the workshop. "Comrade Marchenko, you will have time to state your opinion. Do not interrupt!"

THE LIBRARIAN

Margarita Tikhonovna paused for a few seconds and then continued:

"Those present here no doubt recall those sad events. The Severodvinsk reading room fell victim to forgeries, after which it was closed down by the council. They refused to hand over their Book, and all of them who attempted to resist were killed in a battle with the forces of the council…"

"But that was an official decision," Tereshnikov intervened hastily. "The law!"

"I do not dispute that, Comrade Tereshnikov. I am merely reminding everyone of the substance of the matter. The only Severodvinsk reader to survive was Shapiro. Why pretend other-wise—our district regarded the events in Severodvinsk with great sympathy… Especially since that whole business with the fakes was very shady…"

"Comrade Selivanova! If you please!"

"I beg your pardon, that is my personal opinion… In short, we took Shapiro in as one of us. At first glance he was an ideal reader. He idealized Maxim Danilovich, he was obliging and enthusiastic. He liked to joke. We grew used to him… Well, then… But in November I had an accident. I slipped and broke my leg. I convalesced at home. Vyazintsev brought the Book to me in accordance with the established reading schedule. I was actually opposed to this, I didn't want the Book to leave the confines of the reading room… As a rule, Maxim Danilovich was always accompanied by a personal bodyguard. Shapiro was aware of the schedule. What he did not know was that Maxim Danilovich had left the Book with me before setting off on his way home alone, without any escorts… I will permit myself one small assumption: if Maxim Danilovich had had the book with him, and the attackers had not been simply bandits, then our reading room would have ceased to exist." With that Margarita Tikhonovna fell silent.

"From what you have told us," said Tereshnikov, breaking the silence, "it does not follow that Shapiro was connected with the Gorelov reading room and was carrying out its will."

"A moment's patience. Everything will become clear in a moment… How my suspicions took shape is a long story. Put it down to female intuition. Perhaps because on that fateful evening many of our readers were at my home, but Shapiro was absent, and not in possession of the information that Vyazintsev didn't have the book on him, and he gave the signal to the 'right' person…" Margarita Tikhonovna sighed. "In general, Yegorov's accident, Shapiro's appearance in our library and Maxim Danilovich's death seemed to me to be connected. I concealed my suspicions until the spring, then I informed our comrades about them. They agreed to check Shapiro. Maxim Danilovich's relatives had already laid claim to the inheritance. Two weeks ago I held a meeting of the reading room, at which I said there was a second Book of Memory in Maxim Danilovich's sealed apartment. Supposedly it was a secret that he had asked me not to divulge, but now that Maxim Danilovich's heirs had shown up, the Book needed to be removed. Shapiro, I remember, was excited and said that we could get a huge amount of money for an illegal Book, and he offered to help with his connections… Two days ago I contacted Shapiro and warned him that we had a compulsory gathering on Friday. A problem had arisen: Maxim Danilovich's nephew had arrived. I set the removal of the Book for Monday. To make things more convincing we planted our copy, so that visitors would have something to purloin. If Shapiro had come with them, he would have recognized the Book and seen through our trick, but, as expected, he showed up for the meeting and was arrested. An ambush was set close to the building."

I was feeling really rotten. For me the often-repeated phrase "reading room" was associated only with the village "reading-room huts" of the early Soviet days. It turned out that Uncle Maxim was a librarian, that the people surrounding me constituted a reading room in which he was the central figure, and that a scandal had blown up because of that little book that Kolesov had found on my uncle's shelves.

Every time Margarita Tikhonovna mentioned the surname that I shared with my uncle, a wave of heat flooded across my face, my palms started sweating and my stomach drew in painfully tight. And when the conversation concerned me directly, my mouth filed up with bitter saliva. I did not want to testify.

"Alexei Vyazintsev's visitors showed up in the guise of buyers, after previously writing this letter…" Margarita Tikhonovna took a sheet of paper out of a folder and handed it to Tereshnikov. "You may add it to the minutes… And this is Kolesov's confession, in which he gives a detailed account of his connections with the Gorelov reading room, the saboteur Shapiro's activities and the planned murder of Maxim Danilovich…"

Marchenko surprised me. Despite the fact that everything was shaping up against him and the reaction of the workshop clearly did not express sympathy for the Gorelov group, he remained calm and even smiled, making reassuring signs to his own people.

Tereshnikov compared Kolesov's testimony with the letter.

"Yes, the writing is the same…" he confirmed. He appeared disconcerted. "Carry on, Margarita Tikhonovna."

"At about seven o'clock on Friday we ostentatiously withdrew our surveillance of the apartment and pretended to set off to the meeting—that is, we made it appear that the Book was unprotected. Naturally, we merely moved to another spot and continued to observe the building. When it grew dark, the visitors appeared, having been tipped off by Shapiro. There were four of them and two went upstairs. Half an hour later they came down, and one of them was holding the Book of Memory… We know the outcome: three raiders were liquidated and one was taken prisoner. For the moment I have nothing more to add…"

"Your position is clear," said Tereshnikov. "Now we will hear Comrade Marchenko. He will have to explain many things to us."

Marchenko surveyed the crowd insolently.

"Well, then… Comrade Selivanova has given a remarkable speech… I don't know how I can engage your attention now. You probably won't even want to listen. Why, there is even written evidence! I'm sure you're expecting me to go down on my knees: forgive me, good people, I repent, on my orders the finest of men was killed—the librarian Vyazintsev! Judge me severely, brothers! It was I, scoundrel that I am, who set those fiends on the Shironin reading room. It was I, reckless and shameless driver that I am, who ran down the reader Yegorov in my truck!"

"Should we take that as a confession?" Margarita Tikhonovna enquired contemptuously.

Shouting broke out in the workshop. Insults were thrown at Marchenko. "Dirtbag! Scum!" yelled the people beside us.

"And now," Marchenko said bitterly, "I shall begin. Only there's an epigraph to my story, if you will permit me. A living epigraph…" He gestured with his hand.

Two observers led out Kolesov, swathed in a sheet. He moved his feet with difficulty, his puffy right eye was almost completely covered by a purple bruise, his lips were split and swollen, and a black lock of hair cut across his pale, tormented forehead. Catching sight of Margarita Tikhonovna, Kolesov staggered back, moaned and covered his face with his hands like a child.

Marchenko walked up to him.

"Vadim Leonidovich," he keened, "hold on, my dear man…" Marchenko carefully removed the sheet and then moved aside, holding it as a torero holds his cape. All that was visible was Kolesov's battered face and his legs up to the knees.

"This is how the Shironin reading room questions people!" Marchenko whipped aside the sheet like a genuine conjuror.

Kolesov's body was covered with numerous red lacerations and on his stomach and chest he had repulsive crimson blisters from burns that repeated the outline of an iron.

Marchenko surveyed the meeting with a wrathful gaze.

"Even in the concentration camps prisoners were not tormented like this! Vadim Leonidovich! Show them your back!"

Kolesov slowly turned round and Marchenko confirmed what we saw.

"The Shironin reading room has revived an ancient form of torture: flaying in strips."

Red blotches appeared on Margarita Tikhonovna's cheeks.

"Comrades, don't believe…" she looked round helplessly.

Marchenko, relishing the general confusion, started shrieking.

"Why, after that kind of torture, any one of us would confess to the murder of Tutankhamun! The testimony beaten out of Kolesov by the Shironin sadists is a gory bluff! Vadim Leonidovich, tell them yourself…"

"F-forgive me, comrades…" said Kolesov, stammering. "I… I…"

To my amazement, he started lying.

"We… we arrived. Selivanova asked me, 'Where's the money?' I gave her the bundle and A-a-lik asked for the Book. Shapiro gave it to him, but it was packaged up. Alik started to unwrap it, and when Selivanova said, 'You don't trust us.' And I said, 'Better safe than sorry.' They threatened to take the Book back, and I told them, 'Then give back the money or we'll complain to the council.' And Selivanova said, 'You're not going to complain to anyone!' and stuck an awl through Alik's neck…" At this point Kolesov broke into sobs. "I repudiate all my testimony! Damned fascists! Vicious brutes!" He jabbed his finger towards our group. "I repudiate it! Fascists! I repudiate it!"

"These are treacherous lies!" Lutsis shouted in a loud, clear voice. "Look, his wounds are absolutely fresh! The Gorelovites have only just decorated him themselves!" But his words were drowned out by the general hubbub.

It was clear that Marchenko had won back his lost ground at a stroke.

"Our reader Kolesov slandered himself under hideous torture. I request that his written testimony be disqualified."

"I swear!" said Margarita Tikhonovna, putting her hands to her breast and appealing to the gathering. "Well, perhaps he was thumped in the teeth once or twice, just as a warning! Nobody tortured him!"

"I am astounded!" said Tereshnikov. "I don't even know what to say… At least, until I hear Comrade Marchenko's position."

"Dear fellow thinkers," Marchenko began once the noise had abated slightly. "Yesterday we lost three comrades and one has been maimed. The good name of our reading room has been dragged through the mud… And it all began when the librarian Vyazintsev offered to sell me a Book of Memory that was not registered with the council."

"You shameless liar!" Margarita Tikhonovna exclaimed.

"Selivanova, don't interrupt," Tereshnikov intervened. "You were given an attentive hearing. Carry on, Comrade Marchenko."

"The part of broker between us was played by the reader Boris Arkadyevich Shapiro. Some parties here have tried to portray him as the evil genius of the Shironin reading room, but I have a different opinion concerning that question. Vyazintsev named a moderate price—ten thousand dollars. Our reading room had expanded rapidly and we needed one more book. Vyazintsev explained his actions by the fact that they had no money to register the book legally with the Council of Libraries. As an advance Vyazintsev received a down payment of five thousand dollars from us. Unfortunately we have no documents, nor indeed could we have. Everything was based on a gentleman's agreement…"

"Scoundr-r-rel!"

"Who, Vyazintsev? Oh, don't scold him," Marchenko said with a repulsive smile. "If you can't speak well of the dead…"

"You! You scoundrel!" Margarita Tikhonovna exclaimed, seething. "You two-faced snake! You killed Vyazintsev and now you're trying to slander his good name as well!"

"If you please!" shouted Tereshnikov, suddenly furious. "This is your final warning!"

"Thank you, Comrade Tereshnikov," Marchenko said with a mocking bow and then continued. "Naturally, we never saw the Book. Shapiro told me that on the day Vyazintsev died he apparently had the money—our advance payment—which disappeared. When we asked them to pay us back, the Shironinites gave us evasive replies about mourning and asked us to wait a little while. Month after month, via Shapiro, they fobbed us off with lame excuses and refused to return the advance payment. All we could do was wait and hope that the Shironin reading room would do the decent thing. We couldn't risk making a complaint to the council—by agreeing a deal for the Book with Vyazintsev, we ourselves had broken the law. There were no receipts, and if the matter ever came up, the Shironinites would simply have disowned us. In short, we had fallen into a trap... A week ago Shapiro unexpectedly got in touch with us and informed us that the Shironin reading room was willing to sell the Book, but the price had risen to twelve thousand. We had no option; after already paying the advance, we agreed to pay the extra. I sent four of our readers to the meeting. You know what happened to them. Three were killed, one was maimed, and the money—seven thousand dollars—was stolen. It was deliberately planned financial fraud. The victim Kolesov can tell you about it in greater detail..."

The blood rushed to Igor Valeryevich Kruchina's bald patch and face. Timofei Stepanovich tore at the collar of his shirt. The Vozglyakov sisters started whispering about something, and their mother, Maria Antonovna, sighed and knitted her brows. Tanya's lips turned white. Ogloblin, Larionov and Pal Palych exchanged glances.

"Just look how he's twisted things round..." Sukharev exclaimed in furious admiration.

Lutsis rubbed his temple:

"I suspected from the very beginning that everything would turn out like this..."

"Comrade Marchenko," Tereshnikov protested nervously. "For God's sake, wait. The reader Kolesov cannot testify as a witness in his own right just yet. I am more interested in Shapiro's testimony. Comrade Selivanova, bring him here; we need to slice through this Gordian knot!"

"Oh, yes," said Marchenko, baring his teeth. "They'll bring him this very moment!"

Margarita Tikhonovna had already mastered her bewilderment.

"Unfortunately we cannot call Shapiro."

"You cannot?" said Tereshnikov, raising one eyebrow rapidly in surprise. "Why not?"

"He disappeared. Escaped. Yesterday. And, of course, he notified his masters. Now Comrade Marchenko can slander people to his heart's content."

"I protest!" Marchenko responded vigorously. "Comrade Selivanova is the one who is slandering here. I am telling the honest truth!"

"There is absolutely no logic in your villainous ravings. Most of those present here knew Maxim Danilovich well. He would never have concealed a Book, let alone sold it."

"Well I, for instance, do not know what our deceased librarian could have done and could not have done," Marchenko parried.

"Very well, why do you not accept that if we did have a second Book of Memory we would have legally registered it ourselves?"

"The tax on registration is rather high, and your reading room is small. You only need one copy, so why wouldn't you sell it to wealthier colleagues on the quiet? Let them have the expense. Why pretend otherwise? That is what many people do, and the council closes its eyes to these tricks. But on this occasion it is not a matter of loopholes in the law." Marchenko assumed a more severe expression. "Naturally, we were prepared to cover the fine and pay the tax for purchasing and registration... But we don't have the Book, the money has been stolen, three of our readers have been killed and one maimed... I demand justice!"

"Lies, all lies, from the first word to the last!"

"I'm very sorry, Comrade Selivanova," Tereshnikov stated drily after a brief pause. "It is my job to be objective. You must understand. I have no right to discriminate against Comrade Marchenko's version of events... And then there is your trap and the planting of the Book, which is the genuine and only one. Unfortunately, without Shapiro's testimony, for you the situation is a stalemate, with a distinctly negative bias."

"I request that you hear our witness, Alexei Vladimirovich Vyazintsev."

My heart stopped beating, but Tereshnikov dismissed the suggestion.

"Comrade Selivanova! Shapiro, who has fled, is the only person who could prove you right. And a blood relative of Vyazintsev's is an interested party. I have no doubt that he will tell us what he is supposed to tell us... I wish to appeal immediately to both reading rooms: is there any possibility of resolving the issue of our meeting peacefully? Comrade Marchenko? Can the Shironinites in some way compensate you for the death of your readers? For instance, pay the sum of twelve thousand dollars that has been mentioned?"

"A wonderful idea!" Margarita Tikhonovna exclaimed ironically. "I see the council is irked by our Neverbino privileges! They can't legally hack any tax out of us! They can't turn us into a branch library! But they want their rake-off from the Shironinites. By hook or by crook. Only we paid for our status in lives!"

"I do not understand you, Comrade Selivanova!" Tereshnikov exclaimed, drawing himself up and stiffening.

"Your pretence makes me feel sick! It's quite obvious to any right-thinking individual that the Gorelov reading room is Shulga's project! It's not Marchenko who wants compensation—he's merely an obedient puppet—but Shulga, that is, the council!"

"Margarita Tikhonovna!" Tereshnikov yelled. "You forget yourself! As it happens I too-oo..."—he wagged a finger as soft as if it had been boiled—"...was at Neverbino!"

Margarita Tikhonovna had already calmed down.

"Where would we get that kind of money from? Perhaps I could take it out of my pension? Or Timofei Stepanovich could? Or Tatyana Miroshnikova could pay out of her schoolteacher's salary. Or Igor Valeryevich—everyone knows that our foundry workers are secret millionaires!"

"Don't you complain, Comrade Selivanova," said Tereshnikov. "Life is hard for the whole country! The late Vyazintsev had an apartment. Sell that…"

I was struck by the wild idea that this entire farce had been played out by a good hundred actors in order to take my apartment away from me.

"Denis," I whispered to Lutsis, "tell Margarita Tikhonovna that I agree."

"Alexei?" he said, looking at me in amazement. "What are you talking about?"

"We don't want money!" Marchenko exclaimed with dignity. "The only thing that will satisfy us is the dissolution of the Shironin reading room. And in compensation for the death of our readers we demand the Book of Memory."

"You can have this, scumbag!" said Timofei Stepanovich, weaving his fingers into an obscene sign and symbolically spitting on it for good measure. "Up yours."

"I couldn't put it better," Margarita Tikhonovna said with a satisfied nod. "Up yours, Comrade Marchenko!"

"Did you hear that?" Marchenko asked furiously. "You won't get away with that! Comrade Tereshnikov! Our reading room demands satisfaction!"

"And you'll get it, have no doubt about that!" Margarita Tikhonovna replied.

Lagudov's invited observers all got up at the same time and moved towards the exit.

Tereshnikov cleared his throat.

"I am no lover of violent solutions, but if there is no other option… Ultimately it's not up to me… Thank you for your attention and participation. The meeting is over. The time and place of the satisfaction will be agreed subsequently. The standard limit: forty people on each side. The defeated reading room will be disbanded and its Book will go to the Council of Libraries. I know that opinions in the region are divided. I request those who wish to support the reading rooms in the dispute to draw up their applications and submit them by tomorrow. All participations will be informed by our seconds… What else? I require the signatures of the librarians. Margarita Tikhonovna, are you still the acting librarian? Or is it the young man beside you? How do they put it, from generation to generation, right? Is the younger Vyazintsev now your librarian?"

"Not yet, but I think he soon will be."

"Fill out the documents for him and send them in, they take these matters very seriously now…" Tereshnikov gave a slight bow and walked across to Marchenko.

We were surrounded by the people near us.

"Well, you Shironinites?" asked Burkin. "Will you cope?"

"We'll have to, Vasily Andreyevich!" Lutsis replied cheerfully. "Our reading room's like a Guards regiment!"

"It's not the first time!" Timofei Stepanovich added.

"We'll give you as much help as we can," said Simonyan. "We have five volunteers. And that's not all. There's good news—Garshenin will be with us."

"Thank you, Zhannochka Grigoryevna. Thank you, my dear, we never doubted your solidarity with us," said Margarita Tikhonovna, hugging her gratefully. "Every soldier is precious. And Dmitry Olegovich is a genuine Ilya of Murom."

Burkin beamed with his marshal's face.

"Garshenin? How's he feeling?"

"Excellent. The bones have knitted together and he has completely recovered the use of his arm. He claims that it's even better than before…"

Burkin pointed to me.

"And what about him?"

"I think he'll go with us," Margarita Tikhonovna replied. "Right, Alexei? You are with us, aren't you?"

For some reason I took that to mean I could suddenly be handed on to someone else, like a thing, perhaps to this Burkin.

"I'm with you, Margarita Tikhonovna," I said cautiously.

Burkin sighed.

"Margarita Tikhonovna, don't forget that forty genuine bandits will turn out to fight for Marchenko... Alexei is completely inexperienced. He's barely even read the Book..."

"Alexei hasn't read the Book. He knows absolutely nothing," Margarita Tikhonovna said quietly.

Burkin was dumbstruck.

"Pardon me, but then why the hell did you bring him here?"

He led Margarita Tikhonovna aside and started passionately trying to persuade her of something.

Scraps of the conversation reached my ears. "...If he doesn't want to, I'll understand..." said Burkin. Margarita Tikhonovna protested: "...I believe in him..."

Burkin raised his voice.

"But I'll tell you what will happen. After the resolution of the conflict, even if everything goes well for us..."

"Well, thank you, Vasily Andreyevich! Thank you very much for the moral support!" Margarita Tikhonovna fumed. "Most timely! Why, then, are you helping us, if you doubt our success?"

"In the first place, I'm your friend, so I'm helping... But I'm also a realist! God grant that we get off lightly, without too much blood spilled. Mark my words, after Shapiro's escape they'll slap you with an "A" penalty. The council will tot up its losses for non-disclosure, and then your Vyazintsev..."—he looked at me— "Forgive me, I mean this for the best... As a perfectly normal citizen, Vyazintsev will go running to the militia, and that will be the second "A", for good measure! And there you have it, no more reading room!"

"So tha-a-at's it," Margarita Tikhonovna drawled comically. "With all due respect, Vasily Andreyevich, you're an excellent librarian, but a terrible psychologist…"

"Do you really not understand what you've done? It's not good, it's not honest. Against his will! You have involved a complete outsider… How will you clear up the mess now?"

"He's not an outsider," Margarita Tikhonovna said with feeling. "He's Maxim Danilovich's nephew…"

"I give up," Burkin capitulated in annoyance. "Time will tell…" He glanced at his watch. "And we have just over twenty-four hours of it left. We'll call you, Margarita Tikhonovna."

"See you soon, Vasily Andreyevich."

The workshop gradually emptied. One of the observers took the keys to Kolesov's Zhiguli from Pal Palych.

Simonyan said goodbye to us, once again promising the help of her much-vaunted Garshenin of Murom as she left.

A short man with a limp, by the name of Latokhin—the librarian of the Kolontaysk reading room—came over for a minute. He said he would send at least ten soldiers. This favour was clearly formal in nature and Margarita Tikhonovna signed a document for him.

"But will you not be there yourself?" asked Lutsis.

"Unfortunately," replied Latokhin, slapping himself on his bad leg, "my health won't permit it. My fighting days are over, Comrade Lutsis." Putting the sheet of paper in a red plastic folder, he said goodbye and limped away, taking his people with him.

The first to sum things up was Igor Valeryevich Kruchina.

"Well, now, brothers, things aren't all that bad. Eighteen of us, plus ten Kolontayskites. Simonyan's giving six and presumably Burkin will do the same. We're on the up, Margarita Tikhonovna!" he said and smashed his strong fist into the palm of his hand.

The lights were turned out in the workshop and someone shouted: "Shironinites, the meeting's over. Wrap it up, we're closing the doors! Finish your talking outside!" A steel door screeched and blackness advanced, shutting off half of the entrance. A worker drove the massive bolt into the concrete floor.

We walked out into the yard. Larionov and Ogloblin suddenly realized that the RAF hadn't been washed since yesterday and immediately ran off to get rags and buckets. A minute later they were joined by Tanya, Sasha Sukharev, Pal Palych, Lutsis and Igor Valeryevich.

Timofei Stepanovich and the four Vozglyakovs said that they had to catch the suburban train and said goodbye until tomorrow.

I was left alone with Margarita Tikhonovna. For a few minutes we watched the bustle around the RAF: Lutsis, with his sleeves rolled up, squeezed his rag out into a bucket; Pal Palych tinkered about inside the minibus; Tanya and Sasha washed the rubber rugs; and Igor Valeryevich asked the worker for a little drop of industrial alcohol.

Margarita Tikhonovna suddenly said:

"In many ways, of course, Burkin was right. I apologize for everything you have had to endure during these last two days…"

My eyes started to sting in pity for myself. I implored her in a whisper:

"Margarita Tikhonovna, I won't say a word to anyone, I swear, only please let me go! The militia is out of the question. And take the apartment. I just want to go home. I beg you! My father's seriously ill and my mother's unwell too. She's a pensioner… I'm… e-e-e-er… their only son," I lied hopelessly and stupidly.

Margarita Tikhonovna laughed.

"It's strange… Can a strong, young lad really be so afraid? I think that if I growled now, you'd faint. My poor boy… In actual fact, no one intended to drag you into this…" She paused for a moment. "In principle, you have behaved well, with no hysterics… And you really are very much like Maxim Danilovich to look at, and the boys and girls have already… well, really come to love you and believe in you as a good omen. But of course I'll let you go…"

"Thank you, thank you," I whispered gratefully.

"But I have two requests… Alexei, we have a very difficult job to do tomorrow night, and your presence would give the boys and girls moral support… Well, as the banner of our cause. And afterwards—as free as the wind. All right?"

"Certainly, Margarita Tikhonovna," I agreed readily.

She pondered for a moment and asked out of the blue:

"Alexei, do you believe in God? Only answer me honestly, without any false pathos or sneering."

"I probably do," I said.

"Do you go to church?" Margarita Tikhonovna asked specifically. "Do you confess and take communion?"

I didn't understand what she was getting at and answered cautiously, in order not to startle away her permission to flee.

"No, I don't go to church. Basically, I believe in something, but I don't know exactly what."

"The court understands the facts," Margarita Tikhonovna said with a smile. "Your life is hard, Alexei. Without a god, without inspiration. Nothing but fear. I don't know how you haven't gone insane… But I can give you a present to annul all the terrors that you have been through. I will give God back to you… No, don't be afraid. I'm not talking about some sort of sectarian jiggery-pokery. No one will try to ensnare you. What you will soon become directly aware of is probably one of the proofs of His existence. In order to believe, for some people it is enough to see the sunset in the mountains, or the ocean, for instance. For you it will be a Book. While they're tidying up in the minibus, I'll tell you a little bit about Gromov… After all, you're still completely ignorant…"

THE BOOK

I USUALLY HAVE a good memory for words and details, but I retained very little from the first fifteen minutes—I was up to my neck in ice-cold fear.

A forgotten author, now dead, who had written magical books, was beyond my belief. What I had grasped was that I had fallen into the hands of people who were sick, monstrously cruel, delirious psychos.

I listened to Margarita Tikhonovna without interrupting, evincing an air of calm attentiveness with every fibre of my being. The last thing I needed was to anger her and the other lunatics just like her who were scuttling about nearby.

The history of the Shironin reading room was the thing I remembered best of all, because of the surprising and shameless details with which Margarita Tikhonovna embellished the narrative. This morbid geriatric eroticism finally confirmed my fears.

The reading room had originated with the typist Svetlana Alexandrovna Koltsova. Destiny linked this woman directly with Gromov and seems to have done everything possible to include an unexceptional typist in the ranks of the chosen. She had the good fortune to type out Gromov's manuscript for the Book of Joy (*Narva*). And naturally Koltsova received the published novella as a present.

Life cast Koltsova into the provincial backwaters of Russia for many years. For about fifteen years the forgotten Gromov stood safe and sound on the shelf between Druon and Simenon. One day, out of boredom, Koltsova decided to read the book in which she had once invested her labour.

Koltsova didn't keep the plots of manuscripts in her head, because she never reflected on the text—that slowed down the work considerably. Koltsova opened Gromov's book out of sentimental considerations. In those long-ago evenings she had been involved in a tempestuous affair with the husband of one of her workfellows. Her lover would race round to her place, drink tea and wait until Koltsova, already all of a sweat with passion, tapped out a couple of paragraphs in the name of prudish formality and then surrendered to him right there at her desk. Her lover always took her from behind and Koltsova, with her arms braced against the desk, watched as the penetrating movements set the sheet of paper loaded into the typewriter trembling, rendering its meaning illegible. At the instant of supreme gratification she would deliriously tap her fingers on the keys, leaving an alphabetical code of her orgasm on the paper, and her lover would kiss her tenderly on the nape of her neck. The page defaced by love had to be typed out again.

And so, twenty years later, she took up Gromov's book, permeated with this aura of sensuality. As she read, long-ago scenes from her past life came alive again. The effect of the Book manifested itself in the form of a supremely powerful ecstasy. Koltsova quickly grasped the consistent connection between reading and gratification, after which she shared her discovery with her best friend. Naturally, after a certain time a reading room grew up around Koltsova, and my Uncle Maxim joined it—Koltsova took pity on this cultured individual whom drinking had reduced to a life of physical labour. And apart from that, Uncle Maxim resembled her former lover.

Koltsova was killed, falling victim to a raid by Mokhova's old women, and the Book was stolen. This happened on the very eve of the Battle of Neverbino, in which the reading room participated, and Uncle Maxim fought with great heroism. He was the one who insisted at the council meeting that all reading rooms that had lost their Books through Mokhova's nefarious activities should receive a replacement.

Thanks to Uncle Maxim, the Shironin reading room received a Book of Memory to replace the Book of Joy that had been lost, and it was released from the payment of taxes under the Neverbino exemptions. Formally speaking, the Book belonged to Uncle Maxim, and so by right of my bloodline I had allegedly inherited the position of librarian…

"Alexei! Margarita Tikhonovna!" Denis shouted. "We can go!"

"Thank you. We'll just be a moment," Margarita Tikhonovna responded. She looked me up and down intently, with a vaguely derisive air. "Why don't you say anything, Alyosha? Don't you believe me?"

Her manner was not like Sukharev's crude familiarity or Denis Lutsis's amiable treatment of me as a peer and equal. There was something else behind it. An insistent effort was being made to initiate me into something; attempts were being made every second, against my will, to tap me on the shoulder with a ritual sword, so that I could be considered an insider and judged by their rules. I had to remain extremely cautious and not offer them my shoulder by implication.

"It's hard to answer straight away," I began judiciously. "This information is so unusual, and… But I believe you, yes…"

Margarita Tikhonovna sighed.

"You're only agreeing out of fear. You're probably afraid the crazy old biddy will go berserk and stick a knitting needle in your throat?"

Those words brought me out in a sweat as sticky as honey.

Margarita Tikhonovna went on.

"Forgive me for talking to you like a family member, Alyosha. No one can hear us for the time being in any case. I think it's simpler, more open, like this… Have you never wondered why the apostles betrayed their Teacher, and then later died as fearless martyrs? At first they should have believed, but couldn't, but after

His resurrection they didn't believe—they knew. That's a big difference. And I'm not appealing for you to believe in me either. Very soon, if you so wish, you will know, as Denis, Tanya, Sasha, Pal Palych and Igor Valeryevich do… You can sense that all this time I've been leading you up to my second request. Alexei, I promised that no one would force you into anything. We keep our word. We don't want anything from you; it's simply that we loved and respected Maxim Danilovich, our friend and librarian. We'd like you to declare your final decision once you have read the Book. That is the second request…"

"Are you done talking?" Tanya asked us affably.

"Yes," said Margarita Tikhonovna. "I've given my basic literacy lesson. I had to enlighten Alexei about many things."

"He's a bright lad," Igor Valeryevich said, praising me. "He'll soon get the hang of it."

By this time my fear had almost exhausted itself and run out of steam. I felt indifferent to everything. I wasn't interested in Sukharev's quips, or Tanya's kind eyes, or Ogloblin's story about how thirty years ago in Kazakhstan, when he was still an orphanage boy, he used to catch carp in the river: "They used to swim out into the shallows and stick themselves halfway out to feast on the fresh young grass, and I whacked them with a stick…"

We drove up to Uncle Maxim's building, where Margarita Tikhonovna wished us good night and asked us not to burn the midnight oil, because we would need our strength tomorrow.

I was hoping that when we got back I would be left in peace. That didn't happen. Sukharev, Lutsis and Kruchina followed me up, to guard and protect me. However, they were all considerate and polite. I could tell that these people felt at home in Uncle Maxim's apartment. While Sasha deftly prepared supper—a ten-egg omelette—Denis and Igor Valeryevich made esoteric conversation.

"There's obviously something shady about those Gorelovites," said Igor Valeryevich. "The reading room's not three years old yet, and it's on the ten-per-cent rate. Not a branch library, not even on an annual tax, but the ten-per-cent rate! Who ever heard of the like of that?"

"The council probably decided to try out a new scheme," said Lutsis, munching zestfully on his omelette. "It's very logical. They provoke a conflict and then inflate it at the district meeting. Either compensation or satisfaction…"

"And if the accused side loses," Igor Valeryevich summed up, "the Book becomes the property of the winner: officially the Gorelov reading room, but in fact the library that set it up. Brilliant and simple!"

"But have no fear, Alexei," Sukharev told me with a wink. "It won't come to that."

In the morning Margarita Tikhonovna, Pal Palych, Ogloblin and Larionov showed up, together with three Shironinites I didn't know: Vadik Provotorov, Grisha Vyrin and Marat Andreyevich Dezhnev. This substantial escort was explained by the fact that all seven of them together delivered the Book of Memory, which was ceremoniously presented to me to read.

The new arrivals stayed and the others left. But for the axes and the shoulder belt with two sapper's entrenching tools that were dumped in the hallway, all the indications would have been that these were peaceful people. Marat Andreyevich Dezhnev was a traumatologist, a tall, black-haired man of about fifty. He immediately apologized, saying that he was tired after his work shift, and went to the bedroom to catch up on his sleep. Beside him on the bed he laid a sabre that had been shortened by a quarter of its length, in a scabbard with its end broken off, which, it turned out, he had concealed in his trouser leg.

Vadik Provotorov, small and stocky, with the physique of a wrestler and a nose pushed slightly to one side, was an architect by profession, but he worked as a security man in an amusement arcade. He asked me for a screwdriver and a hammer, tipped out onto the table about thirty metal plates with holes drilled along their edges and a heap of small screws and rivets, then pulled a broad jacket-shaped piece of thick, coarse leather out of his Turkish woven-plastic bag with a check pattern and started dexterously attaching the metal plates to it. The attack by Shapiro the day before yesterday had not had any serious consequences for his health.

Grisha Vyrin, a computer hardware engineer by education, worked for a private firm that sold domestic appliances. To look at, Grisha was more like a provincial rock musician in his frayed jeans and baggy sweater, with long blond hair gathered into a slightly greasy ponytail. He slouched and looked extremely thin, but when he sat down at the table and rolled up the sleeves of his old sweater a bit, the forearms exposed were as powerful and sinewy as a sailor's.

Provotorov, Lutsis and Vyrin stayed in the kitchen and I withdrew to the sitting room—to read the Book.

I couldn't get on with Gromov. Perhaps it was the effect of the mental and emotional fatigue of the last twenty-four hours and two sleepless nights. The novella itself was relatively short. At any other time I would have read a book of that size in a single sitting, but here I was still struggling after more than two hours and not yet even halfway through it.

The plot was as follows. The central character Mitrokhin, a forty-year-old correspondent with a Moscow newspaper, snared in domestic conflicts and problems with his writing, sets off on a long journey. His assignment: to gather information about farms in the Ural region. Mitrokhin stays for a month in the home of state-farm chairman Fomichev. The correspondent conscientiously takes his notebook and makes the rounds of all the farm's various nooks and crannies—the specialized farm units, the cowsheds, the experimental stations and the new school. He meets remarkable people who are passionately committed to their work, such as the teacher Nikodimov, who has set up an agricultural-machinery design club at the Machine and Tractor Station. The club is short of funds to turn a joint invention of Nikodimov and his pupils into reality.

"It's just that we need to produce special vehicles for transporting grain," Nikodimov repeated stubbornly, struggling to keep up with the chairman's broad stride. "Or rather, not vehicles, but all-metal bunkers that are installed on the chassis of Kamaz or Zil trucks. The grain-carrier can transport grain straight from the combine harvester to the elevator without any intermediate sorting. The bunker's airtight, so no grain's lost because of the wind, or the state of the road, or how long the journey is."

Fomichev thought for a moment.

"And how do you deal with bad weather? Grain often gets damp in the windrows and on the threshing floor. Your grain will get ruined. Am I right, Comrade Mitrokhin?"

Mitrokhin didn't answer, and Fomichev exploited the pause for his own ends:

"There, the press agrees with me too."

"But in our grain-carrier that won't happen," Nikodimov persisted. The bunker will be divided into two chambers of equal volume. If the grain's damp, it's loaded into one chamber, and as it moves along it's tipped into the empty one. At the same time the grain is dried by a warm current of air and the chaff and weed particles are separated out…"

"What is it that you have, Yury Viktorovich?" Fomichev asked artfully and answered himself: "That's right, a designers' club and young technicians' station. You attend to them. Your miraculous grain-carrier is just a dream!"

Nikodimov stopped, and Genka and Andryukha froze a little distance away. Mitrokhin looked at Nikodimov, who had fallen behind, then suddenly winked like a young urchin at the saddened young lads and dashed to catch up with Fomichev.

"You do wrong to reject Nikodimov's proposal. I've seen the model myself; it works perfectly. Why not give it a try, and I'll write a big article about it. If it works, you're bound to make the state farm famous right across the country. Is that so bad?"

The chairman's eyes sparkled in the gleeful way that Mitrokhin knew so well.

"Well, OK, try it! I'm sure it will all work out just fine—it has to!"

I made a conscientious effort to read, but I failed miserably. My eyes skidded on the first line and I tumbled precipitately down from the top of the page as if I had fallen off a roof; the paragraphs flitted by like the storeys of the building and I read only the foundation: "Mitrokhin liked the teacher's stubbornness and persistence— anyone else would have given up ages ago and decided the whole business was futile, but Nikodimov kept on searching for something, inventing something and, above all, believing in success."

I set the unfinished book aside and glanced out into the corridor. I could hear three voices in conversation behind the closed kitchen door with its cloudy glass, like a thin patch in the ice on a river. The traumatologist Dezhnev snored intermittently in the bedroom.

Just to check, I picked up the phone—there was no dial tone. And even if there had been, who could I have called? The militia? These people would finish me off before any help could arrive.

I went out onto the balcony. My imagination immediately painted a picture: I cling to the Virginia creeper's shaggy lianas that look like wild-growing string—the fourth floor, the third, the second—I jump and run to the road, catch a taxi very quickly and drive to the station. And I leave on the first train…

Up on the fifth floor the branches were like a network of thin, weak capillaries on the surface of the wall. They wouldn't hold my weight. I could clamber across onto the adjacent balcony, to the neighbours, but if they raised a hue and cry, my uncle's readers would be there before the militia.

"Alexei, finished already?" Lutsis's voice suddenly asked behind me. "You've read it then?"

I told the truth.

"I didn't finish it. I've got a headache."

"That's no good. You were warned about the two Conditions. It won't have any effect without them! Well, that's it; now you'll have to read it again," Lutsis concluded disappointedly.

I didn't want to tell him that I was less concerned about the Book than about the "satisfaction", in which I had promised to participate.

Lutsis went off to the kitchen, and I went back into the sitting room and set about the Book for the second time…

If not for the great unknown that lay ahead, I would almost certainly have coped with *The Quiet Grass*. But a feeling of alarm as persistent as toothache drilled into my soul and wouldn't let me concentrate. My attention evaporated more rapidly with every minute that passed, and my thoughts, like a brainless insect, kept crawling from the page to the window and on farther, spreading their wings and zooming off into the grey skies.

My agitation immediately affected my stomach and every time I shut myself in the toilet I felt desperately afraid that my trumpeting, intestinal terror might be heard in the kitchen. I didn't take the book with me at those times. Who could tell, perhaps seeing me emerging from the toilet with the Book, the readers might have regarded the act as sacrilege. In any case, the novella had to be started again from the beginning. I moved to the sofa-bed and read lying down until I sank into a sleep as black as a lumber room.

I was woken by a subdued conversation in the hallway. The jangling tones of Margarita Tikhonovna's voice stood out as she tried unsuccessfully to speak quietly.

"Denis, how's Alexei? Has he read it?" she asked. "Is he asleep?"

"He seems to be," Lutsis replied quietly. "I didn't go in. I thought it was best if he rested. He couldn't manage it at first, and he started over again. He was in a nervous state…"

"All right, it's time to wake him up anyway," Margarita Tikhonovna said categorically. "We'll go to meet the Kolontaysk comrades now, but don't you all just sit around doing nothing. We assemble at precisely midnight beside the turn for Kamyshevo…"

The voices hovered for a few more minutes and then footsteps reverberated in the stairwell.

There was purple darkness outside the window. I looked at the clock on the wall. In the dark the phosphorescent drops on the hands looked like grave lights—one almost at the top, the other down at the bottom: half-past ten.

"Better make some coffee. I'll wake him myself." The door opened slightly and Tanya appeared in the yellow strip of light.

I pretended to be sleeping. She sat down quietly beside me. The sofa-bed's springs creaked slightly. I breathed in noisily through my nose and turned over onto my side.

Tanya touched my hand.

"Alexander Vladimirovich…"

I turned my head and blinked as if in drowsy bewilderment.

"Eh? What's happened?"

"You have to get up," Tanya whispered. "We're setting off at eleven…"

"I see…" I said, rubbing my eyes vigorously.

Tanya stood up.

"I'll just turn on the table lamp, but I'll turn the shade to the wall, so it won't be too bright…"

Her touching efforts to render my awakening painless were interrupted by Lutsis's noisy appearance.

"Awake already? Excellent!" He clicked the switch and the bright light crashed into my eyes.

"Alexei, go into the kitchen," said Dezhnev, glancing in. "There's coffee ready for you in there. You could have a bite to eat, but I don't recommend it; better take a large cognac, but no more than that—otherwise it'll fuddle you, not brace you… Or should I give you some activated charcoal? That will fix any problems caused by nerves."

"No need," I said, feeling myself blushing. Probably it wasn't only in the kitchen that I had been heard.

Vadik Provotorov was tinkering with something in the hallway. He had changed into camouflage fatigues. The front door was open. I saw Grisha Vyrin. He was already wearing the shoulder belt with the sapper's entrenching tools. He greeted me, picked up two bags and carried them downstairs.

Lutsis came out of the bedroom. He was holding something like a miniature steel casket or a case with a chain attached to it. Lying on velvet in one half of it, like a violin in its case, was the Book. Lutsis closed the lid and an internal lock clicked. Denis was very solemn, as if this was a ceremony for the award of some kind of decoration.

"Are you all set?"

"Almost. I just need to get a wash and have some coffee."

"The coffee can wait. This is something more important…" Lutsis held out the casket to me. It was slightly bigger than the actual Book and proved to be quite weighty. The sturdy steel chain passed through a ring welded to the end of it, so that the Book could be worn like a pectoral icon.

"Put it on," said Lutsis, confirming what I was thinking. "It's your privilege as a librarian and the corresponding badge of rank…"

I asked if I could carry it in my hand for the time being. Denis told me reproachfully that it wasn't a man-purse. I submissively lowered my head and he hung the Book, as heavy as a convict's chains, around my neck.

TERROR

T HE COFFEE IMMEDIATELY made me feel nauseous. I took a rapid gulp of cognac from a bottle standing on the table, but it didn't do much to reinforce my backbone. In the corridor I furtively stopped Marat Andreyevich and asked for the charcoal pills, and in the bathroom I swallowed the whole pack, washing them down with water from the tap. The casket hanging round my neck got in the way, knocking against the washbasin.

The bustle and tension increased. As he moved about, Denis asked again if everybody was ready and then said: "Right then, God be with us…" My heart gave a dull thud, like a stone thrown against a wall.

The familiar RAF was standing outside. Provotorov and Vyrin waited until I walked out of the entrance and got into the vehicle. Igor Valeryevich, Marat Andreyevich, Pal Palych and Tanya were already sitting inside it. Ogloblin was at the wheel with Larionov beside him. I moved up slightly to make space for Lutsis. The floor was stacked with bags full of equipment. The last to climb in were Vyrin and Provotorov.

We drove out onto the ring road, which was almost lifeless, with no cars at all. After we'd gone a few kilometres we exchanged blinks of headlights with a motorcycle that had a sidecar: its motor immediately rattled into life and it followed us. I recognized the Vozglyakov sisters.

We pulled up at a fork in the road with a sign for Kamyshevo. A few minutes later an ancient GAZ bus with a long corrugated snout, like a truck, came trundling up. I saw Margarita Tikhonovna; she waved to us and we set off after the bus.

Soon the asphalt was replaced by concrete slabs and then by stone chips. After that we were shaken about on a dirt road with centuries-old wheel ruts that were like rails, only inverted into the ossified earth. Barren fields lay on all sides of us. The power-line poles looked like trees gnawed away by some plague, and the porcelain insulators on the cross bars looked like fungal growths. Somewhere in the distance, many kilometres away, the tiny scarlet lights of civilization twinkled.

Eventually we stopped and started hurriedly unloading. As well as our people, more than twenty other people got out of the bus—they were the promised helpers from the Kolontaysk reading room and also the volunteers from Simonyan and Burkin.

People prepared for the "satisfaction" in total silence. Margarita Tikhonovna, the elder Vozglyakov sister, Timofei Stepanovich, Sasha Sukharev and a reader I didn't know—Nikolai Tarasovich Ievlev—came over to us. Ievlev was a genuine giant: two metres tall with broad shoulders and a neck like a tree stump. His head was shaved and a deep scar, white on its bottom, ran across his forehead and cheek, looking like the slash made by a baker on a French loaf.

Timofei Stepanovich cast an approving glance at the casket with the Book in it and leaned down over a bag. The old man took out a cap with earflaps that was reinforced with metal plates on the outside and stuck it on his head, then he wrapped himself in a sheepskin coat with links from a well chain sewn thickly all over it and hung an awl on his belt. He took out a cast-iron ball that had obviously been sawn off a dumb-bell—the sphere had the number "10" stamped into it—and put it in a canvas bag which he tied round tightly with a cord, so transforming it into something like a mace. Then, to demonstrate his prowess, he tossed it lightly up into the air, swung it round his head and smashed it into the ground—the sphere left an impressive dent.

Tanya hid her face behind a fencing mask. The Vozglyakovs and Margarita Tikhonovna tied on thick headscarves and put simple builder's helmets over them, while Ogloblin, Vyrin, Pal Palych and Sukharev donned motorcycle helmets; moreover, Vyrin and Ogloblin had replaced the plastic visors with steel ones that had slits for the eyes. Igor Valeryevich Kruchina put on an ancient brass fireman's helmet. Apparently to intimidate the enemy even more, the mighty Ievlev chose a German army helmet for himself, but Provotorov took a Soviet one, and Lutsis had a pilot's helmet, for which he took off his glasses. The navigator Larionov pulled on a tank soldier's leather helmet lined with plastic foam at the back and the traumatologist Marat Andreyevich didn't cover his head at all, putting his faith in his own agility.

There was also an immense variety of armour. Lutsis had made small pockets in all his clothes and stuffed protective metal plates into them. The Vozglyakovs had steel strips inserted into the padding of their quilted trousers and work jackets. Igor Valeryevich donned a genuine cuirass, which made him look like a samovar. Vyrin's leather jacket was covered with Soviet roubles, like fish scales—there must have been at least five hundred coins. Spotting my interested glance, Grisha explained: "I'd been saving up for a motorbike since I was ten, but then the Union fell apart and the money became worthless, so now at least I get some kind of value out of it…"

Pal Palych's suit of armour consisted of parquet flooring blocks, artfully connected together with wire or cords. Marat Andreyevich had crafted a long carapace, down to his knees, out of linoleum. The giant Ievlev wore an arrangement that was rather reminiscent of a musketeer's cloak, made of thick leather, as stiff as wood. Sukharev clad himself in a tarpaulin overall with starry soldier's belt buckles sewn closely all over it, and Larionov had reinforced his fleecy greatcoat with coarse boot soles. In the world outside, Ogloblin worked as a trainer of working dogs and so he had brought special protective overalls, padded mittens and trousers that a crocodile couldn't have bitten through. Tanya was wearing a jacket of felt, fulled to the toughness of a felt boot. Margarita Tikhonovna put on a short sheepskin coat, rendered stouter by thick hemp rope glued all over it.

All the Kolontaysk readers, without exception, kitted themselves out in ice-hockey gear, with gloves, knee pads and guards on their hips and shins, but they all had goalkeepers' helmets with white plastic visors.

Beside the Kolontayskites the battle attire of the Shironinites looked like the topsy-turvy outfits of Tweedledum and Tweedledee from the far side of the looking glass, with the difference that the sight was anything but funny.

Garshenin, who had been praised so highly the day before, came over to us. His appearance was not in the least heroic; he was thin and tall, with a large nose that made him look like a cock. The resemblance was emphasized by the long spikes, as sharp as beaks, protruding from the front and the rear of his boots. Several of his warriors had also equipped themselves with similar beaked footwear. The volunteers were armed with scythes, hay forks on long handles and firefighting gaffs that had been transformed into bear spears with long pointed ends and hooks. Many of them had little shields made of wood or woven out of bast, like Russian peasant shoes.

I observed all this with the curiosity of the damned, until Margarita Tikhonovna turned to me.

"Alexei, why aren't you dressed yet? We're going into action any minute now!"

It emerged that my uncle's motorbike helmet and sections of tyre—I realized what they were intended for now—had been left behind in the cupboard.

"Boys, I'm absolutely speechless… Denis, you got Alexei ready, didn't you?"

"I'm asked him and he said he was all set, and I thought…"

"Hmm, we have little mix-up here," said Margarita Tikhonovna, shaking her head. "We can't let Alexei go out there like this."

I shuddered as hope suddenly surged through me.

"Maybe I can just wait for you here, eh?" I stammered.

A look of amazement flitted across the readers' faces.

"Alexei, don't you distress yourself," Lutsis said guiltily. "I'll give you mine…"

"Wait, Denis," Igor Valeryevich butted in. "Your chainmail won't fit Alexei. It's too small."

"Oh, boys and girls, there's never dull moment with you. We'll think of something now…" Margarita Tikhonovna went over to the people beside us. "Comrades, my dears, I'm sorry, but we have a problem. Alexei Vyazintsev doesn't have a weapon or any protective clothing with him. Please help us out…"

I heard the Kolontaysk hockey players grumble, pointing out that this was no game for little children. How could anyone forget such absolutely essential things? Was it his first time or what? Margarita Tikhonovna replied curtly: "Yes, precisely, the first time."

The Kolontayskites found a fabric builder's helmet with a lining that had a sour smell and two canvas bags, into which they inserted small baking trays. The handles of the bags were long enough for this primitive armour to be hung round my neck.

When he saw the baking trays, Vyrin pulled off his jacket upholstered with roubles.

"Take this, Alexei. It's almost your size."

I declined, hoping that my cowardice might resemble nobility, at least slightly.

"Grisha, what will you do then? You need it more than I do!"

But the implacable Vyrin virtually forced me to put on the heavy armour, saying:

"I'm used to this, I'll manage."

The jacket was a little narrow in the shoulders and the tight sleeves barely even covered my wrists, but overall it fitted quite well. Timofei Stepanovich donated his cap with the earflaps to me. Lutsis gave me his knee pads and plastic thigh protectors. Maria Antonovna Vozglyakova gave me a pair of coarse leather gloves and Ievlev attached an arm cover made out of half a steel pipe to my forearm.

For a weapon I was given a club weighted with a ribbed insert—I think it was some kind of machine part, possibly a gear wheel from some especially large mechanism.

"That's great now!" Lutsis exclaimed, delighted by the way I looked. "Like Bohdan Khmelnytsky with his mace."

I tensed my jaw—when it was relaxed, my teeth had suddenly started beating out bony drum rolls.

"Margarita Tikhonovna," I asked tentatively, licking my lips, which were dry from terror, "how do you know that no one will come out to fight us with guns?"

"Out of the question. It's strictly forbidden."

"Who forbade it? Tereshnikov?"

"It was long before him… It's a rule, an unwritten law."

"But what if they cheat?"

"There are observers and seconds; they make sure everything's fair," Lutsis put in. "Don't worry."

"Just think about it," boomed Ievlev. "You've got a pistol and I've got a sub-machine-gun. Where's the satisfaction in that?"

"That's just target practice!" Ogloblin joked.

"But there are a few dodges," Sukharev summed up. "Take this, for instance…"

He showed me a ball bearing the size of a tennis ball.

"That weighs more than a kilogram. If it gets you in the head, you'll feel it all right."

"Perhaps I can just wait for you here?" I muttered quietly, staring down at the ground. "Really, please…"

Even after all the time that has passed since that moment, I still feel bitterly ashamed of those faltering, cowardly words…

The Shironinites surrounded me in a tight circle. I couldn't see the slightest hint of mockery or condemnation in their heartfelt, sympathetic gaze. Only my parents had ever looked at me like that before, when I did something wrong at home or at school, and

I stood there in front of them unrepentantly, realizing that any guilt of mine was insignificant in comparison with the love and unconditional forgiveness that these people felt for me.

"It's time… Alexei, give the order!" said Margarita Tikhonovna.

"But what shall I say?" I asked helplessly.

"It doesn't matter… 'Follow me!' or 'Forward march!'"

I cast a brief glance over the detachment, drawn up in a column. The Vozglyakov sisters were clutching spades with exceptionally long, sharpened blades. Maria Antonovna was leaning on the handle of a mighty flail with a spiked head that looked like a marrow.

Tanya was holding a home-made rapier—a steel rod honed until it shone, with a brass hand guard welded onto it. Provotorov, Pal Palych, Larionov and Ogloblin had long pikes resting on their shoulders. I immediately recognized the festive stylization that deftly disguised a weapon as the fancy tip on the hand staff of the Soviet flag, with a star or a hammer and sickle set inside the steel quill.

Vyrin adjusted his shoulder belt with the sapper's entrenching tools; Ievlev folded his hands round the handle of an immense blacksmith's hammer; Timofei Stepanovich flung his mace over his shoulder like a wandering pilgrim. Kruchina made sure that his bayonet moved easily in its scabbard. Sukharev toyed with a weighty chain wound round his hand, with three heavy padlocks dangling from its links.

"Right, come on, Alexei," Margarita Tikhonovna's voice murmured again. "We're all waiting for your command."

I cleared my throat, plucked up my courage and said:

"Let's go, comrades…"

I suddenly felt as if I had stepped off a cliff. My throat choked on a cold void as I fell, hearing the world spinning round me, or perhaps it was the wings of the black bat of panic fluttering in my head.

I didn't know the way. Lutsis and Margarita Tikhonovna led me along, and our entire brigade of thirty-five set off after us. We walked through bushes and a dense plantation of poplars, beyond which lay a boundless open field and a lilac horizon. Fear tore through the poplar trees like a demented squirrel, from branch to branch, from dark foreboding to nightmarish realization. In the grassy expanse it scattered into the air, finding no foothold.

And then I heard my own footsteps and saw the people escorting me with different eyes, and my heart stopped racing—or I forgot how to hear it and feel it. I suddenly fancied that I had experienced this menacing calm many times before—only then, instead of the terror that had now receded, I was filled with pride for the people walking with me, for the heroic feat of arms they would perform…

Soon a distinct incline appeared ahead of us and we walked down it to the bottom of a shallow depression about half the size of a football pitch. Our brigade simply disappeared under the ground; walls rising to a height of several metres and tall grass concealed us securely.

Spectators—about two hundred of them—took up positions on the slopes. The observers—about ten, among whom I recognized Tereshnikov—sat separately, with the guards stationed beside them.

The enemy had already set out his brigade in chess formation. Most of the Gorelovites had massive clubs that were like baseball bats, except for the spikes screwed into them. Some of them had identical carbonized steel machetes—clearly industrially produced imports. Spears tipped with flat blades rose up out of the formation. Every soldier was wearing an ancient military bulletproof vest and a helmet, so that the Gorelovites looked just like Pushkin's sea heroes, "all chosen to match".

As soon as we completed our descent, a long line of men holding kayak paddles appeared around the top of the depression. From the glittering, sharpened edges of the steel blades it was clear that these items of sports equipment had been adroitly converted into weapons. As if to confirm this, a man with a paddle, apparently limbering up, performed several vigorous strokes, slicing his blades through he air. It was easy to guess what would happen to anyone who took a blow from a paddle like that…

"Remember, in ancient Rome, the lictors?" Lutsis whispered. "Only they had poleaxes, not paddles…"

"Lictors?" I asked uneasily, as if this were important.

"Or seconds. Those guys with the paddles keep order too. They only intervene if the fight isn't fought according to the rules."

Our brigade stretched out in a double line, divided into three groups. In the centre was the Shironin reading room, the ten warriors from Kolontaysk were on the right flank, and Burkin and Simonyan's people were on the left. I particularly disliked the fact that I was standing in the front row. All eyes seemed to be glued to the casket with the Book.

"What now?" I anxiously asked Lutsis, who was standing beside me. "Will it start soon?"

"When everybody realizes that they're ready," he said, looking straight ahead, like a man under a spell.

"Afraid?" Pall Palych suddenly asked from the other side. "That's because you haven't read the Book. The meaning of life hasn't been revealed to you yet. And without meaning you're always afraid…"

I had recently heard a similar idea from Margarita Tikhonovna, and now Pal Palych had repeated it in his own manner.

"Don't you be afraid. The Gorelov reading room…"—he paused for a moment, pondering how to characterize the enemy—"… is a load of rubbish! They're mercenaries, and that says it all. You should know that there aren't any special fighting techniques or fancy little moves… That is, there are, but that's not the important thing. It's what's inside that matters, the guts, the heart…"

"Your late uncle was a hero to beat them all," said Timofei Stepanovich. He swung the sack down off his shoulder and the fabric-wrapped sphere lay beside his boot. "That means you're a hero too. Blood's thicker than water, or vodka. Understand?"

A man with a Book in his hands mounted the grassy rostrum. He cleared his throat gently and declaimed:

"*The Silver Channel.*"

"Oh, how humane we are this time," I heard Margarita Tikhonovna's sarcastic voice say. "Obviously especially for the Gorelov reading room. A gift from Shulga."

"The convict's getting nervous," Lutsis remarked. "Maybe he's not sure of his own men." He looked at me. "Sit down, Alexei, we've got at least three hours to spare now. We're going to listen…"

"Well, now, thank God," said Marat Andreyevich, crossing himself. "I'm feeling better already." He winked at me encouragingly. "The Book of Endurance. We're alive and kicking, Alexei."

"What Book is that? What's it for?" I asked in relief.

"It's something that has to be done…" said Timofei Stepanovich, turning one ear towards the rostrum and holding it with his hand to amplify the sound.

The reader started at a frantic pace in a staccato gabble, like a sexton in a church: "April began with eddying winds and frost. And then suddenly winter surrendered. Only a few days earlier there was not a patch of earth to be seen in the field, only little bushes showing through the snowdrifts, but suddenly on the south slope tilth appeared, with rooks stalking about on it. When did they arrive?"

I listened inattentively, more absorbed in my own feelings. At first the reader's monotonous, hurrying voice irritated me, but then it lulled me, like the steady beat of the wheels in a railway carriage.

The Silver Channel was a turgid, opaque lyrical narrative. Two characters sleepwalked through the text, from spring to spring: a forester in love with nature and his little son, to whom the poetic beauties of his native parts were gradually revealed. Along the way father and son encountered various people, simple Soviet toilers, and each one had a story for the boy. The culmination of the novella was a long, dreary scene in which children helped old people to build a haystack: how the stooks were driven up, how they stacked them up, topped them off the stack, adjusted them with rakes, pressed them together with poles…

The reader closed the Book and I suddenly saw that the night had turned bright, with a milky moon and white stars that looked like scars.

Our people got to their feet. Timofei Stepanovich stealthily pricked his flabby wrist with his awl and nodded in satisfaction, licking away the drop of blood that oozed out.

Margarita Tikhonovna tugged on my sleeve.

"Alexei, everyone will go running forward, but you stay here. They'll remember you, and if anything happens they won't abandon you. Here…" She glanced round, choosing. "Annushka will guard you. No need to be afraid with her." She beckoned to her. "Anyuta, will you keep an eye on Alexei? All right?"

Anna Vozglyakova shielded me with her mighty shoulder and I felt a little more confident.

Meanwhile on the left flank Margarita Tikhonovna was already conferring with Simonyan's Garshenin; he agreed with what she said, stroking the metal-bound handle of his scythe.

"Alexei," the traumatologist Dezhnev whispered in my ear, "what Margarita Tikhonovna told you is quite right…" He hesitated. "But if the situation does get a bit tricky, for God's sake, don't just stand there waiting for the wedding… Move about, dodge! If you hit out—don't follow through after the blow. Whether you hit the target or not, it doesn't matter. The important thing is to keep moving all the time." He drew his sabre. "I'll try not to let you out of my sight."

Anna, clutching the handle of her spade in her thick, coarse fingers, suddenly spoke to me.

"I wanted to ask…" she said in a voice that proved to be very thick and low. "You studied in an institute, didn't you? Did you have that subject—psychology? You did? Oh! Explain this situation to me. A long time ago, in fifth year, I planted a birch tree in the school garden. Then suddenly this boy there wanted a thin stick, maybe for a cane to play at horses. Well, he started breaking it off my birch tree, and the tree was no more than a cane anyway, so he snapped almost all of it off. And I shouted at him: 'Hey, you, get off that!' And he said to me: 'Big deal! One little branch… It won't do your birch tree any harm.' I said to him: 'And what if everyone goes breaking off a branch? What then?' The little boy suddenly started crying and ran away…" Anna wrinkled up her forehead and her fingers tightened their grip on the spade handle. "The thing is, why did he start crying, eh? I didn't hurt him. I didn't hit him. Maybe you know why?"

In my previous life I would certainly have mocked this simple-mindedness in my heart of hearts, while outwardly passing some slimy comment like: "I wish I had your problems, darling…"

I understood why Anna had started telling me about the broken birch tree. In her own way she had been impressed by the reading of the Book of Endurance, with its endless descriptions of nature. Anna just wanted to talk about some lofty theme, and there was nothing loftier than Gromov. The story of the birch tree seemed to her a perfectly valid pass to those empyrean regions where brainy people like me probably philosophized about something noble and exalted.

While I was still assembling the circumspect phrase "I rather neglected psychology", it all began.

THE SATISFACTION

T HE GAP BETWEEN US and the Gorelov reading room closed
implacably. If only our enemies had shouted something like
"hurrah", it wouldn't have looked so terrifying. But they ran without
a word, with a rumble of boots in the silence of noisy breathing.
Lutsis, Sukharev, Vyrin, Larionov, Ogloblin and Provotorov flung
heavy ball bearings at the attackers. The steel spheres hit home,
and several of the Gorelov warriors tumbled over as if they had
slipped on a wet floor, felled by a direct hit.

Our side rushed forward. I prudently stayed apart, backing
away rapidly and moving as far away as possible from the fighting.

The brigades clashed head on. Garshenin's team, outrunning
the others, ran through the line running at them with their sickles
and tridents. Some were impaled on steel immediately. I saw a long
fan shape of blood spurt out of a pierced throat. The brunt of
the Gorelov warriors' frontal thrust was borne by the Shironinites.
Burkin's volunteers and the Kolontayskites, armed with miners'
pickaxes, struck from the flanks—the appalling steel beaks rose up
above the crowd and fell, embedding themselves in the human strata.

The human mass seethed as it intermingled in confusion. It was
as if, following the invitation to dance, everyone had gone dashing
to find themselves a partner, to start this elaborate swirling, while
those who had not found a partner were filled with fury and started
breaking up other pairs.

A Gorelovite stunned by a ball bearing and crawling on all fours
was hammered into the ground by a terrible blow from Maria

Antonovna Vozglyakova, who did not seem to notice the knife that was thrust into her side, burying the full length of its narrow blade in her padded work jacket.

Igor Valeryevich arched over in a rapid lunge, driving his bayonet into his foe's defenceless lower belly. Veronika Vozglyakova's spade sliced open the face of a Gorelovite pressing forward.

Timofei Stepanovich, despite his age, doughtily held three enemies at bay. Squatting down, he shattered one attacker's knee with a sweep of his dumb-bell mace, and then helped arrived in the persons of Lutsis and Larionov.

Sasha Sukharev bounded out of the crowd, pursued by a berserk Gorelovite. Sukharev's right hand had been transformed into a limp rag; he ran off a few steps, took out a ball bearing, flung it with his left hand, missed and pulled out a long screwdriver. The adversaries clashed together and fell…

A baseball smashed into Grisha Vyrin's unprotected back, but the Gorelovite who had crept up on him lived only for one more moment before Marat Andreyevich's sabre flashed.

Vadik Provotorov ran by with an axe and flung himself at a Gorelovite armed with a machete. A flurry of backs hid them from sight.

A crushing, spiked blow to the face felled Pal Palych. Larionov, grabbing up a sapper's entrenching tool, fervently pulverized a fallen foe until a knife was thrust into his back up to the hilt.

The swingeing blows of Ievlev's hammer tossed into the air fragments of helmets and pink lumps that looked like boiled beetroot.

One of Burkin's volunteers sat down in the grass and started busily binding up the stump of his arm, which was spurting blood like a guillotined chicken. Garshenin jerked convulsively on the handle of his scythe, but the blade had buried itself too deeply in a dead body. Garshenin kicked the body with his boot, but the sharp spur got stuck instead of helping him pull free. Someone brought a club down on his arms, breaking the bones as well as the scythe handle, but Svetlana Vozglyakova laid out the Gorelovite with a precise bayonet thrust just below the collar.

A Kolontaysk ice-hockey player abandoned the fighting and staggered towards me, as if seeking help, then collapsed on his knees and dropped his miner's pickaxe. Slow, thick blood oozed out through the eye slits of the white goalkeeper's mask. A Gorelovite ran up and impaled the man who was already dead, then swung round and impaled himself on Tanya Miroshnikova's swift rapier.

Lutsis finished off a fallen adversary, looked round for another, and missed an attack—the club struck the plastic of his helmet with a resonant thud. As he fell, Denis struck out with his axe, slicing through his enemy's jaw. Ogloblin dashed at the enemy, ran him through with his fork and moved on with the stride of advancing infantry, and the spiked man could barely move his feet fast enough, as if it were some kind of dance...

If someone had said to me that the battle had been going on for no more than three minutes, I wouldn't have believed them.

Suddenly I saw the Gorelovite librarian, Marchenko. I recognized him from his flaming crimson birthmark. The most frightening thing was that Marchenko was dashing straight at me. He had no helmet and his slashed upper lip bounced up and down in time with his running feet.

Marchenko was belatedly noticed by our fighters too. Anna, who had been set to guard me, flung the charging Gorelovite back with the handle of her spade, but someone who had not been finished off grabbed her leg and Anna stretched her full length on the trampled grass. With a swift flourish of his sabre, Marat Andreyevich cleared himself a path through the halved body of a Gorelovite, but it was clear that he would be too late.

I ran to the slope. Looking back for an instant, I saw Timofei Stepanovich fling his sack. The mace struck Marchenko in the back like a comet and felled him. Marchenko growled and started crawling on all fours, slowly straightening up; in the anthropology textbooks, that was how they illustrated the transformation of a monkey into erect *Homo sapiens*.

I hurtled up the slope, stumbled, dropped my flanged mace and clearly heard Lutsis shout: "Alexei, come back!" A second's paddle hummed past just above my head like a propeller.

I slithered back down on my knees and took off the chain with the Book. My first thought was to fling this awkward item aside in order to distract Marchenko. But the moment I looked into his bloodshot eyes with that trembling bulldog's lip below them, I knew there would be no mercy.

And the chain was lying so conveniently in my hand. Then a second thought appeared. I swung the Book like a sling and brought it down on Marchenko's head. The steel case slammed straight into the base of the skull. A vertebra snapped with a repulsive crunch. Marchenko crawled no more; he tumbled over onto his side, working his legs as if he were turning invisible pedals.

"The satisfaction is concluded!" a short, scrawny man of about forty with a terribly mutilated face declared in a loud, imperious voice. Margarita Tikhonovna took off her helmet. One of the lenses of her glasses was broken and her cheek was soaked in blood. Panting as she spoke, Margarita Tikhonovna said:

"Comrade Kovrov, do not prevent justice from prevailing."

There, about fifty metres away from me, the finishing touches were being put to the battle. Kolontaysk fighters were vigorously beleaguering a lone Gorelovite. The Vozglyakov sisters rhythmically raised their spades and thrust them into squirming bodies. Timofei Stepanovich was crawling about, finishing off the wounded with an awl. Ogloblin and Dezhnev drove a solitary adversary onto the slope; the fugitive fought them off, backing away, until he took a blow from a paddle and collapsed, impaling himself on the pike held out for him.

Kovrov turned to the morose Tereshnikov, who shrugged and said in a loud voice:

"In the name of the council the battle is concluded!"

Tanya took off her battered mask; her cheekbone was decorated with a massive contusion. Lutsis was swinging his head
about like a dog, trying to shake out his concussion. Ievlev was
pressing his hand over a wound on his right forearm. Marat
Andreyevich was wiping down the blade of his sabre with burdock. Margarita Tikhonovna, smiling broadly at me, blinked
away the blood that had accumulated under her shattered lens
with a cleft eyelid…

And then I puked up bile as caustic as acid into the grass.

The spectators left the slope and helped to sort out the mutilated
corpses.

Ogloblin and Timofei Stepanovich laid out dead Pal Palych on
the grass with his face shattered as if a tank had driven over him.
Igor Valeryevich carried over the lifeless Larionov with a knife in
his back. Vadik Provotorov had been killed—I hadn't even seen
how that had happened. He was brought out, his throat slashed,
with the purple breathing innards peeping out through it. Maria
Antonovna Vozglyakova had died of stab wounds. Grisha Vyrin
was lying unconscious. Marat Andreyevich examined him and
said that his spinal column didn't appear to be damaged. I realized that I was partly to blame for what had happened to Vyrin.
If not for me, those loyal Soviet roubles would have protected
Vyrin's back.

Our allies had also suffered serious losses. The Kolontayskites
had lost three warriors, only two of Simonyan's six volunteers
remained, and only one of Burkin's volunteers had survived the
battle.

The Gorelov reading room had been reduced to five people.
These survivors huddled together in a bloodied gaggle. The other
thirty-something, including the librarian Marchenko, had met their
death on the field of satisfaction.

THE RETURN

A T FIRST I SQUEAMISHLY wiped the metal corner of the casket on the grass for a long time. My former terror had disappeared and in its place a frozen, unnatural calm, verging on extreme fatigue, had swept over me.

The heavy, pine-tar smell of Vishnevsky ointment hung over the battlefield—Marat Andreyevich and Tanya were rendering first aid to the wounded.

Margarita Tikhonovna's crushed eye was carefully washed and the fragments of glass were extracted from her eyebrow, but she spoke to me in a spirited voice: "Alexei, I'm proud of you, you're a genuine hero!" The blood, mingling with peroxide, bubbled on her cheek. "How can you not believe in higher justice now? The fact that you were the one to crush Marchenko is a sign. I'm glad that I was not mistaken!" And these words settled in my head in a cold, ornate pattern, like hoar frost.

Sukharev's shattered hand was bandaged up with parquet blocks from the dead Pal Palych's armour. During this procedure Sasha kept exclaiming: "I don't feel any pain at all." But it seemed to me that he was simply in a state of shock.

It is true, though, that I didn't hear a single groan or any of the sounds associated with torment of the flesh. Marat Stepanovich merely commented that you could take out an appendix under the influence of the Book of Endurance and carried on hastily applying stitches.

Timofei Stepanovich treated his comrades' shallow cuts with iodine; Nikolai Tarasovich Ievlev gloomily sucked the blood out of his slashed arm and applied plantain leaves.

The Vozglyakov sisters, Svetlana and Veronika, leaned down over their mother's body without a single tear; the eldest, Anna, was sewing up a deep, ragged wound in Garshenin's shoulder with a stony expression on her face, and a Kolontaysk fighter was waiting his turn nearby, pressing a rag to his bleeding wound.

Four observers came towards us, including the deformed Kovrov. He limped on both legs, but walked without the help of crutches. A conversation was held with Margarita Tikhonovna. The fresh white bandage on her eye was already soaked with blood on the inside and her voice trembled slightly, but it was full of dignity. From Kovrov's sparse words I understood that our debt to the Gorelov reading room had been annulled.

Then the observer started talking about the disposal of the bodies. The essence of the procedure, as Denis explained to me later, was as follows. The victors had the right to request an imitation of any everyday death for their dead—a road accident, an accident at a building site, a fire, suicide, but only such that it would not arouse the suspicion of doctors and the militia. This privilege provided an opportunity to give the fallen normal funerals.

The bodies from the defeated side were supposed either to disappear completely or to lie until they totally decomposed, and lost all the terrible marks of battle. Then, at the request of their nearest and dearest—if such people existed in the world of Gromov—the remains could be discovered by the official world, following a tip-off. Until that time the readers were simply considered to have gone missing.

Shulga's library accepted all the bothersome responsibilities involved in the disposal—not, of course, as a free service, but in exchange for the Gorelov reading room's Book.

"Well then, congratulations once again on your victory," said Kovrov.

"The old school's the best, Timur Gennadyevich," Timofei Stepanovich said sadly, drawing himself erect. "We don't have many novices, we pretty much go all the way back to the Battle of Neverbino."

"Yes, Marchenko was inexperienced. He didn't take into account how dangerous it was to go up against you," Kovrov agreed. "You fight seriously…" he said, yawning, so that his jaw crunched. "Now, about this ambush of the purported killers of the librarian Vyazintsev and the missing reader Shapiro… Depending on the consequences, the council will reach a separate decision and then determine the letter of the penalty. I don't think that will be soon. Carry on with your own business, you'll be informed."

Kovrov limped away majestically. But after a few steps he turned back, met my gaze, wagged his finger at me humorously and declared:

"Don't run away any more!"

Naturally, I didn't like this gesture and his derisive tone, but the ultimate meaning of it all only hit me several hours later, on the way home in our RAF.

My memory of events is blurred, as if I observed them through a polythene bag. The observers carried away our dead comrades. We ourselves loaded the stretcher cases into the bus—the others walked to it themselves—and took them to various hospitals, providing them with the cover stories needed to account for all these breaks, cuts, contusions, broken noses and lost teeth.

One of Burkin's volunteers, one Kolontayskite and Grisha Vyrin went straight onto the operating table. The first two had suffered severe craniocerebral traumas and Vyrin had a serious spinal injury. Lutsis had apparently escaped with only a minor concussion. Sukharev was left in the same traumatological department with a rather complicated break of the wrist, together with Anna Vozglyakova, who had a crack in her collarbone.

Margarita Tikhonovna categorically refused to see any doctors, declaring that her injury might look bad, but it was actually trivial. It was impossible to argue with her.

I asked how we could inform the families of Pal Palych, Larionov and Provotorov about the death of their dear ones. Margarita

Tikhonovna's reply shed some light on the membership of the reading rooms, in which individuals with families were the exception rather than the rule. Pal Palych and Larionov had lived as solitary bachelors, Provotorov grown up without any parents and had been raised by his grandmother. It turned out that there was no one to grieve for the dead apart from their fellow readers.

The Kolontaysk comrades prepared to go back home, and we moved from the bus into our RAF, after thanking them once again for their help. Margarita Tikhonovna spoke, and we all nodded in unison. Their leader replied morosely: "One good turn deserves another."

The expression on Veronika and Svetlana's faces was calm, I would even say exalted. I thought of offering them words of consolation, but I couldn't find the right ones. The Vozglyakov sisters said goodbye and drove off on the motorcycle after the Kolontayskites.

Big-nosed Garshenin looked at the stumps of his fresh plaster casts, repeating over and over again: "I'll be all healed up in no time…"

He was temporarily installed in Margarita Tikhonovna's apartment. Then we drove Ievlev and Kruchina home, and the remaining six of us went to my place.

The same conversation continued. Marat Andreyevich declared:

"It could well be that we took out two or three of Shulga's aces."

"Precisely!" Timofei Stepanovich agreed. "I came across some really stubborn lads, and they fought stoutly. For sure Kovrov stopped the satisfaction because only his fighters were left."

"And that means only one thing," Marat Andreyevich concluded. "We've earned ourselves some serious enemies…"

I was concerned that the Shironinites would regard me as indirectly responsible for Vyrin's injury. Margarita Tikhonovna's passionate words made it clear how greatly mistaken I was: "Alexei, don't even think about that! How could you ever get such an idea into your head?"

They showered me with a chorus of praise for a long time, although I think they all realized that my "heroic feat" was not the result of courage, but a fluke.

"I was so frightened for you," Margarita Tikhonovna said agitatedly. "When I saw Marchenko break through and run at you... My heart sank, I couldn't have borne it if anything had happened to you!"

"Ah, come off it!" Ogloblin responded. "Our Alexei's a hero! Just look at the way he clouted him with the Book!"

"Yes, he's got real spirit," Tanya chimed in.

"It's like I told you—blood's thicker than water!" Timofei Stepanovich exclaimed joyfully.

"I'm glad things turned out that way and you didn't lose your head," said Marat Andreyevich, nodding.

Then the rapture faded and we drove on in silence. An overcast Monday was beginning, fine rain was sprinkling onto the windscreen, and the squeaking wipers smeared the drops like twin metronomes.

And that was when I remembered the observer Kovrov's finger, as inexorable as a pendulum, in a completely different light. Overwhelmed by sudden despair, I realized that rhythmically swaying finger was the most terrible part of everything that had happened to me in the last few days. It was the beginning of the new rhythm of a different world, and all the indications were that escape from that world was only possible to the world beyond, and only through an extremely painful doorway. In one night I had been transformed from a witness into a fully-fledged accomplice in a massacre. I had been bound by blood. And in time there would be a reckoning for it. "There's nowhere you can run to..." That was the warning, that was what the moving finger pointed to...

Behind me, Tanya Miroshnikova suddenly started crying. Timofei Stepanovich blew his nose loudly and Fyodor Ogloblin, who had lost his friend and "reverse namesake" Larionov, heaved a sigh. Margarita Tikhonovna furtively raised her handkerchief to her single eye.

Marat Andreyevich rubbed his temples with the palms of his hands, making his hair stand on end.

"The effect of the Book of Endurance has worn off now," he explained with a bitter smile. "The live human emotions have begun. There's nothing to be done. Now we'll grieve…"

Thank God no one guessed that I was mourning for myself, not the fallen.

AT HOME

T HAT EVENING BROUGHT yet another unpleasant conversation with Margarita Tikhonovna. Towards the end I worked myself up to a screaming whisper yet again. My nerves were shattered after the events of recent days. For half a day I had been running through past events time and time again in my memory, polishing them to a perfect, rounded state of terror. An entire appalling, hostile world was reflected in this convex, distorted perspective.

I kept asking Margarita Tikhonovna to let me go, but she patiently reminded me of our previous agreement, of which I had fulfilled only half: the Book of Memory had not yet been read.

I tried to persuade her that no Book would ever change my decision. Margarita Tikhonovna smiled meekly and assured me that destiny itself had appointed me a librarian.

"But Margarita Tikhonovna, you know I'm simply not ready to take my uncle's place here with you. I'm a perfectly ordinary person. I don't possess any special strength or courage. You have a mature collective; choose a new librarian for yourselves…" I appealed to logic and flattery. "Why shouldn't you take the Shironin reading room into your own hands, Margarita Tikhonovna? You're an excellent leader; everyone respects you. You are the most appropriate candidate for my uncle's position," I said falteringly, rubbing my sticky palms together. "If my Uncle Maxim could express his opinion, he would definitely prefer you."

"That won't work, my boy. I shall die soon…" said Margarita Tikhonovna, shattering my hopes. "Breast cancer—and don't look at me with that clumsy expression of sympathy on your face. I've got six months left. A year at most. The most optimistic prognoses…"

I almost said that she could be the librarian for six months, and then the Shironinites could choose another one, that foundry worker Kruchina or the traumatologist Dezhnev, but I suddenly felt that would sound too cynical. So I said nothing and stared drearily out of the window, watching the white scar that a plane had scraped across the sky, as if with a fingernail.

"My heart aches for the Shironin reading room," Margarita Tikhonovna continued meanwhile. "As long as Maxim Danilovich was alive, the problem didn't exist. And my own position was perfectly clear too—I would have served the reading room right to the end, and departed when my time came. I wanted very badly to find a worthy replacement. Something told me that you would be a genuine librarian, like your uncle. Please, first read the Book…"

After all the beating around the bush, we had come back to where we started. Margarita Tikhonovna cut short my whinging by saying that at the moment it wasn't safe for me to travel to Ukraine; there were many forces interested in getting even for the Gorelov librarian Marchenko, and from every point of view it would be better if I stayed here, under the protection of the reading room's members.

She certainly knew the right point to apply pressure to. I immediately fell silent, remembering that Marchenko was not merely some mythical librarian, but also a murderer.

"And I would recommend you not to leave the apartment in general," Margarita Tikhonovna concluded in an pitilessly formal tone, and at the top of her voice, so that everyone heard.

The readers started coming into the room from the kitchen—Tanya, Fyodor Ogloblin, Marat Andreyevich and Timofei Stepanovich.

"Not even to go to the shop?" I asked cautiously.

"Of course not," Margarita Tikhonovna confirmed. "Especially since our reading room has been weakened. And to be quite honest, it will be much easier for us and we will feel less anxious if you are at home, with the Book."

"But how long will this go on?"

Margarita Tikhonovna shrugged.

"About three weeks. Perhaps a month. One of us will be on duty round the clock, but in order to venture outside one bodyguard is not enough. It would be preferable for you to be accompanied by three people at least."

"Alexei Vladimirovich, I don't understand: why do you need to go out anywhere?" Tanya suddenly asked. "We'll buy everything you need, I'll cook for you… I'm a good cook. And I'll tidy up the apartment!"

"Don't worry about money!" Margarita Tikhonovna added. "We take responsibility for your financial problems."

This suggestion met with a positive response.

"That's how we do things here," said Timofei Stepanovich. "Come what may, we won't let our librarian go hungry! So you don't need to worry about that, Alexei!"

"We don't guarantee black caviar every day, but we can manage a perfectly respectable standard," Ogloblin promised.

Margarita Tikhonovna was pleased by the general support.

"Really, Alexei, it will be more convenient for you, and when you need it our girls will come and cook and tidy up."

Apparently what they had in store for me was indefinite house arrest with full board.

In the corridor I checked the phone just for luck and heard the long-awaited dial tone, which set my heart fluttering, although it was too late to call the militia.

"Have they connected it?" Margarita Tikhonovna asked. "That's excellent. I was thinking we'd have to camp here like gypsies to guard you, but if the phone's working then Timofei Stepanovich will be enough for today. You have a stout door here; you couldn't break it down with a canon. I don't believe they are likely to launch a frontal attack, but it's best to take precautions. Let me write down our phone numbers for you. God forbid that anything should happen, but if it does—we'll be here in ten minutes," she laughed. "We'll beat off any assailant…"

I saw that the Shironinites, despite their sorrow, were always trying to lift my spirits.

"Well, Margarita Tikhonovna… Don't forget now," Timofei Stepanovich drawled. "Alexei has shown what he's capable of. The two of us together will see off anyone you like without any help. Isn't that right, Alexei? We'll see them off? Come on, answer me!"

"Yes, Timofei Stepanovich," I said, reluctantly supporting this bravado.

Everyone prepared to go. The warmness with which the Shironinites took their leave both astounded and horrified me, although I tried not to show it. It was clear that these people really did need me.

TIMOFEI STEPANOVICH

T HE TWO OF US were left alone. For a while we sat in the kitchen
and drank tea. The old man enquired about my life—rather
awkwardly, so that the subject was exhausted in a couple of words,
and in the agonizing pauses he nodded approvingly with his large,
shaggy Caucasian sheepdog's head.

"How did you do in school?"

"Not bad."

"And at the institute?"

"Not too bad."

"Qualified as an engineer?"

"Yes…"

"That's a good profession… And did you love your uncle?"

"Yes I did…"

Timofei Stepanovich's grey locks were soaked and matted. His
forehead was gleaming with sweat, and so was his large, spongy
nose, covered in purple veins. The grey stubble covered his unshaven
cheeks like little crystals of salt.

Timofei Stepanovich still looked sturdy, but the bony emaciation
of old age was already apparent in his shoulders. In thoughtful
moments he pushed his dental plate round his mouth with his
tongue and deftly set it back in place with his lower lip.

After drinking his fill and setting down his cup, he sat there,
clasping his sinewy hands with their yellow nails that looked like
cheese rinds and looking straight ahead, his eyes filled with transparent blueness.

I realized that he liked my first qualification, as an engineer, but my second, as a theatrical director, was more of a puzzle to him than anything else, and he hastily tried to make up for this by commenting on my heroism in combat with the librarian of the Gorelov reading room.

"Were you afraid?" he suddenly asked. "I remember my first real fear very well. In April forty-four, I'd just turned seventeen then, my first week at the front…"

I prepared myself for an edifying war story, but Timofei Stepanovich unexpectedly fell silent for about five minutes, as if he and his story had sunk under water, and then he suddenly surfaced with the words:

"And after the war I worked as a mechanic in a depot, got married and raised two sons; they moved away and I haven't had any news for a long time. They're both about fifty. They'll probably be grandfathers themselves soon. My wife died fifteen years ago. She had bad kidneys…"

He sighed and chewed on some thought with his weathered lips that looked as if they were covered in blisters.

"I'm not feeling so good somehow, Alexei. You issue the book to me and at least I can go and have a read…"

The Book of Memory, already extracted from its steel case, was lying on my uncle's desk, and Timofei Stepanovich could have taken it himself; clearly this was the point at which my duties as librarian began. I went to the other room and brought him the Book. The old man took hold of it devoutly and almost bowed, as if he were saying goodbye and thanking me simultaneously, then withdrew into my uncle's bedroom, closing the door behind him. Soon I could hear his muffled mumbling.

Like most of the readers, with the exception of the Vozglyakovs, Timofei Stepanovich was a solitary. His home town was Sverdlovsk. He had been introduced to the world of Gromov eight years earlier, by an acquaintance. A man who worked with him at the railway depot was a member of a reading room, and he vouched for Timofei Stepanovich. The old man matched all the parameters—a widower, a war hero, a courageous and simple man. His first reading room collapsed because its Book was stolen shortly before the Battle of Neverbino and almost all the readers were killed. Timofei Stepanovich had also taken part in that famous battle—he was in the reading room militia. When the former reading rooms were mostly re-formed into new ones, Timofei Stepanovich was taken in by the Shironinites…

The old man read the Book, and I was left to my own devices. At the time it seemed to me that things could not possibly be more terrible. The apartment had become hateful: everything in it was now an embodiment of angst, bondage and fear. The wall-hanging with Misha the Olympic bear was disgusting, the maroon sideboard with the mirror interior that multiplied the glasses and plates was disgusting, the record player and the records were repulsive. There was nowhere to run to and no one to turn to for help.

I went out onto the balcony. The sight of the household trash—prehistoric cans and oilcloths, a dried-out stool, a little cupboard with no doors—made me want to howl and sprinkle the ashes and bony fag ends from the ashtray on my head. I looked out from my imprisonment at the dreary, rainy, crumbling landscape—the soaking-wet high-rises in the distance, the tawdry strip of forest.

I drank the remainder of the cognac, but I didn't get drunk. I turned on the television in the kitchen—quietly, so as not to disturb Timofei Stepanovich. They were showing *The Ballad of a Soldier*, and as I watched the black-and-white images I fell apart completely.

When it got dark, the mumbling in the bedroom was replaced by long, choking snores. My first thought was that the old man was dying. He was half lying on the bed, with a pillow under his back, and his head had fallen forward onto his chest. His face seemed somehow soft and boneless, as if it had half melted. His lower jaw had dropped open, limp and helpless. He was breathing abruptly and fitfully, producing those terrible dying sounds. Under his eyelids his eyes were racing about, as if Timofei Stepanovich were rolling them wildly. I almost called an ambulance, but I had already seen his dental plate lying beside the Book. For some reason the little yellow prosthesis, covered in spittle, reassured me. Timofei Stepanovich had prudently taken it out. Something told me the old man was not suffering a heart attack after all. The snoring gradually become fainter and was replaced by normal breathing. The eyes also settled down and a few pale little tears seeped out from under the eyelids. I hurried out of the room in order not to embarrass him.

After the reading Timofei Stepanovich spent a long time getting washed, and only then joined me in the sitting room. It's hard to describe the change that had taken place in him. A strange emotion, entirely unlike happiness or pleasure, lit up his face. This facial glow was a mixture of muted, radiant rapture and proud hope. The actors in old Soviet films knew how to portray something of the kind when they gazed into the industrial distance.

"There is meaning, Alexei!" he exclaimed, with his eyes glittering. "And death is not in vain!"

His words sounded insane to me.

"Perhaps you should lie down for a while, Timofei Stepanovich?" I asked.

"No need for that," he said, rubbing his hands excitedly. "I won't sleep all night long now. But you rest! Build up your strength…"

And he really didn't sleep a wink until the morning. He poured water in the kitchen, clattered cups, walked up and down the corridor, singing: "We have no barriers at sea or on the land, we fear neither the ice nor the clouds…"

My dawn drowsiness distorted the words and I listened intently, unable to make sense of the string of phrases. I covered my head with a pillow.

"The flame of our heart," Timofei Stepanovich crooned, "and the banner of our country we shall bear through worlds and ages…"

*

And in the morning the doorbell rang. Tanya and Marat Andreyevich had arrived. They had kept their promise of the previous day and bought plenty of food. Tanya deftly emptied out the bags. Marat Andreyevich said something in a muted voice and the old man greeted every grocery that was laid on the table by name: "chicken", "sausage", "onions", "potatoes", "cucumbers"—so that even without getting up, I was acquainted with the contents of the fridge. Timofei Stepanovich loudly approved all the provisions, said goodbye and left me to Tanya Miroshnikova. Marat Andreyevich had only dropped in for ten minutes to help with the shopping bags. After that he would dash off to the clinic.

Sparrows were chirping audaciously on the balcony and there were bright-blue glimpses of sky between the curtains. I had noticed before that sunlight set healing processes to work within me; when subjected to the effects of photosynthesis, my depression of the previous evening would often evaporate.

In one of the neighbours' apartments a radio splashed out a joyful baritone voice: " A-a-nd the last train again got away from me again, and I wa-alk along the sleepers, a-along the sleepers a-a-again…"

I got up off the sofa and managed to get into my trousers at the third attempt. Marat Andreyevich was sitting in the kitchen, browsing through the newspaper *Arguments and Facts*. Tanya had dropped a bloodless chicken onto a flat wooden executing block and was already setting about the carcass with a knife.

"You're awake, Alexei Vladimirovich!" Tanya said with a studied smile. She looked exhausted and older. The purple bruise on her cheek had been painstakingly powdered.

"I hope we didn't wake you," said Marat Andreyevich, setting down his newspaper. "How are you feeling, Alexei?"

"I still can't take in what happened yesterday," I told him morosely.

Tanya froze for an instant, twitched her shoulders, sobbed and quickly raised one hand to her eyes in an attempt to hold back the tears that hand sprung into them. For a moment it seemed to her that she had mastered her emotions. She leaned down over the chopping board again, but shook her head, apologized and walked out of the kitchen. Water started running noisily in the bathroom sink.

I felt awkward that my cowardly attempt to speak openly about my problems had reduced Tanya to tears. After all, she and the other Shironinites had lost four people who were dear to them.

Tanya came back with her freshly washed eyes still pink from her recent tears. The water had washed off her powder, and the contusion on her cheekbone had turned plum blue.

I still didn't know how to correct my mistake, but in order to say something at least, I told her:

"Tanya, please don't address me so formally. There's no need at all to use my patronymic. Just Alexei, or Lyosha…"

"I don't agree with you there," Marat Andreyevich put in delicately. "Respect for seniority is very important for safeguarding relationships, and it has no effect on the quality of friendship. Correctness is not distance: it's a caring attitude towards the person you're talking to, like rubber gloves, if you like—to prevent infecting the friendship… Don't you agree?"

"You've worked out an entire philosophy, Marat Andreyevich," Tanya said with a playful frown, forgetting her tears. "Alexei, how do you like your chicken; *tabaka* or…"

"You know, Tanya, I hate chicken."

That clearly upset her.

"You don't like it?" She glanced helplessly at Marat Andreyevich as if looking for his support. "Why not? It's delicious…"

"Just the smell of it makes me feel sick…"

Tanya implored me piteously.

"The way I'll cook it, there won't be any smell of chicken. I'll marinade it with garlic!"

"Alexei, imagine that it's not a chicken but, say, a giraffe's head," said Marat Andreyevich, rushing to Tanya's rescue. "Exotic

African meat. Look, here are the horns, and the mouth… See, it looks just like that…"

Tanya laughed, and then Marat Andreyevich smiled too—for the first time in three days.

Several months later I shared these touching memories with Lutsis, saying that my state at the time reminded me of some elements of the cult of Tezcatlipoca, in which the victim chosen by the priests as the earthly incarnation of the god was showered with princely honours and then condemned to slaughter.

Denis took this declaration seriously and even took offence for himself as he was then and for the Shironinites. "Perhaps our attitude to you was like some Indian religious mystery, only with the difference that in the final analysis the priests would have sacrificed themselves, and not the incarnate god."

TANYA

EVEN AS A CHILD I imagined human life as a something similar to the cycle of the year and divided it up into months. January was white, swaddled infancy, February was early childhood, with its slow, half-frozen time, March and April were filled with school, and May was provisionally the time for college studies. At the age of twenty-seven I suddenly realized with bitter surprise that the June of my life was already approaching its end...

The people I always felt the greatest pity for were the "August women". I pitied their fading heat, all their ripeness that was still so toothsome, that holiday-resort aura rapidly approaching its end. The tickets have already been bought for the train; in a day or two it will be time to fold up the sunshade, get dressed and leave the sunny beach of vigorous maturity to travel into September and the fifties, with a direct line from there into pension-book October and on into the endless winter, into the shroud and the grave of December, which accepts everyone "from eighty upward" into its geriatric group...

Tanya Miroshnikova was a typical "August woman". That Tuesday I saw her as someone quite different, not in her crude disguise as a "dacha lady", and not kitted out for combat. She had put on a peach-coloured dress—yellow and orange, warm August colours. A slim, well-proportioned woman with wonderful eyes—blue in the sunlight, green at sunset, and grey in gloomy weather. Tanya's loose hair suited her very well—chestnut, with the glint of a wave in motion; if she gathered it into a ponytail, it brought out something touchingly monkey-like in her face. How old was she? Forty, probably. On her bulging, childish forehead three parallel wrinkles had appeared, almost deep enough to be fate lines. The large white pellets of her false pearls looked touching on her withering neck.

Tanya was a teacher; she taught physical education in a school. She had graduated from a teacher-training college. Tanya's sporting career had only advanced as far as a first-level qualification in fencing, but this highly useful skill came in very handy for the Shironin reading room. Fifteen years earlier Tanya had had a botched abortion, after which she never fell pregnant again. Doctors and medicine didn't help, and one day her husband left her. Tanya had been introduced to the reading room by a friend of her deceased mother. At that point Tanya was on the verge of suicide, and the tender-hearted woman spotted that just in time and gave Tanya the gift of a new life and a large family.

I'm sure my rapid acclimatization to the new place owed much to Tanya Miroshnikova's wonderful female charm. She was an easy person to be with—always smiling, she made it easy to like her, and she knew how to listen. She always praised me and supported me, and simply loved me just the way I am: impressionable, nervous, far from the most courageous of men, with only the title: "librarian"…

I remember that on the Tuesday we spent together Tanya and I agreed to find a substitute for the chicken. We settled on fried potatoes and tinned fish. Tanya groused for a while, and then made me draw up a list of what I didn't eat for the future—she was terribly upset when she saw that cabbage soup and jellied meat were both out of favour.

Marat Andreyevich left to go to work, and Tanya and I spent the whole morning sitting in the kitchen. She questioned me eagerly about my past. Unlike Timofei Stepanovich, she was absolutely delighted that I had studied to be a theatrical director. I told her about my old successes in the CJI, and she immediately started assuring me that she had seen me on the television, but I denied it. At the end Tanya exclaimed enthusiastically, "Alexei, you're a creative individual!"

I suggested that she read the Book and she responded enthusiastically, although at first, out of politeness, she said that her job was to guard me, not to read the Book.

She withdrew into the bedroom. But I wandered aimlessly round the apartment, browsed through a novel by Pikul, starting from the middle, and then dozed. When I woke up, I looked through my uncle's gramophone records and then picked up the phone. I tried calling home and got through on the third attempt, catching my mum in. I was already relatively calm, and my voice didn't betray my anxiety. I told her as nonchalantly as I could that I would try to solve the problem of selling the apartment in the next two months—it couldn't be done any quicker than that. Mum immediately started worrying if I had enough money and I assured her that life in the deep provinces was very cheap, that in general I liked the town and I had met some very warm-hearted people in the housing office who had promised to help me find a buyer. I lied, and my mum, entirely satisfied, asked me to keep my father and her informed about developments.

The moment I put down the receiver, Tanya came out of the bedroom. I was embarrassed, because I wasn't sure if she had overheard my conversation, although of course it hadn't touched on the interests of the reading room. But on taking a closer look at Tanya, I realized that she wasn't concerned about trifles like that. Her pink, flushed face was set in an expression of radiant, tender rapture, directed inward. I observed this luminous, incomprehensible condition without moving, afraid to disturb it with a superfluous movement or word.

Tanya came close to me. The pupils of her slightly narrowed eyes were drifting in a disquieting sensuality, as if she had been exhausted by hours of lovemaking that was not corporeal, but fundamentally different in nature. Her mouth was half open and she was breathing in short sighs, swallowing them, so that her throat and her lips produced slightly sticky sounds, like a kiss separating. She spoke with a faint, provocative hoarseness in her voice: "Everything's fine, Alexei…"

That night, when I reached out for my uncle's porn magazines, to browse through them before I fell asleep, I realized that I could manage perfectly well with just that memory of Tanya.

And two weeks later, during her fourth watch, she told me at breakfast with stupefying directness: "Alexei, don't take this the wrong way. You're a young man, you need a woman, and there's nothing shameful about that. It's hard for you to be locked up like this. If you like, I… I promise you there wouldn't be any problems with me. You'd feel better. It's physiological, so it's hard to fight it, and stupid to try. This probably all sounds vulgar… It's just so that you can feel more comfortable. Just for the time being. When things calm down, you can date anyone you like. If I've shocked you or offended you, I'm sorry. I know I'm not exactly right for you—my age… and maybe you have a girl in Ukraine…"

I thanked her, embarrassed—"Thank you, Tanya…"—and prudently avoided accepting this offer.

The point was that literally only a few days earlier I had heard something similar from the youngest Vozglyakova sister, with the simple difference that she had acted quite directly and unequivocally. After informing me that before reading the Book she was always intensely agitated and began sweating, Veronika locked herself in the bathroom and emerged from it naked. Looking at her, I was prepared to change my disdainful attitude to voluptuous figures. The vision before me had the firm curves of a plaster *Girl with an Oar* in a Soviet park.

Glowing white and covered in sunny little drops, Veronika first bewailed my enforced solitude and assured me that she was willing to do everything she could for what she touchingly called my "male comfort". As she spoke, Veronika dried herself with a bath towel, doing it with a quite inexpressible, artless prudery.

I cast an alarmed glance at the small, round apple-breasts, at the strong broad belly, at the wet curly cluster below Veronika's mighty hips, but caution defeated temptation. I was sure that this was simply an attempt to bind me to the reading room with a woman.

I rather demurely changed the subject to my Uncle Maxim. This device worked, and Veronika immediately turned more serious and got dressed. Then she read the Book, and lost all interest in conversation.

The next morning Veronika Vozglyakova was relieved by Marat Andreyevich, and just before she left she whispered to me at the door that the offer to cater to my male "comfort" was still in force.

MARAT ANDREYEVICH

H E WAS A COLLEAGUE of Uncle Maxim's, working with him
in a clinic until my uncle was sacked. Marat Andreyevich
Dezhnev's family life was a failure. He and his wife had separated, although this had been very hard for him—he loved his
two daughters very much. His only joy was the weekends, when
he went to his former wife's home and collected the girls for a
whole day, to go walking with them in the park or take them to
the cinema. For ten years those Sunday excursions were the only
solace of his life.

At the beginning of the Nineties his wife and her new husband
emigrated. Marat Andreyevich accepted his bitter loss in the
realization that the girls would be better off in distant Canada. In
any case, Dezhnev's life became even more emotionally impoverished, and he was threatened by a loneliness he had never
known before.

On one of his dreary Sunday evenings he met my Uncle
Maxim. They were both equally amazed by the changes that had
taken place in the course of a few years. Marat Andreyevich saw
before him a happy, confident man who had giving up drinking for
ever. Dezhnev, on the contrary, astounded my uncle with his seedy
appearance and bitter dejection. Uncle Maxim took pity on his
former colleague and invited him to join the reading room. That
was shortly before the events at Neverbino.

Uncle Maxim was not mistaken in his choice. Dezhnev fitted
into the collective perfectly—a courageous, solitary, cultured

individual. The Shironin reading room respected and cherished Marat Andreyevich.

I'm glad that those first watches were taken by readers like Tanya Miroshnikova and Dezhnev. Their calm, benevolent attitude, exceptional delicacy and wit had a beneficial effect on me.

I greatly enjoyed listening to Marat Andreyevich, relishing the amazing overtones of his wry voice that crackled slightly, like kindling in a fireplace; the picture that it conjured up, in combination with Marat Andreyevich's skinny, slightly stooped figure and the pearwood pipe smoking in his hand, was remarkably serene, and the words "Listen here, Alexei…" sounded like "Listen here, Watson…"

How much I needed that rational, calm dialogue when fear and uncertainty tormented my soul. But the moment Marat Andreyevich struck up a conversation I knew that this phonic therapy would set everything in the right perspective and free me from the bonds of nightmare and suspicion.

Marat Andreyevich willingly shared with me his years of experience in exploring Gromov's work.

"When you get right down to it, Alexei, the Books are essentially complex, extensive sequences of signs and signals with a broad psychosomatic spectrum. They could be called drugs or, even better, programs. Each program-Book is equipped with a resident subroutine—a coded subtext that is activated when the Two Conditions of intent reading are met. The resident routine is screened from conscious awareness and propagates aggressively at the subconscious level, temporarily changing or, it would be better to say, deforming the personality of the reader. Under conditions in which an individual's spiritual activity is suppressed, this induces an abrupt correction of the organism's psycho-physiological processes, resulting in the hyperstimulation of its innermost resources, the nerve centres responsible for memory and emotion. I'm not making this explanation too recondite, am I? The most interesting thing is that the resident routine cannot be identified on the external, artistic level, because it's dispersed across the entire informational field of the program. It's present not only in the acoustic, neurolinguistic and semantic spectra of the Book, but also in the visual spectrum—that is, in the printing: the typeface, the paper, the layout, the format. And also—and this is very important—in the chronological spectrum. What I'm leading up to, Alexei, is this: a pile of photocopies will never be a book published in 1977. There are no methods or technologies in the world capable of transforming a product of the year 2000 into an item produced in 1977. It is also impossible to forge a Book, because it carries the energetic charge of its own time."

I noticed that Marat Andreyevich avoided talking about his own experiences with the Book. This seemed rather strange—as if a driver who chatters eagerly about the technical features of his car for some reason keeps everything that he has seen out on the road a strict secret.

Marat Andreyevich was so personable and charming that I ventured to ask him about the memories that he saw. I quite honestly didn't even suspect that this was a tactless question, and it was a good thing that he immediately enlightened me on the subject of readers' ethics, so that I never again bothered anyone with my idle curiosity.

Marat Andreyevich was taken aback for a moment, but he replied with a smile.

"Alexei, imagine this situation: a man who is happy in love suddenly offers his wife to the first man he meets, so that the other individual can share his delight... Just forget it. No one will give you an answer in any case. You'll only put people in an awkward situation... Agreed?"

After I read the Book, I didn't discover any barriers at all to prevent me from sharing my impressions. May God forgive me, I even envied all the Shironinites, thinking that my memories were simply inferior to their reveries.

THE OTHER READERS

F ROM THURSDAY TO SUNDAY we said farewell to our fallen
comrades. Although we cremated them on the same day, we
buried them one at a time.

I didn't attend the cremation. The others came for me when
the urns had already been taken to the cemetery. Fearing acts of
aggression, Margarita Tikhonovna did not want me to leave the
apartment at all, but I felt that it would be unfair if the readers on
guard with me were not able to see their friends off on their final
journey. So each time I put on the chain with the Book and went
down to our RAF, and we drove off to the cemetery.

The funerals were closely guarded. Close to the wall in which
the urns were immured, in the next row along, half a dozen gravediggers were hard at work. I kept glancing at them in alarm, until
I recognized two of the cemetery employees as Ievlev, armed with
a spade, and Kruchina with a shovel. Igor Valeryevich nodded to
me and Nikolai Tarasovich gestured to me reassuringly, as if to
say that everything was under control.

However, the wake on Sunday evening was a collective one. It
was held at Margarita Tikhonovna's place in order not to attract
any unnecessary attention to my apartment. Timofei Stepanovich
put on his army decorations, and the former shock worker Kruchina
wore his Order of the Red Banner.

I don't remember much about the posthumous tributes paid
to the fallen Shironinites. My constant terror was amplified by the
funeral feast that we were celebrating, and I tried to stun it using

vodka, like dynamite. It didn't help. All my excruciating thoughts floated belly-up on the very surface of my mind and my head spun crazily as if it were tumbling off the block after being severed from my neck. I puked my guts up in Margarita Tikhonovna's corridor and in the RAF and Tanya wiped my wet mouth with a napkin. I didn't have the strength to apologize: I couldn't even speak.

A hungover Monday was the beginning of the second week of my life as a librarian. I got to know the other readers better. On that day Nikolai Tarasovich Ievlev was on duty with me. He was a taciturn man and only livened up when the subject of conversation was the Book.

Ever since his young days he had been a kettlebell lifter and all-round sportsman, and this had given him his mighty physique. In his pre-Gromov days he used to run amok after drinking and overturn cars in the street all on his own. Only the Book had given Nikolai Tarasovich the gravitas that he needed. He worked as a blacksmith.

The deep scar on his face was a memento of the Battle of Neverbino. They said it was left by the hook of the legendary crane driver Dankevich, the female berserker from Mokhova's clan.

Ievlev listened attentively to the story of my life and, as it turned out, drew his own special conclusions—in the morning he brought round a chest expander and two sixteen-kilogram kettlebells.

"But the most important thing is not to forget about the neck. Your neck's as thin as a finger," Ievlev concluded with a sigh. "Go into a wrestler's bridge, support yourself with your head, and then up and down until you get tired. Pump those muscles every day. The neck's the most important thing," he lectured me.

I nodded, but Nikolai Tarasovich clearly couldn't spot the required eagerness in my eyes and he added this cautionary example:

"One of the readers from Kolontaysk took a wallop from a club on his helmet. His skull wasn't damaged, but his neck vertebrae couldn't take it…"

On Sasha Sukharev's day on guard he presented me with a Solingen cut-throat razor.

"If you get the hang of it, the other guy will have to change the photo in his passport at the very least, because he won't have any nose, and he'll be missing one cheek and his ears too," Sukharev said, smiling radiantly like Yuri Gagarin. "Under the laws of the Russian Federation, this is not considered a dangerous weapon," he explained. "It's perfectly fine for carrying about, concealed on your person... You need something that the pigs can't haggle about—a hammer or a nice long screwdriver is good. Slicing through a sheepskin coat with a screwdriver is a piece of cake, and if the pigs nab you with it, everything's in order—I'm going to my girlfriend's place to put up a cupboard. A screwdriver's not that easy to see in the dark either. It's quick: pull it out, jab, and they've got a hole in their liver or their throat. A handy kind of thing."

Sukharev came from a failed proletarian family, and he was well on the way to spending his years behind bars. From the sixth year in school he was in the register at the militia's children's office, and the only reason he wasn't put away as juvenile offender was that the local militiaman was distantly related to his mother.

Prison caught up with Sukharev after the army. He was put inside for two years for hooliganism. Fortunately, in the prison camp he crossed paths with the reader Pavel Yegorov.

Sukharev was released and for the first month he led a dissipated life, but then, as if by magic, he miraculously came to his senses. Naturally, it wasn't the reforming effect of the prison system that had re-educated him. Yegorov, who had been released earlier, had been in time to take part in the Battle of Neverbino, and when the reconstituted Shironin reading room was actively recruiting new members, he remembered Sukharev and found him, and the Shironinites acquired a faithful comrade.

That recruitment of early 1997 also brought in Grisha Vyrin, and the recently deceased Vadik Provotorov...

Grisha Vyrin's family came from a long line of Old Believers. Although the last two generations had not had any religious connections, he was genetically predisposed to life in a closed community, secrecy and a sense of being one of the chosen.

Grisha recovered in record time. In a week the swelling was gone and he was able to move again as he waited for the cracks in his vertebrae to close up. The doctors reassured us by saying that Grisha had got off lightly and in a month or six weeks he would be on his feet again.

I visited him quite often in the hospital. In the course of one of our conversations it turned out that during his college years Grisha had been a member of the Club of the Jolly and Ingenious team.

"There was this song of Anna German's— 'Hope'. I composed a variation, on the theme of the oligarchs:

There was a long squeal of brakes
In front of the expensive shop.
Sad Jewish eyes
Gave me advice from the limousine:
'You just have to learn to lie,
And be a hard-core cocksucker,
For life sometimes to give you
A fresh grouse with sweet pineapple.'"

Grisha laughed bitterly. "Our captain rejected it—said it was too coarse... Alexei, you'd have taken that rewrite of mine, wouldn't you? I mean, when you were the captain?" he suddenly asked with a sickly kind of hope.

I would have turned the song down as well, and it wasn't just a matter of the "hard-core cocksucker"—although that, too, especially in that disastrous combination with those "Jewish eyes" giving out repulsive advice. But what did my truth and the morals of student slapstick matter? I remembered how Vyrin had given me his protective jacket without even a second thought, and I knew that he would have given his life for me and the reading room without a second thought too. And so I said:

"Of course I would! It's a fine parody. It's just that your captain didn't have any sense of humour."

"Thanks, Alexei," Vyrin said with a happy smile and shook my hand.

Denis Lutsis was a genuine aksakal of the Gromov world, a reader with a decade of experience. The tiny Samara reading room from which he had emerged was essentially a family concern. The Lutsises—Denis's parents and close relatives—were Russified Balts. All in all there were eleven of them, and they owned a Book of Memory. Their life of quiet contentment was shattered when their Book was stolen and the older members of the clan were killed. Lutsis's parents and uncle fell in the battle of Neverbino. Denis survived the battle, but he had been orphaned overnight. He decided not to go back home. His surviving female cousins and aunt attached themselves to the new Samara library. Denis fell in with the Shironinites. He wasn't crushed by his heavy loss. He graduated from the history faculty at university and taught in a road-transport technical college.

Denis was a complicated character, easily wounded by a clumsily spoken word, although he didn't usually give any sign of it, preferring to keep his grievances to himself. I quickly learned to recognize this condition of his. If Denis Lutsis suddenly became morbidly pedantic and emphatically polite and looked off to one side during the conversation, it was clear that he had been deeply offended by something. But you only had to ask him what was wrong for him immediately to open up and inform you in a punctiliously bitter manner what exactly had hurt his feelings. For example, Lutsis was dating Svetlana Vozglyakova, but for some unknown reason he made a terrible secret out of it, although everyone knew about their relationship. Even so, he categorically refused to accept any joking on the subject. Fortunately Lutsis didn't bear grudges, and after an apology he thawed immediately.

Like Marat Andreyevich, Lutsis sometimes shared his experience of the Book with me.

"About four years ago I realized that, if I wanted, I could reproduce the text in my mind without the help of the Book. I tried to do it, setting a kind of scrolling text moving in my head. Nothing happened. I thought I'd got the words mixed up, but I checked with the Book—and everything was right. So words that arose in my mind without their graphic equivalent didn't work. I tried reciting the text out loud. After all, at the group's sessions only one person actually reads, and the Book affects the others via the sound. Another failure. Without the Book itself, the sound doesn't work…"

Thanks to Lutsis I rapidly got to know all the names in the Gromov world and found my way round all its twists and turns. Our relationship was one of friendship, without the slightest hint of any librarian–reader line of subordination.

Looking at Lutsis, I simply couldn't understand why Margarita Tikhonovna's choice for the successor to Uncle Maxim had fallen on me. Decisive, experienced, daring, privy to the mystery of the Books from the days of his youth, Lutsis would have made an entirely worthy replacement. Lutsis himself used to say that he wasn't suited to a management role, so he acted as my mentor as far as he was able and time allowed.

In general, from the very first days the Shironinites did everything to keep my confinement as pleasant as possible and make my life comfortable. The Vozglyakov sisters hung new wallpaper in the apartment and painted the window frames and doors. Fyodor Ogloblin laid new tiles in the bathroom and kitchen, put in new bathroom fixtures, installed a new gas geyser and cooker, and started glazing the balcony. So I wasn't lying when I told my parents that the renovation work was going full steam ahead and there was enough money for everything.

A LITTLE DEBT

THE TEMPORARY CALM came to an abrupt end on 27 June. During the afternoon the phone rang. I blithely answered it because I was sure it was my father calling, and I was even ready to serve up his next portion of: "The renovations are progressing, it's a nice town, the people are friendly and food prices aren't high here."

"Comrade Vyazintsev?" a man's voice asked, and I felt the fear flood through my belly like boiling acid.

"Yes," I replied in a dead voice. That form of address—"Comrade Vyazintsev"—could only mean one thing: the call was for the librarian of the Shironin reading room.

"Alexei Vladimirovich, this is Latokhin here. We met at the meeting..."

The gammy-legged leader of the Kolontaysk reading room. I remembered him.

"Good afternoon, Comrade Latokhin," I said.

"Alexei Vladimirovich, we are sure that you will not refuse us your fraternal support..."

"Comrade Latokhin..."

"Alexei Vladimirovich," Latokhin said insistently, "I know you lost four members only recently, but without us the outcome of the satisfaction would have been even more lamentable! And, after all, you did sign a document..."

"Comrade Latokhin," I said, suddenly realizing that I had offended against etiquette, "do not think that we are refusing. I

193

only arrived here very recently, you know. It would be best for you to talk with Margarita Tikhonovna..."

"But, after all, *you* are the librarian!" Latokhin exclaimed in astonishment.

"Yes, but that is still a formality. Margarita Tikhonovna decides everything..."

"What childish nonsense!" Latokhin muttered, and hung up.

That evening a council of war was held on Shironin's Guards Street. Everybody attended except Vyrin. Margarita Tikhonovna came in dark glasses—her left eye was completely covered by the swollen, mutilated eyelid. Sukharev's hand dangled in a gauze sling like a white claw, with the fingertips poking out of the plaster like potato shoots. Lutsis had almost recovered from his concussion, although he felt sick in the car and he didn't read the Book, complaining of dizziness and nausea. Anna Vozglyakova's cracked collarbone had already knitted together, but it still ached.

Unfortunately my hopes of sitting it out as a nominal presence were not realized. After a brief report on the state of affairs, Margarita Tikhonovna dumped the burden of chairmanship on my shoulders.

What had happened was this: our Kolontaysk neighbours were being menaced by a migrant library that had lost all its Books as a result of armed skirmishes and was now trying to collect them back together, like scattered stones.

The nomads' home territory had once been the town of Aktyubinsk. They used to have three Books of Joy, a Book of Memory, a Book of Endurance and a Book of Fury. The readers called themselves Pavliks, after their first librarian, Pavlik. The Aktyubinskites had been rendered destitute not by Mokhova, but by Lagudov a year before Neverbino, and then marauders had hit them really hard, reducing the substantial group to the size of a small reading room. The Pavliks had left their habitual place of residence to save their lives.

There were twelve of the exiles left, and they had a Book of Fury, capable of plunging anyone into a blind frenzy. This Book didn't bring any pleasure, but the aggressive emotion that it imparted was very useful when it came pouring out on the battlefield. It is not clear what the subsequent destiny of the reading room would have been if Semyon Chakhov, a stage designer, had not come across them. He had a stolen list of redistributed books, which showed who had received the books stolen from the Pavlik library. It was the appearance of the list that provided the stimulus for the reading room's revival. The Pavliks decided to restore justice and take the Books back. The first victim was the Orenburg reading room, which was unfortunate enough to own one of the Books of Joy that had once belonged to the Pavliks. The Pavliks slaughtered the reading room and won back the Book. From there their bloody route ran through Chelyabinsk and Kurgan. The Books of Joy were recovered. Ominous news came from Novosibirsk. The Aktyubinskites had taken back their Book of Endurance.

Naturally, the council kept an eye on the Pavliks, issuing warnings and threatening punitive measures, but with no result. The forces of the council always arrived at the battlefield too late, hypocritically complaining that the enemy was too elusive. It was clear to all right-thinking readers that the only reason for this elusiveness was that a ruinous raid by the Pavliks simply played into the council's hands—the provincial reading rooms were disappearing.

The next target was the Kolontaysk reading room, which owned a Book of Memory. According to information received from the council, the Pavliks could be expected in Kolontaysk any week now. The council had promised Latokhin reinforcements, but the reading room's greatest hope was their neighbours. Latokhin was right to be alarmed. The Pavliks had once again become a fully fledged library with a total of up to eighty readers. And apart from everything else, they had a Book of Fury and a Book of Endurance—irreplaceable battle Books; only the extremely rare Book of Strength could be better...

That was what I learned from Margarita Tikhonovna. And then she said:

"I propose that we should hear from our librarian, Alexei Vladimirovich."

Unfortunately, the cowardly question that came to my mind was whether there was any elegant pretext under which we could renege on our debt to the Kolontaysk readers. I was too embarrassed to put the question directly and approached the subject obliquely.

"I'm new here… It's hard for me to judge. Of course, the easiest thing is to regard this as entirely the Kolontaysk reading room's problem and, after all, the Book of Memory did belong to the Aktyubinsk library…"

I paused, but no one volunteered to complete my train of thought and say, "If that's the case, we have no business sticking our noses into all this." On the contrary, they all waited for what would come next.

"We have suffered substantial losses; our own situation is far from easy…"

And again the response was attentive silence.

"Let us honestly consider whether we can refuse the Kolontaysk reading room…"

The Shironinites smiled. My words had been taken for rhetorical irony born of courage—with the bravado of: "Is there powder in the powder horns still?"

"Well, of course we can't refuse," Lutsis said merrily.

"It's as clear as day," said Sukharev, backing him up. "And anyway, we signed a piece of paper."

"Lads, joking aside," Dezhnev put in, "we have to decide how many people we send."

Margarita Tikhonovna nodded.

"A good question, Marat Andreyevich. The Kolontaysk reading room sacrificed three warriors for us. I think we cannot send fewer than four people."

"That's fine," Timofei Stepanovich declared cheerfully. "I'm always ready."

Kruchina, Ievlev and Lutsis raised their hands like star pupils and Young Pioneers.

"Denis!" Marat Andreyevich exclaimed. "Where do you think you're going? What kind of fighter would you make now?... Timofei Stepanovich and Fyodor Alexandrovich will go." Marat Andreyevich looked at Ogloblin, who nodded eagerly. "Well, and, of course, your humble servant..."

"That's three people," Margarita Tikhonovna said quietly. "Who else, Comrade Dezhnev?"

"Let's say Tanya. Or Svetlana. Or Veronika..."

"Svetlana can stay here," Lutsis said stubbornly. "Why her? I'm more use in any case."

"Denis, just think about it," Ievlev boomed amiably. "Three of the Kolontayskites really did die for us, but that doesn't mean we have to pay them back in corpses. What we want is a victory... You need to rest and restore your strength. But I don't agree with Dezhnev either. Why take women?"

"Wait a moment," Marat Andreyevich sighed. "Let's think logically. Comrades Ievlev and Kruchina are the backbone of our reading room's strength. We can't really count on Sasha and Denis—don't take offence, lads, but it's true. Grisha's position is obvious. Margarita Tikhonovna and Anna are not entirely well. Someone has to protect the Book and Alexei. And our beauties are splendid fighters."

"I'm against Svetlana being chosen," Lutsis declared categorically. "Why can't I go, if I'm well?"

"Denis, you're a grown man. Be objective about yourself," Margarita Tikhonovna said sternly.

"Yes, yes, that's right," said Svetlana. "I'd be happy to join the men."

"And I'd be even happier," Veronika laughed.

"Comrades," said Tanya, getting up. "Permit me to share my thoughts with you. Much as I hate to remind you... The Vozglyakov family..."—Tanya's voice trembled—"... lost their dearest member only a month ago..."

When she said that, Svetlana's lips started trembling, Anna

wiped away a tear and Veronika, the youngest, lowered her face into her hands.

"Tanya," Sukharev exclaimed reproachfully. "Why say that? It will take Veronika half a day to calm down now…"

"I'm sorry, but it was something that simply had to be said," Tanya continued resolutely. "Obviously, the death of any reader is an irreparable loss. But a family is something else, after all. Our girls are strong people, but it wouldn't be right to put them through the unnecessary trauma of more emotional stress. Perhaps they've given enough, eh?"

"Tanya, why are you making us look like some kind of egotists?" Anna said in a pained voice. "We're equal here! We're all equally precious!"

"What Tanya says is right," Marat Andreyevich said with nod. "What has egotism got to do with it? You need to recover, to restore you spirits. Am I right, Tanya?"

"Bull's-eye, Comrade Dezhnev. That's why I propose that I go and I urge everyone to back me up! Well, after all, Alexei can't go! Timofei Stepanovich, why don't you say anything? It will be easier for you with me!"

"Thank you Tanyusha," Margarita Tikhonovna sighed. "You've made everything very clear—clearer than I did. Right then, comrades, let's vote…"

"And make it a unanimous 'yes'," Tanya threatened them jokingly. "Abstainers are my enemies for life!"

I felt a strange new feeling. Something like a pang of conscience. The voting came to an end, the others all went home, and the uncomfortable feeling swelled up inside me, so that by the evening my soul's former timid shell felt as tight as a shoe one size too small…

In an attempt to smother this condition, I picked up the Book. This time everything was much simpler; the text didn't slither about, and in two hours I had read the Book of Memory for the first time…

THE LIBRARIAN

I WON'T REPEAT the experience of my false visions. The child-hood tossed to me could easily have been mine. But that's not the most important thing. More thrilling even than the activation of the false memory was its aftertaste. The Book seemed to have opened up an artesian well, and a torrent of forgotten words, sounds, colours, voices, domestic details, inscriptions, labels and stickers came pouring out of it... On the airwaves: the Pioneer dawn, knowledge is a hard nut, but even so, giving up is not our way, at the airport he was met by Comrades Chernenko, Zaykov, Slyunkov, Vorotnikov, Vladislav Tretyak, Oleg Blokhin, Irina Rodnina is written with a capital letter, Artek, Tarkhun, Baikal, fruit and berry ices for 7 copecks, a choc ice on a stick for 28 copecks, a mug of kvass for 6 copecks, milk in triangular packets, kefir in a glass bottle with a green top, chewing gum is pineapple or mint, you can chew Czech erasers too, the Soyuzpechat kiosk sells trans-fers as thin as a film of oil, the best spray gun is made out of an empty blueing bottle, the best smoke bomb out of the two halves of a ping pong ball, the best crossbow with a wooden clothes peg, keys to the apartment are carried on a cord, mittens on elastic, a pen of woven wire, a little figure made of plastic tubing, table football, our squad, our motto: not a single step back, not a single step on the spot, only forward and only all together, remember down the ages, down the years, those who will never come again, the Young Pioneer heroes Volodya Dubinin, Marat Kazei, Lenya Golikov, Valya Kotik, Zina Portnova, Oleg Popov, Lelek and Bolek,

Rubik's Cube, shifting-picture calendar cards, the planetarium, film strips on a projector, the magazines *Jolly Pictures*, *Murzilka* and *Young Technician* with clever tricks on the cover, Orlenok, Salyut and Desna bicycles, on weekdays *The Adventures of Electronic* and *Girl from the Future*, on Fridays *Visiting a Fairytale*, on Saturdays *ABCDEing*, on Sunday *Alarm Clock*, a week is two pages in a diary...

I stood on the balcony. A stormy purple sky extended above the world as evening advanced. The wind flung handfuls of the first drops of rain into my face, cooling it pleasantly. I had already understood everything and thought it through. Once I had calmed down a bit, I went back into the room. I took the motorcycle helmet out of the wardrobe. My uncle's weapon was in there too—I fancied it was a very old geologist's hammer. The long handle ended in a leather loop. The iron claw was rather larger than on a normal claw hammer, and the other side looked like a sharpened four-faceted beak, curved slightly downward, like a combat pick.

Then I phoned Margarita Tikhonovna and told her in a restrained voice that I was going to Kolontaysk.

Margarita Tikhonovna asked:

"Alexei, have you read the Book?"

I don't know why, but I felt too shy to tell her the truth. I mumbled something unintelligible and said goodbye until tomorrow.

It wasn't only the Book that had made me take this step. I'd remembered my terrible twenty-seventh birthday. Anticipating disaster, two weeks in advance I phoned my old CJI colleagues and schoolmates. They responded feebly to the call, promising to come. We were still in touch, although not very close, and if we met in town we used to sit on a bench, have a beer and crack jokes. My friends thanked me and made excuses, saying they were very busy with family and children. I took fright at this human void and invited lots of people I wasn't at all close to—people from work whom I barely even knew.

My birthday arrived. In the morning my parents presented me with a woolly sweater and drove me out into the country—the dacha-plot harvest was just beginning. Then Vovka dropped round for an hour with my nephew Ivan and a chocolate cake. She kissed me and apologized because Slavik couldn't come—he was at home with Ilya, who was ill, but he sent his best wishes and gave me a CD player. Vovka helped to lay the table and whipped my mother's half-finished delicacies into shape. In the evening I waited for my guests...

No one came. Exhausted by a three-hour wait, I gathered up the plates and glasses from the table, put all the chairs back in their rooms, packed the celebratory food into the fridge, grabbed a bottle of vodka and set off for the edge of town as if it were the world's end. I bounced about in the bus all the way to the final stop, hobbled along a deserted earth road and scrambled through brittle wild grass until I reached a cliff. My town was visible in the distance, like a collapsed New Year tree.

I drank the vodka in tiny sips and scalding, drunken tears coursed down my cheeks. "How could this happen, eh?" I asked helplessly. "What have I done to offend you, Life? Wasn't it you who swore in that sweet-voiced quartet all those years ago from the screen of a black-and-white Record TV that it was time-time-time to delight me with jolly friends, a lucky blade and Alice so fine? I sang along with you, Life! I believed you! How cruelly you have mocked me! My third decade is already coming to an end and I have no faithful friends and never will. My weak hand will never know a sword hilt, and my Alice has never gone astray on the next street. Alice so fine is a blond hybrid of Milady and Constance. She never existed, she was a mirage, an acoustic illusion, a spilled "chalice of wine", a puddle of cheap fortified port on a slashed oilcloth tablecloth..."

And suddenly life had settled up with me, admittedly belatedly, and given me back what it had promised, only it had done it too unexpectedly, sneakily, from round a corner, so that I had failed to recognize my happiness and feared it blindly for almost a month.

The reading room received my unexpected decision without any exultant comments, as something to be taken for granted, but I realized that I had passed the examination for the post of librarian with honour.

Timofei Stepanovich said in passing:

"I told you, Alexei, blood's thicker than water!"

The Book had roused my conscience, but it had not made me reckless. I realized that I was a worthless fighter. Especially for me Ogloblin constructed a sturdy and comfortable protective tunic in the style of an Old Russian *kalantar* out of the slabs of Belaz truck tyres that I had found in the cupboard—two halves connected together at the top by a flexible shoulder piece. Attached to the waist was a skirt made of lighter Kamaz truck tyres. Worn over Vyrin's jacket, the tunic didn't restrict the movements of my arms at all. The motorcycle helmet, reinforced with similar tyre slabs, securely protected my neck and ears. I was also hastily taught a few extremely simple but effective moves with my uncle's pick.

I spent many hours at Margarita Tikhonovna's place. She put on her favourite records and, to the accompaniment of 1970s variety music, we discussed exalted, non-Gromovian subjects...

Thanks to the Book of Memory, on one of those evenings I experienced an acoustic revelation that really boosted my spirits... A fanfare sounded in the speakers and the drums rattled out a gallows roll. Soaring above them, fluttering like a banner, was a high boy's voice: "The house was left behind a veil of steppe mist; I shall not soon return to it. Please just stay with me, Comrade Truth, Comrade Truth..."

In my childhood years that song was played quite often on the radio. I can't say that it had made any special impression on me before; I grew used to it and noticed neither the words nor the music. But now the cotton-wool plugs and filters definitely all fell away, revealing a quite different high-frequency range.

It wasn't just the voice of a boy soloist in a children's choir, it was a child skald glorifying heroism and death. The descant in no way diminished the valour of the youthful voice; on the contrary, it filled it with a pure, unclouded resonance, and grandiose pictures

of a Soviet Valhalla arose before my eyes. Death was simultaneously a parade on Red Square and an eternal battle at Dubosekovo
Junction, in bronze, marble and flame. For a brief moment I saw
or remembered my own glorified or forgotten future death. It was
glorious because it was immortal. I was engulfed by gratitude and
exultation.

Unable to contain myself, I shared my feelings with Margarita
Tikhonovna.

"That's right," she said. "There are sacred icons and there are
sacred Books, like ours. Read it often, and fear will lose its hold
over you for ever..."

And so the infantile arsenal of false memory was reinforced with
an acoustic equivalent of the Soviet eternity, which repeatedly
brought me succour in difficult moments. Later, images reminiscent of blurred and grainy frames from a black-and-white news
chronicle accrued around the sound.

In short, when Latokhin called again on 6 July and set a meeting, I was prepared for a battle with the Pavliks. The day before we
left I gave Margarita Tikhonovna the Book for safekeeping. Then
the entire reading room gathered. There was another reason for
that—we were celebrating Marat Andreyevich's birthday.

It seemed as if I was the only one with his heart pierced by
the rusty nail of dread. The others weren't showing any signs, as
if there were no battle ahead. Yet again I was astounded by the
Shironinites' simple courage. These people with nerves of steel could
joke, smile and praise Tanya's salads or Margarita Tikhonovna's
cake to the skies. Only the singing round the table betrayed their
secret agitation, when we all launched into a song about a comrade
flying to a distant land.

I tried as hard as I could to pull a veil over tomorrow, drank a
large glass of vodka to Marat Andreyevich's health and fitted my
voice in with the chorus as best I could: "The beloved city can sleep
in peace and dream, adrift in springtime greenery."

IN KOLONTAYSK

B EFORE IT WAS LIGHT, the five of us—Tanya, Timofei Stepanovich, Dezhnev, Ogloblin and I—went down to the RAF. Our outfits and weapons were packed in large check bags.

I blithely slept through the journey to Kolontaysk. Tormented by a morning-after hangover, I arranged myself as comfortably as possible in the seat, and the sense of movement and the jolting lulled me until I sank into a blank sleep.

In Kolontaysk we were billeted with the reader Artem Veretenov, who had helped us in the battle with the Gorelov reading room. Veretenov lived in private-sector housing and his two-storey house could accommodate a large number of guests. We were put in the bathroom, the attic and the glazed balcony; the summer house was already taken by the more numerous readers from the Voronezh and Stavropol reading rooms. A brigade from Kostroma was in the annexe.

Of course, having such a large number of armed people around was reassuring, despite the inconvenience involved. But I realized something else: if such an impressive force had been mobilized, then a serious battle was expected. There were twenty-seven people in the Kolontaysk reading room. More than thirty fighters had gathered at Veretenov's home, and, according to what he said, reinforcements were still turning up to join Latokhin. The people from Penza were in the Kolontayskite Sakhno's apartment. The Vologda readers were staying with Latokhin. They were even expecting a brigade of at least two dozen from the Council of Libraries.

Such a large number of warriors indicated that the Pavliks were not merely a dangerous enemy, but also very numerous. In recent times the flourishing library had been joined by a large number of surviving remnants, copyists who had been hiding for years from the forces of the council, bands of marauders, unsuccessful thieves and other riff-raff of the Gromov world. It was anticipated that as many as a hundred warriors had already gathered under the Pavliks' banner.

The most annoying thing was that no one could say how long we would have to wait for the Pavliks to show up—a day or a week—and the enforced idleness was depressing.

I didn't see the town; we had been recommended not to go out for walks, and I didn't particularly want to go outside in any case. We quickly got to know all our neighbours. When Veretenov introduced me as the librarian Vyazintsev, someone exclaimed in surprise: "So you're alive, but we were told you'd been killed a year ago!"

Our colleagues turned out to be fine people. Associating with them was both interesting and useful. After all, I had never previously considered the highly complex mechanisms of conspiracy that allowed the reading rooms and libraries to survive in their grim reality of bloodbaths, ambushes and assassinations.

For instance, in the ordinary world the Kostroma reading room concealed itself under the guise of The Association of Lovers of Japanese Culture. The Kostromites' librarian, Ivan Arnoldovich Kisling, was a teacher of Russian language and literature and entirely indifferent to Japan. The reading room was located in a small basement where sambo, the Russian martial art, was served up as a form of karate, and Japanese sword-fighting techniques were taught to allay suspicion. Kisling prudently charged astronomical prices that frightened off anyone who was curious. His little office was crammed with all sorts of pseudo-oriental trash that was passed off as Japanese—in case an inspection committee turned up. The "association" was an official organization, and if the militia suddenly discovered twenty-odd old dragoons' sabres disguised as Japanese swords in the basement, the Kostromite lovers of Japan wouldn't have any particular problems.

The reading room of the Voronezh librarian, Yevgeny Davidovich Tsofin, was concealed behind the screen of a religious organization that functioned as a kosher slaughterhouse. That gave Tsofin's people a legitimate reason for never parting with their long knives, designed for slaughtering cattle. It should be said that Tsofin was the only Jew in their reading room. With his ginger hair, large nose and eternally dissatisfied and disgusted expression, he unfailingly rebuffed any visitors from the municipal authorities. The bureaucrats wisely preferred to stay clear of him. Only once had uninvited guests from the Jewish Centre poked their noses into the reading room by mistake, but the Voronezh readers had seen off their "kinsmen" very promptly. Soon everyone left the reading room in peace and avoided it as a place with a bad smell, which was exactly what Tsofin and his comrades had been trying to achieve. They had shown up for the battle in double-thickness kaftans as tough as wooden planks and turbans that took the place of helmets.

In their ordinary lives the Stavropol readers were a Cossack rural settlement—purely nominal, of course, as it existed only on paper. This fictitious ethnic status allowed the librarian Zarubin and the readers to carry cold weapons. Zarubin was not scrupulous about historical detail and drew his ideas mainly from the "Streltsy" of Ivan the Terrible's time, so that, in addition to swords, pikes and whips, the reading room also made ready use of poleaxes.

The Stavropolites avoided genuine Cossack communities, just as Tsofin's readers avoided Jews, but that didn't prevent the "Japanese" Kisling from teasing Tsofin every now and then by offering to give him the blood of a Christian child or inviting the "Cossack" Zarubin to arrange a small pogrom against the Voronezhites.

We lived quite comfortably. Latokhin took care of everything, even our food, which was very simple: soup made with dried-pea powder, boiled grain, potatoes, bread and meat pies.

On the second day Latokhin himself dropped round to see us with some papers. Under his intent gaze I nervously applied my signature—a squiggle with a pig's-tail flourish—to some document or other.

We were woken at night. A battered old Laz drove up to Veretenov's house and we hastily piled into it. In the bus Veretenov handed out thermos flasks of coffee and little plastic cups.

We arrived at an immense clay quarry—the future battlefield. The quarry had not been worked for a very long time, but the reddish-brown sides bore the marks of excavators' teeth.

Latokhin's fully assembled army amounted to eighty-four warriors. Surrounded by a crowd of armed men, Latokhin attached an icon case containing the Book of Memory, open at the title page, to a pole. He stuck the pole into the clay and a little lamp lit up in the icon case, illuminating the pages.

As dawn approached it became clear, after several tense hours of waiting, that the Pavliks had not had not taken the bait of the Book and the battle was postponed. We set a watch and went back to our buses.

In the morning Latokhin's lads drove up two field kitchens with goulash and a barrel of kvass. Everyone was given an orange worker's waistcoat for a disguise, but this was just insurance—construction wastelands extended for many kilometres on all sides.

We spent the entire day encamped. At sunset the Vologda patrol, walking round the quarry, came across Pavlikite scouts. There were three of the outsiders. A brief skirmish took place; two Pavliks got away and the third, more dead than alive, was lugged to Latokhin's headquarters.

The prisoner looked appalling, as if he had just been dragged out of a traumatology ward, totally encased in plaster, so that even his face could not be seen. The grubby grey bandages were soaked in blood and smeared with clay. I even had the absurd thought that the men on patrol had first broken the man's bones and then rapidly applied the plaster.

But in fact he wasn't dying of broken bones—the fatal blow had been struck by an axe, precisely between his plaster collar and the bandage on his head.

Marat Andreyevich sat down beside the wounded man with a pair of scissors. The removal of the first cast explained everything—the Pavlik's terrible, blood-spattered costume was a well-designed suit of armour, like a medieval knight's. Under the bandages lay not plaster, but heavy plastic, moulded to the contours of the body.

Marat Andreyevich worked away with the scissors in his habitual fashion, ripping apart the dense bandaging.

"By the way, it's not blood on the bandages," he jovially informed the men who had gathered round. "It's imitation, a dye. Only I can't understand what it's for."

"It's a cunning kind of psychological pressure," said one of the Voronezhites. "The sight of him is enough to terrify you, and at the same time it's harder to hit someone in bandages…"

"That could well be it," Marat Andreyevich agreed. "Their librarian used to be a theatre designer…"

The prisoner lay there stripped, like a lobster, and the sections of his shell were heaped up beside him—cuirass, chausses, poleyns and collar.

"He's dying," Timofei Stepanovich said behind me.

As if he had heard these words, the Pavlik took two convulsive breaths, as if he were gathering his courage, and died.

"We won't have long to wait for our visitors now," a patrolman said confidently. "We found a pair of binoculars up there. So they've been watching us. As sure as eggs, the whole band is sitting down somewhere, working through the Book of Fury. That's a couple of hours, three at most—they'll arrive well warmed up in time for night…"

"Comrades, librarians," said the Kolontayskite Veretenov, running up to us. "A few minutes…"

"Alexei Vladimirovich, let's go. Latokhin wants to see us," said the Vologda librarian Golenishchev, adjusting his steel breast plate, worn over a leather trench coat, and striding off towards the illuminated pole with the Book. I followed him.

The improvised council of war was in full spate.

"We form up in a phalanx," said Zarubin. "How many of us are there? Eighty-four?" He thought for a moment, calculating. "In eight rows: with three, five, seven, nine, eleven and fifteen men."

"That's not a phalanx, it's a 'pig'," the Penza librarian Akimushkin objected. "That's unpatriotic, old man. And I'm superstitious, too. We don't want to share the fate of the Livonians, do we?"

"The Teutons…"

"Ah, what's the difference? The dog knights."

Kisling knitted his brows and declaimed in a sepulchral voice:

"The first rush of the Germans was appalling, wedging into the Russian ranks and charging straight through with two lines of horse-drawn turrets…"

"Tvardovsky?" asked Tsofin, who hadn't spoken so far.

"D-minus, Yevgeny Davidovich! Sit down! And what does the younger generation think?"

"Simonov?" I suggested.

"That's an A-plus!"

"I don't understand…" Tsofin said with a humorous frown. "How can a teacher of Russian be called Kisling? I mean, Ivanov, Petrov…"

"Even Tsofin, if it comes to that…" Kisling continued acidly, and everyone smiled.

"Colleagues," Golenishchev said in a conciliatory tone of voice. "It's a 'pig' when the enemy attacks, but when it's our own Russian men, it's a 'wedge'. There's no problem here."

"Then the question is closed," said Latokhin. "Has anyone got a sheet of paper? Better if it's squared—that makes it easier to draw. Aha, thank you…"

He took the notebook held out to him by Tsofin.

A minute later I glanced curiously over Latokhin's shoulder. The truncated triangle looked like a plan of a theatre auditorium.

"The first twenty-seven numbers," Latokhin explained, "are my reading room. And you, comrades, form the flanks."

I chose a spot on the right, immediately behind the Kolontayskites. The Vologdaites and Stavropolites took the centre and the final rows of seventeen men consisted of readers from Penza, Kostroma and Voronezh.

"Comrades," said Latokhin as soon as the all the squares had been distributed among the brigades. "Let's quickly run through formation-training, so we won't get under each other's feet if there's an alarm…"

Due credit to them, all the readers played their parts meticulously, without any commotion or jostling. I deliberately walked up onto a mound of clay. From a height the army, bristling with terrifying scythes, pikes, gaffs and hayforks, looked very impressive indeed.

Time after time we assembled and disbanded the wedge, and Latokhin only left us in peace when we could match a record-standard time—thirty seconds in full battle kit.

But in fact we didn't get much rest. Half an hour later the Pavliks made a leisurely appearance at the far side of the quarry.

THE PAVLIKS

THERE REALLY WERE a lot of Pavliks, as many as a hundred white, blood-spattered mummies. It was a grisly sight. While they were still on the slopes they formed up into a bulging crescent moon, with a curve like a sabre, but they didn't seem to be in any hurry to attack.

I focused on my own feelings and noted with satisfaction that there was no fear. The thoughtful Shironinites had hidden me away deep in the formation. On Akimushkin's plan it was square number thirty-one. On the right I was covered by Tanya, with Timofei Stepanovich, Marat Andreyevich and Fyodor Ogloblin beyond her—I had no reason to doubt those people's fighting credentials. On my left were the Vologda readers, and to reach me the enemy would have to smash his way through the barrier of their mighty axes—in the world outside the Vologdaites were a worker's cooperative of lumberjacks. And the very sight of twenty-plus Kolontaysk "goalkeepers" was enough to reassure me that the enemy would never crush their ranks.

In imitation of the "Japanese style", Kisling's warriors had assembled armoured mantles out of thin steel pipes attached together like straw mats. Zarubin's "Cossacks" looked tremendous dressed in light chainmail vests over red kaftans and carrying poleaxes and sabres. The turbans and kaftans of Tsofin's warriors added a touch of menacing oriental colour to the ranks.

Akimushkin's readers from Penza had come to the battle with their traditional gaffs, scythes and clubs welded out of water pipes or battle-axes decorated with pommels in the form of brass taps. Their padded work jackets, covered with blocks of plastic foam glued to their surfaces, looked like life-jackets. Akimushkin had said the greatest danger was not from stabbing and slashing, but from crushing blows.

It looked as if he was mistaken in his choice of armour. When the Pavliks came closer, I couldn't see any hammers or axes. What I had taken from a distance to be spears looked exactly like rifles with attached bayonets.

I shook the imperturbable Vologda librarian Golenishchev hard by the shoulder.

"What about the general agreement not to use firearms?"

The answer ran through my head: "That's right, the Pavliks don't come under the council. All they want is to get their Books back. What do questions of ethics and honour mean to them! Now they'll fire a few salvoes and Latokhin's army will no longer exist." That was the explanation for the Pavliks' invincibility…

"Well, good for Chakhov, he knows what he's doing," Golenishchev replied. His voice was calm and slightly mocking. "Take a closer look, Alexei Vladimirovich. Those aren't rifles. Only the bayonets are genuine."

The Pavliks' guns turned out to be something like crutches— perhaps originally they had been crutches, only now they had bayonets and massive butts faced with metal.

"I've been told," Golenishchev continued, "that in Novosibirsk they dressed up as Kapellites. A psychological assault. Meaning they did a bayonet charge…"

"Well, naturally," said one of the Kolontayskites. "A bullet's a fool, but you can trust a bayonet."

The Pavliks halted as if on command. There were no more than a hundred paces between them and us.

"Marat Andreyevich," I whispered to Dezhnev. "What now? There aren't any seconds, are there?… Who sets the rules in cases like this? Who monitors everything?"

"Why, no one does. It's the two sides in the fight. Look, Latokhin's already on his way with some lads… Now they'll decide how to conduct the battle. The Pavliks already realize they don't have much of an advantage, and they're tired… Maybe our side will offer to buy them off or suggest some other compromise. Latokhin had good reason to gather all these people. To cool the Pavliks down a bit and make them think… I don't want to make any guesses, but I've got a very good feeling about this, Alexei." Marat Andreyevich smiled encouragingly.

The tense minutes passed one after another. We stood there, craning our necks, looking at the group of five Kolontayskites and the group of Pavliks who were discussing our fate.

I heard my name called and then Golenishchev's. He parted the backs of the Kolontayskites and set off to answer the call, straight through the formation. I thought I'd misheard, but my name was passed through the ranks again: "Vyazintsev…"

"But what do they want Alexei for?" Tanya asked peevishly.

"We'll find out in a moment," said Ogloblin. "I don't like this."

I saw that Kisling, Akimushkin and Tsofin had left their brigades and set off towards the negotiations. Veretenov followed the librarians. When he drew level with them, he confirmed my summons.

"Latokhin is calling for Comrade Vyazintsev…"

"Where to?" Tanya asked cautiously. "Tell him Vyazintsev won't go… Don't go, Alexei!"

"Comrade Veretenov," said Marat Andreyevich. "Let me go instead."

"I don't understand," said Veretenov, confused. "Vyazintsev's the one they want… He's the librarian!"

"There's nothing here to understand!" Tanya said harshly. "*You* go to that Latokhin of yours…"

The Kolontayskites looked at us in amazement.

"Hey, what are you two doing?" I asked quietly. "They've found a problem. I'm sure it's just a standard formality…"

"And what if it isn't?" Ogloblin asked dubiously. "Don't go. Let Latokhin risk his own life, not yours. That's not what we agreed..."

"I won't let you go!" Tanya exclaimed, clinging tightly to my sleeve. "Marat Andreyevich! Come on, tell him!" she said with tears in her eyes.

I felt terribly embarrassed, especially since I'd already made my mark as a panic-monger.

"Marat Andreyevich, please, calm Comrade Miroshnikova down," I said, adjusting my sleeve when it was released, and dashed after Veretenov.

The Pavliks were waiting for a decision. They looked identical, but I assumed that their leader, Semyon Chakhov, was the one in the centre of the group. This man was unarmed, but he was clutching a large bundle of sticky, bloody entrails, with dung flies sitting on the gleaming guts like motionless bronze sparks.

The other negotiators had slings round their necks, and their plastered forearms rested in them like infants in cradles. This was obviously a piece of Aktyubinsk swank, like sticking your hands in your pockets. The white motorcycle helmets on their heads were decorated with artfully applied bandages.

Chakhov had a good grasp of stagecraft. Even his entourage's weapons were eye-catching and memorable. The maces were especially impressive—crude steel wires with clumps of concrete resembling meteorites, studded with broken glass, and forks with scummy deposits of dung on their prongs and deliberately broken handles. The hand of an artist was clear in everything. The weapons, like the Pavliks themselves, made your skin crawl.

Swaying as if he was exhausted, Chakhov wheezed in a low voice:

"We'll wait on one side..." His hands twitched convulsively and he dropped the repulsive bundle. The stage-prop innards unwound and plopped onto the ground. The dung flies didn't take flight—the insects were only scary junk jewellery.

Chakhov walked off and the ribbon of guts crept after him, with the rubbish that immediately stuck to it. I was aware that this was play-acting, but when Chakhov slowly pulled the guts towards him like an anchor chain, I felt a bayonet piercing my belly.

The Kolontayskites exchanged glances with Latokhin and left the librarians on their own.

And then Latokhin said morosely:

"Comrades, I need to consult with you. As I anticipated, the Pavliks don't want a large-scale battle. I tried to resolve the matter by buying them off. Chakhov refused. Then I suggested an honest duel, one on one, with the condition that if he lost, the matter of the Book would be closed, and if I lost, then his library would get the Book. Chakhov says that since six reading rooms have inter-vened for us, it's only logical that I face the music together with my allies, not on my own. In short, he insists on a collective duel, seven against seven... I implored him to limit it to fighters from our reading room—it's only fitting for them to fight for the Book..." Latokhin sighed and shrugged, spreading his hands. "That didn't suit Chakhov. He's definitely a very shrewd and cunning individual, and he understands the lay of the land. I don't know what I should do. I'm waiting for your advice."

"The calculation is simple, elementary," Kisling said with a frown. "If we refuse, there'll be a bloodbath and many lives will be lost..."

"But we were prepared for that," Tsofin said thoughtfully, "the compromise proposed by Chakhov is far from simple. And, to be quite honest, I'm not in great shape..."

My turn to say what I thought came.

"I won't try to hide the fact that I have absolutely no experi-ence. This is only the second time I've taken part in an event like this. Don't think I'm being cowardly, but I might let you down..."

"Come now, Alexei Vladimirovich, don't belittle your abilities," said Golenishchev. "Our scouts reported the jaunty way you cut down the Gorelov librarian Marchenko, and he was no novice..."

"Comrade Latokhin," said Akimushkin, breaking the silence, "you're laying a great responsibility on us. If we mess things up, you'll be left with no Book!"

"I believe in you," Latokhin said with a helpless smile. "Comrades, I'll tell you what I think…" He scratched the back of his head and then said in a flash of inspiration: "You have to understand that it's not a question of physical strength, but… you could call it meta-physical strength. Our cause is just, we shall prevail in any case!"

"But what will the conditions of the duel be?" asked Zarubin.

"The Pavliks are willing to accept the initial rules," said Latokhin, brightening up. "We have an agreed area for the field of battle; anyone can leave it if he wishes, then he's out of bounds and the others continue, and then… it's whoever wins, basically."

"Humane enough, in principle," Zarubin agreed. "OK, lads, I'm for it. A hundred deaths fewer, as they say…"

"I was in agreement right from the start," said Golenishchev.

"Is there any alternative?" Tsofin asked with a bitter laugh.

"I'm the gregarious type," Akimushkin told us. "Vyazintsev and Kisling, what have you decided?"

I nodded, totally overwhelmed by the situation.

Kisling shrugged: "I'm always willing…"

And Golenishchev summed up: "Comrade Latokhin, call Chakhov… We accept his terms."

SEVEN AGAINST SEVEN

I HEARD TANYA burst into tears. Marat Andreyevich scurried between Kisling and Zarubin. Timofei Stepanovich grabbed Latokhin by the sides of his chest, saying something threatening to him. They barely managed to drag the old man off.

Ogloblin came over to me and spoke to Akimushkin and Tsofin.

"I'll just have a few words with Alexei Vladimirovich, all right? Alexei, the most important thing is not to get nervous. Your armour's superb; no one's got anything like it, I've checked—no axe or sword will pierce it, let alone a bayonet… And another thing, it might just help you…" Ogloblin added hastily. "Before a battle I always try to remember a song, best of all from the Great Patriotic War, about heroic death: that immediately puts me in the right mood, it rouses my fighting spirit. Of course, it's not the Book of Fury, but it's still a kind of doping. By the way, Margarita Tikhonovna hinted to me that when you were at her place, you understood all about it…"

This was an unforgivable lapse of memory. I hadn't spent all those hours in Margarita Tikhonovna's home, listening to the voices of Soviet skalds flying out of the black holes of her gramophone records, just to pass the time. I only had a few minutes left, and I had to use them to apply this still-unexplored technique of courage.

Ogloblin waved his hand in farewell and rejoined the ranks. I tightened my grip on the handle of my hammer. Golenishchev was standing just a metre away from me, resolutely clutching his axe, and behind him was Tsofin, who had readied two knives for the duel. The beak of Latokhin's pickaxe glowed dull silver. Akimushkin toyed calmly with his mace, warming up his stiff wrist.

The seven Pavliks facing us also warmed up—smooth, faceless figures who looked like huge white pawns, but with sharp-pointed crutches held at the ready.

"It seems to me at times that soldiers who have not returned from fields of blood were not laid in our earth at all, but turned into white cranes," I started crooning in my mind. "From those distant times until today they have been flying, calling to us. Is this not why so often we fall sadly silently when we gaze up at the sky?" I cautiously examined my own condition—absolutely nothing was happening in my soul. Panicking, I hurried through the next lines. "The weary wedge flies on and on across the sky, flying in the grey mist at day's end, and in that line there is little gap, perhaps a place for me…" But the song dashed from the right hemisphere of my brain into the left one in a mute whine. I thought I must have remembered about this too late, but I stubbornly carried on invoking the spell of avian death: "The day will come when I too shall fly through this grey gloom with a flock of cranes, calling in a bird's voice from the heavens to all I left behind down on the ground…"

Chakhov wound the entrails into a bundle, then suddenly swung back his arm and tossed them in our direction. The Pavliks shot forward like greyhounds, switching places as they ran, and my opponent turned out not to be the warrior I had been preparing myself for. He was almost right beside me when I finally grasped what my job in this duel was. A rush of adrenalin warmed me like a gulp of vodka, my stomach shuddered happily, and I guessed that this was not fear, but deadly fervour.

I saw Golenishchev take a step back to intensify the stroke to come, and his opponent, standing with his back to me, became an ideal target for the hammer. A sharp blow from a bayonet between the shoulder blades only flung me towards my goal. Ogloblin had done a really good job for me—the Belaz tyre tread didn't let me down; it withstood the blow.

I swung the hammer down on the nape of Golenishchev's foe. There was a wooden crack. The next second I felt a cast-metal lightning bolt pierce my boot and run into the ground. A nauseating pain splashed up from my wounded foot into my head and clouded my mind. The butt of a crutch flashed by, scalding my temple, ear and cheekbone with lead. A red jangling drowned my hearing. I fell, and the Pavlik fell on top of me, flinging out his arms. He screamed silently with his mouth pulled inside out, hoisted himself up on his arms and suddenly struck a terrible blow on the bridge of my nose with his forehead—and then the Pavlik's head split open for some reason and a Vologda axe soared up out of it into the sky, like a bird, and the battle ended there…

I had wondered before what it meant "to lose consciousness", picturing it as a state similar to a nightmare or sleep. In actual fact it was much more boring than that. At first I simply didn't exist. Then I appeared, together with the light from the large window, lying on my back with a plaster ceiling extending above me.

I rapidly made sense of the world and immediately felt its first inconvenience: my face was tightly swaddled. I managed to lift my hand with a struggle and saw a drip protruding from my forearm. I was able to touch my face. It felt numb and limp, like a rag.

A man with a moustache, who looked like a veterinary surgeon and an agronomist at the same time, cautiously put my hand back where it should be. He was wearing a white coat and a little doctor's cap.

"Awake are you, biker? Welcome back!"

I realized I had survived, but for some reason I didn't feel any great jubilation. The recent black vacuum didn't seem at all frightening to me.

"Oh, I'll run and tell your family the good news," a concerned female voice suddenly cooed in my ear. "All your relatives have gathered round. Your uncle, your sister and her husband, and your grandfather. They're completely burned out. They didn't sleep all night…" A figure as white as a snowman drifted towards the door, flapping its slippers.

"Righto. And I'll go home, I'm tired," said the man. "Last night your uncle knocked the stuffing out of me, I swear to God. I told him: 'Believe me,' I said, 'I'll try my very best for a colleague and I'll do a great job…'"

"Are you a librarian too?" I asked with half my mouth, my blood running cold at this surprise. The thought that I was paralysed drove out the question of how my Uncle Maxim had "knocked the stuffing" out of him.

"What librarian?" the man asked in sympathetic surprise. "I'm a surgeon. A traumatologist."

"A traumatologist…" I repeated in a mumbled echo.

"You were brought into our hospital last night. Second-degree coma… Don't let that frighten you! In simple terms, it's just a concussion with loss of consciousness for a couple of hours. You went straight into intensive care, and then came here. Your uncle was champing at the bit to operate himself, but I explained to him: 'You can't operate on relatives!' I said, 'Don't you worry about it. We'll do a great job!' So your nose will be just like new; that is, just like the old one—no changes!" He laughed.

"But why doesn't my mouth move?"

"What a droll fellow! You got jabs across half your face. I mean, they gave you anaesthetic. When you were at the dentist's, didn't they ever give you injections of novocaine?"

"Yes… I suppose…"

"You just tell me this… Who goes riding around a building site on a motorbike, and in the middle of the night too?"

"What motorbike?" I asked, just to be on the safe side. But this precaution was superfluous and came too late. I'd already blundered over my librarian uncle, and if the jaunty surgeon was from a hostile clan, my life was hanging by a thread.

"You can fake amnesia somewhere else. Why lie to me? I'm not a traffic cop…"

"I really don't remember…"

And then, to my inexpressible relief, I saw Marat Andreyevich and Tanya. Ogloblin and Timofei Stepanovich were craning their necks round the door.

"What an actor," the doctor said to Dezhnev with a smile. "Do you hear, your nephew here says he's lost his memory…"

"How's that, Antosha?" Marat Andreyevich asked briskly. "You and your comrades decided to hold a rally on a building site, you caught your foot on a steel reinforcement rod that ran straight through you and naturally you went flying off the bike and smacked your head against some planks. And there you have it…"

"Now I remember," I said. "Thanks."

"That's good," the doctor said with a smile. "Well then, you can do your talking and kissing, but only for ten minutes. The patient needs rest…"

The Shironinites perched on my bed like birds. Marat Andreyevich gave me a brief account of the evening's events.

"Alexei, we won. The Kolontayskites kept their book! But if it hadn't been for your heroism, everything could have turned out very differently! Your fearless and self-sacrificing heroism immediately neutralized your opponent and gave us a numerical advantage. He was finished off by Golenishchev, then Tsofin lent a hand and the two of them decided the outcome of the whole duel!"

"If you only knew how proud we are of you!" Ogloblin said fervently.

"Oh, come on," I said, embarrassed. "I just didn't want to die for nothing, without taking anyone with me…"

"Alexei, that *is* heroism," Marat Andreyevich said with conviction. "A feat that even a complex individual like Semyon Chakhov appreciated!"

"If he could see me here," I said, feeling at my gauze-covered face, "he'd take me into his own library. I'm the spitting image of a Pavlik now."

Tanya took my hand and kissed me several times. Timofei Stepanovich sniffed and deftly brushed away a tear, then smiled and reached for his handkerchief.

"Don't say things like that, Alexei!" exclaimed Marat Andreyevich, upset. "Nothing terrible has happened to you. You've got facial contusions. The swelling will go down completely in two or three weeks. Yes, and your auricular cartilage is broken too, but don't worry, it won't affect your hearing, your ear will just be soft. And I think you were really lucky with your foot. The tendons weren't affected. You'll spend another day in bed here, and tomorrow we'll take you home. Everyone's waiting for you!"

"I forgot to ask. What about the others? And Latokhin, is he pleased?"

"We didn't want to upset you…" Marat Andreyevich said and hesitated. "But I think it's best to tell you. Right, comrades? Latokhin died a heroic death. And Zarubin too. Veretenov has replaced Latokhin as the Kolontayskites' leader. They send you their very best wishes and thanks from whole reading room."

"And where are the Pavliks?"

"They left, as they promised. They've gone to Kazakhstan," said Ogloblin, waving his hand in the direction that he assumed was south. "All seven of their men were killed. They didn't beg for mercy; they fought to the bitter end. And by the way," he said with a smile, "the help from the council arrived yesterday… Punctually late."

Timofei Stepanovich snorted contemptuously.

"Missed the boat, as usual…"

"And what happened?"

"Nothing. We politely told them it was all over and done with and in general it's better to serve the mustard when dinner's still on the table, so they cleared off. You're a celebrity for everyone now!"

THE UGLIES

"FIGRUTDIN ANVAR-OGLY GUSEYNOV, Aslan Imanvedi-Ogly Guseynov, Ramazan Rustamovich Dzhabrailov. Rashid Akhmedovich Khaytulayev, Akhmadrasul Khaybulatovich Magomadov, Khasan Panuevich Yusupov…" I ploughed halfway through the list. Millstones started shifting about nauseatingly in my head—the recent concussion still bothered me, especially when I read anything. Conquering the sensation of nausea, I narrowed my eyes and ran over the gaudy string of names and patronymics, like bumps and ruts, to the end of the list: "Iskander Kazbekovich Bachayev, Abdulkhamed Timerbekovich Izmailov, Alvi Bakhayevich Sadulkhadzhiyev."

"Have you taken a look, Comrade Vyazintsev?" the liaison officer asked in a soft voice. My visitor was called Roman Ivanovich Yambykh; he was the one of the orderlies of Kovrov, the deformed observer from the council who had been present at our satisfaction three months previously. I noticed immediately that Yambykh's way of speaking successfully reproduced the menacingly ingratiating manner of his immediate superior.

The liaison officer's appearance was unpleasant—a slimy individual with a wet little forehead that looked as if it had been licked. The middle finger of his right hand was adorned by a blue perforated ring with a little heart in it, and his left forearm bore a green tattoo of a busty violin.

"The final individual on the list, a certain Sadulkhadzhiyev, is an associate of Girei, or Biygireyev, who is the head of an influential criminal organization in the region, with a wide range of activities—from dealing in arms and narcotics to violent robbery, extortion and contract killings. Your dead men met him to discuss, if I might put it this way, the purchase of a licence for appropriating local assets. This is what we know so far."

"You've made a great effort, Roman Ivanovich," I said, handing him back the list. "You remember everyone by name. What other complaints does the council have against the reading room?"

"Don't be sarcastic, Comrade Vyazintsev. We still don't know what the outcome of your vigilante actions will be! And note that this isn't the first time! The flight of the reader Shapiro and the incident with the Gorelov reading room earned you a category "A" reprimand… Haven't you received the council's report yet? They'll send it to you… And straight away—another problem. Possibly even worse than the previous one. Do you really not understand that you have put all of us at risk?"

"Roman Ivanovich, I get the impression that you feel sorry for these Khasbulatovs," said Dezhnev. "We acted in the interests of our common security…"

"Matters of this kind are discussed collectively!" Yambykh retorted. "But you showed once again that you don't give a damn for the council! Am I not right, Comrade Selivanova?"

"Not entirely. First, the individuals who were the source of danger are all dead. Secondly, we did not arouse the slightest suspicion on the part of the authorities or the criminal elements. What more do you want? And thirdly, not even your experts have been able to discover any hidden motive!"

"And they won't, either!" said Timofei Stepanovich, who had remained silent so far.

"Actions are a shout in the mountains; let us wait and see what kind of echo there is. The problem that has arisen is far more serious than it seems at first. First…"—Yambykh smiled venomously at Margarita Tikhonovna—"… the Shironinites attracted the attention of outsiders, and rather aggressive outsiders at that. All this indicates gross violations of the code of secrecy. And permit me to object. Secondly, we have good reason to suspect that the raid on your reading room was prompted by a tip-off. Which means that someone from the outside is trying to penetrate the mystery of the Books. If this information is confirmed, then I am afraid that your reading room will most likely be disbanded."

"The average annual growth of all libraries and reading rooms is two hundred members," Lutsis put in hastily. "More than enough for a minor leak to occur anywhere at all. What has this got to do with us?"

Yambykh nodded.

"Well yes, but *you* have a new librarian… Oho, Comrade Selivanova is ready to kill me!" He laughed with a crackling sound. "Let me repeat, we still don't know what we're talking about here: monstrous bad luck, criminal negligence on the part of the Shironin reading room, or an external conspiracy. Whichever it is, our common security is at stake. Even if formally speaking this has nothing to do with you, there are higher priorities…"

"Does it not seem to you that a certain prejudice can be discerned in this decision of the council?" Margarita Tikhonovna interrupted.

"And does it not surprise you, Comrade Selivanova, that it is precisely the Shironin reading room that finds itself at the epicentre of the problem yet again? Can it really be nothing but malicious fate?" Yambykh asked reproachfully. "I'm not a superstitious man, I'm a pragmatist. Problems pursue those who have deserved them. We are investigating. If there are no consequences from your high-handed behaviour, the business will go no further than a reprimand. I promise that no one intends to persecute you for no good reason. But meanwhile the Shironinites are under house arrest for a few days, and after that we'll see…"

Disaster had descended on us out of the blue a week earlier. Until then everything had been going really well. For six weeks the reading room had been a haven of calm. On 12 July we had returned in triumph from Kolontaysk. A week later my bandages were removed in Marat Andreyevich's hospital. I tried not to show myself outside, feeling shy on account of my appearance. The swellings on my cheekbone and the bridge of my nose stubbornly hung on right until the beginning of August.

Sometimes I looked at myself in the mirror, studying my unfamiliar blue features in alarm. However, the unknown doctor had not deceived me—my nose really did remain as it was before, without any boxer's twists or humps. The foot that had been run through with a bayonet healed up, leaving only a scar that looked like a navel. Marat Andreyevich jokingly called it "the librarian's stigma".

As soon as we got back, I called my parents. The novocaine no longer distorted my speech and I informed them in a cheerful, relaxed voice that I had found a job—running a theatre studio in a local House of Culture. I realized that I would never abandon the Shironinites and I had to prepare my family.

My father took the news calmly; he had anticipated this kind of possibility for a long time, but my mother, on the contrary, started worrying about how I would manage in a strange town, and complained that she couldn't come to see me—Vovka couldn't manage Ivan and Ilyushka on her own. I said that I would be earning decent money and would probably apply for Russian citizenship soon. Then I assured my parents that I would visit them at the very first opportunity.

The Book was still with Margarita Tikhonovna for safekeeping. I had suggested this myself, motivating the request by saying that I found the readers' daily pilgrimages exhausting and I needed complete peace and quiet. The Shironinites didn't argue, but they said that while bed rest did not require a guard, a nurse was necessary. I chose Tanya for this role.

After the events at Kolontaysk I suddenly realized that I had a right to a woman. For the next two weeks Tanya lived with me. For a while I felt rather awkward in Veronika's presence—I really didn't want this powerful girl to feel insulted by my choice. But no matter how closely I watched her, I couldn't spot even a hint of jealousy or resentment in her eyes. I think I made the right choice. Devoted to the reading room and the Book, Veronika had only been concerned for my "male comfort", but Tanya simply loved me…

In short, for a month and a half everything went well. Then suddenly one August evening the phone rang. A slightly embarrassed Margarita Tikhonovna informed me that problems had arisen for the reading room and it was a matter of urgency. She had informed the readers and they were all gathering at my place.

"What exactly has happened, Margarita Tikhonovna?"

"It's too serious for a phone call…"

An hour later the Shironinites were all assembled. Agitated and outraged, Lutsis reported to us on what had happened.

"Yesterday Grisha and I were walking back from Margarita Tikhonovna's place. He had read the Book and I promised to see him home…"

Vyrin had been discharged from the hospital in July. He was making a rapid recovery, although he still needed help. After all, the Book was a powerful emotional upheaval and one of our group always accompanied Grisha on his way back home. This time Denis was with him.

Just outside the entrance to Vyrin's building they had been stopped by two young men who looked as if they came from the Caucasus and had the accent to prove it. These were the Guseynov cousins, Figrutdin Anvar-Ogly and Aslan Imanvedi-Ogly, known by the nickname "the Uglies". Denis had already heard about them.

The older Ugly—Figrutdin—was twenty, and the younger was nineteen. The cousins were still only starting to spread their criminal wings, gradually mastering the simple skills of blackmail and extortion. So far their new gang had only eight members—scraggy and spiteful children of Chechnya and Azerbaijan—and they plied their trade at the lowest level on the outskirts of town, where there were no competitors. After a short time the Uglies and their comrades had subjugated the old people and miserable bottle-collectors in the district and imposed a tax on them. When they grew a bit stronger, the Uglies moved on to the collection points for jars and bottles. When obstinate owners didn't want to pay up, their depots caught fire.

In a long side street outside a small bus station a little market had spontaneously sprung up in the mornings—women from local suburbs brought the surplus from their vegetable plots to sell here. The Uglies set the illegal traders a price for their spots, and if anyone refused to pay they promised to set the cops on them or threatened them with expropriation of their entire stock. The female lawbreakers had no one to complain to, and they agreed to pay the protection money.

The next victims were the private taxi drivers. A threat to burn their cars worked without fail. The people were absolutely terrified of Chechens, and the Uglies had no scruples about exploiting their gang's menacing ethnic profile.

The Uglies first demonstrated their character in a showdown with the gypsies. They suggested dividing up the territory half and half and claimed that their protector, or "roof", was the well-known criminal boss Girei, whom they didn't even know. To avoid a conflict, the gypsies agreed. Half the job was done; now they only had to persuade Girei to take them under his protection.

Securing their status, the Uglies rapidly took control of all the local drug dens, to provide outlets for the future. They were hoping to squeeze the gypsies out at some stage and become the undisputed masters of the suburbs…

"They told us 'the old woman's joint' was being taken over," Lutsis said, continuing his account of the situation. "They said they knew all about us, said they'd been watching Selivanova for a long time. They mentioned Denis's address, and Sasha's…"

"And the worst thing," said Vyrin, "is that they know Alexei's address. They really have been watching us…"

"Let me sum up, comrades," Margarita Tikhonovna concluded. "Absurd as it sounds, some villains have decided that I run a drug den. By the way, today they approached me in person with the same threats. I don't understand anything," she said with a dispirited sigh. "And I used to love the Caucasus so much. I often used to go there on holiday…"

It was quite possible that the Chechens' visit was a subtle provocation, that we were being tested, that someone was trying to set us up. But in such cases the council's machinations never went beyond the bounds of the Gromovian universe, with its own etiquette and rules. The uncontrollable spontaneity of an attack from the outside made it something to be feared. The questions that arose were: who were these intruders; why had they chosen us; and what was the ultimate goal that they were actually pursuing?

We supposed that they had latched onto us through some misunderstanding or annoying set of coincidences that came together in the appearance of ideal bait for bandits. Margarita Tikhonovna had told us there had been whispers among her neighbours before about Selivanova trading in moonshine and telling fortunes for money—all sorts of different people came to her place far too often. The haggard Vyrin and Sukharev with his plastered hand, and I myself, limping and covered in bruises, gave the impression of asocial personalities and provided grounds for gossip. It wouldn't have been too bad, but those words—"We've been watching you for a long time"—determined the Uglies' fate. We couldn't afford to delay.

"Take the wogs out, no messing," Sukharev said simply. "That's the safest thing. They'll never cut loose on their own."

"But how do we do it?" I enquired. "A mass road accident?"

"Too difficult, Alexei," Dezhnev said thoughtfully. "It would be easier to simulate a banal gangland rumble with the gypsies, a knife fight. The gypsies could easily have grudges to settle with the Uglies. They used to run everything, then Girei squeezed them out, and the Uglies are keen to get in with Girei. The cops shouldn't have any doubts. Afterwards Biygireyev can sort things out with the local barons himself if he wants to…"

"I've got an idea," Sukharev suggested. "The lowlifes are always hanging out in the kebab house at the reservoir—you know, the old Village Hut café. They're bound to show up there at the weekend. It's a remote spot; there won't be any witnesses. When the Uglies celebrate, all the normal people leave—they're afraid. No, there won't be any problems with an ambush."

THE VILLAGE HUT

I WAS EXCLUDED from the Shironinites' operation for health
reasons. Vyrin fell under the same edict. Although Denis was
terribly offended, they didn't take him either—our enemies knew
him by sight. For the same reason they had to do without Sukharev's
strong-arm help—he was often at Margarita Tikhonovna's place
and the Uglies could have caught sight of him. Sasha, Denis and I
had to be content with contributing what we could to the theoreti-
cal planning of the ambush.

The Uglies' cars—an old Mazda and an old Opel—were put
under constant surveillance. The Vozglyakovs' motorbike and
Ogloblin's RAF never let the Uglies out of their sight and we
learned all their routes off by heart.

The Village Hut—a summer café on the shore of the Urmut
reservoir—was a dreary, quiet spot: a sandy yard surrounded by
unkempt bushes. The winter pavilion contained a kitchen and a
dozen tables and in the yard there were gazebos with gabled roofs
on log pillars—the village huts from which the café had got its
name. In recent years ownership of the Village Hut had changed
hands often. The present owner had turned it into a kebab house.
Three people worked there—the cook, his assistant and a waitress
who doubled as the cleaner.

The plan was thought through down to the finest detail. An
hour before the Uglies arrived, the staff had to be neutralized.
Kruchina took on the role of cook, support by Ogloblin and Anna
Vozglyakova. Marat Andreyevich and Tanya became a married

couple who happened to drop in when they saw the smoke. Timofei Stepanovich was loitering about outside the hedge, searching for bottles that had been planted in advance. Ievlev was working away with a spade outside the fence, deepening the drain. Especially for the ambush he made ten steel skewers, sharpened the ends himself and added convenient handles, like those on flaying knives. Every possible scenario was worked through for every eventuality, depending on which table our enemies chose to sit at. Who could have known then that this fine-calibrated plan would end in tragedy?…

As soon as the Uglies and their men had got into the cars, of which there were three for some reason—a Mercedes had joined the cavalcade—Sukharev made a call from a public phone in the street to Margarita Tikhonovna, who was sitting by the phone in the first-aid post at the lifeboat station. Svetlana Vozglyakova was on watch outside with the motorcycle. It took her only a few minutes to dash to the Village Hut and pass on the combat alert.

Silent figures in masks crept into the pavilion and tied up the cook, his assistant and the waitress securely. Kruchina, Ogloblin and Anna put on aprons and started preparing for the encounter.

The optimal table was in the central "hut", which was equidistant from all the participants in the ambush. In order to attract our enemies to it, all the other tables were piled high with dirty paper plates and cups covered in grease spots and ketchup. Skewers were placed there in advance.

There turned out to be nine visitors, one more than had been expected. But even this turn of events had been anticipated. The moment they piled into the yard Ogloblin gave them a welcoming smile and lugged a chair over to the central hut. The chortling, guffawing pack seated itself on the benches along the table, four on each side. The ninth member of the Uglies' party was seated at the head of the table. It emerged later that he was Girei's hit man and the Mercedes belonged to him.

The Ugly brothers had not yet been infected with caution. They were satisfied with a genial explanation that the owner was away on business and the previous assistant and waitress had been sacked for negligence, so new ones had been taken on. The older Ugly was then treated to the cook's obsequious assurances that the meat was the very finest-quality lamb.

About twenty metres away, behind the green hedge, a worker was swinging his spade in a ditch. Kruchina apologized for any noise and gloomily blamed the health inspectors for insisting that he deepen the drainage ditch and run it farther away from the yard. A down-and-out darted into the yard and set his eye on an empty bottle; Kruchina hissed at him and the old man meekly withdrew without his booty. Then the industrious cook set to work at the barbecue. Ogloblin brought mineral water, grape juice, lavash, sliced vegetables, green herbs and a spicy aubergine starter. The customers didn't drink alcohol on principle, but they happily smoked suffocating hashish.

Twenty minutes later the kebabs were ready. Kruchina carried five portions to the table, clutching three in a fan shape in his right fist and two in his left hand. Ogloblin walked beside him in his bright apron. Another four huge skewers that looked more like banderillas were protruding from his smoking fists.

A married couple wandered into the yard, but Kruchina immediately shouted at them.

"A private banquet, we're not serving anyone today!" and smiled enchantingly at the hut with the Caucasian party.

The couple loitered on the spot in bewilderment.

Kruchina repeated his message in a severe voice.

"I told you in plain Russian: we're closed!"

Anna, who was clearing the next table, set her rag down and picked up an empty skewer. Ievlev was no longer working in the ditch, but lurking behind the bushes with his spade at the ready.

Kruchina and Ogloblin walked up to the table. All nine men sitting there were gazing at them and looking forward to the food.

Kruchina spoke the key words: "*Bon appétit!*"

Three deadly shafts were thrust simultaneously into the bandit seated at the head of the table. The sharp points of two others protruded from the back of next man, and on his chest fat from the chunks of meat mingled with blood, spreading across the white material of his shirt. Ogloblin ran another two through with skewers. Vaulting over the bushes, Nikolai Tarasovich cut down a fourth man with his spade—the left half of the table died in a matter of seconds. The men on the other side didn't even have time to react. Anna jabbed one of them in the neck with her skewer and Timofei Stepanovich dashed in just in time to crush the back of another man's head with his mace. Marat Andreyevich dispatched the others with criss-cross slashes of his sabre.

But who could have thought that one of the three skewers with which Kruchina attacked would jam against the table, slowing down the other two so that they didn't penetrate deeply enough into the body to end the victim's life. The wounded man was able to whip a pistol out from under his jacket and fire.

Ogloblin fell. Blood gushed out of his head onto the trampled sand in heavy, spasmodic surges. Ievlev swung his spade, severing the hand holding the pistol. Kruchina snarled, driving in the perfidious skewers so hard that the chunks of smoking meat were wodged tight together against the enemy's chest.

Squatting down, Marat Andreyevich turned over Ogloblin, who was already dead.

"Our reverse namesake is dead... Gone to join Larionov..."

"Why did we have to play this stupid game of honour?" Timofei Stepanovich asked the silence that had descended in a bitter voice.

"We ought to have poisoned them," said Anna Vozglyakova. "All their lousy lives weren't worth a single minute of his..."

The operation that began so brilliantly was a disaster. Ogloblin's death cancelled out everything. Timofei Stepanovich and Ievlev carried Ogloblin to the RAF. Marat Andreyevich and Tanya splashed petrol onto the corpses out of a can. A match was struck and the bodies sitting at the table burst into stinking flames. A ragged, blue-flame fringe trembled on the pillars of the little hut.

Our enemies no longer existed, but the reading room had lost another cherished member.

THE CREMATION

S TILL DROWSY, I couldn't tell what had roused me: the phone or the alarm clock. Waking was like coming round after blacking out. I heard steps in the corridor, the gentle clatter of the phone and then Veronika's voice: "Boys, Fyodor Alexandrovich has been killed!"

Suddenly there was a salty taste in my mouth, as if I'd swallowed slimy blood.

Lutsis walked slowly into the room, pale faced. "Ogloblin's had an accident…" he said, bewildered.

Vyrin appeared in the doorway.

"Don't cry, Veronika," he said, glancing back rapidly into the corridor. "Perhaps it's not definite? Perhaps he's just hurt?"

"Marat Andreyevich said he was killed instantly," said Veronika, wiping away a tear. "They've taken him to our place. Now they're all waiting for Alexei, so he can decide what to do…"

Those were bitter minutes for our reading room. Already washed and dressed in his grave clothes, Ogloblin was turning cold on the deceased Maria Antonovna Vozglyakova's metal bed, while we, his comrades, discussed the sacrilegious precautions that required us to act immediately. Ogloblin had to disappear for ever, to vanish without trace and never be found. For decency's sake we spoke of a funeral, but in actual fact we were talking about disposal. Ogloblin could not have a grave.

We took what seats we could find in the Vozglyakovs' small sitting room—some at the table, some on the ancient sofa with a leather back, draped with a tapestry showing deer and the lacy spiderwebs of doilies. Outside it was already dark. The three branches of the ceiling lamp, curved like cows' horns, shed a bony yellow light.

Ogloblin's dog Latka, a decrepit old Alsatian, prowled round the table, breathing in through her black nose the still-imperceptible smell of the corpse and breathing out a pitiful whimpering. Although Anna had lit the small Dutch stove built into the wall, I felt as cold as if I had walked down into a damp limestone basement.

Who could have supposed then that the bullet which shattered Ogloblin's head would strike all the Shironinites in a murderous ricochet? At first the situation seemed clear, although tragic: through some misunderstanding, outsiders who had nothing to do with the Books had set their sights on us. To avoid the bloody events coming to the attention of the council or the militia, we had to dispose of the only clue that betrayed our involvement in the slaughter—Ogloblin's body.

The question was where and how to bury Fyodor. The Vozglyakovs were intending to do it in their own yard, in the shaft of a dried-out well. This idea had to be rejected. The relationship between Ogloblin and Anna was no secret. We understood the eldest Vozglyakova sister's feelings very well, and that only made Marat Andreyevich's justly spoken words even more painful for us.

"Anyuta," he said, "you must have been seen together. It could be anyone—your colleagues at work, or Fyodor's friends. We can't exclude the possibility of someone coming to search your place. And if, God forbid, you come under suspicion, the police will rake through everything here…"

"And what do you suggest?" Anna asked in a faltering voice. "Dissolving Fyodor in acid? Dismembering him and feeding him to the pigs?"

"Don't say that!" said Tanya, putting her arm round her friend's shoulders.

Margarita Tikhonovna didn't participate in the discussion, but sat at one side, remaining silent. The countdown to the deadline that the doctors once set her had begun long ago. She had become thin and drawn, and all the intensity of her will was directed inward, at her organs invaded by metastases. Every time she overcame an attack of pain, she wiped lemon-coloured sweat that looked like pus off her forehead and temples with a crumpled handkerchief. Meeting her eyes just once, I shuddered at that slithering gaze filled with pity and exhausted, powerless love. Looking round at the depleted reading room, Margarita Tikhonovna seemed to see the terrible marks of her own fatal malady on every one of us. There were thirteen of us left…

"I suggest we cremate Fyodor," said Kruchina, getting up from the table. "In my foundry," he explained morosely. "We'll put the body in the cupola. The temperature there is fifteen hundred degrees, everything will burn up without leaving a trace… Well, now, that seems like a beautiful funeral to me," he said and turned away. "Only we have to hurry. The second shift ends soon. If all the cast iron is smelted, they'll stop the cupola. And tomorrow's Sunday—we'd have to wait another day…"

"And how do you imagine doing it?" Timofei Stepanovich asked warily. "There are men in the foundry."

"It's a small section. One cupola's being overhauled, the other's serviced by four pourers and a melter. I'll distract them," Igor Valeryevich reassured us. "I'll find something to talk about."

"What about the charger?" I asked, recalling a word forgotten since the days of my institute practical work.

"There's Uncle Yasha. He's put away his half-litre a long time ago and he's asleep. But the breakers-out will come for the third shift. They'll be sober. We'd better hurry."

"Wait," Timofei Stepanovich persisted. "I can't see how you'll get the body in without being spotted!"

"There's a nursery school on the other of side of our fence. My workers moonlight; they cast graveyard crosses to sell. You know, I don't object. They've got families to feed, they're paid a pittance, and they're not really stealing anything; they make them out of waste… Anyway, they drop the castings over the fence on a rope into that nursery school and pick them up after the shift… So we'll do it the other way round, taking the body into the plant…"

Vyrin looked at his watch.

"Lads, it's three minutes to nine already…"

"Where do you think you're going?" Svetlana asked nervously. "It's night out there!"

"That's right," Veronika put in despairingly. "You're too late!"

"Girls, Annushka, Svetlana, Veronika, my darlings," Tanya sighed agonizingly. "You have to understand that Fyodor's dead; you can't bring him back! And he has to be buried!"

"And another thing…" Igor Valeryevich said and paused for a moment. "I can't take everyone. Three at the most. Otherwise the group will be too noticeable. I'll go in through the checkpoint."

I sensed that the time had come to draw a line under the discussion. Before the sisters could protest I said firmly:

"I agree with Igor Valeryevich. We have to set off immediately. Ievlev, Dezhnev and I will go to the funeral…" The eldest Vozglyakova sister shuddered and lowered her head. "Everyone else has one minute to say goodbye to Fyodor Alexandrovich…"

Ogloblin was carried to the RAF on a blanket. Ievlev took the wheel, with Kruchina beside him to show him the way. I sat by the corpse's head, beside gloomy Marat Andreyevich.

The sad journey took forty minutes. Then the minibus stopped near the nursery school. It was already completely dark and the bushes with branches poking through the hole of the wire-mesh fencing looked like shaggy black shadows rearing up from the ground. We waited until there was no one at all in the street and climbed out of the minibus.

Kruchina whispered: "The last play area on the left. Hide behind the wooden pavilion there. I'll whistle to you." And he strode off towards the plant.

In the distance I heard 'Evenings near Moscow' as rendered by a ragged, drunken choir. The blanket immediately moved back into the RAF. Eventually the group of tipsy companions moved on. Marat Andreyevich and Nikolai Tarasovich lugged Ogloblin out again. The body had stiffened up enough for us to carry him in a vertical position, arm in arm, like a dummy, which made our job a little bit easier. From a distance the standing figure looked like someone who was alive.

We slipped in through the little gate and quickly turned left onto a path. The crunching gravel gave way to soundless asphalt. The wind blew grating sand out of a sandpit with collapsed sides, swings creaked like a ship's rigging. I went first and Dezhnev and Ievlev followed me, carrying their dead burden.

We waited behind the pavilion for the agreed signal. Eventually there was a brief whistle, repeated three times. Ievlev cautiously tumbled Ogloblin over the fence and Kruchina caught him in his arms. Then we scrambled over too.

A long blank wall—Igor Valeryevich said that was the canteen—and clumps of nettles mixed with burdock concealed us on both sides. We crept along the fence behind the shop, the laboratories and the boiler room and came out into an alley that led to the office block. At the entrance there was a massive structure shaped like a hammer and sickle, and the board of honour was attached to the curve of the sickle. Almost immediately I spotted the enamel oval with Igor Valeryevich's face on it. In the photo he was about ten years younger than he was now, with a slightly thinning thatch of tousled hair.

The workshops stretched on one after the other—the assembly shop, the machine shop, the die-forging shop—tall brick buildings looking like aircraft hangars, roofed with duraluminium.

"They've been idle for years," Igor Valeryevich explained. "Our foundry's the only one that's working at full capacity. All those men they let go! There were more than two thousand of them, and now you're lucky if you can find a couple of hundred. Everything's neglected. See those bushes? They used to be trimmed like poodles, and now they've run wild. I remember in the flower beds they used to plant out Lenin in daisies…"

The cast-iron workshop was the last one. For the first few minutes of our journey we could see two black chimneys above the roofs. Smoke was creeping out of one of them in bluish curls.

"That's good," Igor Valeryevich told us encouragingly. "We're not too late."

We stopped at metal gates that were standing open. From a space that we couldn't see yet came clanging and rumbling and the warm, sourish smell of burned earth.

"Wait," said Kruchina and disappeared into the workshop.

"Seryozha, come here!" we heard his voice boom menacingly.

"Greetings to the top brass!" replied a voice from the rumbling depths. "Has something happened?"

"Yes it has!"

I had the feeling that the invisible Seryozha had been grabbed by the sides of his chest.

"I understand everything!" Kruchina roared. "The pay's bad! Inflation! I'm a fucking liberal! But there are some people you just can't talk to nicely! You're like pigs—you shit where you sleep! Didn't I warn you not to get involved with that cocksucker from the trade union! Did I or didn't I? What are you nodding at? Are you aware that Garkusha's going to show up here any time now?"

"What of it?"

"I'll tell you what! They'll press criminal charges! Shat yourself, have you? That's right! That's the healthy body's natural reaction."

"But Igor Valeryevich! We just wanted to do everything right! To tell the truth!"

"A dick's sprouted where the truth used to be!"

"But Igor Valeryevich! Seryozha pleaded tearfully. "I won't do it again! I'll eat dirt!"

"You'll eat shit! For breakfast, lunch and afternoon tea! Get into that lab now! And not a sound out of you! Until I call you!"

A minute later Kruchina stuck his head out and whispered to us.

"Bring Fyodor in…"

We walked in under the smoky, gloomy vaults. The floor in the workshop seemed to be made of earth, its firm bed only showing through here and there in fragments of cast-iron slabs. The two black columns of the cupolas towered right up to the ceiling, with the lattice-work terraces of the charging platforms attached to them. Below them lay ten moulds retaining the imprint of a cross—a graveyard of emptiness tipped over onto its back.

Igor Valeryevich cast a glance at some doors in the distance, behind which the production shift had probably hidden, and gestured for us to hurry. Dezhnev and Ievlev lugged Ogloblin over to a cupola. The steep, almost vertical steps were too narrow for two men and Ievlev carried the body up to the charging platform on his own. We climbed up after him. The blazing, rectangular charging hole of the furnace breathed out a stifling heat. The seething magma droned; it was so piercingly bright that it hurt our eyes.

"Will it definitely work?" Marat Andreyevich whispered. "What if the cupola gets plugged, they dismantle it brick by brick and find some bones or a skull?"

"Impossible. He'll burn up instantly."

Dezhnev and I supported Ogloblin by the legs while Ievlev and Kruchina guided him. The body dived in through the charging hole and disappeared into the flames. The blast of heat that it raised splashed into our blazing faces. There was a smell of scorched rags and red-hot frying pans.

"What now?" Marat Andreyevich asked with a dry throat. "Do we go?"

"What for?" Igor Valeryevich asked in surprise. "Now we have to pour the iron. I'll go and call those knuckleheads…"

They soon came back. Walking at the front was the melter Seryozha, a man about thirty years old with a ruddy, womanish face. The four lanky pourers tramped along raggedly behind him, swaying like feather grass.

Seryozha wiped his crimson forehead with his sleeve and said resentfully:

"I don't really understand it, Igor Valeryevich. Why am I last in line?"

He'd realized that the danger had passed and was venting his injured feelings. Noticing us, he nodded cautiously in greeting and looked at Kruchina.

"They're with me," his boss said.

"Ah…" said Seryozha, meekly accepting the explanation.

As he walked past some sacks dumped against the wall, he suddenly leaned down to one of them and shouted.

"Uncle Yasha, come on, get up! You're fucked now! Know what you've done? Get up, I said!"

The sack jumped up and turned out to be a dishevelled little man

"What's up?"

"I'll tell you! You slept through charging time!"

The rudely roused Uncle Yasha fluttered his coal-black eyelashes and tumbled back down onto the floor.

"And now what?"

"I'll tell you that too. You've frozen the second cupola! I've called in the boss—see? Now how are you going to break out the scum? With your prick? They'll put you in jail!"

Uncle Yasha wrinkled up his forehead pitifully, as if he was going to cry. He looked about fifty, but his little drunkard's face had remained childish, like a midget's.

"All right, Uncle Yasha, I was only joking," said Seryozha, abruptly breaking off his fun and heading for the cupola.

Uncle Yasha blinked helplessly and tumbled back onto the sacks, certain that the cruel joke was something he'd seen in an alcoholic dream.

Meanwhile Seryozha had picked up a gaff and walked up to the tapping spout.

"I'm expropriating one ladle from you…" Kruchina warned him.

Seryozha was flabbergasted.

"But that's… We've got the moulds set up for crosses!"

"That's fine then. I'll just take one cross."

"That… Well… I don't know…" Seryozha drawled. "We've got an order…"

"Seryozha, what's wrong with you? Have you forgotten the meaning of fear?"

"Take them all if you like, Igor Valeryevich!" the tapper retorted furiously. Swearing soundlessly, he jammed the gaff into the tapping hole. Orange and white metal poured out of the hole in the clay and along the trough. The pourers picked up the ladle by its welded handles and carried it towards the moulding frame. The second pair immediately took their place at the trough.

The tenth ladle turned out to be the last one, and it was poured by Kruchina and Ievlev. I guessed that in Igor Valeryevich's scheme this was the ladle in which Ogloblin's burned-up remains symbolically rested. The casting was a multi-purpose embodiment of the cross, the coffin, the deceased and the grave.

We huddled round the cooling mould with Ogloblin in it like an honour guard and stood there until almost three in the morning. Finally Igor Valeryevich carefully extracted the still warm cross from the moulding frame and broke off the channel metal himself. The mould had obviously not been made very precisely—there were gas cavities on the back of the cross—but that didn't really matter. Our dead comrade was back with us again. Staunch and unbending in life, in death he has become iron, I thought with solemn pride.

*

At dawn we arrived back at the Vozglyakovs' place. The heavy cross was thrust into the earth under the crooked old apple tree in the yard, so that Anna could visit Ogloblin's grave at any moment.

Then Sukharev drove the RAF to the reservoir—with Ogloblin's death the minibus had ceased to belong to our reading room. At a secluded spot on the shoreline Sasha stuck fishing rods in the ground and laid out some simple snacks on a newspaper, with an empty half-litre bottle of vodka. If the militia started searching for Ogloblin after his disappearance, when they found the deserted site, the abandoned RAF and the rods, they would think the hapless fisherman had wandered into the water when he was drunk and drowned.

QUARANTINE

T HE ANNIHILATION of the Uglies' gang didn't cause a big
sensation in the town. The massacre near Urmut was mentioned twice in the faceless news on the local TV channel, somewhere between "the Khokhlakov family wish their dear mum a
happy birthday, good health and every happiness" and a homespun
advertisement for the Paradise furniture store. They said: "gangland killings", "the staff of the café were not harmed" and "the
investigation is continuing".

We learned that we hadn't got away scot-free with the operation from the librarian Burkin. The council was holding a session
in Izhevsk, and Burkin had gone there to arrange some business
of his own. It came as a complete surprise to him to hear a report
by a member of Shulga's clan about the events at Urmut. It was
discussed prosaically, without any pathos, with the flat assertion
that the Shironin reading room had carried out an unsanctioned
"clean-up" without warning anybody about it. Someone in the
presidium remembered that Burkin had given us help in the satisfaction, and he was forced to sign a pledge of non-disclosure. Vasily
Andreyevich was very alarmed by all this. He sensed danger and,
in defiance of the law, warned us.

It was too late to guess how our misfortunes had been discovered. Lutsis suggested that there could have been a spy among the
down-and-outs whom the Uglies fleeced, and he could have reported
to Shulga. We had to forestall any possible penalties and report
the incident with the Uglies to the regional prefect, Tereshnikov,

presenting events in the most favourable light. We prudently didn't inform the council that Ogloblin had been killed. The last thing we wanted was inspectors and checks.

At first glance this move—the repentant guilty head that the sword does not hew—worked perfectly. We could not be accused of criminal concealment of the facts. The members of the council shrugged the matter off and muttered that we were obliged to inform them before the "clean-up" at the reservoir, not afterwards. It went no further than that. But unfortunately we had relaxed prematurely.

Yambykh showed up for what seemed like a trifling inspection. And on the next day, positively bursting with his own sense of importance, he declared that the reading room was under house arrest. The problem, which at first hadn't even existed for the council, had suddenly in the space of a single day been inflated to the menacing proportions of a tribunal. And the most tragic thing about it was that the reader Ogloblin, who had disappeared like a little grain of sand in the sea of the world's life, threatened to become a millstone round the necks of all the Shironinites. It was too late now to report what had happened to him; all we could do was hope that our inspectors wouldn't notice he was missing.

Yambykh's people scoured the town for a few days, trying to dig up dirt on us, but apparently they didn't find anything. We didn't want to provoke Shulga's liaison officer unnecessarily and tried to comply with his absurd order not to leave our homes. During this period Yambykh contacted us twice.

Finally we heard from him a third time. "Comrade Vyazintsev!" his voice shouted down phone in shrill, triumphant fervour. "I have important information for you. Get the whole reading room together this evening!" I couldn't tell what the cunning liaison officer was working up to. Probably Yambykh had sniffed something out and now he was trying to call our bluff with this general meeting. Then we would have to explain where our reader Ogloblin had got to. "Roman Ivanovich," I suggested cautiously, "perhaps we don't need to disturb everyone? Why don't I just call Selivanova and Dezhnev? They're our most senior and respected readers…"

Yambykh didn't argue and set the meeting for seven that evening.

"When you get right down to it," I reassured myself for the rest of the day, "why would he want to count us? He can only know about the Shironin reading room from hearsay. Even if he has been shown a group photograph of the reading room, he's hardly likely to have remembered every Shironinite's face." That was what I thought. "Yambykh is only here to find out why the Caucasian bandits latched onto us."

It was that evening when the prickly hospital word "quarantine" was first heard.

"To ensure the objectivity of our review," Yambykh explained sparsely. "By the way, do you have mobile phones in the reading room?"

"Where would we get them, if I may ask?" Margarita Tikhonovna said with lofty indignation.

"Oh, come on… This is the year 2000," said Yambykh, pulling a wry face. "A mobile stopped being a luxury item ages ago…"

"…and became an adjunct of moderate prosperity," Margarita Tikhonovna concluded. "Something that we cannot boast of, I'm afraid. But what's the problem, Comrade Yambykh? Do you need a cell phone urgently?"

"Not at all," said Yambykh, waving the question aside. "The first requirement of quarantine is a total information blackout."

"Meaning what?" Marat Andreyevich asked cautiously.

"We insist that all your reading room's external contacts be cut off for the duration of the review!"

"Do we have to have our phones at home disconnected?" Margarita Tikhonovna asked.

"Unfortunately that's no solution. The entire reading room is ordered to leave the town."

"And where are we to go?"

"A place where you will be isolated. That's what we have to agree on."

"Listen, Roman Ivanovich," I put in. "This is overkill. We have no intention of hindering your work. Why isolate us? We're not jaundice cases…" I smiled, but Yambykh remained sullen and intent.

"Shironinites, stop pretending the purpose of the quarantine isn't clear to you! Do you think we have no idea who warned you about the inspection? Eh, Comrade Selivanova?"

"I simply can't imagine what you mean!" Margarita Tikhonovna said with an imperturbable shrug.

"Drop all the play-acting," Yambykh said wearily. "You understand perfectly well."

A chilly breath of leaf-fall August wind set the curtains fluttering. Yambykh slapped the greasy locks flung up by the draught back down against the nape of his neck. Even the wide-open window was no help against the suffocating smell of sweat seeping out of the short sleeves of his shirt.

"But can't you manage without quarantine?" I asked, trying to coax the liaison officer, but I ran up against the reverse reaction.

"What's bothering you? The fact that you won't be able to swap your secrets?" Yambykh asked with a pointed glance at me. "In that case the question that arises is what about and who with. What will you tell me to report to the council?"

"What secrets, Roman Ivanovich? You imagine plots and conspiracies everywhere. It's damned inconvenient. Our comrades have to go to work."

"Take unpaid leave. You're not children, you'll have to cope. And anyway it's only for two weeks."

"Listen," said Margarita Tikhonovna, refusing to give in. "I'm an old woman, and I'm not in good health. What if I become unwell?"

"It seems that Comrade Selivanova has failed to understand the seriousness of the moment," Yambykh declared in surprise. "The fate of your reading room depends on the result of my investigation! Is that clear at least?"

"Without medical help I can die!"

"You should have thought about that sooner, and not gone organizing massacres before complaining about your health."

"They've given a toady authority," Margarita Tikhonovna exclaimed in a voice trembling with fury. "And he rolls around in it like a dog in shit!"

"We'll pretend I haven't taken offence," said Yambykh, staring indifferently out of the window.

"Roman Ivanovich," I said, grasping at a new idea. "Let us just move out to the country. Some of our readers have a private house outside the town. It's a remote spot with no phone, perfectly suited for quarantine..."

Still looking off to the side, Yambykh tapped out a confused march on the table with his fingers.

"All right," he said after pondering affectedly for a while. "I'll accommodate your request. You can make the move tomorrow. The requirements are the same: all outside contacts and travel are prohibited. I urge you wholeheartedly to act responsibly, or the consequences could be disastrous." He picked up a matchbox from the table, hooked out a match with his nail and clenched it in his teeth, like a cigarette.

"A day's not long enough," I said immediately. "Give us at least until the end of the week."

"What's the problem?" Twisting his grinning mouth, Yambykh poked between his samovar-like crowns with the match.

Margarita Tikhonovna turned away squeamishly.

"It's a bothersome business, Comrade Yambykh," I said, haggling. "Arranging leave, packing things, buying in enough food, organizing transport..."

"You used to have a minibus, if my memory serves me right..."

While I was feverishly trying to think what line to spin him, such as: we sold the RAF to pay our debts and cover our reader

Vyrin's medical costs… Yambykh fortunately forestalled my cumbersome lies.

"OK, I'll give you two days. But no more."

He wrote down the Vozglyakovs' address and said goodbye, promising to visit us.

SCREWED

T HE DAYS PASSED anxiously and uneasily. Although we put a brave face on things, we were in a despondent mood. Things were only going from bad to worse, as if after Ogloblin's death the entire Shironin reading room had been buried under his iron cross.

Of course, everyone understood why the council had taken such severe measures against us. Not only did they know about Burkin's secret assistance, but they had also foreseen his noble and imprudent act, and then exploited it to the maximum. Burkin had damaged himself, and we had been placed under lock and key out of considerations of higher security.

No one talked about our quarantine. On the contrary, we tried to imagine that our imprisonment was a holiday at a country dacha.

The Vozglyakovs' little farmstead lay two kilometres from the nearest village. It was surrounded on all side by a silence that was only stitched along the edge by the clattering of district suburban trains.

The small house proved to be a hospitable refuge. The sisters, Margarita Tikhonovna and Tanya occupied two rooms. Anna whispered furtively to me that she would give Tanya and me a separate little room under the roof, but, to be honest, I found the idea of such open cohabitation embarrassing—it looked too provocative. We gave the little room to Vyrin—it had a hard trestle bed that was perfect for his injured back. We put a couch in the inner porch, where Timofei Stepanovich took up residence; just enough space was left for a camp bed as well, and Marat Andreyevich slept on that.

Kruchina, Ievlev and Sukharev slept in the bathroom, and Lutsis and I spent the night in the hayloft. Anna gave us quilted jackets and the late Maria Antonovna's thick woollen coat—the nights were already cold.

The Vozglyakovs' property was dilapidated and in need of repair, so there was plenty of work for everyone. We strengthened the posts of the lean-to shed for the motorbike, reset the corrugated asbestos on the roof, mended the porch, painted the shutters, straightened up the fence and replaced the rotten shelves in the bathroom with new ones. At one time the Vozglyakovs had kept two cows, but after Maria Antonovna's death the cattle were sold. The only animals apart from dogs were undemanding chickens. We transformed the former cowshed into a woodshed, and in a couple of days Ievlev and Lutsis had crammed it with firewood right up to the roof. Tanya and the sisters whitewashed the cellar and Margarita Tikhonovna boiled up plum jam in a large copper basin.

By the end of a week everything in the house had been transformed and we had only leisure time left. In the evening the reading room divided up into groups according to interests. Timofei Stepanovich ceremoniously pulled tiny barrels out of a canvas bag, calling out the numbers in a ringing voice, and Margarita Tikhonovna, Anna, Svetlana and Veronika covered the matching numbers on lotto cards with buttons. The atmosphere at their table was impeccably childish.

Grisha tipped a chess set with some pieces missing out of its folding board, made draughts out of tar and white bread and played passionate sessions of Russian giveaway with Sukharev. A short distance away Dezhnev, Ievlev and Lutsis were totally absorbed in a game of preference.

Tanya and I, left alone together, played badminton in the garden. The shuttlecock, which looked like dead sparrow, made a special effort to get stuck in the knotty branches of the contorted apple trees all the time. I stirred the dense foliage with a ski pole, the shuttlecock fell down, and down with it fell an unripe winter apple.

It all came to an end in a single instant, rapidly and almost painlessly, like a bone crunching under local anaesthetic. It was the second week of our confinement; lulled into a false sense of security by the steady-paced country life, we now thought that everything would blow over.

On Friday morning a cavalcade of four cars drove up to the farm. Before the booming iron of the gates had even started rumbling to the blow of a fist, the Moscow watchdog Nayda broke into cacophonous, ragged barking and started circling round her kennel, jangling her long chain. Ogloblin's Latka joined in, twisting her vulpine warbling up into the sky like a corkscrew. And it was only then that the gates pealed like thunder.

We weren't expecting anyone. Somehow we'd forgotten the reason that had brought us all together in the Vozglyakovs' house. I hid the case with the Book under a floorboard, took out my hammer and ran to the gates. Lutsis, Sukharev, Kruchina and Dezhnev had already gathered there.

The formidable Ievlev, holding a cleaving axe out in front of him, asked:

"Who the hell is this?"

"Friends, friends," a familiar voice replied. "Open up!"

We drew back the bolt. Standing there in front of us was Yambykh, with two of his staff behind him, as alike as two cobblestones. A little farther away, craning his neck and smiling tensely, was Tereshnikov, looking like a goose in a white cloth cap with a plastic peak and the faded inscription "Theodosia". I also thought I recognized the passenger loitering beside a car, despite the cumbersome glasses with smoky lenses that covered half his face.

"Vadim Leonidovich!" Tereshnikov called. "Come here, don't be afraid. We won't let anyone hurt you."

And then I remembered—it was Kolesov, the false apartment buyer from the Gorelov reading room.

"May I?" Yambykh asked drily and walked in without waiting for permission. "I hope the dogs are leashed?"

He was followed in by a small retinue of men, who squinted warily at our axes. About ten guards remained outside by the cars.

Tereshnikov turned back casually and shouted to them.

"Wait, we'll be back soon! And don't do anything stupid; we're not in any danger."

After that he anxiously assessed the effect his words had had on the Shironinites.

"Genuine cut-throats," he mumbled, jabbing his thumb back over his shoulder. "Maniacs. They don't even need a Book of Fury…" he muttered, nudging along Kolesov, who moved awkwardly, as if he was hobbled.

They walked along our living corridor and stopped in the middle of the yard. Svetlana, with the kennel chain wound onto her hand, barely managed to restrain Nayda, who reared up on her hind legs. On the other side Anna was hauling on Latka's leash, with the dog raging wildly. Tanya, Veronika, Margarita Tikhonovna and Timofei Stepanovich came running up. The powerful dogs and our weapons created the consoling impression that we had our uninvited guests under armed guard.

"Vadim Leonidovich," asked Sukharev, unable to resist, "how's the health? Are you going to buy the apartment or not?"

Timofei Stepanovich tutted admiringly and exclaimed:

"Alive, you louse!"

Kolesov shuddered painfully and looked down at his shoes as he said:

"Comrade Tereshnikov, I would very much like to leave this place as soon as possible."

"You'll leave, all right. But only after you do your job!" Yambykh interrupted him, and then turned to me.

"All your readers are here, right?"

I nodded, with a foreboding of disaster.

Yambykh rubbed his dry, rustling palms together like a fly.

"Well, and what do you say?" he asked Kolesov.

"Come along, Vadim Leonidovich, don't be so timid," Tereshnikov encouraged him.

Kolesov counted us with brief, fearful glances.

"There's one missing. The driver."

I felt the blood rush to my cheeks. My temples flared up treacherously and started running with sweat.

"Well, well…" Yambykh smirked. "Would you by any chance happen to remember the driver's name?"

Vadim Leonidovich hesitated, then briskly pushed back the collar of his jacket and reached into the pocket.

"Fyodor Alexandrovich Ogloblin," he read from a piece of paper, "born 1956… Now can I go?"

"Go on, go on," Yambykh said. "Comrade Tereshnikov, you go with him. And I'll have a separate little talk with the Shironinites here."

"Will you be long?" Tereshnikov asked, backing away towards the exit. Kolesov retreated with him step by step.

"We'll see…" said Yambykh, smiling at our disconcerted faces. "Well then, where have you hidden this reader of yours? Have you eaten him?"

"We haven't hidden him anywhere," said Margarita Tikhonovna. "Comrade Ogloblin is here with us… It's just that we were irritated by the presence of those clowns…" She pointed to the gate that had clanged shut behind Tereshnikov.

"Don't play games with me! What sort of bullshit is this?" said Yambykh, flying into a rage.

"Ogloblin's here," Margarita Tikhonovna confirmed, "but he can't come to us."

"Why? Is he sick? Wounded?"

"I'll explain everything to you in a moment. Let's go," she said, beckoning to me. "It's just over here, in the garden."

The bewildered Yambykh and his companions followed her. I realized what she was going to show them. We walked over to the cross under the apple tree.

"There," said Margarita Tikhonovna, pointing.

"Aha, so he's dead, after all!" said Yambykh, sighing in relief. "God be praised for that!" And then, slightly embarrassed, he added. "I mean, it clarifies the case. So this is his grave then?"

"Not exactly. There isn't any grave. Only the cross!"

Yambykh was triumphant.

"And why did you conceal his death from us right from the very beginning?"

"We didn't wish to alarm the council once again," I said. "It seemed to us that Ogloblin's death was exclusively the reading room's problem…"

"What happened to him then?"

"He was killed. Shot by gangsters…"

"The same ones who took such a keen interest in us…"

How much all this resembled a rout in chess, with the solitary king fleeing from square to escape an enraged hostile queen.

"You say they shot him," Yambykh said with a sigh. "Sad, very sad… I have one other piece of bad news. We'll have to exhume the body."

"Not possible," I said hastily. "The body was cremated immediately."

"So you're saying what's under the ground is an urn? And we don't know whose ashes are in it? Neat…"

"There aren't any ashes either," Kruchina said with quiet menace. "There couldn't be. Our comrade was cremated in my foundry shop…"

"In a foundry shop…" Yambykh repeated in a mocking echo. "Cremated… Now let me tell you what really happened. He ran off, this Ogloblin of yours!" Yambykh snapped. "He ran off! And there wasn't any shooting. The reader Ogloblin fled from you for the same reasons that Shapiro did! And to cover it up you blew away ten gangsters from the Caucasus so that you could write off yet another traitor afterwards. Ah, but then…"—he suddenly softened his tone of voice and spoke in an almost friendly manner—"…it is possible that I could be mistaken on one point. I admit there is the possibility that the fugitive Ogloblin fingered you to the gang…"

It was pointless to object or argue. The Shironin reading room was screwed on all points.

"Well, thank you for your attention," said Yambykh, breaking into a foul smile. "As they say, the show's over…"

A MEDITATION
ON STALIN CHINAWARE

Y AMBYKH AND HIS MEN went on their way, leaving us to await the council's decision. Our prospects seemed dismal in the extreme: violation of the code of secrecy, the flight of a reader, concealment of facts representing a threat to common security, an unsanctioned operation to eliminate probable witnesses—all this was more than enough to add up to another "A" sanction, with the confiscation of the Book and the disbandment of the reading room already waiting in the wings.

The council was taking its time. They were in no hurry to deliver a verdict; they had the Shironin reading room in their pocket anyway. It was just a matter of timing the delivery of the fatal blow.

Our quarantine didn't end with our return to town; instead it assumed different and disquieting forms. Margarita Tikhonovna spent days on the phone, trying to get through to our reading-room neighbours. In a week and a half the world around us had become extinct. There was no response from Burkin's reading room and Simonyan's also remained silent. No one answered the phone in Kolontaysk. A call to Tereshnikov was answered by a polite little patter: "Hello, you have reached number…"

We were becalmed in lethargy. The people around me behaved as if they had suddenly discovered they had been happily dead for a long time already. That was when I started feeling the same fear and unease as I had during my first days in the Shironin reading room.

Nothing else—neither anger, nor fear, nor even despair—would have had such a depressing effect on me as the shroud of pale, bleak, monkish asceticism that was spread over the reading room. Faces became strange, like the photographs on tombstones. Calmly spoken words sounded like a requiem mass, everyone bared their teeth in beatific, martyred smiles that made me want to lash them across the face to rouse them from their trance. They read the Book more frequently than ever, as if they wanted to blot out real life with the apocryphal bookish phantom as rapidly as possible.

Marat Andreyevich became severe and withdrawn. Lutsis and Kruchina were unrecognizable. Some unearthly fire had scorched them from within and now eternal icon lamps glittered in their dilated pupils. This otherworldly solemnity even distanced Tanya from me. Dead before her time, she already made love differently, from a distance, as if she had been sprinkled with earth.

In this ambulatory graveyard the only person to remain alive and emotionally responsive was the terminally ill Margarita Tikhonovna. I had been certain that she would be affected more than the others by this state of suicidally rhapsodic fatalism. On the contrary, she became gentler and more warm-hearted.

"Don't avoid the others, Alexei," Margarita Tikhonovna admonished me meekly. "Zombies indeed! What an idea!" she snorted. "What makes you think they're preparing to die? Quite the contrary, they want to get in as much reading as possible for the future…" Margarita Tikhonovna sighed. "But is it really possible to store up looking and listening? The flesh of memories is ephemeral. They are weak creatures; in order to survive they need to attach themselves to a strong body. The Book of Memory is the best possible donor—a powerful, unfailing generator of a happy past, a paradise regained. Feeble human memory cannot possibly keep up with such a vast, complex mechanism. You realize that yourself!"

"Margarita Tikhonovna, I'm not disputing the merits of this phenomenon, but essentially it's a mirage."

"A fine mirage!" she laughed. "One that's better than the original! How many times have you read the Book? Four? Well, then… But our boys and girls know it off by heart! You still have only your own natural past, but they have two pasts, and one of them is genuinely beautiful. That's what they're clinging to. Only there's a catch: to prevent the past from fading, you have to nurture it constantly, that is, to read the Book. Losing it means losing for ever the ability to immerse yourself in the happiness of the past—not merely recalling it, but reliving it anew, without any loss of sensual immediacy. That is worth so much. The others are all going through a kind of psychological test: are they prepared to die for the Book?…"

I plucked up my courage.

"Margarita Tikhonovna, please don't take this the wrong way. I'm going to be absolutely frank with you. Of course, the Book is very important, but I don't feel that I'm ready to go all the way with it… I mean, it seems to me that if push comes to shove, I can get by without the Book. Very probably I am mistaken, in fact I am almost certainly mistaken, but I don't have any time to come to terms with myself. And I'm tired of the responsibility. I want to be alone…"

Margarita Tikhonovna remained compassionately silent. I was glad that she wasn't surprised or offended. The next morning I passed the Book on to Lutsis for safekeeping, saying that my place wasn't safe. The Shironinites didn't actually require any explanations; my requests were carried out unquestioningly. The entire membership of the reading room took the Book to Lutsis's apartment. Proud of the trust that had been placed in him, he promised to guard it like the apple of his eye.

After a week of solitude I realized despairingly that I didn't have the slightest desire to lead the brigade of condemned men that was called the Shironin reading room. But neither could I abandon these people to the whim of fate. Something had changed in me for ever, and treacherous thoughts of flight stumbled into the bear trap of scaling shame at the very first steps. I sat there, tormented by pity, duty and panic, sipping sour, bitter coffee from my cup and squashing cigarette ends in the ashtray one after another, while hour after hour a sluggish September fly butted stubbornly at the window pane.

On the seventh day the doorbell rang. I pressed my eye to the peephole. The round lens stretched a bulky, elderly woman out into an idiotic tadpole. Her gauzy headscarf had slipped to the back of her head, revealing a parting in her grey hair, and she had a plump bag hanging from her shoulder over an unbuttoned knitted cardigan. The woman was holding a small package in her hands. After waiting for a minute, she extracted another viscous, lingering trill from the bell.

Naturally I didn't intend to open up. Who knew why this creature had come here and whether she had an invisible helper nestling down by the door with a nifty little knife?

The woman trilled on the bell again, swore in frustration and set about the neighbours. At the third attempt she was lucky. An old voice responded: "Who's there?"

"Galina Ivanovna, it's me—Valya!" the woman with the bag shouted. "There's a parcel for your neighbour and he's not in. Can I leave it with you?"

An old woman in a tattered dressing gown appeared.

"Oh, hello, Valechka, hello. And there I was thinking you'd already brought my pension or something… What kind of parcel is it?" she asked, reaching out curiously for the package.

"Will you take it then?" the postwoman asked. "Oh, thank you… I crawled all the way up here to you on the fifth floor; my legs have all swollen up and the black veins have come up." She lifted up her long skirt and showed off her affliction. "I can hardly even walk…"

She took out the receipt while the old woman gasped in sympathy.

"Sign here… What's the new neighbour like?"

"Young…" said the old woman, taking aim with the pencil. "Says he's the nephew…" She nodded significantly. "He brings people round too…"

"They say as the old one was murdered," the postwoman said indifferently.

"That's right. His boozy friends knifed him," said the old woman, scratching at the receipt. "Almost a year ago…"

It didn't look like a trap. I grasped the razor in my left hand and opened the door slightly, without taking it off the chain. If anyone tried to squeeze though the gap, I would have slashed them across the eyes with the razor, and then kicked the body back out.

The women looked round.

"Oh, you're awake!" the postwoman exclaimed, delighted for some reason. "Good morning!"

"Hello," I said, yawning widely just to be on the safe side.

"There's a little parcel for you. I was just asking Galina Ivanovna here…"—she pointed to the old woman—"…if she would give it to her neighbour."

The postwoman looked at the package, then at me. "Alexei Vladimirovich Vyazintsev?"

"Yes. Shall I show you my passport?"

"Why would I need that now?" The postwoman handed me the package and the receipt.

In the kitchen I studied the light package carefully. The mysterious sender was called "V.G." All that was left of the effaced surname was its impersonal, unisex ending "…nko". I strained my memory to recall someone with the initials "V.G." and a Ukrainian surname (some Sayenko or other), but I couldn't. The address, written in ink on the pale-brown wrapping paper, had also been blurred by water. The purple streaks seemed to bear the marks of fingers, or perhaps large drops of rain.

With some trepidation I tore the wrapping open and saw a book. The author's name and title were stamped into the faded sky-blue cover in a severe typeface: "D. Gromov" and below that: "A Meditation on Stalin Chinaware".

A fake! Someone had planted a copy on me. Cold, sticky sweat trickled down my back—the council's crack special troops were already creeping over the walls, their steel-tipped boots not even touching the steps. Another minute and the door would cave in. Rapid, silent men would tumble the traitor to the floor and secure his arms; stern sergeants would enter into their report the confiscation of an illegal forgery—they have unmasked a copyist! Now nothing can save the Shironin reading room and its ill-starred librarian...

I caught my breath and examined the book more closely: *A Meditation on Stalin Chinaware*, Radyansky Pismennik, 1956. The lemon-yellow pages covered with ginger freckles looked untouched. The print was strangely raised. The tip of my finger could feel every word set in the swollen lettering.

I studied the title page. Editor: V. Vilkova—Design Editor: V. Burgunker—Technical Editor: E. Makarova. The cloth spine had an aroma of decrepit paper and stale medicines—a cracked, desiccated bookshelf. The stifling dust numbed my nostrils slightly. An insert with a title in capitals had been pasted to the end sheet: "ERRATA: P. 96, line 9 up. Printed 'away'. Should read 'way'. P. 167, line 6 down. Printed 'glories'. Should read 'glorious'."

The phantom clatter of the enforcers' boots faded somewhat. This couldn't be yet another attempted entrapment by the council, I realized with piercing clarity. The fever heat of conjecture squeezed my head in a tight band. *A Meditation on Stalin Chinaware*—I knew the titles of all the Books in the Gromov world, but not this one. What I was holding in my hands was not a fake at all, but the Gromov Book that everyone was searching for, the renowned Book of Meaning...

My first feverish impulse was to summon all the Shironinites immediately. This find held the promise of wondrous blessing. There was no doubt that the unique Book could be used to buy off the council once and for all and demand the restoration of our immunity in perpetuity!

Halfway to the phone, my rapturous impetus evaporated completely and I turned back into the room. I was trembling in nervous agitation. I was only three hours from the truth. The person who sent me the Book had already been the trailblazer. But who knew about him and what was his Meaning worth?

I was swept away by the presentiment of being chosen. It wasn't clear how long the Book would remain in the Shironin reading room. I had to seize the moment. I didn't think about whether the consequences of reading the Book alone might be disastrous. It took me a long time to still my visual tremors, and my eyes kept slipping off the line I was reading. I gulped down two glasses of cold water. Things went better with chilled innards.

Meditation was written in lyrical, celebratory style, abounding in internal monologues that were rhymed, like prose poems. A former front-line soldier, the Red Director Shcherbakov dreams of restoring production at an old chinaware factory ruined during the war. An incurable romantic, full of the ideals of Pavel Korchagin, he believes that the factory he raises up will supply high-class tableware to the workers of the entire world. He is a simple, honest man. His affected severity conceals a soul that is compassionate and attentive to people's needs and is capable of forgiving anything except cowardice and betrayal.

The senior engineer Berezhnoi is written as a polemical counterpoint to Shcherbakov's image. He has behind him the difficult experience of evacuating factories to the east. He's a professional, and what attracts him in the reconstruction of the factory is the purely technical aspect. Berezhnoi is very far from being a dreamer; he is calculating and pragmatic. He is often right in a merely formal sense. For instance, by compromising on facilities and conveniences in the workers' housing estate, Berezhnoi frees up more funds from the budget for construction, but Shcherbakov judiciously tells him that it is wrong to forget about comforts in the lives of the workers who will man the factory. Berezhnoi finds out that in Moscow the attitude to the project is negative. He immediately retreats and writes a backdated report about the pointlessness of renovating the factory. But Shcherbakov is willing "to go on trial if need be" in order to prove that the project is valid. Shcherbakov's enthusiasm triumphs in Moscow. In addition to all this, a personal conflict flares up between Shcherbakov and Berezhnoi. Berezhnoi falls in love with same girl as the director, and when he discovers that Katya has no feelings for him, he immediately hands in his resignation. Meanwhile, the construction work continues. Close by, the workers' housing estate is growing, and the cultural life is already boisterous...

At a meeting the young design artist Gordeyev suggests producing a dinner service decorated with an image of Stalin. Everyone fervently supports the idea. And then the triumphant moment arrives when the artist removes the hot firing capsule with the new tableware from the muffle furnace. He joyfully carries the fired cups with Stalin's image on them into the office. He is greeted with happy smiles by Shcherbakov, Katya and the new head engineer Velikanov...

Before evening came I had finished reading and prepared myself for a revelation. The alarm clock ticked loudly in tense anticipation, but nothing miraculous was happening to me. I diligently drove all sorts of mental dross out of my mind, so that it wouldn't cramp the space prepared for Meaning. Minute after minute I maintained this void, until, drop by drop, bitter disappointment seeped in and filled it.

I reluctantly admitted that the Book hadn't worked, although I thought I had read attentively, without being distracted by the artistic aspect of Meditation. Perhaps the Book had a concealed inner defect or a lost page, otherwise why had it been sent to our reading room? I scrupulously checked the page numbers—all the pages were there. There remained the faint possibility that I had been careless and missed a line or a paragraph somewhere.

I got up off the bed, moving ponderously, as if a ton of lead had been poured into me. Behind my keen disappointment, somewhere on the outskirts of my mind, a phrase that seemed absurd to me suddenly took shape: "Unsleeping Psalter".

THE SEARCH FOR MEANING

"Is that all?" Margarita Ivanovna asked. "Nothing else, apart from this 'Unsleeping Psalter'?"

For an entire hour she had gazed, mesmerized, at the Book, never once taking her eyes off it and all the while cautiously stroking its cover with trembling fingers.

I called Margarita Tikhonovna almost immediately after the failed reading and told her that a certain V.G. had sent me a package with "curious contents" and that I needed her confidential advice urgently.

We quite often spent time together on our own, so Margarita Tikhonovna wasn't surprised by my request. After complaining briefly that she was tired, she came.

As was only to be expected, she was ecstatic at the sight of the Book.

"Alexei, I had a presentiment that something wonderful was going to happen soon!" she exclaimed. "I never doubted the chosen status of our reading room! Do you understand what has happened? The very rarest, the most essential Book has been found, and it has chosen us, or rather you, Alexei! This is no coincidence—this is the grand scheme of destiny!"

Strangely enough, Margarita Tikhonovna was not in the least concerned about how the Book had come into my hands.

"The name and address are probably fictitious," she explained. "And the people who sent you the Book are dead."

"Why?"

"They guessed that they would be killed soon and didn't want this Meaning to disappear, but they couldn't hand it over to the aggressors either... There have been rumours before that a rare Book had found its way into our region, but there was no way to verify them. To force the Book to the surface, a total purge of all the reading rooms was required. And, as you see, the plan was successful."

"On the contrary," I protested. "We have the Book now."

"But you yourself said only a minute ago that a Book of Meaning is enough to buy off the council," Margarita Tikhonovna remarked judiciously. "They took that into account as well."

"But even so, things don't add up. We would have heard about any battles…"

"Alexei, why do you think the council needed to quarantine us?" Her voice faltered. "We shall never hear of Simonyan's and Burkin's reading rooms again, believe me. And there's no one in Kolontaysk either. We're the only ones left in the region."

I remembered the hospitable Kolontaysk reader Veretenov and the cantankerous, honest through-and-through librarian Burkin, and suddenly had a terrible feeling.

"Maybe they've been quarantined too?"

"I doubt it. Most likely while the Shironinites meekly sat under lock and key, punitive units picked off the undesirable reading rooms one by one. May God grant that I'm mistaken!"

After her initial emotions had settled down, Margarita Tikhonovna examined the Book thoroughly.

"Published in 1956," she said, as if something had dawned on her. "The Twentieth Party Congress—criticism of the cult of personality. It's obvious what happened. The Book was withdrawn from sale; in fact I think it never even went on sale. Gromov made a fatal mistake with his title. But how could he have foreseen that only three short years after Stalin's death the name of the Leader and Teacher would be the worst possible of recommendations?

The fourth Book—that is, the Book of Joy—wasn't written until 1965, when Khrushchev was removed from power. I was always bothered by that break in Gromov's output. Now we have the explanation. In his naivety, Gromov sang the praises of a dead and disgraced leader, and the price he paid was ten years of silence…"

She touched the typographical miracle reverently while I recited the details of my failure from every possible angle. Margarita Tikhonovna herself asked me to do it. She thought that I might simply have failed to notice Meaning or hadn't attached any importance to it.

"It's too large and too complex to splash out all at once," said Margarita Tikhonovna, stubbornly shaking her head. "But Meaning seeks a way to embodiment, it clads itself in minimal, compact forms, in the embryo of meaning, from which it will later reproduce itself to its full extent! You know yourself that everyone who reads the Book of Memory is given his own individual past. That means that everyone who reads the Book of Meaning will be given his own individual Meaning that only he can understand."

"The phrase 'Unsleeping Psalter' doesn't clarify anything for me! It's an arbitrary oxymoron—wooden water, icy steam!"

"For the time being Meaning is in a dormant state," Margarita Tikhonovna said patiently. "When circumstances are propitious it will unfold immediately, you'll see!"

"Wouldn't it be easier for you to read the Book of Meaning yourself, Margarita Tikhonovna?" I suggested.

She reached out uncertainly to the Book, then suddenly pulled back her hand and smiled guiltily.

"I'm frightened…"

"Take it, Margarita Tikhonovna," I insisted. "You'll manage better than me."

"Do you think so?" She paused and then sighed, as if she had taken a difficult decision. "So be it then!"

"And what about the others?" I asked, touching on a sore point. "We ought to tell them about the Book, or they might be offended…"

"You say that very uncertainly," Margarita Tikhonovna remarked astutely. "You feel that the Shironinites are rather unbalanced at present and any additional upheaval in the reading room can only be harmful. Do I understand you correctly?"

I nodded, although Margarita Tikhonovna's way of putting it didn't precisely correspond to my own feelings.

"Relax, Alexei, we're not concealing the Book—we're saving it. Like an ace of trumps up our sleeve." She carefully wrapped the Meaning in newspaper and put the bundle in the very bottom of her bag.

To be honest, I had expected Margarita Tikhonovna to stay and read it at my place, but when I realized that she getting ready to go, it felt too awkward to object. What difference did it make where the Book was? I would actually feel better without it.

"Are you going?" I asked anyway. "Isn't it risky on your own, Margarita Tikhonovna? Anything could happen."

"Who's interested in a sick old woman like me? And what valuables could I possibly have in my bag except for a hundred roubles, half a loaf of Borodinsky and some Validol?" Margarita Tikhonovna laughed.

"Let see you home…"

"It's not worth the bother, Alexei, I can manage perfectly well without any escorts," Margarita responded hastily. "But you'd better stay home and not stick your nose outside unnecessarily. It's quite possible that the reading room is being watched. If they see you with me, they might think the Book of Memory has been left unguarded…"

"All the more reason not to let you go…"

"What foolish nonsense that is!" For the first time those steely notes appeared in Margarita Tikhonovna's voice, but then they immediately faded away. "All right, since our reading room has money to burn, let's call a taxi to take me home. Hang the expense!"

About fifteen minutes later the female dispatcher called and informed us indifferently that the taxi was waiting outside. Just to be on the safe side I asked her for the number of the car.

It was an unnecessary precaution. It was too light outside and there were too many people about for enemies to spring an ambush. The children's swings gave out long, rusty, creaking groans. Little schoolgirls skipped over squares scratched into the ground, raising tiny white tornados on the trampled earth. The old bench women, including neighbours from my floor, greeted us ceremoniously. I escorted Margarita Tikhonovna to the door of the battered yellow Volga and checked that the number matched the one I had been given—and that there was nobody but the driver in the car. The red-haired driver with one freckled hand dangling out of the window, holding a foul-smelling cigarette butt, didn't arouse my suspicions either. The council wasn't likely to employ such an eye-catching character.

I paid the driver. Margarita Tikhonovna got into the front seat, put her bag on her knees and winked at me in farewell.

When I got back in I phoned Lutsis.

"Hi, Denis," I said cheerfully. "Tell me now, how are you getting on? Is everything all right?"

"Glad to hear your voice," Lutsis replied. "By the way, we were starting to get worried," he added with a hint of reproach. "Margarita Tikhonovna warned us not to bother you unnecessarily. She said you were dealing with some important business…"

"I wonder what that was?"

"Listen, Alexei," Lutsis said apologetically, "only, please, don't get angry. I know Margarita Tikhonovna promised you she wouldn't tell anyone. Don't take offence. It's just that there are no secrets in our reading room. In the final event the move would have had to be brought up for general discussion anyway. But I can tell you in advance that resorting to flight wouldn't solve anything. It would just put the problem off for a while…"

"What flight?" I asked, dumbfounded.

"The one you're planning," Lutsis added impatiently. "I know you only want what's for the best. Any day now they'll expropriate the Book, and we won't be able to put up any resistance, and the most rational thing is to flee… But the council will find us anyway. In a month, or a year. Chelyabinsk is absurd. We're not Old Believers… Don't you agree?"

"I do," I said, catching my breath. "Denis, I wanted to ask you something. Do you happen to know what 'Unsleeping Psalter' means?"

"Say the first word again…"

"Un-sleep-ing," I said, syllable by syllable.

Lutsis thought for a moment. "Well, now, Psalter's clear enough—it's the collection of psalms in the Bible. It's used in the Christian services, like the New Testament. They read the Psalter over the dead… But I don't know that much about religion. Why do you ask?"

"I probably just got something confused."

"So what about a general meeting?"

"I don't know. Maybe we'll have one in a day or two."

"All right…" Lutsis hesitated. "Only don't let Margarita Tikhonovna know I mentioned the move to you, OK?"

"It goes without saying," I promised.

I spent the rest of the evening waiting for a call from Margarita Tikhonovna, but it was Lutsis who called.

"Alexei, you weren't mistaken. The Unsleeping Psalter does exist. Grisha was just here, and he explained it. I even wrote it down. The Psalter is read day after day, year after year, without a break. One reader takes over from another, and it's best if it's done with an overlap, so there's no pause, because the devil can slip in through those pauses, as if they were cracks…"

In an instant some gigantic blood vessel swelled up and burst in my brain. Orange heat flooded my eyes. I just had time to say "Thanks, Denis" before I dropped the phone.

I was woken, lying on the floor, by a heavy ache in the back of my head. I raised myself up on my elbows and plum-coloured blood flowed slowly out of my nose, as if it were oozing out of a liver. Nothingness ebbed away and my head started feeling fresher. The words "Unsleeping Psalter" had acquired a specific meaning.

The Book didn't have Meaning; it had a Design for Meaning. It was like a living, three-dimensional panoramic scene in Palekh—the Soviet icon-painting style on a lacquer background that I knew so well from my childhood, which used gold, lapis lazuli and all the shades of scarlet to depict scenes of peaceful labour: factories draped in fluttering silk, luxuriant fields of wheat and combine harvesters. Workers clutched blacksmiths' hammers in their mighty hands, collective-farm women in turquoise sarafans bound up golden sheathes, cosmonauts in starry helmets and fluttering silver cloaks trod the ground of unexplored planets. A vehement October Revolution Lenin flung out his hand in eddying swirls of red, a soldier and a sailor carried an endless banner as light as if it were chiffon, and above them the cruiser *Aurora* pierced through the clouds like a beam of sunlight...

The Design for Meaning unfolded a sphere of black Palekh above me. The sombre events of past and future catastrophes stood out like red mercury on the polished surface. A blow of devastating force came crashing on the point where the heart of my Soviet Motherland was beating like a tiny red diode, and the slim spider-legs of geographical cracks ran out from that extinguished point. The glittering pipes of borders crumbled, the seams of republics split apart, and the ancient, eternal Enemy immediately appeared on the leaky borders of the new, weakened country. He scattered acoustic buoys into the seas, picking up every movement in the depths, and cast a seine of total control into space. An invisible hand with a diamond glass-cutter deepened the cracks of the fragile federation. The schism of the future, crushing and conclusive, is scheduled for these contours. On the approaches to industrial cities special vaults have already been dug, and the only people who have access to them are arrogant Yankees with haughty faces who maintain close secrecy.

The Enemy has perverted everything he has touched. And now the Baltic, with its drowned-man smell, has pricked up its radio-location station ears, welcomed the Enemy into its barracks and opened its ports to his ships. Asia has concreted over its cotton fields, converting them into landing strips for bombers, and put up greenhouses after the Dutch model—to regale the Danish-American, Austro-Italian and Canadian-Turkish soldiers with soya and potatoes.

At the appointed hour the poisonous vaults will explode. Hostile submarines will sail into the Pacific Ocean and the Northern, Baltic, Barents and Black Seas. Morose soldiers in their grandfathers' German camouflage suits will ride through transmuted Ukraine on growling military vehicles. Chechen warriors will fly in from the direction of Georgia in American helicopters. Predatory web-sailed junks will slide across the chilly waters of the Amur, carrying a piratical assault force to Russian shores. Slit-eyed peddlers, Chinks from Khabarovsk and Blagoveshchensk, will take Chinese-made Kalashnikovs out of their check-pattern bags and subjugate ancient Siberia. Japanese forces will land as the masters on Sakhalin, the Kurils and Kamchatka.

The Enemy cannot be stopped. The red button was ripped out of the black box long ago. But even if it still existed, it wouldn't summon any missiles to life. The wombs of the bunkers have been curetted. A Peace Treaty sawed the heavy missiles into pieces long ago. Planes will not take off, atomic submarines will not be launched from their docks. The army's electronic equipment was murdered long ago by the effects of baleful hostile signals. No one will be saved.

But there is a special, secret man with mastery of the occult Heptateuch. He knows that while the Seven Books are read one after another without a break the terrible Enemy is helpless. The country is securely protected by an invisible dome, a wonder-working veil, an impenetrable vault, stronger than anything else on earth, for it is supported by unshakeable pillars—kind Memory, proud Endurance, heartfelt Joy, mighty Strength, holy Power, noble Fury and the great Design.

A vista of countless years upon years unfolded before my eyes. In a little room with velvet curtains on the windows a man sits at a simple office desk. A marble lamp with a green shade pours electric brilliance onto open pages. No one enters the room and no one leaves it. We see the reader from behind, his hunched shoulders, his inclined head in a trembling diadem of light.

He who reads the Books knows no weariness or sleep. Death has no power over him, because his heroic labour is greater than death. This reader is the perennial Custodian of the Motherland. He stands his watch in the expanses of the universe. His labour is eternal. The country under his protection is indestructible.

Such was the Design of the Books.

THE FLIGHT

THE NEXT DAY Dezhnev, extremely alarmed, told me that Margarita Tikhonovna wasn't answering her phone. Taking Sukharev along to help, we rushed round to her apartment, but no one opened the door to us. God only knows all the thoughts that ran through my head while Sukharev dexterously and silently broke open the lock on the door. I was already reproaching myself, because Margarita Tikhonovna, exhausted by her terrible illness, had died, overwhelmed by the stress of reading the Book of Meaning.

My worst fears were not confirmed. The apartment was simply empty. I would have thought that Margarita Tikhonovna had never reached home, if not for one strange fact that roused serious suspicions. Some elusive change had taken place in the little room that served as both sitting room and bedroom. At first I couldn't spot which item had abandoned its long-accustomed place. I probed the room with my eyes. Protruding from the wall above the bed was an empty nail, with a rectangle of emptiness below it. Standing on the dinner table, leaning against the carafe on the brass tray was a photograph of Margarita Tikhonovna when she was still young—a portrait in a wooden frame. In this black-and-white snapshot she bore a certain resemblance to the actress Lyudmila Tselikovskaya. Cutting across the firm neck and the dimpled smile, like a crude slash from an anatomist's scalpel, was an inscription: "To Alexei, as a keepsake".

I picked up the portrait and was overwhelmed by a sense of unbearably bitter loss. Of course, I regretted the loss of the Book of Meaning too, but only in a material sense—it could certainly have been used to raise an incredible sum of money in the Gromov world. Its Great Design of heroic self-sacrifice and individual immortality seemed more like hell to me. More than that, I even suspected that the Book's appearance had been prompted by the similar disenchantment of its previous owners. But there was no longer anyone with whom I could share these thoughts.

Marat Andreyevich muttered in a bewildered voice.

"At least I haven't found her passport. So not all is lost. We'll wait…"

We left the deserted apartment and Sukharev neatly removed all traces of a break-in.

I repent that I didn't have the courage to tell the Shironinites the truth about the Book of Meaning, especially after my visit to the taxi dispatcher's office. The order that Margarita Tikhonovna and I placed was in their records. The red-headed driver made no attempt to hide and told me the disheartening details. He remembered his elderly passenger very well. She really did call in first at 21 Kontorskaya Street, where she asked the driver to wait and soon came out with a small suitcase. Her second and final destination was the railway station.

I forced myself to think that Margarita Tikhonovna was alive and acting for the good of the reading room.

The waiting dragged on for the whole of the next day, but without either sight or sound of Margarita Tikhonovna. By evening the feeble hopes of her return had faded completely.

I calmed the Shironinites and cheered them up as well as I could. But every cloud has a silver lining. The jarring shock roused them from their fatal, listless torpor.

At the meeting, which was held at Lutsis's apartment, the Shironinites voted unanimously for flight. In light of recent events, this appeared to be Margarita Tikhonovna's dying bequest. Feverish preparations began. Everything had to be done quietly, inconspicuously and as rapidly as possible. Items that had any value at all had to be sold. No one thought about making a profit. Everybody clubbed together to buy a capacious trailer, and the essential tools, tinned food and clothing were purchased.

On the night before we fled we paid another visit to the deserted apartment on Kontorskaya Street. I wanted to collect the photograph that Margarita Tikhonovna had given me.

The moment we stepped out of the entrance on the way back, I suddenly sensed that we were being watched, and froze warily. The experienced Sukharev immediately lowered his hand into a bag of tools, took out a claw hammer and handed it to me, while he took a short crow bar and a screwdriver. Nikolai Tarasovich, waiting for us beside the Niva, had clearly also sensed that something was wrong—he was holding a weighty sledgehammer. Lutsis had hidden behind the car.

The bushes growing in an impenetrable wall along the ground floor suddenly trembled, as if from the wind, and two male figures stepped out onto the path.

The first man took a few uncertain steps towards us.

"Have you come from Margarita Tikhonovna's?" he asked in a nervous voice that also sounded desperate to me.

"Perhaps we have…" I replied, playing for time while Denis crept up on the strangers from the rear.

"Then she's home?" the man asked joyfully. "God, we've been keeping watch all day and all night!" he moved towards me confidently, as if he hadn't noticed Nikolai Tarasovich.

Lutsis silently emerged behind the strangers' back and readied his axe.

"And why are you watching Comrade Selivanova?" I asked pointedly.

"You're Vyazintsev, Alexei. Maxim Danilovich's nephew," the man said in a confident voice. "Don't you remember me?" He stepped into slanting light of a street lamp.

I had definitely seen that thin, haggard face with the long crooked nose before.

"You must remember!" the man exclaimed bitterly. "My name's Garshenin. I'm from Zhanna Grigoryevna Simonyan's reading room. And this," he said, pointing to his companion, a stocky, blond-haired man with a boatswain's beard, "is another of our readers, Yevgeny Ozerov. After your satisfaction I..."—he faltered, trying to find the words—"...visited Margarita Tikhonovna. It's the only address we know, so we came here. We haven't got anywhere else to go."

Then I recognized him.

"But of course! They broke your arms that time. Dmitry... er..."

"...Olegovich," the man prompted me eagerly.

"Why didn't you tell us your name straight away?" asked Sukharev, giving Garshenin a friendly slap on the shoulder. "Nikolai Tarasovich," he said impatiently to Ievlev, "put that hammer down, will you? These are our people..."

It was from Garshenin that we learned the whole terrible truth of the last few weeks. How Burkin's reading room caved in to threats at the regional meeting and agreed to pay tribute to the council for the right to use its own Book of Memory—the so-called branch library arrangement—and a document was signed in confirmation. Burkin was counting on this to save his people from certain death. Simonyan categorically rejected all the council's proposals and attempted to leave the meeting. The stubborn librarian's way was blocked by the guards. It wasn't clear who started the fight that immediately became a massacre. Burkin attempted unsuccessfully to halt the bloodshed and was mown down by the indiscriminately swinging axes of Lagudov's and Shulga's warriors.

Caught in a trap, Simonyan's reading room made a desperate attempt to break out. Five readers managed to break through the enemy line, but only Garshenin and Ozerov escaped pursuit. Now they were outlaws, and every library or reading room was obliged to turn them in.

The fugitives made for Kolontaysk, but the new librarian Veretenov's reading room had disappeared. Garshenin and Ozerov discovered the well-concealed traces of recent carnage. Only one of the Kolontayskites had survived—Sergei Dzyuba. He had been buried while unconscious in a common grave at the bottom of an abandoned foundation pit. Dzyuba was lucky that the disposal had not been carried out by the council's professional gravediggers— they always inspected the bodies carefully and no witnesses were ever left alive.

Dzyuba told us how the reading room was lured out of the town by the regional prefect Tereshnikov, but the executioner's part had been played by quite different people—the Pavliks had secretly returned to Kolontaysk. The council also let the vengeful Chakhov have Voronezh, Penza, Kostroma and Stavropol to buy him off.

The basic policy of the large clans was obvious—to use someone else to break down the regional reading rooms, without formally violating the Neverbino convention on immunity. The calculation was simple: some of the recalcitrant reading rooms would be wiped out by Chakhov, which would serve them right—certainly the Pavliks would get another Book of Memory or even a Book of Endurance, but that was no great loss—and some of the librarians, seeing the lamentable outcome of independence, would voluntarily relinquish ownership of their Book and pay membership dues to the council.

Probably a similar humane sentence in the form of a library subscription was being readied for the Shironin reading room. But was it worth waiting for it? Especially since our Niva and the motorbike had unexpectedly been augmented by the Kolontaysk reading room's bus, in which Dzyuba, Garshenin and Ozerov had arrived. It was a genuine salvation for them to find a new reading room; we had completely solved all our transport problems, and the collective had been augmented by three seasoned fighters.

Our impressive convoy set out at dawn.

THE VILLAGE SOVIET

AFTER THE REGIONAL CENTRE we turned into a forest. The tall crowns of the trees locked together over the bus and branches brushed its sloping roof like rustling twig brooms. After half an hour a gap suddenly appeared at the end of the gloom. The trees parted. We shot out of the forest thickets and the sky opened up above us, lofty and colourless, with smoky streaks. The bus bounced and rattled over the deep potholes, and it was easy to guess what kind of sludge the clayey ground was transformed into during prolonged periods of heavy rain. Only Ievlev's Niva would get through here then, but fortunately the regional centre, with its shops, post office and hospital, was only about twenty kilometres away.

Immediately after the forest there was a meadow that had run wild, overgrown with tall grass and dry thistles, a line of black fences with gates in them, and village houses covered in patches of ancient blue moss.

We stopped outside the largest building in the abandoned village. Apparently during its best years it had accommodated the village soviet or some such institution. The traces of an administrative sign were visible on the wall beside the door, and there was a bracket for a flag hanging beside it. Unlike the peasant houses, the single-storey structure had been built with architectural pretensions—after the style of a poor landowner's manor house. There were small false columns at the entrance. The broad porch expanded into a skirt of stone steps. Little green tress had taken root in the cracks in the mossy foundations. The peeling shutters and door had been carelessly nailed shut. Not far from this village soviet was the bristling straw roof of a long, low, log-built shed with one wall missing—a former barn or storehouse.

Inside the building the air was musty and stifling. Grey clumps of spiderwebs hung everywhere, like yarn spun by old women. The previous occupants had not left any furniture behind. Here and there on the ceiling and walls the damp plaster had come away, and in places the planks of the floor were green with mildew. Ievlev stamped his foot and a half-rotten board immediately snapped. Garshenin and Kruchina climbed up into the attic to patch the holes in the roof before evening.

The building had two stoves—a large Russian stove that ran right through two rooms and a smaller Dutch stove. The stoves were very dirty, but looked in good condition. Anna scraped a bucket of ash out of each of them and checked the draught with a piece of burning newspaper. The smoke was safely drawn up into the chimney.

The village no longer had any electricity. Outside the building a transformer cabinet was hanging on a post with its open door creaking. Vyrin and Sukharev immediately set about it with their tools.

Timofei Stepanovich promptly took charge of the new boys Ozerov and Dzyuba and instructed them to clear up the yard.

Dezhnev, Lutsis and I walked round the local area. There was deathly silence everywhere, but I was haunted by the feeling that someone was studying us with suspicious, hostile eyes from the broken windows. The process of decay was still going on: everything was falling apart, creaking, collapsing, dripping, clanking, crumbling into dust. Looking at all this desolation I felt a melancholy uncertainty welling up inside me: was it really possible to build a life here?

We looked through all twelve of the village houses. People had left the village a long time ago and taken almost everything that was useful with them. The only things freely available in abundance were planks, old sheets of corrugated fibre cement and leaky rain barrels.

There was no water in the black shafts of the wells, and down below they were clogged with greasy pond scum. Just outside the village, beside the ruins of the church, the old graveyard had rotted away almost completely.

While we were walking round the village, the women tidied up the village soviet building as well as they could, sweeping out the years of accumulated dust and removing the cobwebs. They dumped all the old lumber, leaves and rubbish in a ravine. Anna managed to light the stove—the whole place needed to be thoroughly warmed to get rid of the mould that had colonized it.

The first night, spent in the bus, was bleak and uncomfortable. The future looked as desolate as ever. I couldn't get to sleep because of nagging rheumatic pains in my foot. The cold and discomfort had set the obstinate bayonet wound aching. I tossed about, listening to the sounds of the night. Long, lingering howls, dreary and despondent, came from the forest and our dogs replied with peals of melancholy barking.

During the night the dank gloom became bloated with moisture; even my hair turned wet and sticky. Every rag in the bus was heavy with dampness.

After a bad night's sleep Lutsis said morosely:

"Why did we ever come out here into the back of beyond? We should have stayed in town…"

"Uhu, they'd have snuffed the lot of us there," Igor Valeryevich objected in a hoarse voice.

"We did right to leave. Even dying's better in the country," Timofei Stepanovich explained ambiguously.

In the morning there was thick mist. When the sun rose, the mist melted away, lingering in the forest clearings. A damp exudation swirled above the wet earth. The hollows were filled with clammy, stagnant humidity and the sweet smell of thick, withering grass. We seemed to see the high, colourless sky through a layer of turbid water and the wind swirled around light streaks of autumn fog. During the day we explored the boundaries of our settlement. To the north and east the forest was impenetrable. The trees grew close together and with every springy step we could sense below our feet a half-metre layer of foliage that had fallen over countless years: your foot could sink into it right up to the knee, unless it struck an invisible root. Beside the meadow close to the forest there were broad weeping birches, bowing their yellow caps almost down to the ground.

In the slope to the west there was a deep ravine with steep sides. Following its bed, choked with briars and burdock, we unexpectedly came out at a river lying between slippery clay banks. The murky, chilly, reddish water carried leaf litter and scraps of birch bark. There were blackened branches rotting in the swampy shallows and skeletal tree trunks lodged in the grey sand.

To the south the hills bristled with prickly spruce. Ancient knotty roots protruded from the crumbly slopes and sometimes we came across large white boulders. We walked along a depression cluttered with fallen trees as far as the brick wall that curved round the back yard of our village soviet. The village was hemmed in by forest on all sides.

We gradually rendered our new home livable. There was a sharp smell of wood glue, paint and varnish in the air. Sukharev, Kruchina, Ievlev and Garshenin knocked together trestle beds, a broad dining table and long benches. I also mastered the carpenter's art little by little and made a spacious kennel for shaggy Nayda. Doddery Latka spent the night in the inner porch.

Thanks to the women's efforts the house started looking a bit smarter. The floorboards were decorated with mats and runners. Curtains fluttered at the windows which still had no glass.

The whole of the next week was devoted to fortifying our homestead. The village soviet that had given us refuge was partly surrounded by a two-metre-high brick wall and low iron railings, like the ones round graves. We took apart the six nearest log houses and used the logs to construct a stout stockade that took in the house and the farm shed standing nearby, which could serve as a garage for the Niva and the motorbike after it was repaired.

The cold wind grew stronger every day and by nightfall the stars were overlaid with hoar frost. We had to prepare for winter and lay in provisions. There were no problems with heating—there was enough firewood for the next few years; the rotten village was our woodpile.

There were still some unbroken windows in the village huts, so Nikolai Tarasovich didn't even have to go into town for new glass. We weren't able to repair the transformer. During the evening readings we had to light candles and kerosene lamps. For next year we were thinking of acquiring a portable diesel generator and already had a place in the yard in mind for the fuel tank.

But we were never to spend the winter there.

The first uninvited visitors were spotted by Timofei Stepanovich. In the morning the old man took a basket and went looking for mushrooms. One day he came running back to us with alarming news—there was a suspicious-looking character wandering along the edge of the forest. It was a mystery what a solitary individual who didn't look like a hunter or a mushroom picker could be doing in these desolate parts. He had a camera or binoculars dangling over his canvas raincoat.

I can't say that we were particularly alarmed by the news. It could be anyone walking in the forest in the early morning. Timofei Stepanovich had probably seen a harmless urbanite, a photographic tourist who wanted to take picturesque shots of rural decay. We didn't have any time for anxiety; every corner of our homestead required attention and repair.

That night we heard dull, rhythmical knocking and scraping noises from the direction of the forest road. In the morning, after making their round of the local area, Sukharev and Kruchina reported that the road had been blocked with fallen trees. It was clear at a glance that the stout oaks had not been felled by the forces of nature, but by the saw and the axe.

We were seriously dismayed by the nocturnal lumberjacks' efforts. Any planned widening of the road could only mean that our isolated existence would come to an end one day and people would appear here. And it was disquieting that the mysterious woodcutters had worked at night and had not dragged the trees to the side of the road. It was still too soon to draw conclusions about definite danger, but the fact remained that the trunks had cut off the way out to the regional centre.

I limited my response to setting up twenty-four-hour patrols. For the whole day and the next night we listened in case the work in the forest was resumed. Nothing of the sort happened. We wanted to believe that the strangers had appeared by chance and now they had disappeared for ever.

The idea that the council might have tracked us down was voiced at lunch by Dezhnev. First a deathly silence descended, and then the reproaches came thick and fast: was it even worth leaving town if we had to scram again after only a month?

"This is going to go on for ever, until they drive us to the ends of the earth," Kruchina said indignantly.

He was supported by the Vozglyakov sisters, who were missing their abandoned farmstead.

"I think you should meet your destiny face to face, and not run away from it," Anna said morosely. "Isn't that right, girls?" Svetlana and Veronika nodded uncertainly.

Timofei Stepanovich changed the balance of the situation slightly.

"What's the point of getting all worked up about it? If they've spotted us, we've got a great chance to die with honour. You don't need all the comforts of home for that, do you?"

"Well, in all honesty, I'm not planning to join the stiffs just yet," Sukharev said cheerfully. "That wouldn't be very interesting.

You've invented a problem!" he snorted. "We just hop in the bus, and then they can whistle for us—search the whole country if they like. 'There's nothing I like better than wandering the wide world with my frie-iends!'" he sang.

"I'd prefer a life on the road anyway," Vyrin said pensively. "That's even more interesting. You spend the night in the open fields. Baked potatoes, singing to a guitar... And you can always find somewhere to earn a bit of money."

"Why not," said Ievlev, scratching energetically at the back of his head, as broad as a spade. "I like that. Install a cooker in the bus, set up sleeping places, get the glass tinted. Make it into a motorized home."

"Sure, step on the gas and away we go," Lutsis grumbled. "They've already closed off the road over there. We'll have to leave on foot, travelling light. Or on rafts."

"Alarmists have the upper hand in our reading room now," said Tanya. "Margarita Tikhonovna would be ashamed of some of you..."

"What's alarmism got to do with it?" Anna asked with frown. "I say there's no point in trembling over you own precious skin."

"And no one is trembling," Marat Andreyevich put in gently. "It's just that this entire conversation is extremely impolite to Alexei..."

The Vozglyakov sisters and Kruchina lowered their eyes.

They were all waiting for what I would say.

"I was the initiator of the move, and I still think it was the right thing to do. It was what Margarita Tikhonovna was planning. I think all this alarm is rather premature. There's no way the council could know which way we went, unless someone in the reading room passed on that information to them..."

For some reason everyone looked at Ozerov, who had turned sullen. He was the only one of the three new readers at the supper table—Garshenin and Dzyuba were on watch. Ozerov was delicately avoiding joining in the conversation. Sensing the Shironinites' eyes on him, he turned crimson and got up from the table so abruptly that the bench shifted back with a piercing screech, taking the substantial Vozglyakov sisters with it.

"What, do you…" Ozerov glowered and clenched his fists. "Do you think that we would snitch to the council?"

"Calm down, Zhenya," Marat Andreyevich immediately intervened. "How could you even think such a thing?"

"It's not a matter of you at all," Lutsis began. "But Dzyuba… Don't get me wrong, I'm not accusing anyone. But, for instance, the only one I knew well was Latokhin. And I can say for certain that Dzyuba wasn't one of the ten fighters who helped us at the satisfaction."

"That's right," said Sukharev.

"Alexei, Tanya, you were there at Kolontaysk," said Vyrin. "Try hard to remember!"

"Why, there were almost a hundred people there," Timofei Stepanovich said with a frown. "Almost thirty from Kolontaysk alone. And they were wearing ice hockey helmets, you couldn't even see their eyes properly!"

"I remember Veretenov very well," I declared. "We stayed at his house… And Latokhin too, of course… I can't say anything definite about the others…"

"Yes, indeed…" Kruchina said thoughtfully. "A fine little business… And you, Yevgeny, did you know Dzyuba?"

"Not personally," Ozerov said cheerlessly, "but there was a reader with that name. The best thing you can do is ask Garshenin. He had more or less close contacts with the Kolontaysk reading room. But wait, how can you suspect Dzyuba? He was wounded!"

"That doesn't mean anything," Anna said dismissively. "Can't we consider the possibility that the real Dzyuba was killed and buried with everyone else, and someone different came with us?"

"This is just crazy," said Ozerov, shaking his head. "We haven't been out of each other's sight! When could he have let the council know where we are now? It's absurd… Are we going to ask to see his passport, then?"

"It doesn't make any difference anyway," said Anna. "If Dzyuba's an informer, he's already done his job. If he isn't, there's nothing to talk about."

"Well, I'm absolutely sure that Dzyuba's not involved at all," said Veronika, collecting up the dirty dishes. "He's a decent guy. He's calm and he hasn't got shifty eyes. Traitors don't behave the way he does. And the council has plenty of spies without him. Maybe someone tailed us on the way and followed us here, Nikolai Tarasovich?"

"I reckon not," said Ievlev. "I was watching; we didn't have a tail."

"Boys and girls," said Marat Andreyevich, slightly embarrassed. "I already regret that I raised the subject… It's much too soon to be sure that the council has found out where we are."

"A council punitive unit wouldn't beat about the bush; they'd just attack," Timofei Stepanovich laughed.

"But in that case, who was it that blocked the road?" Svetlana asked. "And what for?"

"We can't tell," Marat Andreyevich agreed. "So I suggest we clear the obstruction."

"And the sooner the better," Lutsis added.

"Me and Kruchina can do the job in an hour," Nikolai Tarasovich said briskly. "Especially seeing as we've got the Taiga."

"I wouldn't recommend you to use the chainsaw," said Marat Andreyevich. "That rig's too noisy. Take the bucksaw instead."

The dogs started howling.

Garshenin ran in, swinging the door wide open and panting hard.

"Panic stations, everyone," he gasped out. "We've got visitors!"

We went scurrying over to the long shelves where our armour was laid out. The pikes, Anna Vozglyakova's flail and Garshenin's battle scythe were standing in round nests in a low stand.

"What sort of people are they?" I asked quickly, pulling on my heavy armour over my head. The Book of Memory immediately migrated to its case.

"How the hell can we tell, Alexei Vladimirovich?" Garshenin replied, taking hold of his scythe handle reinforced with steel strips. "Five of them. Coming this way. I ran in here the moment we spotted them."

"Only five?" asked Marat Andreyevich, fastening on his sabre. "Not exactly a lot."

"Are they armed?"

"Doesn't look like it. At least, they're not holding anything suspicious in their hands... One has a coil of cable..."

"Repairmen?"

"How would I know?" Garshenin asked in frustration. "It's not written on them. But they're not likely to be repairmen. The best thing they can be is thieves who cut down cables to sell."

"And the worst thing is council spies," Igor Valeryevich continued, wrapping his bayonet in newspaper. "How are they dressed?"

"Normally for the weather. Work jackets, tarpaulin boots. Typical collective-farm style."

"Very suspicious," said Timofei Stepanovich, shaking his head. "No axes, no spades. As sure as eggs is eggs, they've got their little knives tucked away somewhere under their clothes."

"Where did they come from?" I asked, still questioning Garshenin.

"They came out along the road..."

"Did they notice you and Dzyuba?"

"I don't know..."

"And where is Dzyuba?"

"He stayed by the gate."

"We need to close it!" Lutsis exclaimed.

"What for?" asked Anna, dragging her dead mother's battle flail out of the stand. "Let them come in. We'll talk to them and work out what they want."

Nikolai Tarasovich took his sledgehammer down from the shelf.

"If they're just passing by, I wouldn't like to frighten them straight away. Or they'll spread the word afterwards..."

Sukharev thought for a moment and took off his cuirass covered with soldier's belt buckles.

"That's right, why go sounding the alarm too soon?"

"Don't act the fool," Kruchina said harshly. "Just put something on over the top. And take the mace. God helps those who help themselves…"

Vyrin, who had also taken off his jacket, put it back on again and hung the shoulder belt with the sapper's entrenching tools over the top.

We tumbled out into the yard. One side of the gates was open and Dzyuba was standing beside it with his hammer-pick over his shoulder. He waved to us reassuringly.

I looked at the men approaching the village soviet. They had already noticed us. Our guests certainly did look like typical rural residents. They strode confidently onto the yard and took off their caps. Their leader, dressed in a long tarpaulin raincoat reaching down almost to the ground, stepped forward—a scrawny man who looked about forty years old, with straw-blond hair and eyebrows and a moustache weathered to grey.

"Good health to you," he said, screwing up his eyes roguishly. "You know, this isn't the first year we've been walking these parts, and there's been no one living here for a long time, but now it seems there is…" He started and turned round at the bang Dzyuba made as he closed the other half of the gates, using Ogloblin's heavy cross instead of a bolt.

This action clearly made an unfavourable impression on our visitors. They suddenly started shuffling their feet and glancing round rapidly in alarm.

The light-haired one smiled.

"My, my, why do you use a cross to lock yourself in? You must be serious folks. Not Baptists, are you, by any chance? No?"

Timofei Stepanovich, Sukharev, Tanya and the Vozglyakov sisters moved towards the gates. Nayda sat at Veronika's feet, growling deep in her chest. Garshenin, Ozerov, Vyrin and Lutsis hemmed our visitors in from the sides. I stood there, surrounded by Ievlev, Kruchina and Dezhnev. I think we produced an intimidating impression.

"No, we're not Baptists," I said.

"A-a-ah," their leader drawled, as if he was relieved. "That's good… Although if truth be told, it's all the same to us. What's the difference who you are, as long as you're a good man? Isn't that right now?"

Inspired by his own words, he blathered about good people for half a minute, but I'd already spotted his avaricious glance, slipping out from under his pale eyebrows and across the case with the Book that was hanging on my chest. I had a bad feeling and my guts tensed up. Marat Andreyevich was standing beside me and I nudged him gently with my elbow. He turned towards me and said silently, with just his lips: "I see it…"

"So, who are you?" I asked the light-haired man. "What brings you to us?"

"That's… We're a building team. Do you need any repairs done?"

"So far we're managing all right on our own…"

"I get you… But we could give you a hand… And for a good price…"

"Here's a question for you," I said. "Was it you who blocked the road?"

"The road? No, that wasn't us…"

"It's pointless lying!" I exclaimed to startle the stranger into confessing. "We saw you with our own eyes!"

"You did?" he asked, taken aback. "Well, yes, that's right, we did it." He shrugged. "It's a forestry-section requirement. The trees are sick… I just didn't realize what road you meant."

"And why did you leave them lying about? No one can get through now."

"Well, it's not our job to clear them away. We were only told to cut them down…" The foreman glanced round at the gates. "And another thing," he said with an obnoxious grin. "You wouldn't happen to have any hooch to spare, would you?"

"No, we wouldn't."

"We're not asking for it for free. We'd work for it. Don't be shy now. Think about it. In principle, we can work for chow too, right lad?"

"I'm so hungry that I haven't got anywhere to spend the night," Timofei Stepanovich croaked comically.

Nayda suddenly started howling furiously and scrabbling at the stockade with her shaggy paw. I noticed the light-haired man and his companions draw themselves erect.

"Well, then, we'll be going, since there's nothing you need. Open the gates, please."

We looked at Dzyuba. If he tried to pull out the cross acting as a bolt, it meant he was in league with the strangers. I saw Sukharev already preparing to strike with his chain. But Dzyuba completely ignored the request and didn't budge; his heavy brows simply knitted together above his nose in a frown and his fingers tightened their grip on his hammer-pick.

"Listen, guys, come on now," the light-haired man said loudly. "We've really got to go!"

At that very moment our enemies' heads and bodies appeared over the stockade. Before the first one could even throw his leg over the logs he was impaled on the blade of Garshenin's scythe. Dzyuba sank his hammer-pick into the side of the nearest enemy with a crunch.

The light-haired man threw open the flaps of his raincoat and pulled two blunt-nosed butcher's cleavers. His three comrades took out the hatchets and knives that were hidden under their work jackets and threw themselves into the skirmish. However, they lacked the skill to back up their fervour. An abrupt bayonet thrust from Kruchina pierced the belly of one attacker, who collapsed, howling, with his legs pulled up. Nayda growled and clamped her jaws on the fallen man's throat. Dezhnev's sabre flashed and a hand holding an axe dropped onto the sand; the stump flung out a long spray of blood, as if someone had tossed the leftover tea out of a glass. The wounded man was immediately run through by Tanya's rapier and Ozerov's pike.

More and more fighters kept tumbling over the wall. Dzyuba crushed fingers that clung to the top of the stockade with his hammer-pick and the enemies dropped away, howling, on the other side. Two hung there on top of the logs, lifeless, with their arms flung out like shirts on a washing line, and a third, whose trunk had toppled inside, had slipped almost to the ground, but the tops of his boot had got caught on the stockade's points. Nikolai had already run up and was finishing someone off with swings of his sledgehammer.

I had to fight two opponents at once. I swung the hammer, trying not to let the dangerous hatchets get too close. In the heat of the moment it seemed as if the two of them were only parrying my blows. This cowardly tactic maddened me completely, dispelling the final remnants of caution. Eventually my hammer struck an enemy's head with a dull ceramic sound. His contorted face was instantly covered in blood. But the euphoria of the third killing in my life was short-lived. The other man immediately swarmed into me and knocked me off my feet, but instead of hacking me to death, he started trying to pull the Book off me. He panted hoarse obscenities, strangling me with the chain of the steel case. I sank my teeth into his arm and tried to crush his prickly Adam's apple, but the slippy cartilage wouldn't break. My mouth was flooded with blood, as salty as old brine from pickled cucumbers, and I choked on it. Everything went hazy. My enemy suddenly jerked his hand free and hit me in the face several times so hard that I almost lost consciousness. The Book was dragged off me, tearing out a bunch of hair on its way, and I was released. Choking, I pushed a soft piece of flesh out of my mouth and wave of terror swept over me at the thought that I had bitten of my own tongue. I shouted, but instead of words there were only pink bubbles.

The man who had taken the Book from me was lying on the ground, with Sukharev raising his chain with the bunches of padlocks dangling from it and crashing it down on the body that was shuddering in agony.

Down on my hands and knees, I feverishly ran my fingers round my mouth, trying to feel my tongue. My numb, insensitive fingers were immediately smeared with blood and I couldn't understand a thing. Horrified, I wiped the bitten-off piece of flesh on my sleeve. It looked as if it wasn't a tongue after all, but a bite taken out of a wrist. I was racked by a nauseous, retching cough and spat up blood—either my own or someone else's—for a minute. Then Garshenin and Dzyuba ran over to me and lifted me up. Sukharev handed me the box with the Book in it, and I hung it round my neck again.

No more new fighters were climbing in, and the final enemy succumbed in uneven battle on two fronts with Anna and Marat Andreyevich, taking a blow from the head of the flail.

From the side where the yard was enclosed by a brick wall, fresh forces suddenly broke in. The only one left alive at the gates was the light-haired leader himself. He was no longer trying to break through to bolt, but skilfully dodging the Vozglyakovs' spades and Kruchina's bayonet as he retreated along the stockade. "Fuck it, will get you get a move on!" he called hoarsely to his accomplices.

Lutsis, Vyrin and Ozerov dashed to intercept the reinforcements, with Timofei Stepanovich struggling to keep up with them.

The light-haired man launched a desperate counterattack. Svetlana's spade broke under a crushing blow from a cleaver and it was a miracle that she wasn't killed herself. The second cleaver caught Kruchina. I heard Igor Valeryevich give a wild roar, pressing his hand to the spot on his temple where only a second ago he had an ear. Veronika's spade sank into the enemy leader's breastbone with a crunch. He roared. Veronika leaned on the handle with her full weight, pinning her adversary to the stockade. The light-haired man went limp and dangled on the spade like a puppet whose strings have all snapped at once.

Their leader's death did nothing to stiffen the attackers' courage. One of the six immediately fell victim to Vyrin's entrenching tool and Timofei Stepanovich's mace crushed another one's skull. Ozerov's pike transfixed the ribs of a third. A ball bearing precisely flung by Lutsis hit a fleeing enemy on the back of the neck. The man howled, clutched his head and fell, and Nikolai Tarasovich stamped his boot down on the man's shattered neck vertebrae.

One of the fighters who was still alive flung his axe at Ozerov, but luckily it was only the handle that caught him on the chin. Ozerov toppled over and didn't see Marat Andreyevich reach his foe and dispatch him. The sixth hero didn't waste any precious time; he just hopped back over the wall.

"Out there... Only four of them..." Garshenin whispered, pointing over the stockade. "We have to make a sortie to finish them off..."

Ievlev, Kruchina, Sukharev, the Vozglyakov sisters, Tanya and Dzyuba split up and stood at both sides of the gate. Garshenin pulled out the cross, and Kruchina and Ievlev pulled the heavy, creaking gates inward.

Four men immediately dashed into the opening. They ran a couple of steps and then halted. Their astonishment was replaced by confusion. They backed away and took to their heels without thinking twice. The long point of Garshenin's scythe caught the slowest enemy, whose inertia pulled him off the blade, but after running a couple of steps, he ran out of steam and collapsed. Anna flung her spade just above the ground, spinning it through the air like a windmill. A second runner collapsed into the grass with his legs broken and Ievlev was on him in two swift bounds.

Their comrade's dying shriek lent the other two invaders strength. Breaking away from the panting pursuit, they reached the forest and hid behind the trees. They were not pursued any farther. The battle was over.

I was shuddering in an icy fever. There was a deafening pulse beating in the nape of my neck and my eardrums. The adrenalin rush subsided. The spot where my hair had been pulled out started burning again. My black eye swelled up, the eyebrow and eyelid stung. A nagging pain, like toothache, was twisting my swollen cheek. I stood in the middle of the yard and watched Ievlev throw the body of a fallen enemy over his shoulder, while Sukharev and Ozerov dragged another by the legs. The other Shironinites were also coming back.

Garshenin stopped beside me, dishevelled and dirty.

"Victory! Congratulations!" he exclaimed, his eyes glowing in exultation.

"Looks like we squeezed through without any losses," said Dzyuba. "May God be praised…"

"Oh, no, we've got losses!" Kruchina hissed. He was holding his hand to the wound on his head, with blood seeping between his fingers. "I've lost half my ear, dammit! Now I'll have to walk around like a convict!"

"You can cover it with your hair. No one will even notice," Tanya reassured him as she poured peroxide onto cotton wool from a little bottle.

Kruchina took his hand away from his temple, revealing for a moment a crimson stump that looked like a tulip, and applied the lump of cotton wool.

Ozerov got up off the ground unsteadily, his beard covered in blood; Timofei Stepanovich, sitting with his back against the wall, clutched his handkerchief, wearily wiping his face, as purple as a new-born baby's.

There were about a dozen enemy bodies lying around in the yard. Five of them had met their death beside the brick wall. Three were still dangling on the stockade and four storm troopers were lying by the gates, with their light-haired leader squirming nearby.

"Interrogate him, Alexei. Interrogate him immediately," Timofei Stepanovich hissed. "Find out who sent them." The old man could barely even draw breath, as if he had been running hard.

The light-haired man was in a really bad way, and I had to hurry if I was going to get anything out of him.

I walked up to the dying man.

"Listen, we'll try to ease your suffering, as far we're able…" I swung round. "Marat Andreyevich, bring some Analgin quickly!"

The enemy leader's eyes shuddered murkily, like a fish's.

"Where's the Book?"

"Here," I said tapping on the steel casket. "And now tell me who set you on us."

"Show me the Book…" he wheezed painfully.

"All right," I said and set the case on my knee.

He waited patiently for me to find the key and open the lock, even raising himself up slightly. The broad red patch on his caved-in chest glittered as fresh blood flowed into it, as dull and greasy as crude oil.

"There you are…" I showed him the Book lying on the velvet. "And now tell me how you found out about us."

"The wrong one!" he slumped back feebly and looked at me with desolate, weary hatred. "It's a different one!"

"What did you expect to see?"

"The Book of Endurance!" the light-haired man barked out in a fury, and rivulets of beetroot-red blood spurted from his nostrils.

"And who told you we had a Book of Endurance?"

"The old woman…"

"What old woman?"

"A clever old woman! We drew the lot to try first… Three years we'd been waiting for our turn, and then this chance came up… It didn't work…" He stirred feebly. "It hurts… The Book of Endurance…"

"We only have a Book of Memory."

"You're lying," the light-haired man whispered indifferently.

"No, it's true…"

The wounded man laughed, with a gurgling sound in his throat.

"So, the old woman tricked us… I told you she was clever. But you're going to die anyway. No one will get away. The old woman's decided…"

"Has that shed any light on things? Who are they?" asked Dezhnev, squatting down beside us. He was holding a syringe with an analgesic mixture that looked like spittle.

"I can't tell… It doesn't sound like the council. He talked about some old woman. Tried to frighten me with her."

Marat Andreyevich slid the needle into one of the light-haired man's veins.

The man watched the movement of the plunger indifferently and asked:

"Did you kill all my men?"

"Three of them escaped."

"They were lucky…"

He didn't say another word. Soon he closed his eyes. The rustle of his departing breath struggled out through his clenched teeth, like a little moth fluttering its wings in a fragile porcelain throat. His blood-choked nostrils flared like gills and then froze.

"Alexei! Marat Andreyevich!" Tanya suddenly called in a piercing voice that broke into a shriek.

I shuddered and looked round. Startled by the heart-rending cry, the Shironinites were already hurrying towards the stockade. When we reached the site of the commotion, we saw Timofei Stepanovich. The old man was still sitting there, leaning back against the logs. His shaggy head had slumped forward into his chest, as if it had been severed. His right leg was drawn up, but his left one was extended, so we could see the worn-down heel of his dusty boot.

Sukharev and Vyrin laid Timofei Stepanovich out on the ground, and Marat Andreyevich clutched the old man's wrist with its black veins, listening intently for any life that might tremble under the skin, and then, unable to believe his own inconceivable diagnosis, he said:

"Nine satisfactions, Neverbino—he went through them all without a scratch. And now his heart's given out…"

"What kind of crap's that?" Ievlev roared. "What do you mean, his heart?" He pressed his hands down on the bony ribcage. "Breathe, old man, breathe!" he said, buffeting the lifeless body.

Some secret fermentation stirred inside Timofei Stepanovich, and a spate of thick lymph and bodily fluids gushed out through his blue, half-open mouth and splashed onto Ievlev, who cried out and staggered back, hastily wiping the death slime off his face and clothes. Then it was finally clear to me that Timofei Stepanovich was no longer with us, and one more name had been added to the doleful list of the Shironin reading room's losses.

THROUGH THE FOREST

IN HALF AN HOUR Sukharev, Kruchina and Lutsis had dug the old man a shallow, cramped grave. The clayey soil yielded reluctantly to their spades. It was a hasty funeral, with no speeches and no commemorative snacks. The bodies of our enemies were carried to the ravine and covered over with brushwood—there was no time for a more thorough burial.

We loaded all our things, food reserves and weapons into the trailer and the bus haphazardly; all we wanted was to get out of there before sunset.

Meanwhile Ievlev fiddled with the chainsaw, mixing petrol and oil together like an alchemist. The proportions of the liquids weren't right, the second-hand saw was acting up and Nikolai Ivanovich, mentally forwarding his curses to the inventor of the two-stroke engine, took it apart again, adjusted the magneto, cleaned the carburettor, emptied the tank and poured in the new mixture—and then on and on like that, until the Taiga started cackling at the first tug on the starting cord. The chainsaw had no right to cut out that evening.

The goal we had set was far from simple. We intended to break out through the blockage and escape from this trap. If the light-haired man's dying words could be trusted, we were smack in the middle of a full-scale altercation. There were embittered, deprived readers lurking in the forest, and they wanted to acquire a rare and valuable Book from outcasts like us. We couldn't understand what mysterious old woman it was that had set this pack of aggrieved hounds on us.

Our desperate calculations were founded entirely on the hope that the fugitives from the gang we had just destroyed would spread word of the horror they had suffered through the forest and cool the martial ardour of the other marauders. Apart from that, I had a fairly clear idea of the strategy of this campaign of pillage. The horde could not unite. Dividing up a Book between temporary partners was not a realistic prospect. There could only be one winner. That was probably what the light-haired man had meant when he told me they had drawn lots. His men had been given the opportunity to get the Book, and they had lost. Now a new team would try their strength against us. The marauders were taking turns.

The sun was already sinking in the west when the cavalcade set off, fully armed and equipped, into the dangerous unknown. Leading the squad were Sukharev, Vyrin, Lutsis and Garshenin, peering keenly into the twilight of the branches to spot the slightest signs of danger, with the dogs running alongside them. Immediately after the watch unit came the chugging motorbike driven by Anna, with Ievlev and his chainsaw in the sidecar. The bus and the Niva crept along slowly behind them. Marat Andreyevich was driving the bus and Veronika and Svetlana walked alongside the LAZ, protecting its wheels. The Niva was driven by Ozerov. Kruchina and Dzyuba came last, guarding the rear.

Judging from the voices in the avant-garde, we had reached the blockage. The chainsaw's motor roared like a moped rearing up on its back wheel. The buzzing ribbon of steel ripped into the wood. The low-voiced Taiga gave a falsetto howl and made short work of the forest timber. Then it ripped into wood again with a squeal.

After only a couple of minutes the future corridor through the impassable blockage was already marked out and there was a heap of branches lying beside Nikolai Tarasovich. I tried to lift a sawn-off round of log the size of a small butcher's block. The damp wood was as heavy as stone. I rolled it to the bushes beside the road and sensed, rather than saw, figures lurking behind the tangled branches of blackthorn.

In the deep millpond of forest twilight I saw the outlines of stooping shadows, skulking along like black holes that had come to life. There was a vague hubbub running through the forest, safely drowned out by the strenuous barking of the chainsaw. The men who had hidden behind the tangled ricks of blackthorn didn't yet realize that they had been discovered. Signalling to his companions, one enemy hissed: "S-s-s-shh!" Then a long trill of birdsong ran through the bushes. A crow cawed hoarsely in reply and a woodpecker started tapping.

Simultaneously with my piercing shout of "Ambush!" a staff with a long, narrow spearhead was thrust out through the cobwebs of branches as rapidly as a chameleon's tongue. The weak point couldn't pierce the tyre rubber of my armour, as tough as an oak board. A shaggy little body darted out of the bushes straight at me. I swung my hammer. The attacker flung out his arms and tumbled over backwards onto a bush.

A demonic chorus mingled with the roaring of the chainsaw. I looked round. Small, dwarfish creatures were clambering through the forest tangle. Dressed in furs, with cattle horns sewn on above their ribs, and caps with the bony tops of horses', deer's or bulls' skulls. The round faces with narrow eyes and straight, coal-black hair revealed that they belonged to vanishing races of the Far North. They howled, shaking their grandfathers' lances, harpoons and bear spears. There were about fifteen of these men in their freakish animal armour.

Before attacking they shrieked again, levelled their weapons and came rushing down. Latka growled and was immediately picked up on a bear spear and tossed aside like an old moth-eaten fur jacket.

A bloody battle started up on the logs. Sukharev, Vyrin, Lutsis and Garshenin bravely fought off an enemy three times as numerous. Nikolai Tarasovich carried on working away with the saw, hurrying to complete a corridor wide enough to accommodate the bus.

Lutsis sank the upper corner of his axe into a mare's forehead, slicing through the helmet and the skull right down to the chin.

Vyrin's entrenching tools fluttered like the black wings of a swallowtail butterfly.

Garshenin grabbed hold of a harpoon and jerked it towards himself. The long blade of his scythe slid along the handle—straight into a swollen, straining throat. Sukharev swung his mace above his head and brought it down hard on a horned helmet, raising a fountain of powdered bone.

Someone recklessly attacked Nikolai Tarasovich's chainsaw, sticking his fur sleeve right in under the cutting edges as they raced round their ellipse. The saw spat out a tattered bundle of bloody fragments and suddenly choked. The dense nap had jammed the chain, which was designed for timber. Ievlev flung the useless piece of equipment aside and reached out his hands. Even stooping over, he was twice as tall as his squat adversaries and could rely on an unchallenged superiority of muscle power and height. He struck the first one with his fist of iron, neatly dodging a fifty-centimetre-long jagged blade. The face of the animal-headed warrior was flooded with blood from his smashed brow bone. The second one jumped from above. Ievlev caught him in the air by the scruff of his neck, smashed him down hard onto the ground and kicked him in the temple. Then he immediately broke the bear spear that had been dropped across his knee, converting the stabbing weapon into a two-handed sword.

A second troop tumbled out into the road like spilled beads. These warriors entered battle wearing padded builders' helmets with round metal plates on them and home-made boleros of coarse leather with metal plates sewn close together all over them. A heavy mace crunched into the windscreen of the Niva. Ozerov jumped out of the car and rolled across the ground, miraculously dodging a spiked club that ploughed up the earth beside his head, and jumped to his feet. An axe glinted in his hand.

Kruchina, Dzyuba and Tanya retreated in triangular formation. Their attackers prodded at them with bear spears, seeking a gap in their defences, trying to catch a leg or stab a neck or unprotected side. Two of them had already misjudged the distance and paid the price by running onto the ninety-centimetre blade of Tanya's rapier. The axe and the mace clashed resonantly, altering the trajectory of their blows. Ozerov's axe, aimed at the head, fell crookedly, hitting a collarbone. There was a loud crack, as if someone had bitten a large bone in half.

Marat Andreyevich dashed about inside the bus. I had given him the Book earlier and now he didn't know what to do: wade into the battle or sit in the relatively safe bus, waiting for Ievlev to clear the way with his chainsaw.

A bearded man holding a hayfork at the ready dashed towards one of the bus's wheels. Veronika blocked his way. Anna, swinging her flail, rushed to help her sister.

The next second light spears were thrust against my back and my chest. They did no damage, but pain engulfed my calf like a red-hot whiplash. I yelled and pulled out the small harpoon, which looked like a broom, only the twigs were steel spokes tied round with wire.

Men in jute-rope waistcoats came running out. This simple homespun protection took the place of armour for them. They were armed with equal simplicity—stakes with charred points on their ends. Some of them had convex shields woven out of osiers, like baskets.

For some reason the other attackers were dumbfounded by the appearance of this group. The man with the fork forgot about the bus and roared: "Bastards! Where are you going? You've jumped the queue!" And he impaled one of the men without armour on his long prongs.

"Over here, over here!" the bearded man roared furiously. "The Ulyanovites are jumping the queue!"

Hearing his strident summons, some of the warriors from the second troop abandoned the fighting by the trailer and ran to attack the newcomers. In order not to be thrust back by the impact, the armourless men ran to meet them.

Thanks to this incidental strife between the allies, I was given a breathing space and I withdrew, limping back closer to the roadblock. Ievlev was flinging rounds of sawn tree trunks, as heavy as large boulders, felling members of the greatly reduced animal-headed army, crushing heads and torsos.

Lutsis, fending off his adversaries with an axe that had a horned skull stuck on it, shouted:

"Alexei, let's get to the bus!"

In among the trees the orange dots of torches flared up. Another brigade, the fourth of the evening, appeared, walking in such dense formation that it was impossible to tell how many men there were. The polished metal of their breastplates and their pointed helmets glinted brightly. Their visors, with holes in them that made them look like the grilles of stoves, were lowered. Their arms were protected by shoulder plates and bracers, and most of them were holding bladed weapons. Their leader's left fist was covered by a rounded piece of steel, like a boxer's glove, and he used this knuckleduster to deliver crushing uppercuts and hooks. His brigade tore into the armourless fighters as they were dragging their wounded into the bushes, like ants. For a minute the slaughter shifted to and fro between the forest and thickets of alder. The armourless men fought desperately; even when they were felled, they grabbed the armoured men's legs and tumbled them to the ground, in order to thrust a kitchen knife into their adversary and then die.

Reinforcements came rushing out of the forest from both sides. The warriors were clutching crude short pikes, gaffs with triple hooks, clubs studded with nails, and axes. The new forces arrived in two independent groups; acting according to a coherent plan, they ran in and wedged themselves between the bus and the wrecked Niva. Only seconds earlier Anna and Veronika were standing beside me, and a short distance away Tanya, Kruchina, Dzyuba and Ozerov had readied themselves for action, and now suddenly we had been scattered, as if an ocean wave had surged over us.

I saw an axe swooping down, then the metal top-plate of a helmet sent flying by a blow from my hammer. A grinning mouth contorted in a scream, flooding a ginger beard with blood. A bayonet jabbing in the rush, a jagged-toothed bear spear darted to and fro.

The knobbly iron apple of a flail slammed into my helmet. For a moment I was stunned by the piercing clang of bronze, and the pain shot into my neck, as if someone had driven a spike between the vertebrae. I collapsed onto the sticky earth, no longer aware of anything but the agonizing chime that had flooded my ears. I pulled the helmet off my head, as if it were the only source of the unbearable sound. Someone's boot turned me face up. I made out Anna, aiming her heavy flail with two hands. The hawkish claw of a triple gaff was thrust into Veronika's underbelly. I was grabbed by the scruff of my neck and dragged along. I gulped in air three times. My hearing returned abruptly and painfully.

A black silhouette leaned down over me and asked distinctly in the squeaky womanish voice of a eunuch.

"Your name?"

All I could see of the face was a thin-lipped mouth and a plump chin with a dimple. Everything else was covered by a mask with a horizontal slit for the eyes.

There was no reason to be secretive and I answered, squinting at the iron stump on the end of the speaker's left hand.

"Vyazintsev."

"Then live." The figure got up and a dark patchwork of leaves swayed above me.

"Nikolai Tarasovich, Alexei's here!" Lutsis's voice shouted somewhere near me.

The warrior walking away deftly caught the clanging axe on his glove and slashed with his own sword.

Someone threw me over his shoulder and carried me. The ground swayed like a chiming bell. A woman trilled piercingly, as if she were giving birth. Nayda crawled along with a broken back, dying. An animal-headed whaler flung a harpoon from a distance of three metres. Sukharev strained in awkward amazement to get a look at the sharp point that had suddenly emerged from his back…

Dezhnev dragged me into the bus.

"How are you?"

"All right…" I collapsed onto a seat.

Veronika was lying on the floor beside me with her padded jacket pulled up and her trousers lowered to her pubic mound. She was pressing her hands to her lower stomach, which was slashed into three parts. At every breath dull, almost blue, blood spurted out through her cramped finger. Anna was frantically trying to plug the wound with a bunched-up rag.

Garshenin was trying to drag limp Sukharev into the bus. The harpoon, which had pierced right through Sasha's body, had stuck in the narrow doorway, and his dangling head shuddered with each jerk.

Twice the bus heeled over steeply with a jolt. Unfamiliar voices yelled outside. Stones smashed into the windows, sending showers of glass splinters flying. Garshenin and Vyrin jumped onto the step, followed by Ievlev.

"Quick! Get a move on!" he yelled hoarsely to the remaining Shironinites.

"Get into the car!" Garshenin told them in a cracked whisper.

As if they had heard Garshenin's advice, the remnants of the first two brigades pushed small trees in under the bottom of the Niva and overturned it. The armoured brigade, the same one that had dealt so skilfully and cruelly with the deprived readers from Ulyanovsk, dressed in their yellow peasant bast, was crowding round our comrades, preventing them from breaking through to the bus.

"They won't make it!" Vyrin raged.

With every second they moved farther away—Lutsis dragging Svetlana, Tanya criss-crossing with her rapier. Kruchina waved in farewell, telling us to continue our flight. Ozerov and Dzyuba, with their backs together, had fused into a single, unassailable fighting organism, stabbing with a pike and lashing with an axe. The road took a turn and they disappeared from view...

"Marat Andreyevich!" I roared. "Reverse!"

The breaks squealed like a stuck pig. Our inertia first pressed me against a seat. Then it flung me onto the floor, slippery with blood. Veronika's head bounced off her sister's knees and Sukharev, posthumously freed from his harpoon, flew off the seat and tumbled over.

"Marat Andreyevich!" Vyrin yelled raucously. With his head stuck out of the window, he pointed to the road, where a new danger was lurking directly in out path. Up ahead, about a hundred metres from the skidding bus, there was a tall new roadblock, twice as wide as the first one. There were armed men swarming beside the tree trunks, as massive as museum columns. A moment later they came running in a dense, roaring pack—at least fifty raging warriors...

"Marat Andreyevich, go back!" I howled. "We'll pick up our people and go to the village soviet! Turn round!"

The rounded snout of the bus slammed into our enemies' backs. The mighty blow flung a spreadeagled body up onto the windscreen and tossed another, waving its arms about, up into the air like a bull.

Garshenin thrust his scythe out of a broken window like an oar. The black blade sliced through an armoured torso. Nikolai Tarasovich and Anna exited as a landing party and now they were hammering the adversary right and left. Blood spurted as Vyrin, clinging to the door handle, slashed with his entrenching tool. The formation scattered and our enemies dashed to the edges of the road in panic. Then I saw the Shironinites. There were only four of them. Kruchina in a slashed cuirass and dented fireman's helmet, with a slim dart that looked like an antenna protruding from his hip. Tanya's hair had clumped into coarse, bloody plaits and her forehead was dissected by a ragged, bleeding wound. Dzyuba lowered his hammer pick and covered his face with one hand, as if there was a blinding light shining into his face. Ozerov staggered back as if he had seen some forbidden miracle.

"Why? Igor Valeryevich groaned a moment later. "Now we'll all die!"

I read reproach in Tanya's eyes. She hadn't wanted us to come back either. The expression on Dzyuba's and Ozerov's faces, soaked in blood as if they had been flayed, was not joy, but bewildered despair. Hoping for nothing, condemning no one, they had been willing to pay with their lives for our chance to escape, and we had foiled their plan.

Then I saw Lutsis stretched out on the ground. He was frozen in movement, as if he were crawling on his belly. Svetlana was lying farther away with her head in a murky puddle of blood that looked like a halo…

I heard an inhuman roaring and a loud trampling moving closer. It sounded like a gang of growling throats straddling a herd of crazed horses. On a high note the shouting merged into a wolf-song to the moon. The hoarse voice howled of a Book, of the horrors of suffering endured, of imminent delivery from torment. The improvization, with neither rhythm nor metre, like the keening of women at a funeral, flew through the forest. And men came back, full of deadly determination, to finish what they had started…

"Everyone into the bus!" I yelled, rousing myself from the enchantment of terror. "That's an order!" Then I turned Lutsis over onto his back and stumbled along, dragging him to the door. Ievlev picked up Svetlana. Overwhelmed by new grief, Anna was almost dragged along by Kruchina.

Rasping blows hammered against the sides of the bus. The motor roared. Slashed tyres burst. Riddled with spears, the LAZ tore its way out of encirclement, picked up speed and hurtled out of the forest…

That was how I remembered those fleeting seconds for ever: the road, bodies, the rattling, sagging bus. For the last few metres we were already travelling on tyre rims that stuck in the ground…

The village soviet was guarded by a small group. They barely managed to close the heavy log gates before the bus smashed through them in a spray of glass, squeezed in between the logs of the stockade and stopped dead, becoming the new gate. Half of a bloodied torso in a padded work jacket, with its head twisted unnaturally, protruded from under the bumper that had ploughed up the ground.

A minute later the yard was ours again. This battle was the shortest of all. A small Yakut with a broad, flattened nose deftly dodged Dzyuba's hammer pick, dived under Garshenin's scythe and caught Ievlev's leg a glancing blow with his pike, but couldn't avoid the hammer and died without a sound, as if he didn't even feel his death. Vyrin's entrenching tool turned a deadly somersault as it flew through the air, burying itself deep in the face of the third guard with a crunch, and blood spurted out of the man's dissected eye. The fourth guard tried to escape by squeezing between the bus and the stockade, but got stuck and was mercilessly dispatched by Anna.

BREATHING SPACE

T HEY HELPED ME clamber onto the roof of the bus. From
up there I surveyed the road that cut across the dreary
meadow like a cartridge belt—our pursuers had long ago changed
their run to the jogging pace of a trek. Small scattered gangs
were seeping stealthily out of the forest, but they were in no
rush to storm us.

Our enemies occupied the huts farthest away, on the outskirts of
the village. The campfires of numerous bivouacs blazed up in the
meadow; axes started tapping. Then I realized that the combined
army had called a halt; nothing could be expected to happen in
the next few hours, and I could get down.

When I reached the ground I felt blood squelching in my boot.
The frenzy of battle was gradually receding. Bruises I hadn't felt
before flared up under the tyre rubber. My forehead was burning
as if it had been bandaged with a dressing of crushed glass.

Ievlev pulled a long fragment of the snapped-off tip of a Yakut
pike out of his leg. Vyrin took off his jacket cautiously, to avoid
causing himself unnecessary pain. The roubles had left crimson
imprints on his back and sides. Dzyuba could only see with one
eye—the other had almost disappeared under a blue swelling. On
his left hand, instead of a middle finger and little finger Ozerov
had wiggling scraps of skin and gnawed chicken bones. He hadn't
even noticed when it happened to him. Kruchina had taken a
close swipe to the jaw with a club and the sharp spikes had ripped
deep into his cheek and chin. Marat Andreyevich had paid for

ramming the gates with a rib broken against the steering wheel and numerous contusions...

Smeared with their own blood and the blood of others, mauled and weary, the Shironinites gradually revived. The emerging physical pain brought with it the bitter realization of irreparable losses. The failed breakout had cost us dearly. Sukharev and Lutsis had been killed; Svetlana and Veronika had bled to death...

My throat constricted as if it were caught in a prickly noose when Anna fell on her sisters' bodies and started wailing. Tanya wept and even stern Igor Valeryevich sobbed. Grisha could barely hold back his tears. Marat Andreyevich's face had turned to stone and his teeth were clenched. Nikolai Tarasovich turned away so that no one would see his eyes. Ozerov, Dzyuba and Garshenin stood there with their heads lowered...

But, alas, there was no time for grieving. We carried our dead comrades into the house and then Marat Andreyevich started treating our wounds. By sheer luck, all the medical supplies were in the bus. Ozerov's crushed fingers were removed immediately. He bore the amputation manfully, without a single groan. For more than an hour Marat Andreyevich treated and stitched up ragged wounds, staunched blood, applied splints to cracked bones, wound on bandages and rubbed ointment into bruised and battered shoulders, sides and backs.

Relentless pain poked about with a needle between my neck vertebrae and fanned glowing coals under the dressing where my leg had been torn by a harpoon. I greedily ate a full pack of analgin and then asked for another one. Soon my body lost all sensitivity.

As far as our strength and medical analgesia permitted, we reinforced the yard, rolling out metal barrels that had not previously found any use in our home life and setting them along the wall. We set a platform of planks across the metal bottoms so that we could get above the stockade and repel the attacking enemy from up there. The cobblestones that had been used to pave the paths were gouged out of the earth and piled in heaps. The rear windows of the bus were blocked off with logs. Only after we had prepared the village soviet for a storm did we allow ourselves a brief breathing space. The stalwart Ievlev and Garshenin volunteered to be sentries.

In the porch I collapsed, exhausted, onto the couch, sticking the first bag that came to hand under my head. A sharp corner jabbed into my temple. After contemplating the discomfort, I pulled out the wooden frame with Margarita Tikhonovna's photograph in it. I read the dedication, noting to myself that the recipient of this kind memento was unlikely to survive the next day. There was no hope left, just as there was no trace of my former despondency.

Following the established tradition of the world, before facing deadly danger, I had to put my earthly affairs in order. After a moment's thought I quickly came to the conclusion that I didn't really have any. Neither did I feel any fear in the face of the imminent battle.

For the sake of decency I remembered my father, my mother, my sister and nephews, but somehow I felt neither love nor tenderness. I gazed into my family's faces with surprised indifference. They seemed to me like pale copies of a dream from last year. It was absurd and ridiculous to feel any familial emotions for these ghosts. The city where I had lived for almost thirty years, my school, my two institutes, my former wife, my work—it had all become a stupid, unreal game, like some boring popular film that I had watched many years ago in a summer cinema in the Crimea.

A sticky sense of unease forced me to open my eyes. It was simplest of all to blame this incomprehensible coldheartedness on the analgin, which had numbed my feelings as well as my body, but I knew another explanation. I had read Gromov too often. The Book's implant, full of sparkling happiness, had invaded the entire space of my memory, simultaneously rendering my own childhood worthless. I had to make a serious mental effort finally to convince myself that this sequence of faded portraits, burned-out events and blurred landscapes was once my real life.

I spent a long time splashing cold water onto my face out of a bucket, and the apparition that had restricted my breathing relaxed its grip. To be honest, I no longer understood what I had been afraid of. Alexei Vyazintsev's self-awareness was not in any fundamental danger; he had always remained himself, regardless of the nature of his memories.

I reminded myself yet again of the strict mental discipline without which the Book would undoubtedly herd the events of my childhood into the reservation of forgetfulness. But then this touching concern was also absurd. Was it worth taking care of this ordinary past, or feeling compassion for its morose shadows, if soon there would be no present, and no future either?

A campfire was blazing in the yard. The entire reading room gathered round the flames. Ievlev sang a front-line song about a dark night. Ozerov pensively tested the blade of his axe with his thumb. Vyrin dozed, leaning on Marat Andreyevich's shoulder. Tanya honed the point of her rapier with a whetstone. Anna was a frozen, hunched-over stone idol. Garshenin strode round the edge of the village soviet's roof with a pair of binoculars—watching over the surrounding area.

Thunder rumbled somewhere far beyond the forest, as if someone had run across a booming metal roof. In the black sky, lilac veins swelled up and faded away, but no raindrops fell.

"How are you feeling, Alexei?" Marat Andreyevich asked solicitously.

"Fine... I slept a little bit."

"Well, now, sleep's good," Marat Andreyevich agreed. "Take this, I've been wanting to return it for a long time..." He handed me the case with the Book.

I took the solemn attribute of my post as librarian, put the chain round my neck, sat down between Dzyuba and Tanya, and looked round at the silent Shironinites. Ievlev broke off his song, Kruchina and Ozerov set aside their weapons. Vyrin stood up. They were all expecting something from me, perhaps some farewell words.

"There are a couple of hours left before dawn," I said, opening the little steel doors of the case. "There won't be another chance. I suggest that we listen to the Book…"

I cleared my throat and began without any intonation or expression, as if I was listing off the printed words. By the end of the reading my voice was hoarse and had lost all its resonance. My back was numb, the lines crept about like graphic gnats, but none of that mattered at all. I had known many of the paragraphs off by heart for a long time, and I only had to touch the text for it to leap out of its own accord. I whispered the end of the final page and slammed the cover shut.

There was a smell of gangrene and death from the direction of the ravine to which we had carried our enemies a day earlier. The wind drove along grey clouds and the rushing moon was a bleached, smoky-white blob. Scattered dewdrops appeared on the long blade of a rapier stuck into the ground. The same sparkling water drops, glinting on Ozerov's axe and Kruchina's bayonet, were suddenly transformed into round, glassy, magical decorations on a tree, reflecting the New Year and the entire, blindingly festive, happy world of my childhood. The kaleidoscope of remembrance took a bend, flinging out the crystal pattern of a new memory…

THE ASSAULT

CROWS FLEW IN from out of nowhere, anticipating carrion. They called in their repulsive voices, like the cracking sound of tearing rags. My memories immediately blurred and dimmed.

I stood up. The Shironinites also got to their feet. The bustle and hubbub outside the stockade indicated that the enemy had begun preparations to storm us. The combined army numbered about sixty and was divided into three independent brigades, each standing slightly apart from the others. Their shared claim to the Book would not allow them to follow a common strategy. They were simultaneously allies and rivals, which made our task significantly easier. We would not have to fight the whole mass, but only separate groups. It was a different matter that the enemy kept throwing fresh forces into the battle, while we were so weary that we could hardly stand.

The first and biggest brigade was mostly armed with peasant weapons—pitchforks, axes and knives. These readers had clearly not taken part in the fighting yet and were burning with impatience. God only knows what these people's professions were and what their lives had been like, but now they had all become warriors. They peered at us intently and there was demonic obsession in every face.

The second brigade was a composite one, cobbled together out of our acquaintances of the previous day. I saw padded building workers' helmets with metal plates sewn all over them, and horned animal skulls. Hunting harpoons, bear spears and lances mingled with gaffs and clubs.

The backbone of the third brigade was the seriously diminished group of armoured warriors. After the skirmish at the roadblock there were only four of them left. But they had been joined by reinforcements—fifteen men. They didn't look like warriors at all and had no armour of any kind. Instead of weapons they carried strange-looking curved troughs with ladle-like hollows and broad bags hanging on their shoulders. The armoured men were fiddling with a device that looked like a mobile building-site compressor, connecting up boxes of some kind and laying out wires. The warrior with the iron stump was running everything.

Garshenin came over to me and reported in a quiet voice.

"There's another brigade behind the brick wall. Twenty men. I think it's so that we can't get away through the ravine…"

Vyrin built a little artillery pyramid of ball bearings beside my foot and scrambled up onto the platform. Clutching a weighty cobblestone in each hand, I followed the enemy's manoeuvres intently.

The warrior with the metal stump completed the preparations and declared in a shrill, squeaky voice:

"Music by Pakhmutova! Lyrics by Dobronravov!"

The commander of the first brigade gave an inaudible command. The ranks shuddered, walked forward and spread out into a broad formation. Six readers picked up a trimmed tree trunk that looked like a gigantic pencil.

Maintaining their line, our enemies moved towards the village soviet at a jog, holding their axes and pitchforks ready in front of them. Every third warrior was carrying a sledgehammer on his shoulder.

The air was filled with a strange crackling sound, like dried-out brushwood bursting into flames; then a deafening symphonic fanfare roared out, followed by the booming explosion of a drum, and then violins played a snivelling, jet-plane glissando. A rumbling baritone voice filled all the space within sight.

The banner of the morning sky.
In life the first step is important.
Hear the winds of furious attacks
Blowing above the country!

The rousing song rushed through the air in several directions simultaneously. I saw a double loudspeaker attached to a crooked power-cable post. And there was another pair of stentorian trumpets standing on the compressor.

The melodious call of the soviet skald spread over the forest, summoning warriors to the attack. I didn't even pause to think how the enemy came to know about this technology of bravery. Probably the discovery of using musical stimulation to stifle fear was not made by Margarita Tikhonovna or the late Ogloblin.

And again the battle continues,
Your heart is restless in your chest,
And our Lenin is so young
And young October lies ahead!

I suddenly felt an emotional exultation I had never known before. The majestic song, the lack of sleep, the stupefying medicines, the memories, the expectation of death at any second—it all heated my feelings to a seething ecstasy, a muscular frenzy.

A shower of stones mingled with ball bearings flew out from behind the stockade. The barrage was so sudden that our enemies never even reached the wall with their battering ram: they lost impetus, dropped the heavy timber and scattered, trying to dodge this precisely aimed death.

The thunderous voice sang and sledgehammers drubbed against the logs of the stockade, sending chips flying, but the stout timber didn't yield. The long pikes of the defenders of the village soviet attacked the reckless hammer-men from above. The agile points seized on every swing to jab into an exposed artery on a neck, to thrust in under a collarbone, to tear the tissue of muscles, to drive their tips right into the heart…

The song ended, the skald fell silent, but even before that the attack had choked on blood and the brigade had withdrawn. Eight prostrate bodies were left under the stockade.

In the unbearable icy silence the shrill-voiced eunuch in the pointed helmet shouted again:

"Music by Pakhmutova! Lyrics by Dobronravov!"

The frosty air was filled with rustling and scraping. The crackling needle of the invisible gramophone circled the record again. Orchestral brass responded with the pounding rhythm of train wheels, and piercing trumpets of doom played a towering line. A choir of a hundred young crystal-clear voices soared.

Ring out, you bell of fearless valour!
All who are young are on the road!
We have been issued a map of victories!
The stations of our working glory
Are our gift to our native land.
Remember their names well:
Love, Komsomol and Spring!

The song inspired the battered brigade, driving them back to repeat their storm. Without taking a second for rest, our enemies slung a reserve battering ram up onto their shoulders and rushed at the village soviet in a new wave. The berserk assault force moved closer with every second.

The second assault did not last long, but it was bloodier. They formed up to protect the battering ram with a living shield and only scattered just before the wall, clearing the way for the decisive blow.

I felt my elbow joint tear apart every time a smooth cobblestone flew out of my crooked fingers. I kept my eyes on one stone, following its trajectory. The projectile dented in an enemy's cheek with a dull plop, as if it had landed in wet earth. The man struck his head against the tree trunk and went limp. The massive battering ram, deprived of one pair of its legs, swayed abruptly and veered to one side. Someone got his boot tangled up with the dead man and stumbled. The weakened battering ram didn't strike the stockade, but fell against it, knocking out a log. The commander of the brigade clambered in though the gap that had appeared and Marat Andreyevich attacked him from above. The sabre whistled and the face distorted by savage fury was sliced across by a slanting crimson thread. It opened, spilling out its deep, fleshy innards. The commander staggered back. Dzyuba tossed another warrior out of the breach with a precise swing of his hammer pick. There were no more takers.

An incessant hail of stones continued to fall on their heads, smashing helmets, breaking arms, crushing knees. Suddenly Garshenin, Dzyuba and Kruchina hopped over the wall. The men outside had not been expecting a daring sortie like this. Before the enemy could gather his wits, the black blade of the scythe had already sheared through someone's neck, the hammer had butted right through to a backbone, like a horn, and the bayonet had jabbed into a belly. After carrying out this lightning raid, the defenders of the village soviet withdrew through the breach and stones started flying down from the wall again. The attackers collapsed and scattered in disorder, urged on by the sonorous choir.

> Once again the blizzards swirl,
> And a song teaches us courage,
> And you are with us for all time,
> Love, Komsomol and Spring!

A scraping acoustic nail rasped out from all the speakers. The choir fell silent. Only the natural sounds of death remained.

Leaning out from the stockade to stab an enemy better with his pike, Ozerov was caught on the curved prongs of a pitchfork. Spiked through the stomach, he screamed horrendously and they dragged him off as a trophy.

To make up for their losses in the lottery, our enemies threw themselves on Ozerov's prostrate form and ripped open his chest while he was still alive and then, working together from the sides, they broke out all his ribs, like wooden battens. We watched in helpless fury as this performance of diabolical cruelty was played out to the accompaniment of heinously obscene oaths. To work off their rage, before they fixed the break in the wall, Vyrin, Ievlev and Kruchina jumped over the stockade and finished off the stunned and wounded with a few blows from a spade, a hammer or a flail.

The shattered brigade was suffering its own tragedy. The readers had exhausted their reserves of strength. Spent and bitter, they gave way to new challengers. The second, composite brigade entered the battle. Shields made out of sections of fencing were raised above the withered grass. The animal-headed men sheltered securely behind them and all we could see were the tops of their helmets and a bristling array of harpoons, lances and bear spears.

Vyrin smacked a cobblestone down on the planks.

"The last one…" he said in a quiet, despairing voice. "What are we going to beat them back with?"

"With these," said Ievlev, laying out dead men's axes. "We can throw them."

Our Niva came trundling along the road with its overworked engine snorting: it had been transformed into a siege engine. A mighty pointed stake ran right through the interior of the car, with its pointed head protruding a metre in front of the hood.

The moment the Niva had taken up battle position, the "shields" started advancing. The next moment the reinforcements of the third brigade formed up into a free line with wide intervals. The men readied their curved troughs and placed something in the round hollows of the ladles.

"Music by Basner! Lyrics by Matusovsky!" the DJ eunuch announced.

A low bass voice replete with subterranean tragedy intoned to a funereal air.

The grove was haze up on the hill
And in the sky the sunset blazed.
Now only three of us left
From eighteen stalwart lads in all.
How many of them, our good friends,
Were left there, lying in the dark,
Beside a distant unknown village,
Set high upon a nameless hill?

The "shields" started running and the Niva roared towards us, throwing out a cloud of petrol fumes. The hands holding the ladles all flew upward and fell simultaneously, as if they were lashing whips. I thought I heard a swarm of mayflies go buzzing past close by. Something crashed into the top of the stockade, shattering into pieces, and a sharp fragment from it bit into my cheek.

The ladles flashed again. A buzzing horde of insects soared into the air and a moment later a second barrage descended on the stockade, smashing splinters out of the logs. Before I even realized that we were being bombarded, Vyrin was flung off the platform with a strange crunching smack.

"Slingsmen," Marat Andreyevich howled desperately. "Get down!"

I dropped onto the planks. Vyrin was squirming about on the ground with his head shattered. Grisha didn't have a face any longer, the stone ball had smashed it to mush.

The stockade shuddered; the barrels and the planks were overturned. The Niva's oak bowsprit crashed into the gap and the loosened logs were sent tumbling. Deprived of support, part of the wall collapsed. Following the car, our enemies poured in through the breach in an unstemmable flood. But although the battering ram had thrown them to the ground, the Shironinites still managed to organize their defence. The first enemy line ran straight onto pikes or were struck down by spades and axes. The onrush faltered, fell back and then flooded forward again. Animal-headed men stubbornly climbed in through the breach, grunting and growling, ready to give their lives in order to topple, tear, strangle.

I rushed over to the spot where my comrades were fighting. A bloody ruck had formed beside the breach and the trampled earth was slimy and slippery. In the intense crush I couldn't get a proper swing and I poked with my hammer, looking at the drink-soaked Siberian faces contorted in fury, at the fading eyes, still as pitiless as ever, at the bare, grinning teeth with clumps of foam clinging to them…

> And in that firing line I stand again with them!
> Beside a distant unknown village,
> Set high upon a nameless hill…

The bass voice drawled out the words of the refrain mournfully and the music stopped. The needle wheezed and there was a click. Warriors in armour and slingsmen appeared in the breach. There was no one to change the records. Strengthened by the reinforcements, our enemies pressed forward. The carnage shifted to the centre of the yard. The soldiers of the fourth group, the ambush brigade, climbed nimbly over the wall, hurrying to bloody their weapons.

The continuous swirl of spattering blood, clashing metal, yelling and groaning scattered us. Lancemen forced me back against the deepest section of the stockade. Their rapid lunges seemed to trace out an invisible but precise semicircle, within which I remained invulnerable, and I watched as my reading room melted away.

Tanya thrust her rapier into the eye slit of an iron visor and the sharpened rod pierced through the back plate of the helmet. The rapier stuck solid. The ponderous carcass fell abruptly, disarming Tanya. She parried a downsweeping club with an arm that snapped instantly under the brutal blow. An axe sheared through the mesh of her fencing mask and its hooked back emerged in a flurry of bloody spray.

Dzyuba was caught from the side of his swollen eye and hoisted up on a pitchfork. He jerked his legs about as if he was struggling with all his might to do chin-ups on a bar. Slingsmen stoned Garshenin to death from a distance, and a few warriors from the second brigade were also caught in the murderous hail—they collapsed with the backs of their heads smashed in, never knowing from where death had struck them.

Anna knocked the helmet off the head of the advancing shrill-voiced eunuch with her flail. For a moment a flabby woman's face was revealed, with peroxided hair and thick purple lipstick smeared on the lips. The second blow of the flail crushed a dyed tress into the temple bone with a soft, bloody crunch. The next moment a spiked gaff bit into Anna's neck. She fell, still clutching her trusty flail, and an animal-headed warrior in shaggy fur boots jumped onto her prostrate body and started stabbing her furiously with his lance. Ievlev's massive hammer smashed his howling face to smithereens.

Kruchina forced his way into a crowd of careless slingsmen. Working deftly with his bayonet and a captured hatchet, he struck rapid blows that were fatal to these lightly equipped soldiers, unskilled in the subtleties of hand-to-hand combat. The death-dealing ladles and bags full of stone balls were useless against the swift blades. The slingsmen fled from this overwhelming rampage of stabbing and slashing in a disorderly gaggle, and they would have suffered even worse as they fled if the warriors of the ambush brigade hadn't covered them.

I kept trying to break out of my phantom cordon of invulnerability, but lunging lances drove me back again. I saw Marat Andreyevich backing towards the village soviet, strewing his path with enemies hewn down by his sabre. A horned head went tumbling onto the reddish sand. A warrior in a padded helmet with round metal plates fell and sprawled across the ground. A slim harpoon thrown by someone scraped across Marat Andreyevich's cheek, striking out scarlet sparks. One of the lancemen besieging me shuddered, his backbone crushed. Ievlev's hammer flung a second one aside. The third lanceman swung round and ran for it. But Ievlev and his fatal hammer were not the reason for his fright.

The picture that unfolded before me finally hurled me out of reality. Like some fantastic, monstrous vision, a gigantic woman appeared in the breach of the stockade. She was wearing a dirty orange waistcoat over a vast, outsize knitted jumper that looked like smoked fibreglass, and blue trousers tucked into boots. Her swollen rhinoceros shoulders were covered by a flowery shawl. The woman's face was puffy and red, and there were curly, chemical-yellow tresses that looked like matted sheep's wool dangling from under her helmet. She was dragging an immense hook on a rusty, creaking wire cable, and with a few flourishes of her mighty hand she set the gigantic mace twirling so fast that the cable merged into the rippling, flickering air and the hook became transparent.

With my clouded mind I didn't realize immediately that in these fateful minutes a legendary warrior of the Mokhova clan and awesome mythological relic of the Gromov world, Olga Dankevich, had appeared before my very eyes. Trampling the bodies with her elephantine legs, she walked within the impregnable three-metre radius of her mace as it looped the loop and whistled through figures of eight.

I saw the pale terror that suddenly swept over the faces of the stormtroopers. They pressed their backs hard against the stockade in order not to be taken for enemies by mistake.

Marat Andreyevich weighed a heavy pitchfork in his hands and flung it at Dankevich. But even before his throw the humming propeller had tilted. The hook swung a metre above the ground, sand swirled up into the air, and the invisible cable, better than any shield, knocked the seemingly weightless pitchfork aside, flinging it over the stockade. The hook's next revolution grabbed up Dezhnev, swung him round like a sputnik in orbit and smashed him into the log corner of the remote dwelling with a crunch of breaking bones. Blood gushed out of Marat Andreyevich's mouth and his eyes froze, still open.

With two minutely precise swirls of her mace Dankevich first knocked away Kruchina's bayonet, reducing the hand that had been gripping the weapon to ragged tatters, then flattened the fireman's helmet. The hook buried Kruchina's fallen body in the sandy ground, leaving it in a deep crater.

Ievlev cried out in fury and pain. The tip of a bear spear that had been thrust through him from behind crept out of his chest, as long and broad as a sword. He fell to his knees, thrusting his hands and the spear tip into the sand.

Alone, shackled by black despair, I saw my dead comrades and the dozens of enemies they had killed. The reading room had bled to death and, like a true librarian, I was leaving it last.

Holding out my hammer, I stepped into the shadow of centrifugal death. The invisible cable sheared through the air, whistling just above my helmet. Dankevich suddenly smiled with her iron-toothed mouth and called to me in a vodka-hoarse voice: "Come here, I won't touch you." The skittish words sounded like the wind: "Come closer, my little one. Stand here by the fat woman. I'll take you out…"

I waited for a shattering blow followed by darkness, but the cable whistled even higher above me…

A warrior's duty and loyalty lifted dying Ievlev to his feet. In a few fleeting strides he was already beside Dankevich and he pressed himself against her like an ardent lover who had crept up furtively, so that the long tip of the spear that had doomed him sank right into the burly woman's flesh.

Dankevich swayed, and her drunken smile was replaced by a mask of bewilderment. She retched up spittle with a slight purple tinge. The hand holding the hook's cable remained raised, but the hook sank lower as the radius of the mace shortened with every turn. Dankevich breathed heavily, like a bulldog, and blood flowed down her fat chin, dripping onto the worker's waistcoat. The cable stopped moving and the hook buried itself in the sand. Fused together, the two bodies collapsed heavily to the ground. Nikolai had died before that moment, not knowing that he had defeated Dankevich.

THE APPEARANCE OF GORN

I SUDDENLY FELT an attack of irrational fear, as if in some inconceivable fashion, in the heat of the battle, I had failed to notice that I was killed long ago. I didn't understand what was happening. It wasn't as if I had ceased to exist for my enemies, but simply that they looked at me without any predatory greed, as if they had already taken the coveted Book. Just to make sure, I touched the cold top of the case with my hand—the Book was still there. I was standing on both my feet, and I definitely wasn't seriously hurt. No one tried to disarm me. I was removed from the action, an object of taboo. All of my recent adversaries' behaviour had taken place outside the context of the fighting, and perhaps that was why I realized that the attack really was over and done with. Fury had degenerated into turbid weariness and indifference, and I merely contemplated the same bedlam of pain and blood that had lodged in my memory since my first satisfaction.

The yard was transformed into a genuine junk pile of the dead. The wounded groaned: there were many of them with hacked-off limbs or mutilated faces; some squirmed about on the ground, some who had lost their minds crept about on their knees, covering the back of their heads with their hands. The warriors who had survived attended to the wounded and maimed and sorted out the dead according to their fighting brigades. Blowing out smoke, the Niva rolled out from behind the stockade and dragged away the logs that had been knocked down.

Severe-looking women appeared, camouflaged as road and construction workers—blue padded work jackets, padded trousers, soldier's tarpaulin boots. On their heads they wore headscarves or beaver-lamb caps with earflaps, the colour of tarnished bronze. Like Dankevich, every one of them wore an orange waistcoat. The women were armed with hammers on long handles, crowbars and shovels. Soon they filled the yard. They didn't help with the clearing—they merely observed, or rather oversaw.

The attackers' actions betrayed their nervousness. They hurried, quarrelling quietly among themselves. I realized that everything was being done with wary, alarmed glances at the stony faces of the working women. Eventually they dragged the compressor into the yard, as heavy and bulky as an armoured car. They set out boxes on our home-made table—an amplifier and a portable record player.

People formed up in their brigades in front of the village soviet as if it was a military parade. The air was filled with a kind of mute solemnity. A woman in an orange waistcoat lowered the arm of the pickup onto a record and the speaker broadcast 'The March of the Enthusiasts' with an admixture of butter seething on a frying pan.

On the work-days of great building projects,
Amid the merry rumbling, flames and clanking,
Greetings to you, land of heroes,
Land of dreamers, land of scientists!

An old woman stepped into the yard through a breach cleared in the stockade. She was leaning on a cane, but it was clear that she only required this additional support as an attribute of her age. The old woman walked lightly, with the majestic nobility of an erect reptile, some ancient humanoid lizard. Her small head was framed by silvery fluff that had been painstakingly shaped into a hairstyle. Set in her wrinkled, lipless face, with a scaly covering of pigmentation, was a pair of prominent, lacklustre eyes, attentive but motionless, as if they had been drawn on an eggshell. The pointed nose and chin created the impression of a tortoise's open beak. The crop, as wrinkled and soft as an iguana's, ran under the lacy snow-white collar of her blouse. All her other clothes were black—the severe tweed jacket, the long skirt, the shoes. Her elbow was pressing against her side an old-fashioned leather handbag with a large clasp in the form of two small spheres.

The old woman stopped beside me and gave an almost imperceptible sign—not with her hands, but with her ossified eyelids covered in blue veinlets; she simply moved them slightly—and the music stopped.

"Alyoshka…" the old woman said in an affectionate voice. "Don't be afraid." Suddenly she smiled.

The decrepit, cracked voice jumbled the feelings in my head.

"We'll sort out the people…" She walked round the intertwined bodies of Dankevich and Ievlev.

"Olka," the old woman continued, "has been killed too…" Her serpent's glance paralysed my eyes. "That's bad…"

She spoke curtly, packing the meaning into the minimum number of words, strained through her teeth, as if she didn't have enough air for long phrases. The trembling, guttural bleating and the note of hoarseness had disappeared, or become insignificant. A colossal imperious power shone through every gesture she made and every turn of that little head. This grand, noble lady, bearing the signs of the elect on her proud, superb visage, deigned to notice me. I realized joyfully that she was not angry, but was scolding me, like an imperious progenitrix scolding her mischievous grandson. I gave heed to her, entranced.

"Ah," she said with a wave of her hand. "I'm not sorry! I was sick of Olka… She thought too much of herself."

Then the grand lady surveyed Ievlev and said respectfully:

"A gallant knight…"

She looked at me again with surprised indulgence.

"But you're weak… You succumb easily…" Then she took pity and bestowed a radiant smile on me. "Let's introduce ourselves. Polina Vasilyevna. My surname's Gorn. Have you heard of me?"

I nodded.

"Ritka spoke highly of you… Give it to me," she said, sticking the cane in the ground and holding out her free hand.

I meekly took off the case.

"How does it open? With a key. Or is there a mechanism? You open it," Gorn told me.

I hastily pulled the key out of my pocket and unlocked the case.

Gorn turned to the stormtroopers

"A hitch… I was wrong! What can you expect from an old woman?… This is the Book of Memory!"

A sigh of disappointment rustled through the ranks. The commander of the ambush brigade stepped forward.

"How could that happen, Polina Vasilyevna?" The croaking, cracked tone of his voice stung my ears, pampered by the velvet speech of Gorn. "You promised us a Book of Endurance! What have we spilled our blood for?"

"Still not content?" was all that Gorn said. "One step forward… Briskly, now… Briskly…" she said, urging him on.

"Polina Vasilyevna! I implore you!" the commander said, shaking his head and clenching his jaw muscles. "Stop these jester's tricks. The Book of Power won't affect me in any case! Comrades!" he exclaimed, addressing his men. "You wake up too! Don't allow yourselves to be swindled! We demand a Book of Endurance!"

Most of the soldiers in the ambush brigade seemed to wake from a hypnotic trance. After a moment's hesitation, ten soldiers followed their commander. Four remained unpersuaded and carried on standing in the assembled ranks along with eleven soldiers from the first storm brigade. There were also seven soldiers from the second storm brigade and ten slingsmen standing there.

Encourage by this support, the rebel added:

"Polina Vasilyevna, we carried out your orders. Now we expect you to keep your promise…"

"Look... Now he talks..." Gorn rasped unexpectedly. "He demands... Who is he?..."

The enchantment of her voice had evaporated. Her appearance was also transformed. I looked at Gorn, but didn't see that proud turn of the head—only a birthmark with blue warts peeping through the thin covering of hair on the gaunt crown of her head. This birthmark really did look quite repulsive. Blinking away my mirage, for a brief moment I saw in front of me a decrepit old woman with pink bald patches on her trembling, desiccated head.

Gorn evidently realized that her spell had faded.

"Wait a moment, Alyoshka... I'll sort out... The problem... With this egotist..." The tone of her voice gathered charm and strength again. The ugly birthmark was not so much inconspicuous as visually insignificant. "It's a shame," Gorn said in a loud voice, addressing the brigades, "that there is no Book of Justice... The one-hander forgot to write it... It would be a good idea... for some... to read it..." She jabbed her handbag in the direction of the group of conspirators. "Do you all want to grab the prize? They're demanding it for themselves!" Gorn exclaimed with exceptional inspiration. "And what about them?" The handbag pointed to the surly ranks. "Didn't they fight? Haven't they lost friends?"

For me, and probably for the weary, dismal majority, the meaning wasn't particularly important. I was conquered by the confident voice, the facial expressions, the nervous impulse, the gesticulations. Gorn persuaded, explained, commanded. I felt a thrill of joy at seeing the miraculous effect produced on the gathering by Gorn's speech. The ambush brigade really hadn't played a decisive role in the battle. They were the last to become involved and more of them had survived. But that didn't give them any special right to claim the trophy won in battle by the entire army!

It was as if the Shironin reading room had not perished half an hour ago, as if people dear to my heart had not accepted a martyr's death! Once again I forgot that I was being shamelessly duped by the Book of Power. The moment in which a mental effort could have halted the enchantment had been missed.

Gorn baited the doubting readers, eroding their will.

"Do you want to cheat your comrades?" she rebuked the rebels menacingly. "To rob them?"

Poisoned by this venomous eloquence the warriors in the first three rows whispered furiously among themselves. No one remembered the broken promise and the Book of Endurance any longer. Why would they? A handful of villains were planning to take away their hard-won reward.

"Don't listen to her!" the commander of the ambush brigade droned in a pitiful voice. "She's trying to set you on us!"

He spoke in vain; they didn't believe him. The female guard closed round Gorn in a tight ring. From behind their backs she shouted: "They are traitors, thieves and saboteurs! Kill the saboteurs!"

A massacre began. The renegades resisted desperately, but the odds were uneven. For a few minutes the small plot of land in front of the village soviet was once again transformed into an arena of death.

Gorn contemplated the carnage with a smile.

"That's it… Serves them right… What an idea… 'Jester's tricks'…" The men's resistance to the bookish spell had stung Gorn to the quick.

"All done, Polina Vasilyevna!" a beast-headed warrior announced, shaking his harpoon over the fresh corpses. "There are no more saboteurs!"

"I congratulate you on your victory!" Gorn shouted and gave me a cunning wink. "Hurrah!"

The brigades didn't sense the note of mockery and guilelessly took up the cry. They were genuinely happy and they gazed at Gorn with devotion in their eyes.

The women in padded jackets parted, allowing Gorn to step forward. She surveyed the battered army that had shrunk to twenty-five men in a day.

"Comrades," said Gorn, "we are united by the bond of blood and the Book... What could be stronger? Nothing! Remain as one reading room... My advice... Who is your leader? All right, you'll work that out yourselves. But now... I keep my word... Here!" She flung the Book of Memory, as if she were tossing a bone from the dinner table. The Book soared through the air, fluttering its pages, and fell. Several men threw themselves on it straight away.

Gorn spoke in a confidential whisper.

"I bet you that by evening there'll only be half of them left... Who gives a damn? Right, Alyoshka? Let's go into the house. We'll have a chat, there's something I want to talk about... Where are you going?"—that question was for the mercenaries. "Not so fast! What about cleaning up after yourselves? Get some spades... And dig graves..."

Gorn pulled her cane out of the ground. I saw that it didn't end in a rubber tip, but in a point, like an alpenstock. The old woman swung round and strode towards the village soviet. I obediently followed her.

A fierce-looking middle-aged woman with a scorched cheek tagged on after us. Gorn called her Masha. This creature was apparently the old woman's orderly. She was carrying a tightly stuffed travelling bag with the metal cap of a thermos flask jutting out through the parted zip.

The guards remained outside—two large female workers with hammers froze by the door. Only the orderly Masha went into the room with us. After assessing the modest decor, she immediately selected for her mistress the only chair with a high back and arm-rests, and solicitously placed a small cushion, as flat as a pancake, on the hard plywood seat. She set a shaggy pouffe under Gorn's feet. Then Masha took a telescopic stand out of the bag and on the round surface set out the thermos flask, a steaming cup of an infusion with a minty smell, a small sugar bowl and a spoon.

My hammer, my armour and my helmet had been taken from me at the entrance by the guards, but even so, the vigilant Masha searched me again. The Solingen cut-throat razor was found in the pocket of my trousers. The orderly continued the search with especial zeal, shamelessly rummaging in my crotch and between my buttocks with her tenacious fingers. After the search Masha wrapped Gorn in a rug—the old woman accepted her attentions without letting go of her handbag and rested her dangerous cane against the arm of the chair. Masha lit the stove and left.

Gorn was in no hurry to start the promised conversation. At first she stirred sugar in her drink for a long time. Suddenly she asked:

"Perhaps you'd like some tea? It's healthy, mint…" Without waiting for my agreement, she took the cap of the thermos flask, splashed a generous amount of hot liquid into it, dropped in two lumps of sugar and stirred it. "Take it…"

The thin metal had heated up in a second. As if deliberately, Gorn had filled it with tea right up to the brim. I almost dropped the scorching hot cup, but managed to set it on the floor, scalding my palm in the process, and sat down on the low bench. The tips of my fingers swelled up in red blisters.

Gorn gave a crooked smile.

"As they say in Ukraine… If it's hot, blow on it, you fool. Burned yourself? No? Want to ask something?"

"Yes, Polina Vasilyevna. Why wasn't I killed?"

"An interesting question… Because you're needed…"

"By whom?" Hard as I tried to maintain my courage, my voice trembled. "Your Mokhova?"

"Lizka?" Gorn worked her bloodless lips and sighed briefly. "Lizka's gone… Lizka was killed… By Selivanova… A grievous blow… An irreparable loss… We've been in mourning for a month…" However, I didn't hear any particular sadness in her voice. "I'm in charge now…"

"Selivanova?" I asked, flabbergasted. "Margarita Tikhonovna? She killed Mokhova?"

"Why, yes," Gorn confirmed impatiently. "Ritka-Margaritka. That louse. She came to see Lizka… They had a talk… And then she stabbed her. With a knitting needle, in the throat… She said: 'Lizka betrayed the ideals'…"—at this point Gorn threw her hands up in the air—"What ideals?"

"And where's Margarita Tikhonovna now?" I asked, guessing the answer in advance.

"In accordance with martial law…" Gorn said harshly. "Is that clear enough?"

"I think so. You believe that a reader of the Shironin reading room could only have killed Mokhova on the orders of the librarian. And now you've decided to take revenge…"

Gorn stopped looking serious and snorted.

"What an analyst… Ritka was one of us! She always was!" Gorn laughed good-naturedly. "Selivanova was planted even before Neverbino. A year before… And not only Ritka. Lots of them. They had a mission. To collect information. And report…"

I realized that Gorn was telling the truth, but I still couldn't imagine the principled, transparently honest Margarita Tikhonovna as a devious agent of the Mokhova clan.

"It's child's play," Gorn continued. "We wiped out the local crowd. Completely… So there wouldn't be any witnesses. We took the Book… Ritka went running to the nearest reading room: 'Take me in! Mokhova's destroyed us!' A refugee. So they took her. Felt sorry for her… See how simple it is… But Selivanova's one of us, a Mokhovite."

All of this was just too much to take in. I didn't condemn Margarita Tikhonovna for her two-faced life. My memory refused to betray our long conversations on summer evenings, the old gramophone records, the tea from the old electric samovar, the biscuits and, finally, the terrible chaos of September, when only Margarita Tikhonovna's moral support helped me remain as librarian and retain my mental fortitude.

"Of course, she got used to all of you," said Gorn, as if she were reading my mind. "In five years! She settled in… Ran wild… Stepped out of line… She got attached to you. But she didn't forget her duty. She brought the Book of Meaning…" Gorn snapped open the catch of her handbag. "Here's the Book… Unique… The most important one of all. But it didn't work. Perhaps you can guess why? There was an insert at the end. With misprints…" She abruptly opened the book at the back flyleaf and scraped her nail across a scuffed stripe with traces of glue on it in the middle of the page. "But now there isn't any insert… It's gone… Disappeared… It was there but it vanished!" Gorn's pupils flashed with orange blast-furnace fire. "Ritka said…"—the appalling, imperious voice pressed down hard on my brain with all its crushing hypnotic power—"…that you have the insert. Give it to me. I'm asking you nicely… And you won't be killed, I promise… On my word of honour… Where's the insert? Give it to me!" she repeated magisterially.

At that moment I would have complied with any request from Gorn. Shackled by a devout, abject timidity, I replied:

"Polina Vasilyevna, I haven't got anything. I swear to you!"

"Look into my eyes, you little bastard!" said Gorn, transfixing me with terror. "Into my eyes! Tell me the truth! Or I'll kill you! Cruelly!"

"I swear, Polina Vasilyevna," I whispered, crushed. Icy sweat mingled with tears on my cheeks, Terror stirred my hair like regiments of fleas.

"I haven't got anything!"

Gorn suddenly tempered the intense heat of her fury. The imperious voice died away. A hot shudder surged though my body. My teeth chattered and I felt a damp heat in my back, as if I had woken from an exhausting malarial delirium.

"All right, all right, stop shaking," Gorn said morosely. "I can see. You're not to blame… It's that bastard Ritka and her cunning games…"

I picked up the overturned cup with trembling fingers. My heart was pounding dully, as if it were inside a tank. The air could barely seep into my paper throat, crumpled by terror.

"Ritka, Ritka…" Gorn muttered in annoyance. "Even after death you play your dirty tricks, my friend. I'll tell you what, Alyoshka…" She pondered for a moment. "Let's think logically… The first thing. Ritka had ideals. Concerning Meaning… That was why I killed her. She just wanted power… The second thing. Ritka would have kept the insert safe… At any price… And the third thing. To do with you, Alyoshka. She had plans. Grandiose plans. She loved you… That's why you're still alive… Ritka calculated correctly… You're the only thread now… You croak and the insert's lost. And the Meaning is lost… You know everything… Subconsciously, of course… Since you were a friend of Ritka's…"

Gorn looked me over curiously.

"Ritka said you read the Book of Meaning… Is that right?"

"Yes, I did."

"With the insert?"

"Yes."

"So that means…"—the old woman's voice had a rapid, chiming note to it, the ring of a coin that is spun like a top—"…you know the Truth?…"

Gorn swung away abruptly, as if someone had slapped her across the face. Hard nodules of fury swelled up on her notched cheeks. Apparently the old woman's pride was wounded because the Meaning had not been revealed to her—the great and sagacious Gorn, the empress of cruel old women—but to that worthless creature Alexei Vyazintsev, the librarian of the obliterated Shironin reading room…

"Alyoshka," she said in an almost plaintive voice. "Tell me about the Meaning… Sit a bit closer."

The Book of Power was still working, and I kept nothing back.

THE LITTLE GRANDSON

"I THOUGHT ABOUT IT SO MUCH..." Gorn murmured. "What it would be like... Meaning... Eternal labour... And personal immortality... They say... While Moses was copying out the Torah... The angel of death couldn't take... His soul." Gorn moved her hand and the thin gold bracelet of a watch showed from under her sleeve. The old woman gave a long, drawn-out moan: "Oo-oo-ooph-ooph-o-okh..."

I felt the slightly rotten breath of unclean teeth and sick bowels brush across my face. I hadn't noticed when the transformation took place in Gorn. It was as if the hooked, peeling nose and disproportionately large, flabby ears had suddenly emerged from inside her. The moles and numerous senile warts on her face—on her narrow, dried-up forehead and cheeks—were flooded with buckwheat-coloured pigment.

"We've sat here too long, Alyoshka... It's time to read. The Book of Strength. I read it twice a day... After all, I'm ninety-five... My natural life is over. Only the Book keeps..." Gorn grimaced malignantly. "Don't like the look of me? Old? Ugly? Not a queen any longer? Not an empress? That can be rectified... I'll just read the Book of Strength again... And you'll respect me again."

I felt inexpressible shame and revulsion for my minutes of vile, squalid toadying to this decrepit creature whose malicious will had condemned my friends to death...

"What's it go to do with me?" Gorn exclaimed astutely. "Ritka gave the village away... The killing was done by those out there..."—she pointed out of the window—"I wanted the Meaning. Do you hate me? Do you want to take revenge? Well, you shouldn't…" Gorn's knotty fingers tightened on the cane leaning against her chair. "I saved him from death," said Gorn, singing her own praises. "I strictly forbade anyone to lay a finger on him… What? You don't believe me? You're an interesting one… All the readers croaked… For some reason he's still alive… And where's his gratitude?" That hoarse tone of voice that had lost its power to enchant or charm was still able to convince. "And aren't you ashamed?… To kill… an old woman?… Alyoshka… Ay-ay-ay…" A long, slim blade suddenly glided out of the cane. The blade froze a centimetre away from my face. I didn't even have time to recoil from it. "Do you see?" Gorn asked me mockingly. "I'm more agile than you. One movement of my hand… And you're gone…"

"You won't kill, me," I said cautiously, pushing the sword blade aside with my palm. "You want the Meaning."

"Well, not all that much…" she said with an affected yawn. "What's the big deal? The veil of the Soviet Mother of God over the country…"

Realizing that Gorn was trying to conceal her emotions, I said confidently:

"But it gives immortality! And even the Book of Strength doesn't help you there, Polina Vasilyevna…"

"I like living," Gorn admitted. "I don't like dying." The blade swayed in front of my face for a moment and slid back into the cane with a click. "But all the same. We haven't got the insert. So what good is the Meaning?" However, she said that in a perfectly friendly voice. "It's funny… Ritka was a fool… What was that she said?… Er… Er… Ah, that's it… 'I left the Meaning to Alexei… As a memento…'" Gorn laughed with a rasping sound. "But you don't remember anything… What kind of a memento is that?"

At that moment I knew where the insert from the Book of Meaning was. I stared down at the floor trying not to betray my agitation.

"Don't be sad, Alyoshka," said Gorn, interpreting my slumped shoulders and lowered head in her own way. "I won't touch you for the time being. I give you a month... You're on probation... But hurry. Don't weaken. Rack your brains. My patience isn't elastic... It will snap."

"Polina Vasilyevna..."—meanwhile I had thought up a question to allow me to weigh up all the prospects of my unexpected discovery—"...was it your idea to play music during the fighting?"

"No. It was Ritka's idea... A placebo. But it helps... Not everyone... It depends on their character. On their age... Their cast of mind... And then you have to... get the right song... We're figuring things out little by little. For some we'll put on a record. For others we'll brew up an asthma remedy. Herbs from the chemist's... That has a bracing effect too... Various means. But you must agree... Giving out the Book of Fury... or Strength... to all sorts of riff-raff..." Gorn nodded contemptuously towards the window. "They can do without. Without a Book more of them will croak... Right?"

"Did you meet Margarita Tikhonovna a long time ago?"

"A good long time ago..." Gorn said sombrely. "Ritka's mother, Valentina Grigoryevna... was next to me... in the ward. In the old folk's home... We all started with her... With Valentina Grigoryevna... You could say we were the pioneers. She brought Ritka. When was that?... Eighty-six... Fourteen years ago... Ritka wasn't even fifty yet... In her prime..."

"And what about Margarita Tikhonovna's mother? Is she still alive?"

"She is... Only she's in a demented state. She used to oversee the Manitogorsk region... Now she's been punished. Don't get upset. She's taken care of..." Gorn gave a cunning smile. "Are you trying to get me off the subject here?"

"No, Polina Vasilyevna. I just asked."

"What else are you interested in?"

"Well, let's say the insert is found. What happens to me then?"

"You won't die."

"I see…" I said and plucked up my nerve. "I need guarantees, Polina Vasilyevna."

"Guarantees?" said Gorn, amused and surprised. "For you?"

"The moment you get the insert, you'll eliminate me."

"I won't kill you… Isn't my word enough for you?"

"Not really, Polina Vasilyevna."

"You're getting impudent, Alyoshka," said Gorn, growing tenser. Her thin, colourless lips flooded with blue.

"You'll distort your promise or interpret it in a way that suits you. Perhaps you won't kill me yourself, but someone under you will. If not them, then the mercenaries…"

"You're strange, Alyoshka," Gorn said reproachfully. "Funny. Your life's hanging by a thread… And you're haggling like a Yid… But you haven't got any bargaining counters."

"I'll remember where the insert is, Polina Vasilyevna. Definitely. It's just a matter of time. The more reliable the guarantees are, the sooner I'll remember… And one more thing…"

"Yes?" said Gorn, leaning forward. "I'm listening carefully…"

"Don't use the Book of Power to influence me again. It leaves a very humiliating feeling behind."

Gorn snickered.

"You don't like the Book… And my will is humiliating… Very high and mighty! You've got carried away by your arrogance, Alyoshka."

"You're the one who's arrogant, Polina Vasilyevna. You don't want to negotiate on anything. Out of sheer caprice and conceit you're willing to sacrifice the Meaning and immortality…"

Gorn made a strange sound, like a creaky cupboard door opening and swaying to and fro. When she finished laughing, the old woman said:

"Ritka was right… There is something about you… I understand… I can arrange things… Not even my command… Will make them kill you… On the contrary, they'll tear poor me apart instead… Do you like that idea, Alyoshka? You'll be the boss…

The leader… But I also require guarantees… You're asking for a lot… And in exchange… Zilch. Empty promises. That's not really fair, is it?"

I met Gorn's gaze and realized that I'd fallen into a trap, like Gogol's character Khoma Brut. The grey mirrors of my dismayed soul immediately reflected a mental pandemonium dominated by terror and guile.

"Alyoshka! You green, snotty-nosed kid!" said Gorn, leaning back in her chair in elation. "Very bright!… Attaboy! Well, let me hear it, don't be shy… There, you see… Just as you asked… Without the Book of Power… All up front, no tricks… And if you decide to get awkward… I'll call my girls… They're real craftswomen when it comes to torture… Oh, believe me…" Gorn suddenly turned serious. "There, you see, Alyoshka… And where are… your guarantees now?"

I hated Gorn and despised myself. In the morning I was still prepared to die in battle, and suddenly in half an hour I had lost all the resolve built up over six months. The explanation for it all was simple: I wasn't daring by nature and the main motivation for my actions had always been shameful fear of what people around me would think. The reading room had perished, and I'd been left alone with my essential inner self—and that inner self didn't want to die in battle, or under torture, and accepted any conditions in advance, simply in order to survive.

I tried to build up a stock of shame. When it appeared, I felt even more disgusted. I didn't feel the kind of powerful, creative feeling that lifts the coward into the attack. It was the tearful morning-after repentance of the drunkard who has drunk away the money for his children's bread—the feeble spasms of a puny conscience, which dissolve in that glass to cure the hangover.

I tried in vain to make myself abandon all the ruses and stupid hopes. I told myself that putting things off would only prolong the torture, exhorted myself to accept a worthy death: "They'll kill you in any case. Before it's too late, wring this old woman's neck and die with dignity!"

The Book of Power had broken me fundamentally. I refused to listen to the voice of sombre truth, knowing in advance that I would give Gorn the insert that Margarita Tikhonovna had hidden in her photograph, and then I would wheedle and whine and try to squirm my way out of things.

"All right, Alyoshka…" said Gorn. "I'm not a spiteful woman… I'm warm-hearted. This is how we'll do it… You'll be the 'grandson'. From now on, you're not Vyazintsev. You're Mokhov. We'll keep your first name—Alyoshka. So as not to get confused. How old are you?"

"Twenty-seven…"

"You look younger… About twenty-three… Alyoshka Mokhov… Born in 1978… Your story is this: Lizka gave you away as a baby… In the maternity home… And I found you… You are the legitimate heir… How's that for a guarantee?" Gorn shuffled her beetling brows expressively. "And let's dot all the i's and cross all the t's once and for all… So there won't be any misunderstandings… No grudges… For what happened to your readers… If it wasn't me, it would have been Lagudov or Shulga…You were doomed… No matter what… Accept it… You'll be just fine with us. It'll be nice and calm. If you start feeling down—we'll find you a girlfriend. An old woman who's a good housekeeper. About fifty years old… Don't get nervous. I'm joking again… Let's run through it one more time. Your name?"

"Alexei Mokhov," I said, feeling on my skin the chill of the irrevocable crossing of another Rubicon. "But won't we need documents too?"

"Don't let that worry you… I still know some people. We'll set you up with a passport… Don't get distracted. What was your mother's name?"

"Tatyana Andre—"

"Alexei! Don't be stupid!" Gorn shouted art me. "She was called Yelizaveta Makarovna. Remember that well… You childhood was spent… Well? Answer!"

"In an orphanage."

"Correct. Did you graduate from a college?"

"Two. A Polytechnic Institute and a —"

"The Polytechnic will do. A talented orphan… Alyoshka Mokhov… Grew up in an orphanage… Made his way, got on in life… Wonderful. And now tell me… Where did Rita stash the insert from the Book?"

"I think it's in the back of the frame of Margarita Tikhonovna's photograph…"

"And of course, the photograph has been lost…"

"No, it's here."

"Where, in the hut?" asked Gorn, looking round nervously. "Where? Did you hang it on the wall?"

"In my bag. With my personal things. In the porch, beside the trestle bed. It's a big, check bag…"

"We'll find it."

"But I'm not absolutely certain. It's an assumption…"

"Mashka! Mashka!" Gorn suddenly called in a piercing voice. Her orderly burst in, flinging the door open with a crash.

"Mashka! Stop!" said Gorn. Then, savouring my fright, she carried on in a quiet tone of voice: "Look in the porch. There was a check bag…"

"There's a dozen of them," the orderly boomed in a deep, hoarse voice. "It's like a den of speculators…"

"Bring them here," Gorn ordered, giving me a saucy wink. "You've done me proud, little grandson!"

PART III

The Curator of the Motherland

THE BUNKER

I HAVE MORE than enough dramatic talent and artistic restraint to keep an ending secret, even when I know very definitely what it is. All that I have at the present moment is the closed space around me—a room eight paces long and the same across. A ceiling three metres high with a quietly purring, milky neon lamp on it. The sun's light doesn't penetrate in here. On two walls side by side there are dummy window frames, stage decorations flanked by heavy blue curtains. Landscape photo wallpaper has been stuck in the window spaces, representing the false views from the insultingly fake windows: one of Red Square in the morning, the other a view of a large city at night, with the tracer-bullet lines of car lights. And hanging on the wall like a small pictorial window is a reproduction of the painting *The Ice Has Gone*: a chilly bend in a little grey river, a sky the colour of frozen lead, an earthy bank, the ochre of thawed patches, snow, birch trees, a meadow on the far side of the river as red as a cow's hide, and a distant fringe of forest.

The door in the room is real, made of riveted gunmetal, with a round peephole and two strong bolts—perhaps that's why the room reminds me of a war bunker. The bolts aren't shut, but the door doesn't open anyway. The mica peephole is always black, its lens covered on the other side by a little curtain inaccessible to me—the peephole was designed for the convenience of those who are on the outside. Earlier I used to sit at the door, waiting for light to quiver in those black optical depths and indicate that, although locked in, I was still under observation. But alas, nothing

351

ever trembled in that bottomless, spellbinding blur. I'm afraid it is simply not permitted to observe me. After all, I am a sacred figure.

One of the walls contains the shaft of a dumb waiter. The only part showing on the outside is the cover, which looks like the damper of a stove. The dumb waiter comes to life four times a day. I say "a day", but that's an arbitrary definition. I don't have a clock or a watch to tell the time by. If the dumb waiter contains a plate of soup as well as other food, I assume that lunchtime has arrived, and that outside the bunker it is day, and I put a tick in an exercise book. There are a hundred and sixty nine of them and I presume that a few days might have been missed—I didn't start keeping a calendar of my incarceration immediately. I have been under lock and key for more than five months, and outside it is March or April 2001.

I can't complain about the quality of the food—it's regular canteen fare. The standard breakfast is vermicelli with a meat patty, salad and tea. Lunch is pearl barley (or pea, or rice) soup, mashed potatoes with a large frankfurter, bread and stewed-fruit water. The afternoon snack is cocoa and a curd-cheese pastry. Supper is a potato cake with sour cream or perhaps, for a change, flapjacks with jam and tea. The side vegetable sometimes changes: instead of mashed potatoes there might be boiled buckwheat or millet; instead of soup there might be clear broth or thick cabbage soup. On my nominal Thursday the frankfurter is replaced by fried hake. I have plenty of food.

I used to send regular notes in the dumb waiter with requests to increase the standard ration, but nobody responded to my requests. There's a radiator in the bunker. The rusty pipe oozes hot water, which doesn't affect its heating function at all. I have appropriated a glass and now I put it under the sparse rusty drops. In about one "day" it fills up to the top.

About two months ago I started laying in reserves. Of course, I can't keep meat products—they go off. The only thing I set aside is bread, and I have almost a kilogram of rusks...

It is not possible to get washed in the bunker. The problem of personal hygiene is solved by a large packet of cotton wool and a five-litre canister of medical spirit. Every three "days" I moisten some cotton wool and wipe down my body. Sometimes I pour some spirit into the compote and treat myself to a cocktail. In the morning and the evening, in addition to everything else, the tray bears a fragrant strip of chewing gum—a substitute for a toothbrush.

For answering the greater and lesser calls of nature, I have a porcelain bedpan. Our dumb waiter is divided into two parts. In the top is the tray with the plates and glass, and in the bottom is the bedpan. I felt ashamed the first time sudden acute anxiety instantly affected my intestinal tract. But all the awkwardness is far behind me now.

There is an excellent writing desk in the bunker—natural oak, a time-honoured office design, with a fabric-upholstered top. One of its corners is broken and crushed—I tried to use the desk as a battering ram and hammered on the door with it. There is a table lamp with a green shade. There are Books laid out on the fabric desktop. So far there are six of them.

After about two months they sent down a Book of Strength that roused wild hopes in me—they couldn't simply "bury" such a valuable rarity of the Gromov world. I even ventured an attempt to blackmail my jailers, writing notes saying that I would destroy this extremely rare, and quite possibly unique, copy.

The Books of Power, Meaning and Joy arrived, and I shuddered. The neon light went out and the air in the bunker immediately condensed into a prickly fish's backbone in my throat—I realized why the librarian Alexei Vyazintsev had been locked up. After short intervals I received the Books of Fury and Endurance...

Every time I raise the cover of the dumb waiter, I pray that the Book of Memory will not be there, although I know that one day it will happen. Such is the will of Polina Vasilyevna Gorn.

In a drawer of the desk there were about ten ballpoint pens, three simple pencils and a pencil sharpener. In addition, I have six general school exercise books—four with squared pages and two with lined pages. I wiped my behind the very first time with squared pages, and then my jailers took pity on me and sent down toilet paper.

In the first week they sent down the cotton wool and medical spirit, a comb and a Kharkov electric shaver, with signs of having been used; below the blades there was a lot of coarse, grey stubble that looked like a boar's bristles—probably the old women used it to shave their hormonal moustaches. I kept my clothes on for a long time, but by the end of a month they were impregnated with the smell of sweat. I gave in and put them in the dumb waiter. In return they sent me hospital pyjamas, a dressing gown and stretched woolly socks.

For sleeping I have a couch—a sturdy, pre-war model. Instead of a pillow I have a cloth bolster under my head. There's no sheet, but I do have a grey hospital blanket. In addition to the desk and the couch, there is a chair in the bunker. A fine chair with a soft back. True, it is a bit rickety, but that's my fault. I smashed it against the door and then put it back together again.

The way the dumb waiter is built makes it impossible to climb into the shaft. And squeezing into the actual niche of the lift is quite out of the question. No matter how tightly I might curl myself up, there's no way a man 190 centimetres tall can fit into a box the size of an oven.

I have studied the walls of the niche carefully. It is set in a solid metal beam that moves up and down the shaft in the manner of a lift. When the niche is in line with the cover, the cover opens and I can take out my food. For the rest of the time the cover is cunningly pressed closed by the edges of the beam. Using the Book of Strength, I have bent the cover slightly and seen the blank metal behind it.

I have tried to break through the wall several times. Behind the bricks there was concrete, and I abandoned any attempts to scrape through it with a splinter of wood. Soon I came into possession of a pair of nail scissors, but I felt reluctant to blunt them. Now I formally perform the ritual of "digging-out" with a disposable plastic spoon, which is already half used up.

My schedule is simple. I write or I read a Book—Endurance or Joy, depending on my mood. Twice a day I perform the ritual of "digging-out" by scraping diligently at the wall with the spoon. After supper I arrange myself on the couch and sleep until the dumb waiter creaks again.

I have got used to the views from the "windows". I usually read by the "Avenue at Night". But the writing goes better beside "The Kremlin in the Morning"—that's where the desk is. In essence, nothing has changed since Polina Vasilyevna Gorn first brought me to the bunker—a former book repository. At that time I could still walk out of here…

I look at the dreary landscape in the wooden frame, and in my mind's eye I see a different murky river with slippery banks. If you turn your back to the water and walk through the channel of a ravine for about ten minutes, you can climb up to a charred stockade. There is nothing there to remind you of the people who recently moved in here, the heroic defence of the village soviet, the blood and the death, but the deep ravine is a common grave, concealing for ever the bodies of thirteen Shironinites and about seventy of the deprived readers who attacked us.

Leaning my hands against the low window sill, I glowered as I watched the victors, supervised by morose female workers, carrying the bodies out of the yard. By evening all the seriously wounded had died—during the day they groaned, asked for water, tossed about, but at sunset they calmed down and went quiet. Then they were also carried into the ravine.

After dismissing her orderly, Gorn went through the bags in person. In one she discovered a portrait. Gorn broke it with a crunch, impatiently smashing the glass under her heel. She beat out the shards of glass by hammering the frame against the table. The photograph fell out and a small piece of paper with the title "ERRATA" swirled through the air to the ground…

IN THE OLD FOLK'S HOME

T HE NEXT EVENING a UAZ van with a red cross on its side
      rushed us to the Old Folk's Home. I don't remember the
roads we followed. I slept all night and half a day. The plain-
looking exterior of the van concealed a perfectly comfortable
interior, fitted with a couch, a chair and a fold-down stool. Gorn
magnanimously let me have the couch; she took the chair and
Masha, the orderly, installed herself on the stool. Gorn immediately started reading the Book of Strength. The vigilant Masha
carried on guarding me. I stopped fighting my exhaustion and
passed out.

I awoke in the afternoon. Gorn was reading again. I surrepti-
tiously observed her, then dozed off again, until I was woken by
lively chattering—it was Gorn talking to a sleepy Masha. After
the Book, Polina Vasilyevna was clearly feeling an exceptional
access of strength. The old woman amused herself for a while
with little round pieces of foil that she folded in two or in four,
depending on their size, and then set them out in a line on the
broad armrest of the chair. Then she twirled around in her
fingers a little rod that looked like a large nail, but was soft,
as if it was made out of plasticine, and easily preserved the
impression of every squeeze of her gnarled fingers. A silly kind
of march started playing in her handbag and she announced
triumphantly:

"I'm bringing something!… It's a surprise!… No, not that!…
A grandson!…"

The old woman moved back the curtain and gazed out into the night for a long time. Out of the corner of my eye I saw smooth whiteness flying by, reminding me of flying above the clouds.

"It piled up overnight…" Gorn commented. "Winter…"

"He's awake," Masha suddenly said in a hoarse voice.

Gorn immediately swung round. Her face lit up in a smile.

"Alyoshka! You do like your sleep!"

She leaned down to the armrest, took aim and flicked her nail, as if she were playing at Chapayev. A piece of foil was sent flying and struck me a palpable blow on the cheek; it turned out to be a bent coin.

"Arise, arise, you working folk," the mischievous old woman said as she bombarded me. "Battery, take aim! Fire!"

"Stop it, Polina Vasilyevna," I said angrily. "That hurts."

Gorn burst into joyful laughter.

"Want a bite to eat? Mashka, give him some! Don't be greedy! He's a great boy! Our treasure! Our own flesh and blood."

The orderly handed me a sandwich in a greasy paper bag and poured me a glass of tea from a thermos flask. I wasn't feeling hungry, but I obediently chewed the sour bread and stringy smoked sausage.

"Need to go to the toilet?" Gorn asked solicitously.

I thought and nodded.

"Number two, number one?" she asked, with a wink at her orderly, who knocked with her fist on the partition dividing us from the driver's compartment and called: "Lusya, stop!"

The UAZ swerved to the shoulder of the road and stopped.

"Only don't run off," Gorn told me. "We'll catch up with you anyway… And put something on… It's turned cold… You didn't answer me… Shall I give you some paper?"

"There's no need…" I hissed through my teeth.

"Whatever you say… Masha, escort him…"

The snowy steppe washed over me in a chilly wave. Masha let me go ahead and climbed out after me. Swaying slightly on legs that were still unsteady after sleep, I stopped beside some frost-covered clumps of burdock.

Without taking her stony guard's eyes off me, Masha used one hand to hold up the edge of her padded jacket and the other to pull down her trousers. She squatted down not far away. The yellow fluid gurgled as it ran between the coarse soles of her boots. Masha suddenly asked.

"And are you really Mokhov, then?"

"Yes," I said without blinking an eye. "Alexei Mokhov."

"You look like Yelizaveta Makarovna." The orderly's voice sounded kinder somehow, and it had lost its spiteful hoarseness. She pulled up her trousers and adjusted her padded jacket. "Let's go then, love… Or else, God forbid, you might catch cold."

I was looking forward with awe to seeing a bustling Babylon, an indomitable fortress of aged Amazons, but what I was presented with was a neglected soviet building—a long, three-storey, red-brick barracks-style structure surrounded by a wall made of concrete slabs and prison-style gates with peeling paint.

The door of the UAZ was swung open by a fat woman with a sheepskin jacket thrown across her shoulders like a Caucasian felt cloak on top of a white coat. The fat woman's face was rather beautiful, but it was disproportionately small, like an elegant carnival mask set on a pig's face with numerous chins and a bloated neck.

"Good afternoon, Polina Vasilyevna!" she gasped out joyfully. I was accorded a cautious bow. "How was the journey, Polina Vasilyevna?"

"Fine, Klava, fine…" Gorn supported herself on the hand held out to her and climbed out of the vehicle. "Report on how all of you here… have been getting on."

I rejoiced in my heart that our arrival had not caused any serious commotion. The very last thing I wanted was to find myself in the centre of a jubilant or, on the contrary, morose, glowering crowd of decrepit female fanatics whose cruelty was legendary…

But there wasn't any crowd as such. About a dozen old women wearing astrakhan coats with the same old-fashioned cut were staggering along the paths of a small park between flower beds with a light covering of snow. Nurse-overseers were keeping an eye on them. All in all I counted about twenty fighting-fit inhabitants, including the welcoming escort of eight taciturn female bodyguards. The garrison was small even by the standards of the most average reading room.

We went straight towards the building, with Gorn and the wheezing Klava leading the way. Masha and I walked behind them. Klava recounted the news.

"We've received the annual reports from Novosibirsk, Chita, Irkutsk and Krasnoyarsk. There's sad news from the Khabarovsk region—the regional prefect Shipova passed away at the age of seventy-nine. We've had correspondence from Tver, Vladimir, Lipetsk and Ryazan. And the most important thing. There…"—Klava handed Gorn an impressive stack of paper—"Stenographic reports and summaries. We recorded Piskunova, Belaya, Shvedova…"

"Not now," Gorn said impatiently. "I'll look at them later… No, all right… Let me have them…"

The escort drew level with the herd of astrakhan coats. One old woman left the others and hobbled towards us, pushing her way through the bodyguards.

"Polya, Polya," she squealed pitifully. "Where have you been?"

"Reznikova! My beauty!" said Gorn, stopping and tenderly putting her arm round the old woman's shoulders. "Are you married?"

"Polya… Polya…" The old woman caught hold of Gorn's hand and pressed the palm against her own cheek. "So long? Where were you?" Reznikova's seeing eye watered and glowed with the joy of recognition, while the other, with the dense, milky cataract, shimmered with insanity. "Polya… Where were you?" she repeated tearfully.

"I'll tell you later."

Something inside the old woman made a liquid intestinal sound.

"Reznikova… My sunshine…" Gorn said tenderly. "Nadya-Valya-Galya-Tonya!" she shouted to the nurses. "Get everyone back to the wards! Wash them, dress them, feed them… And prepare them for a reading. Beginning at fifteen hundred hours…"

Reznikova was led away. She resisted desperately and howled something incoherent. The other old women also became agitated. One tried to take her clothes off, another seized her chance to grab something that was lying on the ground and stuff it in her mouth, trilling sickeningly, like a cockerel, when the nurse tried to extract the filthy thing from her ward's mouth. Startled by her cries, the old women scattered in all directions.

"Girls!" Gorn exclaimed irritably to her escort. "Don't just watch! Catch them! Masha! Do you need a special invitation?"

The bodyguards and the orderly ran to help the nurses. The old women who had relapsed into dotage were not particularly agile. They were quickly herded together into a knot and led towards the entrance in the left wing of the building.

"Listen, Klava," Gorn suddenly asked. "How's Rudenko?"

"Fine," the fat woman replied. "What's going to happen to her? She smeared the walls with shit again…"—she laughed—"If only that energy could be used for peaceful purposes!"

"She's a good housekeeper!" Gorn said admiringly. "And tough. It even makes me feel envious. Have they tidied up the wards?"

"Yes, Polina Vasilyevna. Komarskaya and Pogozhina were on duty. They whitewashed the walls too, though they swore themselves blue in the face…"

"Hey, you!" Gorn suddenly shouted to the bodyguards who were holding the aged fugitives by their astrakhan collars. "A bit more politeness there! They're really getting out of hand, the riff-raff!" Gorn watched the old women leave with a morose air and sighed: "There, Alyoshka… Take note… If you've got money, it's 'yes sir, no sir'… If you don't have money, it's 'bugger you'… That's the *gloria mundi* for you… They only needed to get weak… And there's no more respect… Not for age, not for title… It's just that they've been without the Book of Strength… For more than two weeks… So their brains have given up…"

Klava moved ahead of us, ran up the steps of the porch and pulled open the glass door.

"Please, come in…"

We walked through a hall that was like an aquarium and into a corridor that ran off to the left and the right. Facing us at the centre was a broad stairway of speckled stone with plaster banisters. The landing between floors was decorated with a semicircular stained-glass window with a sky of heavenly blue, two drooping ears of wheat and a crimson star. Filtered through the different-coloured glass, the sunlight spread itself on the floor in a hazy petrol rainbow.

To the right of the stairway, a woman in a white coat was sitting behind a perspex window with the word "Administration" on it. She was holding a telephone receiver to her ear, evidently informing the upper storeys that the boss had arrived.

"Klava," said Gorn. "Go on… Get the equipment ready."

"Yes, Polina Vasilyevna," the fat woman said with a nod and darted up the stairs. I was left alone with Gorn.

The corridor was genuinely gloomy—poorly lit and as long as a Metro tunnel, and in both directions it ended in twilight and shadows.

A line of matt spheres glowed on the ceiling, like an unknown planetary system of dull, identical moons, but they only lit up themselves, not the twilit expanse of the endless corridor.

"Let's go," said Gorn, and led me along the corridor. The scuffed blue linoleum squeaked repulsively as if I weren't walking, but being pushed on a hospital bed. I heard the voices of nurses and the sandpaper shuffling of numerous slow soles from a distant stairway.

"Well, Alyoshka, are you disappointed?" Gorn suddenly asked. "Were you expecting more?"

"It's strange that there are so few people…"

"In recent times… many things have changed. Out of the old guard… only fifteen are still alive… You saw them… The ones who were walking in the yard… Former generals, regional prefects, centurion-mums. Before, each one of them had… three or four hundred people… under their command… So much for your Lagudov!…" Gorn lowered her voice to a half whisper. "I've been trying for more than a year to persuade them to take well-deserved retirement… But I can't do it… Be extremely cautious… They're only dead wood for now… After the Book of Strength they'll be themselves again. These ladies are very dangerous… and still influential… I'm afraid they won't go for the hogwash about… a newly discovered grandson… The younger ones will believe it… But you can't fool the old ones… God only knows what ideas they might get into their heads… Don't go wandering round the Home… Just to be sure… I'll give you Masha… Don't take a step without her… She may be stupid… But she's as strong as they come… Yes… And don't even think about mentioning the Book of Meaning to anyone… And in general… until the initiation, try… not to let anyone see you…"

"What initiation?"

"You have to be… consecrated as the grandson… Urgently… Without any precise status… you're an empty space… No one will stand up for you… And the elders… will be against any 'grandsons' in any case…"

"Perhaps you shouldn't read them the Book of Power yet?"

Gorn frowned jokingly.

"Are you suggesting I should kill them? With Alzheimer's and Pick's? My battle comrades?"

"You misunderstand me, Polina Vasilyevna," I said hastily.

"Don't make excuses… I understood perfectly well… We're here." Gorn stopped in front of a door with a plaque that said "Director" on it and fiddled with her keys. "Basically, you're think-ing… along the right lines. In my time… I suggested an idea to Liza… I had serious doubts… that one of the elders… as my Masha would put it… was playing the rat… That is… hiding Books that had been found. Each of them effectively had… her own network of agents, with spies and scouts… fighters, theoreticians, couriers, suicide operatives… How could we find out? You can't climb inside someone else's head… And, after all, they're experienced and cunning… There's no way to get them to talk openly…"

The ponderous luxury of Gorn's office was impressive. The walls were faced with a honey-coloured, semitransparent material that resembled amber. The gleaming parquet floor was decorated with patterned inserts. Most of the furniture matched the ornate decor. An old writing desk crowned with a slab of marble, an armchair as sumptuous as a throne, a carved baroque secretaire, a grandfather clock that looked like an expensive coffin, a branching chandelier with garlands of crystal, velvet curtains, a palm in a tub. Discordant notes among all this lordly magnificence were struck by the office cupboards crammed from top to bottom with papers, the black leather sofa, the glass coffee table, the television, the two-chamber safe, the typewriter and the telephone.

Gorn flung the papers that Klava had given her onto the table.

"Come on in and make yourself at home," she said, pointing to the sofa. "Being secretive is an intellectual effort… When the personality deteriorates… control is lost. It's like wine… it loosens the tongue… And drunk or gaga… fundamentally it's all the same. We needed our colleagues suddenly to become more stupid… How could we do it? Why, elementary. Under some pretext or other… deprive them of the Book of Strength… After a week the lack of constant input… already affects the brain… It all happens confidentially… A stenographer is attached to the suspect, and she documents every word… Naturally, there were some innocent victims. To make an omelette, you've got to break some eggs… A few veterans pegged out. A stroke, or kidney failure, or a heart attack… But the important thing, Alexei, was that we caught the 'rat'. Or rather, she gave herself away. And you know who it was? Valka Rudenko, your Selivanova's mother. A long time ago—five

years now—she hid… a couple of extremely valuable Books. Valka
didn't live with us—she said her health was good enough… That's
the way we do things here… Those who can live independently,
without the Book of Strength, live outside in the district. I can see
now that Valka wanted to… stay in the shadows… But two months
ago she moved into the Home… With a diagnosis of 'cerebral
atherosclerosis'. She wanted to use the Book as treatment… Valka
was above suspicion… No one was checking her especially… But
since the opportunity arose…" Gorn laughed. "Thank God, all
the stenographic reports… came straight to my desk. Absolutely
appalling facts surfaced. Valka had a Book of Meaning, and she
gave it it to someone… Who exactly, we couldn't find out… Valka
was completely off her trolley… She couldn't string two words
together… I didn't report everything to Liza… Why upset her?…
Liza was absolutely raging anyway… Bearing in mind her previous
services… Valka was banned from the readings… Let her die on
her own… Then Ritka Selivanova showed up… with a Book of
Meaning… And that set the cat among the pigeons… The insert
was missing… Ritka was killed… At least we found out… that the
Book of Meaning had been sent to you… I won't try to hide my
curiosity, Alyoshka… I was intrigued why Valka sent the Book to
you… What is it that makes you so special? And you had the insert
too… Our agents got busy… They found your village… Organized
people for the attack… And that's the whole story… It's a month
now since Lizka died… Valka paints the walls… with her own shit…
It's horrible… But on the other hand… she would have resented
what happened to Ritka. And taken revenge… But when's she's
crazy… she can't even remember… her own name… Later, if you
like, you can pay her a visit…" Gorn looked through the sheets
of paper as she spoke. "No sedition… As pure as turtle doves…"

"What are those?"

"Stenographic reports…"

"But who have you recorded? Rudenko again?"

"No… the other lovely ladies…"

"The ones you abandoned to their fate?"

"Don't be sarcastic," said Gorn, suddenly angry. "I had no choice…" She hastily stacked the sheets into a pile and got up from the desk. "I had to go away… They'll only turn senile… I'll die without the Book…" Gorn opened the upper chamber of the safe and hid the papers away. The phone trilled. Gorn answered it and replied curtly: "We're starting in fifteen minutes… Damn… That interrupted my train of thought… I forgot what I wanted to tell you…"

"Polina Vasilyevna, may I phone home?"

"Where?" Gorn asked in amazement.

"You know, home. To my family. My parents or my sister. They haven't heard a word from me for a month now… They'll be worried…"

A wooden mask of cruelty suddenly seemed to cover Gorn's face.

"Your mother… Yelizaveta Makarovna Mokhova… is dead," the old woman said with pitiless, slow emphasis. "And the librarian Vyazintsev is dead… There is only Alexei Mokhov… He doesn't have a sister… And if Mokhov thinks that he is still… a little bit Vyazintsev… Alexei Mokhov will be dead too… Any more questions?"

"Yes…" I said in a depressed voice. Gorn's crude rebuke had reminded me yet again what a dangerous escapade I had got involved in. "When's the initiation?"

"I think it will be the seventh of November. We'll combine two celebrations… In the meantime, you'll get used to things, settle in…" Gorn looked at the clock. "I'll be back… in about four hours… Lock yourself in securely… Don't open the door to anyone. How can I keep you amused? By the way, have you ever seen the one-hander?"

"Who?"

"Well, Gromov."

"Why the one-hander?"

"What, you mean you didn't know? For crying out loud! Ritka didn't tell you? No? That's strange… Gromov lost his right hand…

at the front. He wrote with his left hand... We've got... his photograph. Shall I show you it? In *By Labour's Roads* there's only a pencil portrait. Ah, yes... You've only... read two Books..."

Gorn walked over to some shelves crammed full with many years of archive material. The lacquered spines of notebooks, folders and thick journals protruded from them.

"I think it's here..." Gorn pulled apart the plastic covers that had glued themselves together and dragged out a thick envelope. "Who have we got here?... E-e-er... Hello there!..." She turned round. "Have you seen Lagudov? No?" She handed me a dog-eared, faded photo that was once coloured, with a long white crack across its glossy surface. The snapshot showed a small group of people huddled together in friendly style, like a set of pan pipes.

"Lagudov and his inner circle?" I asked at random.

"No. This is 1981. A birthday at the publishing house..."

"Where did you get this from?"

"A company secret..." Gorn said with a smile and a wave of her hand. "There isn't any secret... Just normal intelligence work... We cadged it from Lagudov's wife... We gleaned... a lot of useful things from her...."

"And which one here is Lagudov?"

"The third from the right... There's a woman in a blue dress... with ruffles... and he's perched beside her... A real opera-singer type..."

Lagudov turned out to be a portly, well-fed gentleman with a dense thatch of greying hair. His dramatic appearance was spoiled by flabby cheeks and a chin the size of a small dumpling.

"And this is Gromov," said Gorn. "In this snapshot... he's already almost seventy... We appropriated it from his daughter. At first we wanted to initiate her into the cause... but then we changed our minds... Lizka was afraid of the competition..."

Staring out at me from the black-and-white photo was a distinctive old man with a thin face, who looked more like a physicist than a lyric writer, wearing glasses. His forehead was bony, as if it were faceted, and emphasized by a receding hairline on both sides. The horn-rimmed spectacles had slipped down his nose and the slim legs had lifted up above his ears, so that Gromov seemed to be looking through the lenses and over the top of them at the same time—with two glances. This produced a strange impression.

"A good portrait," I said, giving the photo back to Gorn.

"I like it too… The one on his grave… is the same."

"Where is he buried?"

"In the town of Gorlovka… in the municipal cemetery… Right, now, Alyoshka… Recognize this?"

The next photograph was of me. Slightly out of focus, because I had been caught in movement—my waving hand looked like ethereal pigeon fluff. Kruchina and Sukharev had also been caught in the frame, but they were completely blurred and cloudy, like ghosts.

"Our photocorps's work," Gorn explained. "Taken back in June… For the archive… Who would ever have thought it?…" She shook her head. "The new Shironin librarian… A pawn… A nothing… A tiny little screw…" Gorn held up her hand with the tips of her fingers bunched together, as if she was straining to make out something microscopic. "And the Book of Meaning… Even now… I can hardly believe it… All right then," she said with a start, "I'll go… You remember, right? Lock yourself in… Don't put a foot out in the corridor… Don't get bored… Take a rest… Watch the television… Only quietly… Don't attract attention…"

The moment the door closed behind Gorn I turned the key twice, but I still didn't feel any calmer. On the contrary, I now found myself face to face with a feeling of dangerous uncertainty, as acrid as heartburn. Pounding away in my head was the thought that I had to use this pause I had been given to analyse things. I strode round the office witlessly, repeating to myself, like an incantation: "I have to think everything through carefully." But there wasn't anything to think through. That is, I had plenty of thoughts, but they didn't require analysis. Everything was absolutely clear as it was: I didn't have the slightest degree of control over the situation and by acting independently I could only make my position worse.

I suddenly realized that I had been wanting to go to the toilet for ages, and now it was too late; Gorn had gone. I didn't torment myself, but simply took a leak into the palm tree's pot. Then I sat down at the desk. For a few minutes I was tempted by the phone, but after a moment's thought I decided not to violate Gorn's prohibitions. Maybe the line was monitored, and I didn't want to get on the wrong side of Gorn.

I spotted a print-out that Gorn had forgotten on the desk:

NATALIA ALEXANDROVNA SUPRUN. BORN 1915.
SEVENTEEN-DAY CASE HISTORY.

Week 1. S is anxious about the lack of readings. Irritable. Spends most of her time in bed, tries not to move or speak. Believes that in this way she reduces the use of her body's energy to the minimum and so prolongs her life.

Start of week 2. Sunday–Thursday. Emotionally heightened mood. Agitated. Gluttonous. Immediately after eating, she forgets about it and demands a new portion of food. Obsessed by the idea that the woman next to her in the ward, T.A. Kashmanova, is wearing her slippers. Becomes abusive and aggressive. Takes the slippers and reads out to Kashmanova the supposedly special inscription on the sole: "This is Suprun's slipper. Kashmanova is strictly forbidden to wear it."

End of week 2. Friday–Monday. Has lost the ability to keep herself clean and tidy. Finds it hard to get her bearings in the ward. Fussy and rude. Often becomes quarrelsome. Walks with a short, mincing stride, grabs everything that comes within reach, grates her teeth and laughs unnaturally. Happily sits by the television and makes conversation with the presenters. Her sense of taste is distorted. She picks up rubbish and earth outside and puts it in her mouth. Forgets the names of things. Instead of "alarm clock", she says "temporal", instead of "pencil she says "written", instead of "glass" she says "drinkable".

Start of week 3. Does not understand what people say to her. Her facial expression is frozen. Active. Broad, sweeping movements. Afraid to change her clothes, starts shouting and protesting. Keeps asking the same question all the time: "How much?"—then runs away without waiting for an answer. Wanders aimlessly around the corridors. Fingers the folds of her dress one by one. Takes matches out of a matchbox and puts them on the floor, then puts them back again. Sings the same set of words over and over to a definite melody and rhythm.

My attention was caught by the clamour of a vast nesting ground of birds of prey coming from the yard. I walked across to the window and my eyes were dazzled by a welter of orange waistcoats and padded work jackets. There were so many of them, perhaps a hundred and fifty or two hundred clamouring women. A truck slowly crept into the yard, pulling a compressor behind it. Another truck disgorged more female workers from its canvas belly. In only half an hour the almost extinct home was engorged with fresh strength.

Of course, I didn't switch on the television. It seemed to me that someone was walking to and fro outside the door—I pressed my ear to it and heard the linoleum squeaking as regularly as a pendulum. The invisible steps affected my nerves, and I tried to make as little noise as possible.

The marble slab was piled high with post. Some envelopes had already been opened, and until it got dark I passed the time reading this correspondence—mostly boring reports on the housekeeping.

*

Gorn appeared four hours later, as she had promised. She was not alone. Masha's jowly face peeped in round the door. Probably the orderly had been watching me in Gorn's absence.

"How did everything go, Polina Vasilyevna?" I asked cheerfully. "Well?"

"*Alles gut…*" Gorn said with a nod. "Although one reading is not enough. The girls have more strength… More than enough, in fact… But they don't have much more wits… They'll be their old selves again in a couple of day… You'll meet them then…" Gorn studied the desk and turned towards me. "The curious cat…"—the old woman's voice trembled with reproach; starting with a gentle tone, it suddenly slid down to a harsh crackle, like someone stepping on spilled sugar—"… ended up dead."

I took offence.

"I haven't touched anything, Polina Vasilyevna. Check for yourself…"

"Too much knowledge… can be dangerous, Alyoshka… But then, who are you here? That's right… The grandson… The future heir… Of the biggest clan of all… We'll educate you…" She went over to the shelves and tugged on a wide cloth spine with her nail. "There—you can browse through it at your leisure. Lots of useful things…"

"What is it?" I asked, taking the loosely assembled volume out of Gorn's hands.

"The Chronicle of the Home. And not only that… A little bit about everyone…"

I opened the cardboard cover with red corners. The close-set text had been typed on tracing paper. Blurred by carbon paper, the print was as fluffy as wool thread.

"Right, let's go, Alyoshka, let's go…" said Gorn, hurrying me along. "We'll get you quarters for the night. You're probably hungry. You can get something to eat at the same time…"

*

In the corridor we ran into fat, breathless Klava.

"Polinochka… Vasilyevna," she babbled, stifling as she breathed. "The room for our… e-e-er… respected guest…"—the fat woman bowed to me—"…is ready… All first-rate… They put in the couch, and a really fancy desk, a chair and a lamp…"

"Thank you, Klava," said Gorn. "Get over to the kitchen… to Ankudinova… Arrange for some supper…"

"Aye, aye," said Klava, raising her palm to her curls in a military-style salute, and dashed off down the corridor at top speed. Near the central stairway she turned a corner and disappeared from view.

"Remember, Alyoshka," Gorn told me, jabbing her finger at one door after another. "Administration, accounts… dental surgery and physiotherapy room… massage and dressings… after that, the linen room… the housekeeper's room… cloakroom… utility room… The two upper floors are all wards…"

From the main stairway and the alabaster banisters a more modest stairway led downward. We walked down it into an echoing basement.

"Here are the storerooms… The kitchen." Gorn drew air in through her nose and wrinkled up her face squeamishly. "It stinks like a cheap public canteen…"

The air in the basement was permeated with a warm onion stench. From behind the tiled wall I could hear the battlefield clatter of kitchenware and the cooks' owlish laughter.

"It's just that they had *rassolnik* for lunch," Masha put in. "The smell hasn't worn off yet."

"It's just that they boil up slops for lunch," said Gorn, mimicking her. "What sort of people are they?… They've grown idle in just three weeks… What's the point in trying? The old women are all gaga… They'll eat it anyway… Ankudinova's lost all sense of shame. I'll have her sacked and out the door before she knows what's happening!"

"Polina Vasilyevna, you shouldn't say that," Masha boomed in her deep voice. "The *rassolnik* was delicious. I tried it. And the potato cakes were tasty too."

"And now she has an intercessor to plead for her," Gorn carried on ranting. "The idle gossips are working hand in glove... They're as thick as thieves... And Klava too... Where the hell has she got to?"

I sensed that Gorn's grousing was contrived. She was clearly nervous, but I couldn't tell why. I suddenly felt terribly uneasy, and an invisible, icy hand ruffled up the hair on the nape of my neck, leaving it standing on end.

"Where are we going, Polina Vasilyevna?" I asked with affected indifference.

"To the bunker."

The basement ended in a broad ramp that ran down to a depth of several storeys.

"It used to be a bomb shelter," Gorn explained to me as we walked. "Then the Books were kept there... Now it's your personal study..."

We wound our way through concrete catacombs for about another minute until the path ended abruptly at an impressive metal door with a large wheel for opening and closing it, like in a submarine; it looked like the armoured entrance to a bank safe.

"Hard a-starboard," said Gorn, spinning the wheel. The unlocking mechanism clanged and the old woman pushed against the heavy door. The slab of steel slowly drifted inward. Gorn went in first and switched on the light. "Come in, Alexei, make yourself at home."

The bunker turned out to be a normal living room, not musty, and quite cosy to look at—an impression that was greatly assisted by the decorative windows framed with dark velvet curtains. Even the desk and couch that Klava had promised were there, and also the chair, in a white slip cover. The pipe of a ventilation shaft or rubbish chute protruded from the wall.

I immediately had the feeling that I'd seen this interior before, only I couldn't remember where—perhaps it was in a dream.

"They've fitted it out well... Good for them," said Gorn, prais-ing the bunker. "A luxury suite. In an Intourist hotel." She patted the wall proudly. "Three metres thick, no aerial bomb could ever penetrate it. The safest place in the Home. You'll live here for now… Until the initiation. No one will bother you. Just look at those bolts."

I looked round.

"And what are the windows here for?"

"To make it beautiful," said Klava, who had come up behind me. She was holding a tray with plates on it. Leningrad *rassolnik*, potato cakes with meat stuffing, sliced. Stewed-pear water. *Bon appétit…*"

"Thank you."

"You don't like it here?" the fat woman asked, genuinely disappointed. "A bit gloomy, right?"

"It's bad that there isn't a toilet or a washbasin…"

"You can't put in plumbing in a day," Klava sighed. "It's a lot of trouble. The lavatory's close by. Just a short walk down the corridor…"

"Don't be awkward, Alyoshka," Gorn intervened. "I'm sure you can run to the toilet without spattering the whole place."

"Polina Vasilyevna, you warned me yourself not to go out anywhere."

"That's true, I did. So don't hang about. Once you've relieved yourself, it's straight back… To the bunker."

"You can have a bedpan for the nights," Klava suggested. "I'll just bring one."

"And what about getting washed?"

"Masha will take you… to the shower unit tomorrow. She's personally… responsible for you…" Gorn gave her orderly a severe glance. "Answerable with her head, her ovaries and all her other innards…"

Masha and Klava laughed.

"Don't be sad, Alyosha…" Gorn said encouragingly. "The guard is only a temporary measure. Once you're a boss… you can wander about wherever you like…"

THE VIEWING

F OR THE NEXT three days not very much happened. I spent them locked away, only leaving the bunker in order to relieve myself. I was regularly provided with food and everything I needed by Masha, who was sometimes replaced by Klava. Gorn was busy with some business or other connected with my initiation. Perhaps she was preparing the ground with the old women who had awoken from their dementia.

I slept for long periods—that was the effect of the fatigue that had accumulated over recent weeks and, in addition, the bunker, with no natural lighting, encouraged lengthy sleep. For the rest of the time I studied the Chronicle. For the most part it was written in the dry style of minutes. Events and names were listed in a monotonous fashion: who found what Book, where and when and then set up a library or a reading room and when they were killed or, on the contrary, eliminated a rival. If the author doubted the authenticity of an event, then various sources with versions of the disputed episode were cited. In places there were tables and even maps on which arrows indicated the routes followed on foot by those long-forgotten distributors of Books, the wandering apostles. At the end of each chapter there were numerous notes, annotations, appendices and commentaries.

The Chronicle of the Home did not fit into this general style, betraying the author's emotional partiality. The text was thick with graphic metaphors, often breaking into frank adulation of Gorn. At times it gave the impression that it wasn't the pharmacist

Yelizaveta Makarovna Mokhova who was the real leader, but Gorn. And in all likelihood that is the way it was. At the very dawn of the Mokhova clan's expansion, Gorn sidelined her young boss, giving her the outwardly striking role of a sacred leader. The true power was focused in the hands of Gorn and several dozen old women. I had already realized that under the very best scenario the role prepared for me was the similarly formal role of "grandson". I didn't know what Gorn needed this for. At that time I wasn't concerned with such global questions. I read the description of the ritual of adoption with intense revulsion—I didn't want Gorn to think up some disgusting, unhygienic procedure of anointment that I would have to go through. Knowing Gorn, she could easily extract Mokhova's body from the grave for theatrical effect and stage the mystery of my birth for several hundred women. I told myself that I would have a word with Gorn and ask her to keep the ritual of initiation as simple as possible.

Thanks to the Chronicle, by the end of the third day I was fairly well versed in the history of the Gromov world. Recalling the sycophantic recommendations of Dale Carnegie, I learned off the names of all the "mums" who were still alive: Aksak, Nazarova, Sushko, Reznikova, Voloshina, Suprun, Fertishina, Kashmanova, Kharitonova, Guseva, Kolycheva, Temtseva, Tsekhanskaya, Sinelnik.

In the evening Masha came for me. She usually behaved in a relaxed—I would even say flirtatious—manner, as far as that was possible for a tough old woman with huge tattooed, mannish hands that she shyly hid in her sleeves, like in a muff. But this time Masha was extremely serious, with no clowning about.

"The elders want to see you," Masha informed me quietly and significantly.

"What did Polina Vasilyevna say it was?" I asked keenly. "The initiation?"

"Nah… The viewing. They're going to get to know you. They're celebrating the return in the canteen. Polina Vasilyevna said for you to get you dressed up for the occasion. So that you look presentable…"

Masha took me to a storeroom full of things left over from when the male half of the Home was exterminated. There were hundreds of suits hanging on crossbeams, looking like emaciated hanged men. Most of them were old-fashioned and decrepit.

"What size are you?" Masha asked, arming herself with a long stick with a hook on the end.

"Fifty-six…"

"Not an old man's size…" Masha scurried about between the rows of clothes, hooking everything that caught her eye and then laying it out in front of me. "Don't you worry. These aren't cast-offs. They were saving these for when they died, for the coffin. It's all clean, never even worn."

I rejected the shirts out of hand because of their proverbial closeness to the body and limited myself to a dark-blue sweater. Masha hunted out two good quality suits for me: the jacket from the black suit fitted me, and so did the trousers from the grey one. Then we set off for the viewing.

I remember how agitated I was as I walked up the broad stairway, leaning with my hand on the cool white convex surface of the banister. While still on the steps I heard a piano accordion playing—the runs were too shrill for a button accordion. A guitar jangled and I heard indistinct choral singing, mingling with trills of laughter in the background.

"They're cutting loose," Masha said approvingly. Nonetheless we walked straight past the canteen, which was ringing with voices and music. Masha opened the next door.

"This is the serving room," she explained. "Polina Vasilyevna's instructions. She wants to give the others a surprise. I'll go and tell her in secret that I've brought you."

The din of the celebrations was on my left, beyond a thin, impalpable partition with a broad square window loosely covered by a zinc shutter. Something started jangling in a cupboard built onto the wall.

"Oh, Ankudinova's sent the dessert," Masha said. She opened the doors, took out four oven trays and put them on the table. The room was filled with the pleasant smell of something baked with apples.

"You wait a few minutes. I'll soon be back," Masha promised, and ran off.

I pressed my eye to the crack between the shutter and the serving window.

The canteen was long and narrow, like a railway carriage. It had been illuminated with strings of little lights—the tiny glow-worms were scattered thickly across the ceiling and the walls, glittering like deep-ocean plankton. Black silhouettes moved about in front of my eyes, clinking bottles and erupting into explosive peals of jackal-like laughter. Somewhere very close to me a knife scraped lingeringly across a plate, and this porcelain screech set my teeth on edge. The merry-making was taking place between tables that were set out in a horseshoe. I saw fat Klava holding an accordion on her knees. She was playing 'The Blue Scarf', and half a dozen old women were weaving a cautious reel round some chairs. Polina Vasilyevna Gorn was sitting at the head of the horseshoe table, surrounded by her broad-shouldered retinue. She had her chin propped on her hand and was frowning slightly at the insistent noise as she listened carefully to Reznikova.

Before I could guess what the fun was all about, Klava suddenly broke off the tune, squeezing the bellows of the accordion shut. The old women squealed and made a dash for the chairs. One of them didn't get a seat and she jostled helplessly for a while and then retreated with a shrug.

"Guseva's out! Let's hear about Guseva!" the more agile old women trilled gleefully, stamping their feet. Their resemblance to little girls frolicking about during the break at school was comical, and they even called each other by their surnames.

"What shall I read about this victim?" Klava asked the group in a loud voice.

Guseva threatened her companions.

"If you take it out of week three, I'll never forgive you…"

The victorious women consulted and announced: "Day eight!"

Klava picked up a tall stack of papers, found the sheet she needed, cleared her throat and read out:

"A letter from Guseva to the elder Maksakova… 'Zhenechka send me a comb please please I really need a comb because Tsekhanskaya took my comb and lost it and now I haven't got a comb and they didn't give me a new comb so I really need a comb now what else can I write to you I'm fine Polya has gone away don't send any reports but please please send a comb now what else can I write to you come and visit don't forget and there's nothing else to write greetings to Vera Yuryevna and do please send me a comb…'"

Guseva dragged the superfluous chair off to one side. Klava started playing 'On the Hills of Manchuria' and the reel round the remaining chairs started up again. Klava deliberately played for a long time, teasing them, so that the old women and the spectators were soon exhausted by the tension. Someone even shouted out: "Stop mocking us, Klavka!" Then the accordion suddenly fell silent and the old women dashed for the chairs. Kashmanova was out and she was sentenced to a stenographic report of her fifteenth day of dementia.

Kashmanova gasped resentfully and threw her hands up in the air.

Guseva, who was out just before her, started reading with a gloating note in her voice.

"Uses too much lipstick, mascara, rouge and powder. She has plucked her eyebrows. Always carries a bottle of nail varnish around and constantly paints her nails. Wears beads, brooches and clip-on earrings. Flirts with an imaginary admirer and takes her clothes off. Takes the stenographer and nurses for her rivals and at such moments becomes aggressive. Sexually uninhibited. Constantly talks about sexual relations and masturbates openly. Wants to go to the Caucasus 'to enjoy the grapes and other pleasures'. Believes she is twenty years old and ought to get married. In the same tone of voice she says: 'And then I went down on my knees and gave him a French job…'"

The canteen shook with laughter.

"You great fools!" Kashmanova exclaimed, putting on an imperturbable air. "What's so unusual about that? Normal female behaviour! And you're all stupid fools! Especially Aksak and Yemtseva!"

Two old women on the chairs giggled contentedly.

Klava struck up 'The Autumn Waltz'. I saw Masha. She walked round the tables that had been moved together and went straight to Gorn. Masha leaned down to her leader's ear and told her something.

Klava switched tactics and the accordion growled to a halt after only a brief moment. The one caught was an old woman by the name of Tsekhanskaya.

"Stenographic report, day nine," Kashmanova read out in an expressive voice. "She has forgotten what her toes are called. She calls her big toe a 'thumb' and the others 'the ones that are smaller'. When she sees a syringe she says: 'Oh, they've brought the crystal!' If anyone tries to tell her that it's a syringe she asks in amazement: 'A syringe? Then what's crystal?' She claims that foreign agents have put their words in her mouth. She thinks 'blouse' but says 'sun'. She complains that people read her thoughts from her eyes, especially during the daytime. She asks to be locked in a dark room. She does not control her urine and stool…"

Several tables struck up a song to tuneless chords from a guitar.

Once there were four friends who lived a life of fun,
Chasing women, drinking vodka, beating up the wogs…

"Klavka!" the old women cried excitedly. "Let's show the young kids how it's done! Give us 'Evenings on the Ob'!"

379

"Polya!" said Gorn's companion, hammering her fist on the table. "You don't understand! If the reading's done right, you don't need any lighting. The light appears out of the reader!"

"Reznikova!" said Gorn, raising her voice. "There's no proof of that!"

Lines sung in a jaunty chorus rammed like a truck into a couplet about the adventures of the four friends.

> Please, my darling, help me out.
> On these sweet Ob evenings
> I love to dance and jig about.
> Learn to play the accordion!

> Ivan Ivanich picked them up!
> Ivan Stepanich brought them home!
> Ivan Kuzmich took off their clothes!

…the lead singer chanted in a loud, hoarse voice and the tables picked up the next line:

> And Ivan Fomich fucked them all!

…but the laughter that followed was drowned in 'Evenings on the Ob'.

> I going to dance with you and kiss you!
> Learn to play the accordion!

In the middle of this musical bacchanalia, Masha came back to the serving room.

"Let's go," she said. "They're expecting you."

I was suffering all the torment of a new boy at school who is exhibited for general examination by an unfamiliar and hostile class. When we walked into the canteen a swampy silence fell. The old women with their permed hair, bright make-up and festive clothes, the female bodyguards with their broad shoulders, bestial jaws, gaunt drinkers' faces and tattooed arms—the entire dangerous gathering studied me cautiously.

"This, colleagues," Gorn said after a long pause, "is Alexei Mokhov… I've told you… about him… He really does… look like Lizaveta Makarovna… doesn't he?"

"Uhu," Reznikova laughed dourly. "The way a pig looks like a horse…"

The old women smiled. They found the manoeuvring amusing.

"Polya," said the frail Tsekhanskaya, stroking the hair trimmed in fashionable curls at her temples, "the resemblance to Liza is very approximate." The "mum"'s little sparrow head was set on an equally delicate bird's neck.

"He looks a bit pale to me," Kashmanova said mockingly. Her robust, greasy nose looked rather like the heel of a yellow lacquered shoe; her cheeks were covered with a sprinkling of fine moles. "He doesn't suit us…"

"We'll feed him up," Gorn snorted.

"It's not that simple being our grandson," an old woman with red cheeks, vermilion lipstick, a bright flowery skirt and green knitted jumper told me. "Not everyone could handle it."

"He's a talented boy," said Gorn. "He'll get the hang of it."

"We need to test him," said a thin old woman with luxuriant purple hair hanging loose over her dress. "Set him an examination."

"Now you're talking sense, Kharitonova," said Guseva. "Let's take him on probation…"

It was obvious that not a single one of the fourteen took the story about a newly found grandson seriously. But on her other hand I didn't notice any open aggression in the old women's attitude. It was the bodyguards who worried me. They rubbed their hands together in a distinctive, masculine fashion, exchanging mocking glances, grinning with their stainless-steel crowns and scratching with coarse hands at the crotches of their padded trouser legs that were tucked into tarpaulin boots.

Even Masha, who was standing beside me, sensed that the massive women's fury was slowly rising and told them.

"Easy now, easy. No nonsense…"

"You're not being very welcoming, girls," Gorn said with a brief sigh. "We'll leave you…"

"Take him to the bunker, Polya," Reznikova agreed. "Out of harm's way…"

I confess that I felt tremendously relieved when Gorn and Masha finally accompanied me out of the canteen.

"Congratulations, Alyoshka," said Gorn, in what I took to be a hypocritical tone of voice. "You made a good impression."

"I don't think so…" I glanced round at Masha walking a little distance behind us and whispered furtively to Gorn: "They didn't believe you. About me being the grandson."

"Of course they didn't believe me. They're not… complete idiots…" Gorn pulled me closer by my sleeve. "Alyoshka, you blockhead, they're not concerned… about family connections… Lizka was a unique factor… of stability… She died… and the Home needs a new… focus for the balance of power… A kind of amulet… At weddings you often see a replacement father sitting beside the bride. You'll be the same kind of ritual relative… with formal responsibilities. Not difficult, but very important. I'll explain what it's all about… in more detail… later… So don't worry… It's all been agreed…"

Instead of going downstairs, for some reason they took me to the side staircase that led up to the second floor.

"I want to introduce you to another individual," said Gorn, turning back towards me on the final steps. "Of course, she doesn't deserve it… But we'll be magnanimous… Right, Alyoshka?"

"Polina Vasilyevna," I balked. "I'm tired of meetings. Perhaps tomorrow?"

"Don't be stubborn… What's so hard about meeting an old lady? We're here." Gorn stopped in front of a door and fished out a bunch of keys. "Tomorrow, Alexei, will be too late. We read her the Book especially… so that she could… talk to you. In a few hours she'll go out of her mind again, and we won't reanimate her any more. Seize the moment… Masha will wait in the corridor… Then she'll show you to the bunker."

Dense blue light spread symmetrical rhomboids from the window frame across the floor. The only thing in the ward was a bed with a high barred metal footboard and headboard. An old woman was lying on the sheets with her nightshirt pulled up. Her arms were spread and her hands were secured to the metal bars of the bed with broad straps. Her legs were immobilized at the ankles in exactly the same way.

"Necessary measures of restraint," Gorn said with a sigh. "Who knows what wild ideas she might get into her head?…"

She walked up to the bed.

"How are you feeling?"

The old woman stirred.

"Better than the lot of you."

"Sorry about the straps. When the Strength stops working… we'll untie you…"

"Thanks in advance. I won't be able to thank you later; I'll forget all the words." The old woman swayed the mesh base of the bed, setting the woven metal rustling.

"Can you guess why I've come?"

"To show me Vyazintsev," the old woman said simply.

"I thought… you'd find it interesting… to meet him in person. Come here, Alyoshka," said Gorn, beckoning to me with her finger. "She doesn't bite. Not yet…"

I took a few steps towards the bed, trying not to look at the swollen legs covered in blobs of varicose veins and the taboo curly shadow in the depths of the nightshirt. I had already realized that the old woman tied to the bed was Margarita Tikhonovna's mother.

"How long do you need, Valya? Will ten minutes be enough?"

"Yes."

"Only don't frighten him…"

"Go, Polya, go. Celebrate the resurrection of your comrades in arms. Let them enjoy their extreme amusement—deliberately going without the Book of Strength for a while and then reading out to each other what they all got up to."

"A game's not a game without some risk…" said Gorn, then she nodded to us and walked out.

"Hello, Alexei." The old woman's imperious face was covered with deep wrinkles that looked as if they had been incised with threads. The mottled hair, combed up and back, had fused into a growth that resembled a shelf-fungus on a tree. The flaccid ears ended in large lobes as doughy as wet white breadcrumb.

"Hello, Valentina Grigoryevna."

When she heard her name the old woman raised her beetling grey eyebrows.

"Was it Polina who told you?"

"She said it was you who hid the Book of Meaning."

"That's right, I hid it," the old woman confirmed in delight. "What else?"

"Your daughter in my reading room was…" I began and immediately regretted it. The old woman might not know that Selivanova had been killed, and the bitter news could be a blow for her.

"They told me Margo was no longer alive. I'm not suffering. I'll go completely out of my mind soon and lose the ability to grieve. I wouldn't want you to hold a grudge against her. I was the one who advised Margo to keep you on as the Shironinites' librarian…" The old woman flinched as if from cold. "It's drifting over my thoughts," she complained. "White and suffocating, like cotton wool. Soon it will smother them altogether. The illness is taking its toll… Would you mind not squinting at my body like that! I find it offensive."

I hastily turned away to look towards the wall and asked:

"Valentina Grigoryevna, it was you who sent me the Book of Meaning, wasn't it?"

Knots of muscle tensed, swelled up and disappeared under the gelatinous, trembling skin on the crucified arms.

"The Book was found in ninety-four. I had quite a large team of uninitiated agents working for me. The usual mercenaries. We didn't explain anything to them. It was easier and safer that way. Katerina Cheremis, who worked in the Moscow archives, phoned me: 'Valentina Grigoryevna, I've got a Gromov for you. *A Meditation on Stalin Chinaware.* A lucky find: the entire edition was pulped, but this copy was miraculously preserved in the publishing house's museum.' I was sure it was the wrong Gromov. There wasn't any book with that title in the bibliographies. But even so I went to Moscow. And what a surprise…" The old woman shifted restlessly. A baleful, damp flame blazed in the almost lashless eyes, the thin, bloodless lips filled with veinous sludge and swelled up like overtaut tendons. "You've read the Book and you know that it's a temptation. I couldn't resist either and I read it. And instead of a revelation I was given just one single word…" The old woman started breathing more rapidly. The wrists restrained by straps swelled up under the subcutaneous impulses of demonic energy. "Can you imagine how many people have died and how much blood has been spilled for the sake of three syllables that sound like a Russian merchant's surname—'Vyazintsev'? Not very much, is it? Not at all what I and fifteen hundred 'mums' were expecting. No, I decided not to destroy the Book. I eliminated the dangerous witness Cheremis. And then I set about transforming the clan. It had run to seed. We managed to dump almost all the superfluous 'mums' at Neverbino. After the battle Margo sent me a list of the new reading rooms, including the one that she had joined. I came across the librarian Vyazintsev…" The captive body strained at its bonds and the parchment cleavage of breasts that had mummified long ago appeared in the dangling neck of the nightshirt. "I didn't tell Margo about the Book of Meaning; she was only supposed to keep an eye on developments in the region. For many years I was consumed by frustration. Why some Vyazintsev or other? What if I defied the Book of Meaning and killed its incarnation? What then? How would the Books wriggle out of that?" The dry, desiccated nostrils fluttered as if the old woman had caught the scent of a quarry, the fine membrane of skin on the hollow of her throat trembled sensitively. "Vyazintsev was eliminated. But the Book kept on speaking his name. Margo reported to me that a nephew had shown up… I told her that she had to keep a close eye on you…" The old woman suddenly thrust her rump hard down into the metal mesh and jerked forward abruptly, and only the straps held her back. "It's nothing to do with you, you little bastard! Even the fact that you received the Book—that's a pure coincidence! My reason was clouded! I was obviously starting to lose my mind! You're not special! You're just one of a set of circumstances!" If she hadn't been speaking, I would have said that she was simply clacking her jaws, trying to take me by the throat with her gums, as pink as an Alsatian's. "The Book is free to choose its nominees! To point to anyone drawn into its range of influence! If you're not here, it will name someone else!" The old woman suddenly ran out of strength, fell back onto the pillow and half-closed her eyes. "But Margo didn't understand that. She was afraid that Lizka would kill you…" The old woman yawned benignly. "That's all now. I'm tired. I'm finished. Go away."

UNDER LOCK AND KEY

IN THE MORNING I got up, but the door of the bunker wouldn't open any more. I couldn't believe that this had happened and I kept calling: "Hey, is anyone there? Masha! The bolt's got jammed!" No one came. I tried shaking the door, but soon gave up—I was the only one that got a shaking.

A wave of intestinal panic swept over me. I grabbed the bedpan out from under the couch and squatted down. Then I turned out the drawers of the desk in a desperate search for paper. Several exercise books came showering out. I plucked a few pages out of the closest one and wiped myself.

After that I felt a bit better and set about trying to free myself with renewed energy. I took a run up and flung my body at the unyielding door. I shouted hysterically, straining my vocal cords to the limit: "Polina Vasilyevna!" At first threateningly: "I demand!" And then pitifully: "I implore you!" And then threateningly again: "I order you to open up. I am Alexei Mokhov!"

All in vain. I lost my voice and bruised both my shoulders. Exhausted, I lay down on the floor and hammered at the door with my feet. I stopped when my battered feet were a cramped block of pain.

It suddenly dawned on me that this had all been set up. They were observing me in secret! But of course! This was the examination for the position of "grandson", and I had done absolutely everything possible to fail it. Demonic howling, lowered trousers, intestinal cramps, convulsions on the floor. Appalling. Only a stout-hearted prisoner could count on freedom and power; a coward and nonentity didn't deserve any leniency—that was what the old women had decided. I almost groaned aloud in the realization that all was lost.

I had to correct the shameful impression that I had made on my secret observers as quickly as possible. And I had to do it so that they wouldn't realize I had seen through their game.

I called on my old acting skills to help. I laughed wearily, drew myself erect, spat on the floor and declared: "Why, the bastards…" I thought it sounded rather good. Firm, with a derisively hoarse note. A courageous, cheerful man had amused himself by acting the fool in front of the door for a while and then stopped. So what if he had relieved himself—that was only normal. He wasn't the kind of fellow you could frighten with a solitary cell. Now he'd just perform a few push-ups on the floor, then sit down at the desk and browse through the exercise books…

There were six of them… a black one, a light-blue one, a grey one and three brown ones. Ancient exercise books from immemorial Soviet times, in oilcloth bindings. I hadn't seen any like them for a long time—they had disappeared from the shelves many years ago.

The black one had been started. On the cover someone had written: "For Recipes". Inside, the exercise book had been divided up into chapters. "First Courses", "Fish Dishes", "Desserts", "Salads", "Drinks". There weren't any recipes: the headings were followed immediately by blank pages.

The brown exercise books were untouched, but I looked carefully through them all the way to the stanza of typographical free verse on the end flysheet.

POLINKOVSK CARDBOARD AND PAPER PLANT
GENERAL EXERCISE BOOK
Item 6377-U *96 pages*
Price: *84 cop.*
State Standard 13 309–79

In the grey exercise book the price had been crossed out and a new one written in, in ink—1.65 copecks. Below it was the signature of the person who had crossed out the old price.

Inside the light-blue exercise book there was a page from a tear-off calendar for Thursday, 14 October 1999. There was some kind of astrological nonsense on the front of it.

The sun is in Libra, ruled by Jupiter. Dawn: 07.57. Sunset: 18.33. Take care with you words and feelings; it is advisable to pray and express positive moods and attitudes. Do not overdo sweet foods. You should avoid influencing the liver, gall bladder, blood and skin. Illness of the lungs and bronchi may be treated. The Sun's stone is labradorite. The Moon's stone is jacinth.

Out of curiosity I turned the scrap of paper over and my heart fell like a stone, tearing its way through my insides. Printed there in tiny little ant-letters was this:

Feast of the Veil.

This feast has roots that go back deep into the pagan past, when our ancestors celebrated the meeting of autumn and winter. Folk beliefs linked the name of the Veil with the first hoar frost, which "veiled" the earth. After Christianity came to Russia, the festival was celebrated in honour of the Holy Virgin and her miraculous wimple—the Veil or *omophorion* that she extended above the people praying in a church, protecting them against "enemies both visible and invisible".

In ancient times the Feast of the Veil marked the beginning of weddings. Believing in the power of the Veil to expedite matrimonial union, girls ran to the church early in the morning and lit candles to the feast. There was a folk belief that the one who lit her candle earliest would be the first to marry.

In ancient times they used to say:

On Veil Day until lunch it is autumn, but after lunch it's chilly winter.

Veil Day, heat the hut and pray!

Granddad Veil Day, cover the earth with snow and me with a bridegroom!

After Veil Day, a girl will roar like a cow.

The blood rushed to my head in surges of heat. I leaned down lower over the desk, afraid that my face had set into a plaster mask of horror. For a long time I couldn't catch my breath. The air had been snatched away, as if I'd been plunged into a hole in the ice on a river. Thank God, I'd realized that they were watching me and I didn't give myself away; I checked myself in time. I knew only too well what the word "Veil" signified in Gromovian terminology...

A scrap of paper that flew in from the previous millennium. It is always here in front of me. My Black Spot and everlasting calendar. From that first day the bunker's time was frozen at 14 October, an eternal Feast of the Veil...

The pulsing of blood in my head faded away and my breathing returned to normal. My pounding heart clambered its way back up, fastening back together with an excruciating zip the innards that it had ripped in its haste. I forced myself to believe that the calendar page was not a subtle message from Gorn but a stupid coincidence, a misunderstanding.

I was distracted by the sudden rumbling of an invisible mechanism in the wall. I dashed headlong to the hatch. Standing in the niche was a tray of food and a clean porcelain bedpan, smelling of bleach.

Purely for form's sake I shouted up the lift: "Open up, open up!" The only reply was a tinny echo in the shaft.

I took out the tray: a meat patty with mashed potatoes, salad and tea. I wasn't hungry, but I ate. Calmly, with dignity, posing for the observers.

Then I put the bedpan full of liquefied terror in the lower compartment of the niche and the tray with the empty plates in the upper section. I closed the hatch. Inside the wall gearwheels started squeaking and a cable creaked...

I carried on performing for my audience for a long time—I blustered and swaggered, passing insolent comments; as soon as my vocal cords recovered, I bawled out songs—in short I played the part of a dashing, devil-may-care blade. Except that I slept with the ceiling lamp on. I tried it without any light, but the cosmic blackness of the bunker was immediately transformed into airless terror. That was more than I could take.

I stealthily studied the ceiling, walls, false windows and scenic photographic wallpaper and failed to discover any concealed spying devices. Apart from the peephole, there was nothing looking into the bunker, so I had been giving my performances of manly courage for the door.

The identical days rolled by, differentiated only by the side dish served with the patty. There was no one admiring the valiant prisoner; no one replied with any signals from which he could conclude that his behaviour had been duly appreciated. There was just the indifferent dumb waiter, delivering food and a bedpan to me four times a day.

The light bulbs were a greater blow to me than even the calendar page. They sent one with every lunch. I took out the tray, and there on the napkin was an electric bulb. Matte, sixty watts. At first I was glad. Then I felt terribly afraid, although I didn't give any sign that I had guessed: they wanted to provide me with plenty of light for future use. As an experiment I sent one back, and the next day they sent me two. The torture ended when I had accumulated forty or more of these bulbs.

One day I realized that my jailers weren't interested in my character and I stopped playing the stout-hearted hero. The only thing I still couldn't come to terms with for a long time was that I had been totally abandoned. The dumb waiter, although one-sided, was still a means of communication, and I insistently tried to establish a dialogue, writing extensive complaints addressed to Gorn, always starting with: "Dear Polina Vasilyevna…"

I requested her politely and urgently to explain the reasons for my incarceration and reproached her for breaking her word, although I knew that, formally speaking, Gorn had kept her word—I had been granted my life and immunity from harm.

In between the reproaches and demands, I tried to cadge petty concessions: give me another blanket, or vitamins and a television, or paracetamol and fresh newspapers. I didn't receive anything.

However, I can't claim that they didn't respond to me at all. Gorn had her own ideas about a prisoner's requirements. She sent me cotton wool and neat alcohol without any reminders. And they gave me an electric shaver and nail scissors, which I hadn't dared to ask for.

Every single day I scribbled letters and put them in the dumb waiter beside the dirty plates. Naturally, I never got an answer. No, I'm lying. They sent me an answer once. But not in the form of a letter.

It happened like this: I flew right off the handle and sent Gorn an abusive letter. It began with the words: "Gorn, you're a fucking bitch and a shitty whore!" Before breakfast I poured out onto paper my entire arsenal of obscenity. I was really hoping that this unprecedented boorishness would spur Gorn into a response.

And so it did. They sent me my lunch as usual, and floating in the glass of stewed fruit was a thick, ripe-green gob of spit. That was the entire correspondence, if I may call it that. However, I concede that it might not have been Gorn who spat in my drink, but the cook. She could have taken offence for her boss.

I apologized at length over several pages, saying that my nerves had given out. I didn't receive any indication that I had been forgiven, but no one spat in my drink any more. And I was thankful for that much.

I somehow became firmly convinced that they hadn't stuck me in the bunker in order to do me to death. They fed me and took care of me, which mean they must need me alive. And if Vyazintsev's life had some value, that meant that Vyazintsev's death must be undesirable. There was only one way to check this assumption—act out a suicide and lure my jailers into the bunker.

I didn't know what I would gain from the guards appearing in the bunker—I couldn't really expect to escape, and when I was exposed I would become a laughing stock. I had to think the whole thing through properly. After running through numerous possibilities, I chose a hunger strike. In the first place, death would be conveniently stretched out over time and Gorn might relent before things became critical. In the second place, it would be harder to unmask my pretence—how could they tell just how emaciated and dehydrated I really was?

I stealthily laid away reserves of bread, hiding it in my blanket... After I had accumulated about a loaf and a half I wrote a farewell letter.

The breakfasts, lunches and supper were sent back untouched. I fed in the darkness on dry bread, and then crept to the radiator to drink, hoping with all my heart that Gorn had not discovered this extra source of water. After slaking my thirst I turned on the light and withered away dramatically in open view. For the first three days I continued to use the bedpan—my body was still processing its remaining reserves. After that the bedpan went back up empty too—what could it have been filled with? The proud prisoner wasn't eating or drinking.

I arranged a special little privy out of paper and relieved myself there. And I urinated under the radiator, into the natural drain between the floor and the skirting board. And all this in total darkness. The radiator gave me two glasses of water a day at the most, so to some extent I did suffer from lack of fluid. In addition, my concentrated urine had a foul sewer smell. Thank God, the meagre bread diet had a positive effect on the consistency of my stool, which was dry and hardly even smelled at all.

It was the fifth day of my hunger strike. No one seemed in any hurry to visit me. To enhance the effect I coughed like a consumptive, clutching at my stomach with my "withered" hand as if I was stopping a wound—hunger pains. I drew my cheeks farther and farther in, imitating extreme emaciation, and sup-ported myself against the wall when I walked—a performance worthy of an alumnus of the Institute of Culture. Then I lay down on the couch, covered myself with the blanket and lapsed into feigned sleep. I was hoping crazily that soon the bolt would clatter and Gorn would walk into the bunker. Then I would have raised myself up on weak arms, forced apart my dried-out lips—in my grief I had eaten my entire store of stale rusks under the blanket and now I was terribly thirsty—and said: "Get out… I want to die…" and collapsed, with my sunken chest slumping back onto the couch.

Perhaps I was misled by the lack of a clock and I started expiring too soon. The enclosed space gave rise to a different sense of time. Later I tormented myself with the idea that I was in too much of a hurry, but on the other hand everyone's body has its own limits, and the old women had to take that into account.

The bolt didn't clatter. Gorn didn't come. I urgently needed to pee. I gave in and crept down onto the floor. The dumb waiter clattered—it had brought lunch. I suddenly felt disgusted: I was lying on my side under the radiator, easing my bladder in brief rivulets so that it would have time to seep away. The bunker smelled like a public toilet, and up there no one cared what was happening to me.

In a frenzy I got up, switched on the light and opened the hatch. I took out the bedpan and pissed like a human being. And I tipped my entire privy into it as well. I couldn't give a damn what the old women would think when they saw the three-day heap.

I dragged the tray out of the niche and greedily gulped down the soup. The main course was schnitzel with mashed potatoes— I thought I had never tasted anything more delicious in my life. And that was the end of my hunger strike. I put the plates, licked completely clean, back into the dumb waiter. The mechanism's gear wheels squeaked and the echo of the shaft cruelly distorted the mechanical noise into croaking laughter.

I made my second, and last, attempt a month later. I decided to commit suicide again—this time by slashing my wrists. The "blood" was made of water, ground brick and a portion of strawberry jam. I mixed the ingredients together in a glass.

In the morning I sent a letter and stood in front of the door— my jailers had to see my Roman hara-kiri. I crushed a light bulb under the sole of my shoe, picked up an extremely thin petal of glass off the floor and ran it across my veins (not even a scratch) and turned away quickly. I had filled my mouth in advance with the brick-and-jam ersatz, and I spat it out, then showed my wrists covered in "blood" to the peephole and sat down at the desk to die—with my back to the door. I kept adding small amounts of blood from the glass, so that it flowed off the desk in a thin, convincing trickle. I thought it was a realistic picture.

It took great self-restraint to show the strength gradually draining out of me, to melt way slowly, like a snowman. I laid my cheek on an exercise book and froze. And then the mental count began: one, two, three, four, five… and on up to sixty—a minute. Sixty minutes—an hour. With every hour that passed I persuaded myself to remain patient and be a little more dead… The night passed. The dumb waiter woke up as if nothing had happened. But the old scumbags hadn't even thought of coming! Even if they had seen through my amusing hunger strike, they had no right to have any doubts about veins! I really had almost died!

The truth was hard. No one was watching me. Or if they were, they couldn't give a rotten damn for my ignominious dramatic efforts. In a fit of fury I hammered the chair to pieces against the door, but then I put it back together again. From that day on I knew for certain that if I croaked, the bunker would simply be loaded with a new "grandson".

I discovered unexpected positive aspects to this unpleasant discovery. Round-the-clock acting was terribly exhausting. I was finally able to relax. I wasn't crushed by the sense of isolation that suddenly flooded over me. I ate regularly, rubbed myself down with alcohol, combed my hair, shaved and did my exercises. After a month of shoddy acting my shoulders were cramped into a proud bearing. I suffered fits of terror less and less often. An inexperienced diver feels the discomfort of immersion in his chest for the first few seconds. But he only has to get past that urge to breathe in—and there's still a long way to go to genuine asphyxiation…

I thought up something to do to occupy my mind. After all, it was no accident that they had provided me with exercise books and a bundle of ballpoint pens.

In my long-ago childhood I had imitated the example of the Young Communists of the Sixties, who sent time capsules with greetings to themselves into the Communist future, by writing letters to myself. Sometimes I wrote and sealed the envelope, agreeing with myself that I would open it in ten years' time. That was how I learned to my surprise that a person's handwriting ages together with him. Often I cut into the soft, bluish bark of a poplar, imagining that some time, years later, when I grew up, I would touch those scars on the tree and remember the boy in a knitted blue jacket and a woolly "cockerel" cap scraping at the trunk with his key, and that would be a greeting sent across the years.

Working with a view of the Kremlin was absorbing; I didn't feel at all like crazed Nestor, scribbling his *Tale of Bygone Years*. I wrote, and in the pauses I turned off the lamp and rested in the dark. The pitch darkness transformed the bunker into a black box and I was the recording mechanism inside, which would one day be found and read. The grey exercise book came to an end and I started on a brown one…

My first despondent leisure hours as a chronicler were enlivened by the Book of Strength (*The Proletarian Way*). The storyline was this. It is five years since the blast of war fell silent. The country is rebuilding its economy on a peaceful basis. During the war years the plan was fulfilled by superhuman effort and extra-long work shifts. The new life requires not merely enthusiasm but also innovative thinking. Many difficulties arise on this path, including the conservatism of certain enterprise managers. A difficult situation has arisen at the Proletarian Mine. The engineer Solovyev, a former front-line soldier, is at the centre of the plot. He tries to break down the established ways of doing things in order to mechanize work at the coalface. Solovyev is opposed by Basyuk, the head of the mine, who is obsessed with the stereotypes of wartime—to fulfil the plan at any price, even by last-minute storming tactics. Basyuk is not capable of understanding that the grandiose prospects of peacetime construction require different tempos and levels of productivity that cannot be achieved with outmoded equipment. The failure to modernize safety systems results in an accident. Basyuk tries to shift all the blame for what has happened onto Solovyev. It takes all the determination, grit and candour of such seasoned war veterans as the Party organizer Chistyakov and the coalface workers' foreman Lichko to ensure that the genuine culprit receives his deserved punishment…

After reading the Book of Strength I tried to break down the door; a pointless and painful endeavour, the excess of unnatural power almost left me a cripple. I didn't notice that I had given myself a hernia lifting the extremely heavy oak desk that I used to ram the unyielding armour plate. The door didn't budge, but the oak started to crumble. The effect of the Book wore off, and I was racked by fierce pains in my stomach and back. It was no wonder—the Book activated the secret reserves of physical strength of the individual reader. At that moment my maximum strength was limited by the constraints of my body, and even a grenade launcher wouldn't have blown that door in.

I managed, at the cost of skinning my fingers, to bend the hatch cover of the dumb waiter slightly, but I only convinced myself that there was no escape through the shaft—a block of steel with practically no gaps closed it off at the top.

I had clearly damaged the hermetic seal of the bent hatch cover, because sounds from the invisible kitchen started reaching the bunker: radio-station jingles, music, the voices of the cooks, the clatter of kitchenware in sinks.

Always at the same time, between breakfast and lunch, a retro music station played Soviet variety music. The programme lasted for about half an hour, and I allowed myself the pleasure of stopping work and listening to Pakhmutov, Krylatov or Frenkel.

I made yet another attempt to communicate by letter, sending two brief blackmailing epistles: I threatened to destroy the Book of Strength. But they sent me the Book of Power (*Fly On, Happiness*). This short novel in just over two hundred pages was a paean of praise to the heroism of the virgin-soil pioneers. At the summons of the Party, young people have come from every corner of the Union to assimilate previously uncultivated lands. Yevgeny Lubentsov has only recently graduated from an agricultural academy and has been invited to stay on for postgraduate study. The prospects before him are tempting: to finish his Ph.D. and to live in the big city. However, in the spirit of Pavel Korchagin, Lubentsov decides to go to the virgin lands as an agronomist. He deliberately chooses a backward Machine Tractor Station. Lubentsov has to demonstrate great organizational talent in order to get the station working properly. He gradually learns to understand people. At home he was in love with Elina Zaslavskaya, an attractive-looking girl whom he regarded as talented and high-minded. But on the virgin lands he comes to know the value of collectivism and comradeship, and this helps him to see through Elina's essentially bourgeois nature. For her, heroic, noble labour in the name of the people and the country is nothing but romantic nonsense. Lubentsov realizes that Elina cannot remain his friend and companion for the rest of his life. He finds a new love in the ploughwoman Masha Fadeyeva...

From the artistic point of view the book was a lot weaker than *The Proletarian Way*. The negative characters were written too grotesquely, like caricatures in the magazine *Krokodil*. The text was indelibly stained with the newspaper ink of populistic leading articles: "They joyfully appreciated the grandeur and beauty of nature, its wisdom and generosity, and spared no efforts to set the golden ears of wheat waving above the empty land."

Unfortunately there was no one for me to influence with my Power. No one saw the majestic expressions of my face; no one heeded the imperious modulations of my voice. I hurled my lightning-bolt glances at the walls, the door and the dumb waiter in vain.

The third Book they sent was one I was already familiar with—the Book of Meaning, with its neat insert. The fourth was the Book of Joy (*Narva*), a military novel about anti-aircraft gunners. Leaving aside the short lyrical passages with descriptions of the lives of the main characters and several pastoral sections at the beginning of the novella, the plot unfolds in the space of a few heroic days. February 1943. An anti-aircraft and machine-gun platoon from a ski battalion has dug in on the western bank of the Narva River. Supported by tanks, Hitler's forces attack the positions of the Soviet warriors. The defence is headed by Lieutenant Golubnichy. The main forces of the battalion wage stubborn battle against the enemy's tanks and infantry along a small bridgehead on the other side of the river. It is impossible to get the heavy gun across from the eastern bank to the western one—the ice on the Narva is broken. By the end of the day there are only three members of the machine-gun formation remaining—Golubnichy and two privates, Martynenko and Tishin. In the evening Lance-Corporal

Sklyarov manages to get through to them and deliver ammunition. After a powerful mortar attack the German forces advance again. Martynenko is killed. Golubnichy and Sklyarov, both wounded, load the ammunition belts and Tishin runs from one machine gun to another so that the enemy won't guess that there is only one warrior left unwounded at the position. When the Fascists break in, Golubnichy sends a signal rocket to call down the fire of our artillery on himself. The flames of explosions rage above the position and the Hitlerites flee in panic. Units from a Guards' rifle division arrive and make a forced crossing of the Narva...

Joy in its pure form had no admixture of merriment and jocularity. There was only exultation and jubilation of the spirit. All the bitterer was the shift of mood when the feeling of rapture was replaced by a withdrawal full of hopeless despair.

I had no doubt that the pragmatic Gorn had the role of a sacrificial "reader" in mind for me right from the beginning. How bitterly I regretted that I had not been killed at the village soviet together with the other Shironinites. Someone who is destined to be hanged should pray to his rope and make confession to his piece of soap, because if he decides to drown instead, it will be torment. I would gladly have exchanged the job of running round in closed circles for a glorious and rapid death from a hook or an axe.

For many days I used the Book of Joy like vodka, to numb my fear, immersing myself twice a day in an iridescent state of ecstasy. I tried to time the reading so the final pages would coincide with the retro music programme. That way the effect of the Book lasted for almost twice as long.

As a result of this binge reading I even had hallucinations a few times. I heard footsteps outside the door, heard the bolt opening with a rusty screech, or I heard the late Margarita Tikhonovna's voice in the shaft of the dumb waiter, discussing my lunch menu with someone. She was trying to persuade them that "Alyosha has hated chicken since he was little".

I realized that I was being hoodwinked by auditory hallucinations, but even so I shouted to her and asked her to get me out of the bunker. For lunch I was given macaroni and a pimply chicken leg…

This went on until they sent the Book of Endurance. The anaesthetized indifference to everything that this Book induced suited me far better: unlike Joy, Endurance left almost no fleshly hangover.

I deliberately read the Book of Fury (*By Labour's Roads*) without observing the Conditions. I didn't want to reduce myself to the state of a berserk. I had no one to fight and, in addition, I was afraid of damaging myself in my blind fury.

I can say in brief that the Book told the story of a working-class dynasty, the Shapovalovs, and how a small factory for repairing agricultural equipment grew into a metallurgical combine with automated production lines, and the village of Vysoky grew into a city.

I waited for the seventh and final Book, the Book of Memory. I had no doubt that it would appear. The dumb waiter had turned from a provider of food into an instrument of exquisite torture. My heart was in my mouth every time I opened the cover. After all this exhausting agitation I couldn't eat a bite; I even suffered from nervous vomiting. Only the artificial endurance saved me.

I didn't need to wonder exactly how the old women would force me to start reading the Books. The mechanism of compulsion was obvious. When the dumb waiter fell silent, Alexei Vyazintsev would be faced with a fairly simple choice: starve to death or become the talisman of the country. I feverishly stuffed the drawers of the desk with bread.

Of course I was aware that no matter how much I stored up, the rusks would run out. There was no escaping the fate of the reader and curator; I could only drag out the time, hoping that something unimaginable might happen "on the off chance". What if there really were only one copy of the Book of Strength after all? What if Gorn and the fourteen elders had been weakened and died long ago? That meant that sooner or later the leadership would change up above. The new female ataman would want to recover the invaluable Book from the basement. They would have to reach an agreement with me, and I would haggle…

This state of suspense was worse than having my conviction put into effect. But they left me alone for three months as if on purpose. My storage bins were bursting. Like a miser, I arranged the slices of bread I had saved into loaves like bricks—I had fourteen and a half of them. These reserves would last me until summer, and even longer if eaten like Leningrad siege rations.

I was bored now; my writing task was basically completed. I had begun with a brief overview of the Gromovian universe, on the basis of materials found in Gorn's archives, and also described my own brief time as a librarian, the glorious death of the Shironin reading room and even my first months in the bunker. Now the narrative had taken itself by the tail. There was nothing left to reveal, except by supplementing what had already been written…

One morning in April or May I opened the cover. The Book of Memory was lying in the top and the bedpan in the bottom. There wasn't any food or water.

CURATOR OF THE MOTHERLAND

"We owe an irredeemable debt to our Motherland. Her gifts to us are priceless. The ruby-red stars of the Kremlin shine for all of us, warming us with the rays of freedom, equality and brotherhood. What else is needed for happiness? Our Motherland is kind and generous; she does not count our debts. But there are moments when she reminds us of them. That means the Motherland is in danger. And our debt must be repaid to her in courage, steadfastness, valour and heroism."

I learned this excerpt off by heart in the third year at school. Our school, which was named after Lenin, was preparing for the May festivities. The bosses of the district party committee were expected. Under the supervision of a department head from the local school board our frightened headmistress personally knocked the stuffing out of the juvenile orators who were privileged to tread the boards of the school-hall stage, which stank of polish. For the final few days the chosen ones were excused from classes and drilled from morning to evening. Even now if I am woken up in the middle of the night I can still rattle off without a hitch: "We owe an irredeemable debt…" This excerpt has remained branded into the skin of my memory.

I had already been a Young Pioneer since 22 April, but for the sake of the holiday they took away my necktie and those of several other third-year pupils, so that our visitors from empyrean realms could participate in the ritual and welcome us into the ranks of the pioneers for a second time.

"If we compare countries with ships, then the Soviet Union is the flagship of the world fleet. It leads the way for the other ships. If we compare countries with people, then the Soviet Union is a mighty knight who conquers his enemies and helps his friends in need. If we compare countries with stars, then our country is the Pole Star. The Soviet Union shows all the peoples of the world the way to Communism."

This is the extract that I was given at first, and then it was replaced with "We owe an irredeemable…" At the time I was very upset. I liked the solemn words about the flagship, the knight and the star better. Not even the words themselves, but myself proclaiming them, as sonorous as a ship's bell.

Changes were made to the script, the head of department placed the "Union" right at the very end of the programme, and the excerpt was given to some older girl whose father was the chairman of the district soviet executive committee. And the sensuous paragraph about Lenin—"For ever shall the human river flow to the Mausoleum"—was read by the proud son of the first secretary of the district Party committee

The stupefying smell of polish fogged my reason, which was already wrought up to the absolute limit. I declaimed my section after: "Our country's shores are washed by twelve seas, and two more seas lie set upon its land" and shouted my text out into the hall without hearing my own voice, deafened by the beating of my heart. We were applauded. The secretary of the Young Communist League district committee knotted my necktie and pinned the Young Pioneer badge onto my white shirt…

And now, from out of oblivion, the country that has disappeared has presented the grubby promissory notes that I rashly signed so many years ago, demanding payment in steadfastness, valour and heroism.

It was all quite fair. Although there was indeed some delay, I have received the incredible happiness promised by my Soviet

Motherland. Granted, it was a false happiness, instilled in me by the Book of Memory. But what difference does that make? After all, in my genuine childhood I believed absolutely that the state which was eulogized in all the books, films and plays *was* the reality in which I lived. The earthly USSR was a coarse and imperfect body, but dwelling apart in the hearts of romantic old men and the children of prosperous urban families was its artistic ideal— the Heavenly Union. When the mental dimension withered, the insensate geographical body also died.

Even when society regarded hatred of one's own country and its past as a badge of good form, I intuitively steered clear of the debunking novels that screamed with the gluttonous voices of seagulls about various Gulag children of the Arbat walking about in white clothes. I was embarrassed by literary half-truth, and especially by its morosely frowning authors, hammering on the table with the reverberating skulls of victims of the bygone Socialist era. This skeletal rat-a-tat-tat changed nothing in the way that I felt about the Union. When I grew up a bit, I loved the Union, not for what it was, but for what it could have become if things had turned out differently. And is a potentially good man really so very much to blame if the difficulties in his life prevent his splendid qualities from blossoming?

And there was another key moment, the significance and paradoxical character of which only became clear to me years later. The Union knew how to make Ukraine a Motherland. But without the Union, Ukraine has not managed to remain one...

The country in which both of my childhoods—the genuine and the fictitious—were simultaneously located was my genuine, unique Motherland, which I could never deny. And the Book of Memory lying on the tray was my call-up papers from it.

Of course, I didn't reason in this philosophical manner from the very beginning. At first, the moment I saw the Book, my legs went from under me, as they say, and fear drove the blood into my solar plexus so fiercely that for a few minutes I couldn't take a proper breath, but only open my mouth. It's strange: I had spent three months preparing, but the fateful day still caught me by surprise. I reached out for the Book of Endurance, but put it down—I wouldn't have got through a single page. With my teeth clattering against the glass, I drank the water I had already gathered, filled the glass up to the brim with medical spirit and downed it in one. My throat and oesophagus were charred. A pillar of fire struck me in the head...

It helped. I realized that when the suffocating heat receded, as if the part responsible for fear had burned out for ever. I have nothing left to be afraid of. I have calmed down for ever.

* * *

It was the second week at my post. There were heaps of rusks and I was not suffering from hunger. There was a suspicious noise in the radiator and the yields had fallen slightly. During the last twenty-four hours only a glass and a half had accumulated. The heating season was clearly coming to an end, and soon they could turn the water off completely.

In the morning my personal clothing was in the lift and also— an unexpected surprise—the late Grisha Vyrin's jacket. Someone in Gorn's female brigade must have taken a fancy to this unusual trophy on that occasion at the village soviet and appropriated the anonymous dead man's cuirass.

I didn't feel the slightest shudder. I simply pulled on the jacket that smelled slightly of smoke over my sweater and felt perfectly protected.

They sent me a Solingen straight razor. I took this as a joking reference to my "slashed wrists" and felt offended. I stuck the razor in my pocket and drank my rusty "tea" through pieces of rusk.

Those were probably the most serene days since I had been incarcerated. I could even have killed myself, if only I had wanted to—I was not by nature inherently afraid of death. In fact, almost until the third year in school I was sure that I would grow up to be a soldier and one day I would be killed, and a solemn salute would ring out over my grave. Most often I imagined death with a grenade. I'm fighting off my advancing enemies' fire. My sub-machine-gun falls silent—the clip in my pistol is empty. I conceal my last grenade under my tunic so that I can easily reach the safety pin. I raise my arms, emerge from cover and say I have an important message for their commanding officer. He comes over to me—the complacent enemy—his soldiers surround me. And then I pull out the safety pin with my teeth and depart into eternity, into the granite forms of a monument and the gold letters on the commemorative plaque: "Senior Lieutenant Alexei Vyazintsev died a hero's death…" For the minutes that my fantasies lasted, my eyes blazed with tears and my cheeks burned with the heat from the martyr's flame of that unexploded grenade…

Now that I had grown up, my task had been simplified for me—I had been offered a simplified version of heroism. I don't even have to die. On the contrary, to live for ever for the good of the Motherland—what is there to be afraid of in that?

I was not particularly worried about what would happen if I suddenly broke off reading after, let's say, a year. Whether I would emerge from hibernation like a bear or crumble into dust, whether the much-vaunted mechanism of immortality supposedly embedded in the Books would even work…

* * *

I suddenly started dreaming of people I had killed. I didn't have nightmares at all, but calm, epic dreams. In one I was transported into the dismal landscape that adorned my wall. I wandered through birch trees, breathed the damp coolness, chewed on melting snow, glanced across the river. On the opposite bank a little Pavlik, as white as if he were woven out of cobwebs, was scurrying about, shouting something and waving his plaster arms around, but the wind carried away his weightless words.

In another dream the Gorelov librarian Marchenko came to me. He brought a rejigged song for the Institute's Club of the Jolly and Ingenious team: "Though grieving and alarmed, do not stand in the doorway, I'll show up when the snow melts." I objected that this was gruesome humour about corpses. But the Shironinites sitting around me said that I was wrong and the parody was very funny...

I tried to remember my family as little as possible. It was too painful to think of what they had endured in recent times. The first squall of grief had probably already blown itself out. Six months is a long time. They'll come to terms with their loss. Our fecund Vovka will have a third boy and they'll name him after me—Alexei.

* * *

Lulled by the Book of Memory, in the darkness I fell into a doze with my ear pressed against the radio and slept through the first part of the musical broadcast.

"...from the film *Moscow-Cassiopeia*..." the female presenter announced in a joyful, breathy voice, merging her words into the surging bell-chime violins of the orchestral introduction.

The night has passed as if a pain has passed,
The earth is sleeping, let it rest.
The earth, just like the two of us
Still has ahead of it
A journey as long as life.

In the pitch-black abyss of the ceiling a planetarium of the universe suddenly lit up, a cosmically infinite mantle of stars, a magical, tilted swirl of minute heavenly bodies, like a distant reflection of sleeping cities, observed from the fast-moving window of a train that is hurtling past nameless lunar way stations, mysterious non-human dwellings that entice with orange shards of electricity, past a purple sky with the blinking scarlet bead of a nocturnal plane, past cast-iron railings above anthracite rivers, past the smell of industrial iron warmed by the sun, the black plumes of poplars with the peacock flashes of semaphores.

I shall take the chirping of the birds of earth,
I shall take the gentle splash of tinkling streams,
I shall take the light of storms' sheet lightning,
The whisper of the winds, the empty winter forest.

With agonizing, sobbing tenderness, I listened to the simple conversational melody, devoid of all pretentious affectation. The words about parting and the long road ahead moved me to the depths of my soul. The voice was a solicitous mentor, deftly stuffing my kitbag with everything essential, everything that might be needed on an expedition from which one is not fated to return...

I shall take the memory of earthly milestones,
I shall swim through fields of ripe, dense flax.
There in the distance, there beside the blue stars,
The Sun of Earth will shine to me.

I shall take this whole big world,
Its every day and every hour.
And if I should forget anything,
I doubt the stars will welcome us...

Something infinitely dear, woven out of poplar fluff and rays of June sunshine, touched my cheek and flooded my meagre saliva with the taste of pear drops and the viscous intoxication of Hematogen candy, then turned its youthful face towards me and waved its hand once in farewell.

The warm, happy tears were cooling in my eyes. I knew that I would no longer need the rusks and the rusty water, wearing down the glass drop by drop...

* * *

What year is it outside now? If the Motherland is free and its borders are inviolate, then the librarian Alexei Vyazintsev is keeping his watch steadfastly in his underground bunker, tirelessly spinning the thread of the protective Veil extended above the country. To protect against enemies both visible and invisible.

I would like to think that on a summer evening someone walks along the high road outside town, past cherry orchards and glittering tin-plate roofs. The sunset has spread along the horizon in a thick beetroot trickle. Mulberry trees beside the road rustle and drop berries into the dust. The shoulder of the road is covered in mulberry blots. A slow truck with a loose, rattling frame has daubed a stroke of warm petrol fumes through the air; a goods train has clattered by behind a distant embankment; the wind has pulled the tall grass erect by its topknots…

This has not happened yet, but it will be so.

I shall finish writing the final words. I shall place the notebooks—a black one, a grey one, a light-blue one and three brown ones—in the niche of the lift. I shall close the hatch.

Then I shall sit down at the table. I shall pluck up my courage. I shall open the first Book. I shall start in chronological order, with the Book of Strength.

* * *

I shall never die. And the green lamp will never go out.

THE WORLD OF YESTERDAY
STEFAN ZWEIG

'*The World of Yesterday* is one of the greatest memoirs of the twentieth century, as perfect in its evocation of the world Zweig loved, as it is in its portrayal of how that world was destroyed' David Hare

JOURNEY BY MOONLIGHT
ANTAL SZERB

'Just divine… makes you imagine the author has had private access to your own soul' Nicholas Lezard, *Guardian*

BONITA AVENUE
PETER BUWALDA

'One wild ride: a swirling helix of a family saga… a new writer as toe-curling as early Roth, as roomy as Franzen and as caustic as Houellebecq' *Sunday Telegraph*

THE PARROTS
FILIPPO BOLOGNA

'A five-star satire on literary vanity… a wonderful, surprising novel' *Metro*

I WAS JACK MORTIMER
ALEXANDER LERNET-HOLENIA

'Terrific… a truly clever, rather wonderful book that both plays with and defies genre' Eileen Battersby, *Irish Times*

SONG FOR AN APPROACHING STORM
PETER FRÖBERG IDLING

'Beautifully evocative… a must-read novel' *Daily Mail*

THE RABBIT BACK LITERATURE SOCIETY
PASI ILMARI JÄÄSKELÄINEN

'Wonderfully knotty… a very grown-up fantasy masquerading as quirky fable. Unexpected, thrilling and absurd' *Sunday Telegraph*

RED LOVE: THE STORY OF AN EAST GERMAN FAMILY
MAXIM LEO

'Beautiful and supremely touching… an unbearably poignant description of a world that no longer exists' *Sunday Telegraph*

THE BREAK
PIETRO GROSSI

'Small and perfectly formed… reaching its end leaves the reader desirous to start all over again' *Independent*

FROM THE FATHERLAND, WITH LOVE
RYU MURAKAMI

'If Haruki is The Beatles of Japanese literature, Ryu is its Rolling Stones' David Pilling

BUTTERFLIES IN NOVEMBER
AUÐUR AVA ÓLAFSDÓTTIR

'A funny, moving and occasionally bizarre exploration of life's upheavals and reversals' *Financial Times*

BARCELONA SHADOWS
MARC PASTOR

'As gruesome as it is gripping… the writing is extraordinarily vivid… Highly recommended' *Independent*

THE LAST DAYS
LAURENT SEKSIK

'Mesmerising… Seksik's portrait of Zweig's final months is dignified and tender' *Financial Times*

BY BLOOD
ELLEN ULLMAN

'Delicious and intriguing' *Daily Telegraph*

WHILE THE GODS WERE SLEEPING
ERWIN MORTIER

'A monumental, phenomenal book' *De Morgen*

THE BRETHREN
ROBERT MERLE

'A master of the historical novel' *Guardian*

3